After spending three years as a die-hard New Yorker, **Kate Hewitt** now lives in a small village in the English Lake District, with her husband, their five children and a golden retriever. In addition to writing intensely emotional stories, she loves reading, baking and playing chess with her son—she has yet to win against him, but she continues to try. Learn more about Kate at kate-hewitt.com.

Chantelle Shaw lives on the Kent coast and thinks up her stories while walking on the beach. She has been married for over thirty years and has six children. Her love affair with reading and writing Mills & Boon stories began as a teenager, and her first book was published in 2006. She likes strong-willed, slightly unusual characters. Chantelle also loves gardening, walking and wine!

D0279124

Also by Kate Hewitt

Princess's Nine-Month Secret
The Secret Kept from the Italian
Greek's Baby of Redemption
Claiming My Bride of Convenience
The Italian's Unexpected Baby
Vows to Save His Crown
Pride and the Italian's Proposal

Also by Chantelle Shaw

Her Wedding Night Negotiation
Housekeeper in the Headlines
The Italian's Bargain for His Bride

Innocent Summer Brides miniseries

The Greek Wedding She Never Had
Nine Months to Tame the Tycoon

Discover more at millsandboon.co.uk.

First Published in Great Britain 2022
by Mills & Boon, an imprint of HarperCollins*Publishers* Ltd,
1 London Bridge Street, London, SE1 9GF

www.harpercollins.co.uk

HarperCollins*Publishers*
1st Floor, Watermarque Building,
Ringsend Road, Dublin 4, Ireland

A Scandal Made at Midnight © 2022 Kate Hewitt

Her Secret Royal Dilemma © 2022 Chantelle Shaw

ISBN: 978-0-263-30086-4

06/22

A SCANDAL MADE AT MIDNIGHT

KATE HEWITT

MILLS & BOON

CHAPTER ONE

'AREN'T THEY THE most incredible things you've seen?'

Liane Blanchard gave a rueful laugh of acknowledgement as Ella twirled around, blonde curls flying, her musical peal of laughter echoing through the living room, its windows open to the summery breeze wafting in from Central Park.

'That's certainly one word for them,' she replied with a smile. With five-inch platform heels, encrusted with diamantes and made entirely of glass, the shoes really were incredible. They also looked painful and potentially impossible to wear, not that either of those, Liane knew, would put Ella off for a second. 'You're wearing them to the ball, I presume?'

'Of course. I've got quite a plan for these shoes, as it happens.' Ella winked as she slipped the shoes off, replacing them in the layers of tissue paper in the silver shoe box that came from one of Manhattan's up-and-coming fashion designers. As a self-made social media influencer, Ella was often getting samples from desperate designers who longed to be the next big thing, just as she did. 'You should see the dress I'm wearing. It goes *perfectly* with the shoes.'

'Not made of glass, I hope?' Liane joked, only to have Ella give her another wink.

'No, but the fabric version of it! But don't worry, don't worry.' She held up one hand as she shook back her long, tumbling blonde hair. 'It's perfectly decent. Not *too* see-through.' She giggled while Liane smiled and shook her head wryly. Ella was twenty-two, gorgeous, and as happy and carefree as a lark. At twenty-seven innately quiet and cautious, Liane sometimes felt like she was the only thing keeping her younger stepsister from falling head-long into disaster—or at least chaos—again and again.

'What a ridiculous pair of shoes.'

Along with her mother, Liane amended silently. Amelie Ash stood in the doorway of the living room, tall, grey-haired and unsmiling as she looked down her long thin nose at the ridiculous shoes Ella had just put back in the box.

'They are ridiculous, aren't they?' she agreed cheerfully as she put the lid back on the box. 'That's the point.'

Liane had always admired the way Ella refused to let her stepmother get her down. They'd blended their families when Ella had only been six, a cherubic little girl with rosy cheeks and candy floss curls. Amelie, the daughter of two awkward preteen girls at the time, had not taken to her at all.

It hadn't helped that her new husband, Robert Ash, had loved to lavish presents and attention on his only child, since her mother had died when Ella was just a baby. And yet even though Ella had certainly been indulged by her father, Liane reflected with affection, she hadn't actually been *spoiled*. At least not too much. She was simply high-spirited, full of fun—and the complete opposite of her stepmother—as well as Liane—in every way.

'Where on earth are you wearing them?' Amelie asked with a sniff.

'To the ball, of course!'

Liane tensed instinctively as her mother's face became pinched, her cold grey eyes narrowing, lips pursing like a particularly withered prune. She knew that look, had seen it many times over the years as life—as well as her daughters—had continued to disappoint her mother, and she'd done her best to mitigate against it, placate and persevere and please, usually to little avail.

'The ball?' Amelie repeated icily. 'Ella, my dear, you are not going to the ball. You weren't invited.'

For the merest second Ella's laughing expression faltered, and her china blue eyes widened as she shot Liane an uncertain, questioning look.

'No, she wasn't invited,' Liane interjected quickly, 'but she's coming as my guest. I checked with the assistant handling the RSVPs, and plus ones are allowed.' She could have never gone otherwise, knowing Ella would have to stay at home. She'd offered to give Ella her own invitation, as she wasn't much of a one for parties, but Ella had insisted they go together.

Her mother's lips thinned. Liane knew she would much rather Ella didn't attend what was billed to be *the* event of the season—a ball hosted by the notoriously reclusive hotel magnate Alessandro Rossi, to celebrate a hundred years of his family's luxury hotels, for the crème de la crème of New York society. Not that they could actually count themselves one of that number, but Liane's father, Michel Blanchard, had been a minor diplomat and a casual acquaintance of Alessandro Rossi's father, Leonardo, a long time ago. Liane had been as shocked as anyone when the invitation on thick, creamy card had been slotted through their letter box, although her mother had been smugly exultant.

'Of course we'd be invited,' she'd scoffed, preening. 'Your father was a dear friend of Leonardo Rossi's. You know how he lent him money when he needed it.'

A hundred francs at a casino, thirty years ago, hardly the lofty business deal her mother made it seem. Of course Liane did not say any of this. She had long ago learned to hold her tongue around her mother; it made everything easier for everyone if she placated rather than poured oil onto the flames of her mother's ire.

In any case, she was looking forward to going to the ball, admittedly with some apprehension; as a French teacher working at a girls' school on the Upper East Side, she'd chosen to live a quiet life with her mother and sisters, rather than step into the spotlight that Ella launched herself into, again and again, in pursuit of fame and fortune. Liane had no interest in either; the losses she'd experienced in life had taught her to be cautious, to stick to the shadows. When you didn't, you got hurt. She'd seen it with her father, she felt it with her mother. Putting yourself out there could hurt, and Liane had decided long ago that she'd rather not even try.

But, she thought as Ella put the shoe box away, attending a ball would certainly be a nice change, even if she knew she would stay on the sidelines as she always did.

'I doubt you have anything appropriate to wear,' Amelie remarked with another sniff as her stepdaughter came back into the living room. Ella might own the house they all lived in, given to her by her father with the proviso that her stepmother and sisters could live in it for all their lives, but otherwise she did not have a penny to her name and was dependent on her stepmother's grudging generosity.

'Oh, but I do,' Ella replied sweetly. 'A fashion designer friend of mine has made the most glorious gown—don't worry, Belle-Mère, I promise I won't embarrass you by wearing rags.'

Which was hardly her mother's concern, Liane knew. No, her mother's concern was quite the opposite—that gorgeous, laughing Ella would show her and her sister Manon up, which she undoubtedly would, without even trying. Liane was used to it, Manon didn't really care, and her mother became coldly, quietly infuriated. She had aspirations of her daughters marrying wealthy, well-connected men, the kind of men who would be guests at the Rossi Ball. Liane couldn't see it happening herself. She'd be afraid to say boo to a man like that, if truth were told, while Ella could turn flirting into a competitive sport.

'How fortunate for you,' Amelie stated coldly. 'Liane? Has your dress come back from the seamstress?'

'Yes, I picked it up this morning.' Liane forced a smile even though she partly dreaded wearing that old blue bag of a dress—a castoff of her mother's, hardly flattering, yet all they could afford.

'And just in time too, considering the ball is tomorrow night,' her mother replied, and, with another narrowed look of dislike for her stepdaughter, Amelie stalked out of the room. Liane gave her sister a sympathetic look.

'Don't mind her.'

'I never do,' Ella assured her sunnily. 'But you haven't shown me your dress. Let's see it.'

'It's nothing much—' Liane said hurriedly, knowing what an awful understatement her words were.

'Oh, come on, Liane! I bet you'll look amazing in it. Show me?'

'Very well.' She never could resist her sister's puppy dog eyes. 'But it really isn't much at all.' With a sigh she headed upstairs, Ella following her to her bedroom on the first floor, its long sash windows facing the house's narrow back garden, Central Park visible in the distance. Ella had the small room at the top of the house by her stepmother's decree, but she had always insisted she didn't mind.

'More privacy,' she'd assured Liane when she'd offered to switch. 'And you know what a night owl I am. I'd hate to disturb everyone with my noise.' Liane still felt guilty. Ella had been short-changed in so many ways since her father's death three years ago, but she never put up a fuss, no matter how her stepmother tried to limit her life.

'Now show me this dress,' Ella commanded as Liane reached for the plastic-swathed gown hanging from her wardrobe door. 'I hope it's sensational.'

'Nothing like yours, I'm sure.' Liane eased the plastic off the gown. Her mother might have pretensions of her and Manon catching the attention of an eligible man like Alessandro Rossi, but their limited budget did not stretch to ball gowns that would serve such a purpose.

The powder-blue dress had been her mother's and a local seamstress had updated its debatably classic look. Amelie had insisted it was still in style, but Liane had her doubts. So did Ella.

'Thank goodness you got rid of the ruffles,' she said as she eyed it critically. 'Otherwise it would have been pure nineteen-eighties, and not in a good way, unfortunately.'

'I know.' Liane suppressed a sigh. She was used to looking like a wallflower, with her pale, washed-out looks—or so her mother said—but wearing a forty-year-old dress took even that to its limits. 'I don't really mind. I'm not one for parties anyway, Ella, you know that. And no one will be looking at me anyway, I'm quite sure.'

'Still, this is *the* party of the year,' Ella protested. Liane couldn't help but notice she didn't even argue her second point. 'You can't wear something you could find in a thrift shop.'

'Ouch.' Liane pretended to wince. There was too much truth in her sister's words. Even with the seamstress's help the dress looked far too dated and worn, bagging about her bosom and hips, the material possessing the unlovely sheen of cheap satin. But what did it really matter? As she'd said and Ella had silently agreed, no one would be looking at her. They'd all be looking at Ella, and she was glad of it.

'Look, you can't wear this,' Ella declared as she slid her phone out of her pocket. 'Not to this party. It might be fine for Manon—she really doesn't care about dresses—'

'She's wearing black, as she always does.' Manon loved her work as an administrative assistant in a law office and couldn't care less about fashion or finding a husband. She was only going because their mother had absolutely insisted and, as they both knew when it came to their mother's machinations, it was easier to go along than to resist. Easier to stay silent than protest against her constant barrage of criticism, because her daughters disappointed her as much as her husbands had.

'Of course she is. Let me text my designer friend. I think she was working on another gown, and it would be perfect for you. Violet to match your eyes.'

'Oh, I don't know,' Liane protested, not wanting Ella to go to such trouble.

'I'm telling you it would be perfect—'

'I'm not wearing something transparent,' Liane warned her.

'Of course not,' Ella answered with a laugh as her fingers flew over her phone. 'That one's for me. Trust me, Liane, it really will be perfect. You'll be the belle of the ball!'

'Hardly,' Liane returned. 'That's a position reserved for you.' Ella took to the spotlight naturally, and always had, much to Amelie Ash's ire. Liane knew their mother had always wanted her and Manon to be more like Ella, sparkling and sociable and charismatic, even as she'd disdained and even despised her stepdaughter for being exactly how she was. As for herself? She'd be happy enough to stand unnoticed on the sidelines as she watched Ella take the world by storm. Still, she decided with a smile, she was feminine enough to feel it would be nice to wear a pretty dress while she was doing it.

The party was in full swing as Alessandro Rossi stepped out of the elevator onto the penthouse floor of Hotel Rossi, his family empire's flagship hotel in the centre of Manhattan. From the open doors of the ballroom he heard the tinkle of laughter and crystal, the strains of the seventeen-piece orchestra. All around him the city stretched out, a carpet of darkness lit by the golden blur of streetlights, matched by the glitter and sparkle of crystal chandeliers and champagne flutes, not to mention the hundreds of thousands of dollars' worth of jewels dripping off most of the women in the room. The Rossi Ball, the first of its kind, had been hyped to be the event of the year in the city, as it had to be. The publicity was the only reason he was having this tedious affair in the first place.

Straightening his black tie, his eyes narrowing as his hooded grey gaze swept the crowded room, Alessandro stepped into the ballroom—and then froze when he heard a tiny strangled yelp. *What the...?*

'I'm so sorry,' a woman said. Her voice was soft, with a gentle trace of a French accent. 'I didn't mean to get in your way. I do apologise.'

Considering he'd stepped on *her* foot, he had a feeling he was the one who'd got in the way. He hadn't even seen her. Alessandro's eyes narrowed as he glanced down at the woman in question—barely coming to his shoulder, with white-blonde hair piled on top of her head and a small, slender figure encased in swathes of gauzy violet. She was standing behind a potted palm by the door, which was why he hadn't seen her. That, and because she was also rather petite. She tilted her head back to gaze up at him with eyes the same colour as her dress as she tried not to wince. She was, he realised, hopping on one foot.

'I apologise. I hope I didn't break your toes?' He'd meant to sound charmingly wry, but the woman gave him a level look.

'Only my pinkie toe, which I can live without, although I might walk with a limp from now on. Don't you need pinkie toes for balance?' She spoke so sombrely that for a horrified split second he thought she was serious—and then her smile emerged, reminding Alessandro bizarrely of a cuckoo clock—it popped out and then it was gone, and it left him smiling in return, strangely lightened.

'I thought you were serious,' he told her.

'I think I am.' Again with the glimpse of a smile, so fleeting and precious, making something long dead flicker inside him, come to life. 'But don't worry, I'll live.

Clearly this is a punishment for my pride. I shouldn't have let my sister convince me to wear these ridiculous shoes.'

Alessandro's mouth quirked. 'It's been my experience that most women wear ridiculous shoes.'

'What an insulting generalisation.' She wasn't laughing but it felt like she was, and it made him want to laugh as well. *Strange*. He generally wasn't one for levity. 'I assure you I am the proud owner of several pairs of sensible shoes, and not one even slightly ridiculous pair.'

He nodded towards her feet. 'Excluding these.'

'These belong to my sister.' She reached down to lift the hem of her gown to show him the shoes in question, along with a pair of slim ankles. The shoes were stiletto-heeled and dyed violet to match the dress. 'Truly ridiculous,' she proclaimed with another smile, this one reaching her eyes.

Alessandro had certainly seen more ridiculous shoes in his time, but he decided not to say as much. As reluctantly charmed as he was by this funny, elfin woman, and as much he had an odd longing to prolong the conversation, he needed to begin the tedious and unpleasant business of meeting and greeting his guests, get the necessary publicity photos and then make a strategic retreat. Focus on the task at hand, as he always did, with resolve and determination. No distractions, no temptations, nothing to deter or derail him from his chosen course.

'Very fetching, I'm sure,' he told her, his tone instinctively several degrees cooler than it had been previously.

He watched, feeling an inexplicable sense of loss, as a shuttered look came over her face, like a curtain coming down, all the light and sparkle suddenly gone. She let go of her dress so the hem hid her feet, the gauzy material brushing the floor. 'Thank you, indeed. Clearly I've already taken up too much of your time. I do apologise.'

Before he could reply, she took a step back and then another, the crowd swallowing her up within seconds while he simply stared. Strange woman. *Beguiling* woman. No, he told himself, just strange. And rather mousy, really, with all that pale hair and skin. Colourless, although her eyes had been extraordinary, like amethysts...

He gave himself a mental shake as he turned back to the ballroom. He needed to stop thinking about some nobody woman who would do nothing to further his cause. The only reason he was here was to generate positive publicity for the Rossi brand—a prospect that filled him with both determination and ire.

He hadn't realised when he'd taken over as CEO of the sprawling family empire from his father last year just how much the hotel side of the business had started to falter. Leonardo Rossi had seconded his son to Rome for ten years, to oversee their European assets and investments, the main source of the Rossi wealth. While Alessandro had been solidifying their financial business, his father, no doubt too busy with his latest *amour*, had let the hotel empire's flagship hotel in America run nearly into the ground, simply through mismanagement and indifference. It was stunts like this one that were supposedly going to save it, according to the consultant Alessandro had hired.

'The Rossi brand has become associated with stuffy, old world gentility,' the branding specialist, a woman who barely looked out of grad school, had told him bluntly several months ago, when Alessandro had flown into New York to find the flagship hotel only half full at one of the busiest times of the year. 'At least in America. People want to stay somewhere exciting and cutting edge, somewhere young and new.'

'The Rossi brand is over a hundred years old,' Alessandro had pointed out dryly. 'We are never going to be young and new.'

'Which is why it's time for a reinvention.'

Initially he'd been against the whole idea. Rossi hotels were the best in the world—the epitome of elegance, luxury, class. They did not need reinventing, and the last thing he wanted to do was to chase after a fleeting trend. The Rossi name was built on the idea of stable dependability; the world around might change, but its timeless elegance and luxury did not.

And yet, as he'd toured the New York hotel, he'd realised *something* needed to change. Rooms were empty. Guests were mainly octogenarians. The branding consultant, he'd been forced to concede reluctantly, might have had a point. He could turn around his family's fortunes just as he'd done with their investments, but it might need a different approach.

What he realised was he didn't want to change anything about the hotels—they were still timelessly stylish and luxurious, an oasis of peace in a bustling city. What he needed to do was simply change how they were perceived. Hence this party, along with several others over the next few weeks, each one at a different Rossi hotel, with him in attendance, showing how *fun* he was, which was, he knew, something of a joke. He wasn't fun at all. He didn't want to be. Fun was for layabouts and useless charmers, people who skated through life by other people's hard work, tumbling in and out of love because they were led by their emotions, capricious as those could be,   .

and caused pain and suffering in their wake. People like his father. That was not who he was at all, who he'd chosen to be, but for tonight, as well as for a few others, for expediency's sake, the camera could lie.

He moved through the crowds, offering brief smiles to anyone whose eyes he met, stopping to make idle chit-chat with whoever waylaid him. Several of the glossier gossip magazines were here, discreetly taking their paparazzi shots. Alessandro made sure to pause and pose as needed, his relaxed smile hiding his gritted teeth, the tension that was twanging through his whole body.

He hated parties. *Hated* them. Had despised them since he'd been about three years old and had been trotted out as a prop for his parents to show their marriage wasn't the train wreck everyone knew it to be, paraded around like some sort of show monkey. Just the memory made an icy sweat prickle on the back of his neck, his stomach clench with remembered anxiety he'd long ago forced himself to move past. Their pathetic little stunt had never worked, but still they'd tried. Over and over again. It had given him a decided aversion to socialising of any kind…as well as marriage.

As he took a sip of champagne, he aimed a discreet glance at his watch. How long would he have to socialise, showing everyone the obvious—that Rossi hotels were the best in the world? And yes, they were *fun*.

'Of course,' the branding consultant had told him at that meeting, her smile a bit mischievous, 'what you really need is a representative for the hotel—someone young and fun and cool who comes to all these parties.' She'd given him a pertly expectant look, while Alessandro had merely stared back.

Was she implying she would be up for the job? He

wasn't about to hire some wannabe starlet to gush and gallivant about the hotel, however, whatever this well-meaning woman said. 'I cannot imagine who that would be,' he'd told her. 'For the moment I'll settle for a few judicious publicity shots.'

How many had they taken now? Eight, nine? Surely that was enough? He looked down at his watch again. He'd only been here for fifteen minutes. Unbelievable. He already felt both wired and exhausted by the attention, the chitchat, the speculation, *the memories.*

'Here's our little darling boy. Come here, Alessandro, and show everyone how much you love us.'

No matter how many obedient hugs and smiles he'd given, it had never been enough. His mother would drink herself into a stupor, his father would embark on another affair. And they would scream and rage at each other, with him always at the centre, being used.

He'd always vowed he would never let himself be so used again.

He pushed the memories away as he glanced around the ballroom, and it wasn't until his gaze had skated over half the people that he realised who he was looking for. Her. That funny little woman with the purple eyes and the smile that wasn't. He shook his head as if to clear it, and that was when he caught sight of the woman holding court in the centre of the room—and he wondered how he had ever missed her.

She was objectively gorgeous, first of all, with long, tumbling blonde hair, a figure that was both curvaceous and slender, encased in sparkling gauze that made her look like a mermaid, and an almost naked one at that, considering the nearly sheer gauze of her dress. But, beyond her obvious good looks, she had a mesmerising quality about her, something that made it hard to look away. He found himself taking a step towards her, and then another, intrigued by the way she held court in the middle of the room.

She was surrounded by a crowd of admirers, men as well as women, the men discreetly—or not—ogling her figure, the women simply wanting to be in her reflected radiance. She tossed her hair over her shoulder and her cerulean gaze met his for an instant, causing him to hesitate mid-stride. Her eyes widened and her smile curved with a catlike knowledge. She fluttered her eyelashes, but in a way that made it seem like a joke, like she was mocking herself—or him. He kept walking.

From the corner of his eye he saw a flash of violet as a small, svelte figure move quickly out of the way, sidling along the wall. He hesitated, almost turned, compelled by some deeper, instinctive desire to find *that* woman, as different as she was. To see her smile again.

Then he retrained his gaze on the Princess holding court in the middle of the ballroom. *Focus*, as he always did. He would not be guided by emotion but by reason, for here, surely, was the new face of Rossi Hotels.

CHAPTER TWO

LIANE WATCHED ALESSANDRO ROSSI walk towards her sister like a man on a mission. He wouldn't be the first—half the men in the room had already been swept up in her orbit—but he would certainly be the most eligible. She forced herself to quash the tiniest flicker of envy she couldn't keep herself from feeling as he stood in front of Ella, one hand in his pocket, his manner relaxed as he gave her a slow, smiling look.

From her position behind a potted plant Liane could study him unguardedly, taking in his tall, powerful figure, well over six feet. She barely topped five feet herself and standing next to him had made her feel small, but strangely in a good way. Delicate. When he'd gazed down at her she'd felt warmed right through, as if by the sun, as if she'd *swallowed* the sun. Silly to think like that, of course. Most likely he'd simply seen her as an amusement, maybe even an irritation. He'd certainly dismissed her quickly enough.

Besides, he was far more suited to Ella than to her. With his close-cut hair of burnished midnight, those iron-grey eyes and a face that looked as if it had been sculpted from marble, his classic good looks complemented Ella's blonde goddess-like beauty far more than Liane's less striking looks.

'You must make more of yourself, Liane,' her mother often complained. *'You're so pale and mousy, you completely fade away.'*

Once, on her mother's bidding, Liane had tried to do just that—carefully applying make-up, wearing a nicer dress to work, putting her hair up in a chignon, adding earrings and a necklace. She'd felt both shy and hopeful as she'd stepped through the doors of the school.

The results had been, to Liane's mind, disastrous—or at least humiliating. The receptionist had raised her eyebrows and smirked. *'Ooh, who are you trying to impress, then?'* The girls in her class had tittered behind their hands. *'Have you got a date, Miss?'* they'd asked, shooting each other looks. But worst of all had been the teachers Liane had overheard gossiping about her when she'd been in the staffroom, marking papers in the corner—they hadn't even seen her!

'What on earth has got into Liane? Who is she trying to impress? She looks absolutely ridiculous.'

'There is such a thing as trying too hard, isn't there?' They'd shared a look as they'd laughed. 'Poor thing. I suppose she just wants to be noticed for once.'

Liane had shrunk back into her chair, desperate not to be noticed right then. After the women had left, she'd gone into the bathroom and scrubbed off all the make-up. The next day she'd returned to school in her usual serviceable blouse and skirt, her hair back in a neat clip, her face devoid of make-up. The receptionist had given her a pitying look as Liane had marched past, her head held high, determined never to try to be noticed again. There was a reason some people naturally sparkled and shone—and some people didn't. Besides, if you didn't try, you didn't get hurt, and the shadows were a far safer place than the spotlight.

As for the spotlight… Liane turned back to Alessandro Rossi and her sister. They were like Venus and Apollo, she mused, or perhaps Venus and Ares, for there was something almost warlike about Alessandro Rossi's hard profile—the lines of his cheek and jaw were unforgiving, like two slashes of a blade. While Ella was softness and light, Alessandro was all hard, dark planes. Yet together, like two demigods of high society, they worked, that much was obvious, for the whole crowd was watching, cameras snapping, as the orchestra struck up another tune and Alessandro took Ella in his arms.

She was not going to feel jealous, Liane told herself severely, because that would be utterly absurd and frankly shaming. She'd had a few minutes of awkward chitchat with the man, about *shoes*, of all things. Ridiculous shoes. The fact that he made her heart skip a beat and a blush come to her cheeks when she thought about him now meant nothing. Nothing at all, except perhaps that she was completely inexperienced in matters of romance and flirtation, which she already knew perfectly well.

'Ella is the centre of attention, as usual,' Manon remarked sourly as she came to stand beside Liane, moving a palm frond out of the way. 'How does she manage it?'

'She's beautiful and funny and nice. Why wouldn't she?' Liane smiled and shrugged, while her older sister tracked Ella and Alessandro with a frown. 'Don't be jealous,' she entreated quietly. 'She's never spiteful about it, you know.'

'I'm not *jealous*,' Manon replied with a huff. 'I'm just bored. I didn't want to come to this wretched ball in the first place, and Maman has been throwing me at any man under the age of sixty. It's humiliating. Why is she so desperate to see us married off? You'd think it was the eighteen-hundreds or something.'

'She wants to see us provided for, and that's the only way she knows how.' Despite her mother's stern ways and near-constant barrage of criticism, Liane couldn't help but feel a rush of sympathy for her—she'd had two husbands, both of whom had died and left her with little more than pennies. She still managed to eke out an existence of shabby gentility, depending on a few small investments and her reputation to at least give the pretence of gracious living, but it wasn't much, and Ella inheriting the house had been a very bitter pill to swallow. Of course she wanted to see her daughters provided for— and, as she reminded them on many occasions, working as a teacher and a secretary was not adequate provision, not in her view, anyway.

'Why are you two standing in the corner?'

Liane tensed as her mother sailed over, dressed as always in widow's black, a martyr to her disappointments for ever. She eyed Liane critically. 'I don't think purple suits you. The blue would have been better.'

Manon rolled her eyes. 'The blue was terrible, Maman.'

Amelie sniffed. 'I suppose Ella gave you that dress?'

'Just to borrow.' As usual Liane felt the need to smooth things over. 'I'll wear the blue next time, Maman.' There probably wouldn't be a next time; it wasn't as if she went to balls every day of the week.

Amelie turned, her eyes narrowing as she took in the sight of Ella and Alessandro together. 'Making a spectacle of herself as usual, I see.' She poked Liane between her shoulder blades. 'Why don't you go over and say something? I saw you talking with Rossi earlier, so you've made his acquaintance.'

'Only because he stepped on my foot…!'

'Well, say hello again, then.' Amelie poked her again, hard enough that Liane was forced to take a few steps towards Ella and Alessandro.

'Maman…' she whispered, horrified, while Manon smothered a laugh.

'Yes, do go over, Liane,' she chimed in. 'I'm sure they'll both appreciate it.'

Amelie nudged her again, so Liane found herself standing alone on the edge of the dance floor, frozen in embarrassment. People were looking at her, sensing that something was going on, waiting to see what she would do.

'Go on, Liane!' Amelie barked, loud enough for people nearby to hear.

Liane closed her eyes. Why did her mother have to be so pushy? And why did she let herself be pushed?

'Are you hoping to cut in?'

Her eyes flew open as, mortified, she saw Alessandro and Ella standing before her. Oh, no…

'I…' The syllable came out in a squeak. Alessandro looked bemused, Ella sympathetic.

'Yes, go on and dance, Liane. I'd like to sit down for a bit.' As easily as she did everything, Ella drew her by the hand towards Alessandro. Before Liane even knew what was happening, Alessandro had taken her in his arms and Ella had disappeared. A pity dance, she thought miserably. How awful. Yet even so she couldn't keep from being affected by the citrusy tang of his aftershave, the muscles bunching his arm as she rested one hand on his shoulder, and his hand spanned the dip of her waist, warm and heavy.

'You know Ella?' Alessandro asked as he gazed down at her, moving her about the floor with grace and ease while Liane did her best to keep up.

'Yes, she's my sister.'

'How surprising. You two are nothing alike.'

A flush came to her cheeks at the implied criticism. Of course she already knew she was nothing like Ella. 'We're stepsisters, actually.'

'Ah, I see.'

His knowing tone both annoyed and hurt her. Why did *everyone* have to see her as someone less than? She wasn't envious of Ella, but she was so very tired of not being appreciated for herself—someone who didn't crave the spotlight. What was so wrong with that?

'The two of you look very well together,' Liane remarked, a touch of acid to her tone. 'The belle and beau of the ball.'

'You think so?' Alessandro looked only amused. 'Then why did you cut in?'

Colour washed her cheeks. 'I did not!'

'You seemed as if you were about to.'

She was not going to admit that her mother had pushed her onto the dance floor. 'I was just trying to get Ella's attention,' she improvised stiffly. 'My mother wanted to speak to her.'

'Ah, well, then, why didn't you say so?'

'I didn't have the opportunity,' she snapped. Why was he so…*smug*?

'Don't look daggers at me,' Alessandro remarked mildly. 'I'm only teasing.'

A remark that put Liane into a complete tizzy, because

she had no idea how to take it. Was he teasing? Or was he just being contrary? Or maybe she was? She shook her head, her gaze on the floor as they continued to dance.

'You're really quite something,' Alessandro remarked as he whirled her around a final time, the music coming to a finish with a swell of the orchestra. 'I can't decide if you're a mouse or a virago.'

'Oh, a mouse, most certainly,' Liane managed, stung by his verdict. In truth she didn't know which was the worse one to be. 'And look, here is Ella, waiting for you. How perfect.'

She turned away, not trusting the look on her face as she walked quickly from the dance floor.

'Liane—' Ella began, and she shook her head.

'Please, go and dance.' She didn't wait to see if Ella did as she'd bid. She didn't want to look.

The rest of the evening passed interminably. Alessandro danced with Ella again, and then stayed by her side as they laughed and chatted, moving through the various groups mingling in the ballroom. Liane made sure never to be near them; she didn't want to be the butt of one of Alessandro's remarks again.

Would Ella fall in love with Alessandro? she wondered. Ella, she knew, loved to fall in love, something Liane had never been able to understand.

'Don't worry, my heart can't actually be broken,' Ella had told her more than once. 'It's made of rubber—it practically bounces! I *like* falling in love, Liane. It's the best feeling in the world, like tumbling through stars! You should try it.'

Liane always smiled and said nothing because she had no intention of doing something so reckless, so dangerous. A heart was a very precious thing and she guarded hers closely, waiting for the right moment. The right man, if he even existed. She hoped he did, but on her bad days she wondered.

She was twenty-seven years old and she'd only gone on a handful of dates, none of them leading anywhere. She hadn't yet found anyone who would make her want more, or dare for the daydream she cast for herself in lonely moments—a hazy world of children and dogs, love and laughter, ease and comfort. The kind of home she'd once had and lost, with the death of her father so many years ago. The kind of life she longed for but was afraid to try to find.

Liane glanced again at Alessandro and Ella. They were standing very close together in the centre of the ballroom. He was murmuring in her ear and she was smiling in that teasing, catlike way that Liane knew she practised in the mirror. She'd seen her do it. Her stomach cramped and she turned away. She was happy for her sister, very happy, of course, but that didn't mean she had to take a front row seat to the unfolding of her fairy tale romance.

A balmy breeze blew in from the penthouse's terrace and Liane moved through the crowd to step outside, enjoying the sultry air on her face. The terrace ran along all four sides of the impressive ballroom, affording a panoramic view of the city. Liane moved away from a few chatting couples, hardly needing the reminder of her own single status.

She'd never minded so much before; she was generally happy with her job, happy with herself. Content, at least. *Mostly*, even if she liked to daydream.

As she gazed out at the city she found herself thinking

about Alessandro. The mocking gleam in his eyes, the way his mobile mouth had quirked. He was infuriating and annoying and yet even when she'd been angry she'd felt *alive* in his arms. She could remember exactly how humour had flashed in his eyes, turning them to silver, and how, strangely, the way he'd looked at her had made her feel *seen*, in a way she hadn't before…

The distant chiming of a clock somewhere in the city had Liane giving herself a mental shake. Was it midnight already? Time to go home, then. She'd find Ella first, and—

She drew her breath in sharply as she caught sight of a familiar slender figure on the pavement far below, dressed in gauzy silk and diamantes, her dress flowing out behind her in a silken stream as she ran down the front steps of the hotel. *Ella*. Why was she leaving the ball in such a rush? Liane's stomach cramped with anxiety. What had happened?

She whirled away from the terrace, stumbling through the doors to get back into the ballroom and downstairs to find her sister. She had to push her way through the milling crowds, catching snatches of gossip as she headed towards the bank of elevators.

'Who is she? Whoever she is, she's clearly captured *his* interest—'

'The Prince of Manhattan's found his Princess, then? He's always seemed so remote—'

'But she just disappeared. Ran out like the building was on fire—'

Finally Liane reached the elevator and stabbed the button to go down. She scrabbled for her phone in her handbag, but when she dialled Ella's number there was no answer. Her sister was awful about answering her phone, which was somewhat absurd considering how glued she was to social media.

'Phones aren't for *calling* people,' she'd told Liane once, as if stating something patently obvious.

The elevator doors finally opened and Liane hurried in, counting down all twenty-four floors to the magnificent lobby, all marble and crystal and gilt. It was empty now, for everyone was still up at the ball, but as she came outside onto the steps she stopped suddenly, her breath coming out in a rush, for while her sister might have disappeared, Alessandro Rossi, looking as devastating as ever, was standing right in front of her.

'You again.'

Alessandro Rossi narrowed his eyes in speculation as he surveyed Ella's stepsister, who had stopped abruptly in front of him, her chest heaving. He realised he was enjoying the sight, more than a bit. Her hair had tumbled from its pins and lay over her shoulders in disordered silvery-gold waves. Her cheeks were flushed, her eyes sparkling—not so colourless after all, then. Right now she looked vibrant and alive, like a tiny, perfect jewel.

'Where's Ella?' she demanded breathlessly.

'I have no idea.' He lifted the glass shoe he'd found lying on the step, like some sort of art installation or perhaps a weapon, glittering under the streetlights. 'She left this, though.'

Liane stared at the high-heeled shoe with a flash of recognition, as if she'd seen it before. 'She *left* it?'

'So it would seem. It was lying rather artfully on the steps as I came out. Just the one, of course, like the fairy tale.' A deliberate ploy? But what on earth for?

Liane pressed her lips together and then gave a short

nod of acceptance, perhaps understanding. Alessandro's eyes narrowed further. He'd sensed the connection between Ella and her stepsister; Ella had spoken about her with careless affection, while Liane seemed to have appointed herself as Ella's minder. 'Do you know what this is about?' he asked, his tone turning terse.

'What do you mean?'

'I get the feeling something is going on. Something has been planned.' And if there was one thing he hated it was being used for someone else's purposes. He would not be that boy trotted out into the living room years ago, obediently hugging his mother and father while everyone watched and his parents pretended. No, never again.

'Nothing has been planned,' Liane said, but she sounded cautious. Uncertain.

Alessandro didn't know how or why, but something about this whole bizarre scenario felt like a set-up. Why had Ella run off like that, without so much as a word? She'd made such a scene, sprinting through the ballroom, her hair and dress both flying out behind her. Rather fetching, really, if a bit clichéd and overdone. *A bit staged.* What was really going on? 'Do you know where Ella went?' he asked.

'No.' She pressed her lips together and again Alessandro felt there was something she wasn't saying. Something about this whole situation definitely felt off, and he intended to find out what it was. He was not about to be played, not by Ella, not by her mousy stepsister. Not by anyone.

'Are you sure?' She nodded, and he gave her a measured look. Was he being fanciful in seeing something vulnerable and strangely touching in the determined tilt of her chin? In any case, he needed to get to the bottom of this absurd little drama—and quash it. 'Why don't we conduct this conversation somewhere a bit more private?' he suggested, his tone as cool as hers.

Something sparked in her eyes, although the look she gave him was guarded. 'And where would that be?'

'I have a private suite in the hotel.'

A huff of maidenly suspicion escaped her in a gust as her body straightened, practically twanging with indignation. 'Your private suite!' The words were full of outraged incredulity, almost making him smile. She sounded like a scandalised spinster.

'It is fully staffed, and has a study,' he assured her, 'but if you're worried for your virtue, as far as I'm concerned the hotel bar will do just as well, trust me.'

Colour flared more deeply in her face. 'I'm not sure what more I can tell you,' she answered stiffly, 'but as I am concerned for my sister, I would certainly like to hear your account of the evening.'

So she would take him to task! Again he had the urge to smile; he found, bizarrely, he was enjoying her display of spirit. Virago more than mouse, then. 'Very well,' he said, and gave a little courtly bow. 'After you.'

With her head held high—and even then only reaching a bit past his shoulder—she marched past him, back into the hotel, while Alessandro followed, pocketing the shoe.

The hotel bar was a comfortable bastion of leather and mahogany, tucked in the back of the lobby, the only person in sight the weary bartender polishing glasses behind the bar. He snapped to attention when Alessandro stalked into the space, lifting two fingers and pointing to a bottle of whisky glinting in the cabinet behind him before guiding the woman to a discreet nook in the back.

'I realise,' he said as he sat down and the woman perched stiffly opposite him, her back ramrod-straight, 'that I don't actually know your full name.'

'Liane Blanchard.'

'You're French?' She nodded. So he'd been right about that accent. For some reason this pleased him. 'What are you doing in New York?'

'I thought you wished to discuss my sister.'

'It's all relevant, I assure you.'

'Is it?' Again with that chin-tilt, the flash of violet in her eyes. She might have been pale and small but she still had fire, even if he wondered whether she realised she did. 'Perhaps I should be the one asking the questions.'

'Oh, do you think so? And why is that?'

'Because my sister ran off into the night, clearly distressed—'

'On the contrary, she wasn't distressed at all.' Alessandro cut her off, his tone turning cool as he recalled Ella's bizarre antics. 'We were having a discussion and she suddenly took off, without a moment's notice.'

Liane cocked her head, scepticism evident in her eyes. 'Just like that?'

'As a matter of fact, yes. Just like that. And left this shoe.' With mocking deliberation he placed the shoe on the table between them. 'Now that is what I call a ridiculous shoe.'

A smile burst across her face like sunlight and then disappeared. He found he was grinning back just for a second, everything in him lightening despite his instinctive suspicion. 'All of Ella's shoes are ridiculous,' she conceded, 'but these more than most, it's true.'

He didn't miss the deep affection in her voice; clearly the sisters were close, and yet so very different. Ella had been bubbly and gregarious, laughing and light and easy to talk to, if a bit, well, *insipid*. He'd been bored, but not as bored as he usually was, and the paparazzi had almost certainly taken the publicity shots they'd needed. He'd been ready to call it a night before Ella had decided to, by sprinting out of the ballroom.

And meanwhile Liane was quiet and contained, yet with those beguiling flashes of fire, those incredible eyes…still waters ran deep, and Alessandro supposed hers ran very deep indeed.

The bartender appeared with the bottle of whisky and two glasses and Alessandro tossed the shoe onto a chair to make way for their drinks.

'I don't drink whisky,' Liane informed him coolly after the bartender had left.

Unperturbed, Alessandro poured a finger of whisky in each glass. 'There's always a first time.'

She folded her arms and attempted to stare him down. 'You're rather…controlling, aren't you?'

'I prefer to think of it as being hospitable.' He proffered her the glass, and after a second's pause she took it. 'But by all means don't drink if you don't want to. It seemed rude not to offer you a whisky when I'm having one myself.' And with that he took one long, burning swallow, grateful for the heat hitting the back of his throat.

Liane put her glass down without giving it so much as a sniff. 'I'm worried about my sister,' she stated almost defiantly.

'I told you,' he replied calmly, 'she was in no way distressed. At all.'

'I know what you said, and in truth I'm inclined to believe you.' She paused, pursing her lips, a little wrinkle appearing in the creamy smoothness of her forehead. 'But she can be quite—impetuous sometimes about things. And to leave the ball that way…' She let out a soft gasp of realisation, biting the soft fullness of her lower lip, and Alessandro's gaze narrowed. 'Of *course*,' she whispered, and then she let out a little laugh, a sound that reminded Alessandro, bizarrely, of the bubbles in champagne. He wanted to hear it again, even as he recognised he'd been right. Something *had* been going on, and Liane knew what it was.

'What?' he demanded. 'What do you know? What's so funny?'

'It's not funny really, but it's classic Ella.' She sighed as she leaned back against the leather cushions of her seat, her body relaxing so for once she didn't look so up-tight, so anxious. 'Ella might have told you; she's something of a social media influencer, although she's just getting started. The glass shoes were given to her by some up-and-coming designer—she must have left one on purpose. The clock strikes midnight, Cinderella at the ball, et cetera.' She sighed, shaking her head. 'And she's gone off wearing one shoe, and is now probably going to vlog the whole thing as some modern take on the fairy tale.'

He frowned, feeling not much more the wiser. 'Vlog?'

She wrinkled her nose, letting out another one of those tinkly little laughs. 'A video blog. I'm a social media dinosaur, but even I know what a vlog is, although I suppose that's because of Ella.'

'So this is nothing more than a publicity stunt,' he surmised slowly, hating the thought, and Liane nodded.

'Yes. Something like that. At least I think so. That would be Ella's style.'

He wasn't surprised, based on what he already knew of Ella, and yet he still felt distrustful. Irritated too, because he did not want to be used in her little ploys and games. And yet, he told himself with the cold logic he prided himself on, he'd basically been using Ella for publicity, making sure they were snapped together to promote the hotel and make it seem so *fun*. If all the while she'd been using him, well, there was a fitting sort of rightness to it, or there could be, even if it went against every instinct he'd ever had. He never allowed himself to be used, not since he'd been a helpless child.

No, if anything, he was the one who would do the using and, considering all he had learned, Ella Ash would suit his purposes admirably. Their association would not end here, for both of their benefits. And if this intriguing woman came as part of the bargain…

'Very good,' he told Liane, and tossed back the rest of his whisky, levelling his iron gaze on her own startled one. 'Then you can help me find her.'

CHAPTER THREE

'ALESSANDRO ROSSI WANTS to see me?'

Ella's eyebrows rose in two golden arcs as she lounged back on the sofa in her pyjamas. A small knowing smile curved her mouth. 'Must have been the shoes.'

'It must have,' Liane agreed, 'or the gorgeous dress or your stunning looks or your sparkling personality. Perhaps all three—or four, even.'

Ella laughed, tossing her head back against the pillows. 'Stop it, I'm blushing.'

Not as much as she'd been blushing last night, when she'd been sitting alone in that bar with Alessandro, remembering how he'd looked down at her with such amusement. *I can't decide if you're a mouse or a virago.* Well, she'd been a virago last night, stung into tart replies by his own self-assured arrogance. This wasn't about her, Liane reminded herself. It was, as ever, about Ella.

'He wants to meet you at his office this afternoon,' she told her stepsister, 'so you ought to get dressed.'

'But it's Saturday.' Ella's eyes fluttered closed as she let out a deep, breathy sigh. 'And I'm exhausted. I was out till five in the morning, you know. Alonso was having a party in Soho—'

'I guess you didn't turn into a pumpkin, then.'

'It's the *carriage* that turns into a pumpkin, Liane. Get your fairy tales straight.' She laughed as she opened her eyes. 'Wasn't that an amazing stunt, though? I put the video up at two o'clock this morning and it already has *fifty thousand* hits.' A bubble of delighted, incredulous laughter escaped her as she reached for her phone and started scrolling. 'Sixty thousand now! Liane, I'm practically viral.'

'Amazing that the term is a compliment.'

'You know what I mean.'

'Yes, I do. What video was this?'

'Of Alessandro finding the shoe, of course.' Ella leaned back against the sofa, a smug smile curving her lips.

'You filmed him?' Liane asked, uneasy at the thought.

'Of course.'

Judging from what little she knew of the man, Liane doubted he would be pleased. He'd certainly acted suspicious last night, demanding to know why Ella had left— and not out of concern either. He seemed, she thought, a quiet, controlled sort of person, someone who prized restraint over emotion. Someone utterly unlike Ella. She sighed and glanced at her watch. It was already past noon, and last night Alessandro Rossi had asked—demanded, really—that Ella appear at his office in midtown at two o'clock sharp. Liane's first instinct had been to refuse on principle; Alessandro Rossi alarmed her as much as he fascinated her, and she wasn't entirely sure what he wanted with her stepsister. Then she realised how beneficial a meeting with him could be for Ella's career aspirations, such as they were. Not that she knew much about social media influencing herself, but still.

Even though he'd only arrived a few months ago,

Alessandro Rossi was already one of the most famous men in the city—handsome, wealthy, powerful, reclusive and thought to be of Italian nobility. Finding out what he wanted with Ella would surely be the savvy thing to do. *And it has nothing to do with you wanting to see him again.*

'Don't you want to start getting ready?' Liane cajoled. 'This could be your big break, Ella.'

She stretched one foot, studying the silver nail polish on her toes. 'What do you think he wants?'

'I have no idea.' That wasn't entirely true. When Alessandro had said he wanted to find Ella last night, he'd assured her it was for a business proposition.

'Legitimate,' he'd added sharply when Liane had looked somewhat scandalised. 'I don't have to hire mistresses, Miss Blanchard, if that's what you were thinking. Trust me on that score.'

'I wasn't—' she'd protested rather feebly.

'I can read your expression perfectly. That's not what this is about. At all.' Which had reassured her to a rather ridiculous degree, even as she'd told herself not to be a fool. Alessandro would never think of her that way. It wouldn't even occur to him.

'Then what is it about?' she'd asked, doing her best not to blush as she imagined what Alessandro Rossi's *mistresses* might be like.

'A business opportunity that will advantage your sister's interests as well as my own. Now, please get her to my office at two o'clock sharp tomorrow if she wants to know the details.' And he'd handed her his business card by way of dismissal.

'No idea at all?' Ella pressed, lifting her head to regard Liane from her lazy sprawl on the sofa. 'What did he say to you?'

'He did mention some sort of business proposition,' Liane allowed, 'but I have no idea what it could be. Still, I imagine it might be worth listening to, at least.' Normally Liane would have advised caution—a word her sister did not take too much to heart—but she was honest enough to acknowledge that she was, somewhat guardedly, encouraging her sister to attend this meeting not just because of the opportunity it could provide but because she wanted to see Alessandro Rossi again. She wasn't sure whether she trusted or even liked him, but when she was in his presence she felt...electrified. More alive than she'd ever felt before, as if every nerve and sense had sprung to quivering life. Which of course was ridiculous, and yet...

True.

'So?' she prompted, nudging Ella's foot. 'Are you going to go?'

'Oh, I suppose.' Ella yawned hugely. 'I mean, for curiosity's sake more than anything else.'

'What did you talk about with him last night?' Liane asked.

'I don't really remember. Basic chitchat. Dull stuff, mostly. He can be charming, but it felt a bit like an act. Almost like he didn't really want to be there.'

'He's known to be somewhat reclusive.' According to the tabloids, anyway. Alessandro Rossi did not socialise or appear in public except for work, something that had made him an enigma, and an attractive one at that.

'In other words, boring.' Ella yawned again, her eyes fluttering closed, and Liane couldn't believe her sister was going to let this opportunity slip through her fingers. Typical Ella—ambitious only when she felt like it.

'Ella.' She nudged her foot again. 'If you're going to go you should have started getting ready ten minutes ago.'

Ella cracked open an eye to gaze at her speculatively. 'Why are you so determined to get me there?'

Don't blush. 'It's a good opportunity for you. Or at least it might be.'

'I suppose.' Ella let out another enormous yawn as she stretched languorously and then finally, in a tangle of golden limbs, rose from the sofa. 'Oh, all right, okay, I'll go, if just to satisfy your curiosity.'

'I'm not—' Liane began, but Ella just laughed all the way upstairs.

At two minutes to two o'clock they were standing in front of an imposing skyscraper that looked to be made almost entirely of opaque black glass that soared up to the summery blue sky, a beacon of dark modernity in the middle of the city.

'Wow.' Ella lowered her sunglasses to survey the building with appreciation. 'He owns the whole building?'

Liane nodded at the discreet gold plaque to the side of the door on which was written 'Rossi Enterprises'. 'It appears so, or at least his family does.' She'd done an Internet search on Alessandro Rossi that morning, forcing herself away from all the articles of spurious speculation in the online tabloids and on gossip sites, heading for a simple encyclopaedia entry that told her Alessandro was the only son of Leonardo Rossi; his father had handed the business to him last year and retired to Ibiza; there was no mention of his mother. He was notoriously reclusive, with very little known about his private life, and Rossi Enterprises was worth billions.

'Well, then, maybe this is worth satisfying your curiosity,' Ella proclaimed and with a glinting smile for Liane she sashayed inside the office building and promptly charmed the grim-faced, black-suited man at the door, who told her Mr Rossi was expecting her.

Liane's stomach tightened with nerves as they soared upwards towards Alessandro Rossi's penthouse office. She wasn't nervous about seeing him again, not precisely, more about him seeing how she reacted to him. This silly schoolgirl infatuation she had stupidly developed over a stranger needed to stop—especially if it showed on her face. She couldn't bear to be revealed in such a way, and she had a sense that Alessandro would be able to guess exactly what she was thinking—and feeling—which was a rather horrifying thought.

Why did she have to react to the man this way? If anything, his high-handed manner should annoy her and nothing more. Yet even now her body was tingling with anticipation, excitement fizzing through her veins, simply at the prospect of seeing him again.

A solemn-looking assistant in a sleek dark suit met them at the elevator and escorted them to an imposing pair of wood-panelled doors. Liane could feel her heart thumping as Ella went in first, head held high, looking as fabulous as she always did in a tastefully clinging yellow sheath and matching open-toed heels, her hair in glossy golden waves about her shoulders. Liane slipped in behind, staying near the wall as Ella strode towards Alessandro's desk.

'I heard you had a proposition for me,' she said, *almost* making it sound dirty.

Alessandro rose from behind his desk in one fluid movement, his face expressionless, his powerful body encased in an expertly tailored charcoal-grey suit that brought out the silver in his eyes. He looked powerful and remote and completely in control and, stupidly, Liane's heart fluttered. She really needed to get to grips with these absurd feelings of hers. Fortunately—or not—and just as she'd expected, he wasn't even looking at her.

'Miss Ash. So glad you could meet me. Please, sit.' He gestured to one of the leather club chairs in front of his massive desk, the floor-to-ceiling windows giving a panoramic view of the city, glinting skyscrapers all around, Central Park a haze of green in the distance. His gaze flicked once, very briefly, to Liane, revealing nothing, yet even so Liane felt as if she'd been jolted with electricity, a second's blazing connection—at least for her. 'And you, Miss Blanchard, as well, of course,' he added smoothly. Was there a hint of humour in his voice? Liane wasn't sure, but she blushed anyway.

'Thank you,' she murmured as she came forward. She perched on the edge of her chair as he stood behind his desk, surveying them both, before he reached down to retrieve something.

'I believe this belongs to you,' he told Ella, bringing out the silly glass shoe with a mocking flourish.

Ella, always rising to the occasion, laughed and raised one slender leg. 'You should see if it fits first,' she told him with a deliberate flutter of her eyelashes.

'Very well,' he said, his face expressionless. His gaze flicked, ever so briefly, to Liane, before he removed her sister's sandal and, without any innuendo or enthusiasm, slid the glass shoe on her foot.

'A perfect fit,' he remarked dryly as he stood back.

Ella's eyes danced. 'So this is when you ask me to marry you, right? And we live happily ever after.' She tossed her head back, giving a throaty laugh. 'Somehow I don't think that was the business proposition you intended to put to me.' She flipped off the glass shoe and replaced her sandal as she gave him a forthright look, the glass slipper dangling from one manicured finger. 'So, Mr Rossi, what exactly is this business proposition?'

Ella Ash was a firecracker, that much was obvious. Alessandro kept his gaze even and expressionless as he fought both amusement and annoyance at her blatant theatrics. His suspicions from last night were clearly confirmed today; she was the type of person who was constantly performing, needing an invisible audience everywhere she went. A lot like his mother had been, and exactly the kind of exhibitionism he hated, and yet in this case she might be just what he needed, at least for a brief time. For the sake of Rossi Hotels.

His gaze flickered once more to Liane. He found he couldn't stop looking at her, trying to gauge what emotion seethed behind those opaque violet eyes, her mouth pursed, her hands in her lap. She wore a plain blue shirtdress, a rather matronly outfit, and yet he was still conscious of her lithe curves, the way the belt at her waist emphasised its slenderness. She was perfectly petite, delicate in every way, and he found her far more fascinating than the obvious Ella. Gold compared to gilt, he reflected, before banishing the thought.

He turned back to Ella. 'My business proposition is simple. Rossi Hotels is in need of a younger ambassador. Our brand of unparalleled luxury, comfort and privacy has not been translating as well to the social media generation.' He quirked his mouth wryly, inviting Ella into the joke, if there even was one. He hated the whole concept of courting publicity, but he hated failure even more.

He'd spent the last ten years building Rossi Enterprises back up from the ashes after his father had so carelessly let it burn near to the ground, and he'd be damned if he let any part of it smoulder away now, simply because the millennial generation needed to see something on Instagram before they paid money. At least with this he could control the attention, the narrative.

'Is that right?' Ella cocked her head. 'I will say, the hotel did seem a little stuffy to me.'

He forced a small, tight smile of acknowledgement. 'So, as I'm sure you've been able to guess, this is where you come in.'

'Do you want me to feature the hotel on my vlog?' Her eyes widened. 'Because the video of you finding the glass shoe has got…' she paused to reach for her phone, scrolling with lightning speed '…two hundred thousand views! Can you believe it?'

'What?' His voice sharpened as he stared at her hard. 'What video?'

'You mean you asked me here without even seeing it?' she exclaimed with a peal of delighted laughter. 'Look.'

She handed him her phone and, frowning, Alessandro gazed down at a somewhat blurry video of, he saw, himself, walking down the steps of his hotel. The camera zoomed in on the glass slipper, lying so artfully on the ground, and then on his face as he picked it up, turned it over in his hands. She'd put text over the last image— *OMG, the Prince found my slipper!! What next??*—which made Alessandro suppress a wince. Seriously, this stuff was both excruciating and infantile, and yet it seemed to work, because in the few seconds it had taken for him to view the damned thing the video had garnered a thousand more views. Insane. And not in a good way. He had a whole churning mess of feelings about being secretly filmed and viewed, being trotted out and *used*, and none of them were good.

Right then and there he fought the deep-seated instinct to fling the phone on the floor, ground it to crushed glass beneath his heel and show Ella Ash the door. *How dared she use him?* He, who would never let himself be used.

And yet, pushing down those heated emotions, he forced himself not to react. He'd suspected she'd been using him last night; now his suspicions had been confirmed. It didn't change his own purpose.

No, he would choose for it not to. Choose control and restraint over anger and emotion, as he always did. Choose to be unlike either of his parents, led by emotion and desire, careering into desperation and misery and using him in the process. Silently he handed the phone back and Ella pocketed it. Liane, he saw out of the corner of his eye, hadn't said a word, although she was definitely looking apprehensive, her violet gaze darting between him and her sister, golden lashes sweeping down when she caught him looking at her.

'So,' he surmised in a clipped voice, 'you took that video of me from some hiding place, I presume?'

'An Uber in the street.' Ella was flippantly unrepentant. Was this sort of behaviour normal among this generation? Alessandro wondered. At thirty-four he was only twelve years older than Ella, but right now he felt utterly ancient.

'And posted it without my knowledge or consent?' he pressed, his voice hardening.

Ella's eyes widened. 'Is that even a thing?'

It was debatable, Alessandro supposed, considering he'd been in a public place, but he was not going to argue the legalities of taking and posting footage of another person right now. 'Just what was the purpose of your little glass slipper stunt, may I ask?'

'My friend Alonso Alovar made the shoes. It was meant to be some publicity for him and, trust me, it's working, because his website has already crashed from all the orders.'

'How did they know they were his shoes?'

'From the hashtags.' She shook her head slowly, her eyes dancing with amusement. 'Do you even know how social media works?'

No, and he didn't really have any desire to know, had never needed to know. Oh, he understood that things went viral, and people got pathetically famous for fifteen minutes through some absurd post or other, yes, *fine*, but it didn't affect real life. His life. The world of business and banking, investments and enterprise, stocks and bonds and cold, hard cash. Except perhaps now it might. Unfortunately.

'I've never had a need or interest in using social media,' he told her levelly, 'but, as I stated before, I am interested in engaging with the medium for the purposes of publicity for the hotels.'

'Don't put that in a tweet,' Ella quipped, and he shook his head in exasperation.

'This is what I propose—for you to join me on a brief tour of the Rossi hotels that I have been planning. It's our centenary this year, and there will be parties hosted at each hotel to celebrate the anniversary throughout the next week. In fact, there is one in Los Angeles tomorrow night.' He'd only been intending to make a brief appearance at a few of the events, but that would have to change now. He'd have to go to every one and stay for at least an hour, chatting and mingling, with Ella at his side. How interminable.

'A tour?' Ella's eyes rounded, her lips parting. 'You want me to go on a tour with you?'

'Yes, the idea is we would go together and it would be covered publicly by the magazines, et cetera.'

'Together?' Ella asked, her eyes dancing. 'I mean, *together* together?'

She was teasing him, but Alessandro decided to take her seriously. Best to be clear about what he wanted—and what he definitely didn't. For a second he had an urge to look at Liane again, but he resisted it. 'Together for the purposes of publicity only, I assure you. As charming as you may be, Miss Ash, this really is a business proposition and nothing more.'

'And then I post about it all on social media?' she surmised, her voice rising in excitement. 'A whole series—like a story, one post per day? We could follow on from the glass slipper—Prince Charming finds his Princess! What happens next? Where do they go? It would be *brilliant*.'

'I had not considered such an angle,' Alessandro replied, 'but it might be effective.' It sounded like an awful, cheap gimmick to him, but it seemed this was what the world had come to. 'The main thing is that you highlight the hotels, not some ridiculous story.' He glanced at Liane, who was looking rather severe. 'Do you disapprove?' he asked and, startled, she jumped a little, her gaze skating away from his.

'Why should I disapprove?'

He didn't know exactly, but he still sensed that she

did. There was something distasteful about the whole thing, even *especially* to him. He didn't court publicity. He hated attention. This was not the way he operated at all, and yet here he was. For the sake of the hotels. For the sake of Rossi Enterprises. And this time he would be in control.

There's no other reason you're doing it, is there?

He banished that sly internal voice as he gave a dismissive shrug. 'You tell me.'

Liane didn't meet his eyes as she answered. 'I don't disapprove, Mr Rossi, although it's not for me to disapprove or approve. This is Ella's decision.'

'Indeed.' He turned back to Ella. 'There are two Rossi hotels in America—one in Los Angeles and the one here in New York, and three in Europe—London, Paris and Rome. The parties are planned over the next week.' Which was a fair amount of time to be gallivanting around the world with Ella Ash in tow, but he could work remotely and it would also provide him with the opportunity to check in on each hotel, which he'd been planning to do over the next few months anyway. All in all, a worthwhile exercise, or so he hoped. 'I'll remunerate you for your time, of course, and provide you with accommodation and travel, as well as the necessary wardrobe accoutrements.'

'I can provide the wardrobe,' Ella assured him. 'This will be an amazing opportunity for some of the designers I work with. Trust me, you won't be disappointed.'

He gave a brief nod of acceptance. 'Very well. All I ask is that I see and sign off on every message or photo before you post it.' He might not be social media savvy, but he knew well enough how things could spiral out of control online and he had no intention of being made a fool of. Ever. Already he feared this project was ill-advised. At least it was only a week.

Ella cocked her head, pursing her lips. 'Agreed, but you've got to trust me. Judging from what I've seen so far, what you think works on social media might actually not.'

He inclined his head in terse acknowledgement. 'Naturally I'm willing to take advice on the matter, but I will have the ultimate say.' Of that he would not be dissuaded.

'Okay.' She smiled at him, a dazzling display of teeth and eyes, all sparkle and shine, making him wonder just how much there actually was underneath.

'So you agree?' he asked, raising his eyebrows.

'Yes, but I have one condition.'

'Oh?' His tone cooled. 'And what is that?'

'Liane comes with me.'

Liane made some small, startled noise, her hand flying to her mouth. Alessandro glanced at her, noticing the way her eyes widened above her hand, as soft and purple as a bed of pansies; clearly she was as surprised as he was by this suggestion. 'I am not opposed,' he stated, realising with a slight jolt just how much he meant it.

'Good, because I need Liane.'

He raised his eyebrows. 'Need her?'

'For moral support and companionship.' Ella's tone was staunch. 'She comes or I don't.'

'No need for ultimatums.' He was not, he realised, opposed to the idea at all. Quite the contrary. He glanced at Liane, who was still looking rather shocked, a blush turning her cheeks a delicate pink. 'Are you able to take time off work?' He realised he didn't even know if she worked, or what she did with her time, her life; he basically knew nothing about her at all.

Slowly she removed her hand from her mouth, still

looking shaken. 'I'm a teacher and we broke for summer vacation last week, so, yes…in theory.'

'In theory? You are willing to accompany us?'

Liane glanced at Ella. 'You don't really need me, do you, Ella?' she asked quietly.

'I do,' Ella insisted. 'You're sensible and no-nonsense and I'll fall to pieces without you. You know I will. I always do.' She reached for Liane's hands, squeezing them in her own. 'Please, Liane. I need you. Truly.'

Liane glanced uncertainly between Ella and Alessandro, clearly torn. Why was she so reluctant? he wondered with a pinch of irritation. At least he thought that was what it was. He was offering an all-expenses-paid trip to some of the world's top destinations, while staying at a series of luxury hotels. She should be thanking her lucky stars or, really, *him*.

'Well?' he asked, a touch of impatience in his voice.

Liane took a deep breath, and then she nodded as she squeezed Ella's hands before releasing them. 'All right,' she said, her tone making it sound as if she were agreeing to something frightening or dangerous rather than a luxury vacation. 'I'll do it. I'll go.'

CHAPTER FOUR

SHE REALLY NEEDED to pinch herself. Liane glanced out of the window of the private jet at the cerulean sky, a few fleecy clouds scudding by. In a little over an hour they were going to be landing in Los Angeles. How crazy was that? Forty-eight hours ago Alessandro Rossi had stepped on her toes. Now she was in his private plane, about to jet around the world. Not that he'd looked at her once since taking off. Or even Ella, for that matter. It was as if, once this bizarre deal had been agreed, they'd both more or less ceased to exist.

She glanced at Ella, who was sprawled in the wide leather seat across from her, fingers flying over her phone as usual. Liane almost wished she was interested in social media the way Ella was, anything to distract her from her own circling thoughts, the uneasy, anxious restlessness coursing through her.

Why had Ella insisted she come along on this crazy trip? And why had she agreed? Of course she knew the answers to both questions—Ella had always counted on her common sense, and she'd agreed because she never said no to her sister.

And because you wanted to spend more time with Alessandro Rossi.

Even if he wasn't looking at her. Even if he almost certainly hadn't thought about her once since suggesting this plan.

Unable to keep herself from it, Liane glanced at the seat diagonally from hers, where Alessandro was poring over some papers on the table in front of him, dark, straight brows drawn together over those hooded eyes. His lashes fanned his cheeks as he read—thick, dark velvety lashes that still somehow made him look masculine. Strange, that. He shifted in his seat, recrossing his legs, and Liane breathed in the citrusy tang of his aftershave.

She turned back to the window, determined to focus on the blue sky and not the man across from her, whose very presence made her senses swim. A party tonight in Los Angeles, and another in London two days after that— it made her head spin. Her mother had been stunned by the sudden turn of events, but also unbearably, pragmatically hopeful.

'This is your chance to make a good match, Liane!' she'd exclaimed. 'Finally, you can find yourself a husband. Do not waste this opportunity. Make the most of yourself, if you can.'

'Alessandro Rossi doesn't have eyes for me, Maman,' Liane had told her, trying to sound rueful rather than forlorn.

'Not Rossi, of course,' Amelie dismissed. 'He's above your league, to be sure.' Liane did her best not to look stung; she knew her mother was only speaking the truth in her usual blunt way. Alessandro Rossi was way, way above her league. 'But someone else, perhaps?' Amelie suggested. 'Someone who works for him, an assistant or acquaintance? You are bound to meet many eligible men in your travels. You must keep your eye out, and make sure to look your best. I will pack the blue gown.'

Circa nineteen eighty-three, Liane had thought with a shudder. Her mother was well-intentioned if decidedly misguided. 'And what if I don't want to get married?' she'd asked, half teasing. 'What if I don't want to hook a man like a fish?' Not that she even could. She wouldn't even know how to try. She'd always hoped one day a man might sweep into her life, and her into his arms. She wouldn't have to go looking for love because it would find her, bowl her over.

'Bah.' Her mother waved her hand in dismissal. 'What else would you do with a man?'

The memory made Liane both sigh and smile now. Despite her mother's near-constant criticism, she felt sorry for her, soured by two expedient marriages that hadn't turned out to be so expedient after all. Her own father had been a lovable gambler, and Robert Ash had been extravagant in his largesse and hopeless with money. Amelie had been left nearly destitute—twice. No wonder she had become both bitter and pragmatic, taking out her disappointments on her daughters. Manon had learned not to care, but Liane still had to work not to let it hurt.

She wasn't sure whether her mother had been deeply in love with either of her husbands, but she suspected she'd at least felt some affection for them. Not the fairy tale, though, she thought with a sigh. Perhaps such epic love stories, glass slippers included, were really only for fiction. She certainly hadn't seen any evidence for them, just the manufactured appearance of them on social media, and yet still, she knew, she secretly yearned for it to happen to her one day. Not the glass slipper, but the Prince. The sweet and sure certainty of finding a man who understood her, who loved her, who *saw* her truly. She didn't necessarily believe there was only one man out there for her, but she hoped there was at least one. Somewhere. Some day…but not, she reminded herself, today.

'How many views now?' she asked her sister, and Ella looked up from her phone.

'Six hundred thousand. It's insane.' She glanced at Alessandro, her eyes full of humour. 'How come you're so famous?'

'Because my family is one of Italy's oldest noble lines and has been foremost in European investments for one hundred years,' he replied without looking up from the papers he was reading.

'And yet you need me.' Ella's voice was full of laughing flirtatiousness.

Alessandro looked up then, one eyebrow quirked. 'Consider this more of a social experiment than anything born of true necessity, Miss Ash. The Rossi hotels are merely one branch of the business as a whole.' He shrugged, returning his gaze to his papers. 'My fortune is hardly dependent upon them, but naturally I wish them to succeed, and if engagement with social media is necessary…' A pause as he made a tick on one of the papers. 'Then so be it.'

'Oh, and here I thought I was saving the day,' Ella teased.

Alessandro gave her a level look before one corner of his mouth reluctantly kicked up, making Liane's heart flip-flop even though he wasn't looking at her. Ella's smile widened and she batted her eyelashes with her usual laughing drama before turning back to her phone.

Excusing herself with a murmur, Liane rose from her seat. Alessandro had invited them to explore the jet when they'd first boarded, but Liane had been too overawed to do anything but sit down and buckle up. Now she left the main cabin for the ones beyond, curiosity warring with an uneasy restlessness at being here at all.

She certainly didn't need a front row seat to the quips flying between Alessandro and Ella. Alessandro might have said he had no interest in romance, but Liane was quite sure Ella could convince him otherwise if she chose to—and why wouldn't she?

The cabin beyond the main seating area was styled as an office, complete with a wide mahogany desk, the curved walls lined with specially built bookcases. Liane trailed her finger along the titles—classics of philosophy, poetry and history in a variety of languages. She wondered if Alessandro had read them all or if they were just for show. She selected a volume of poetry and let the book fall open naturally to a well-worn marked page—*Demain, dès l'aube*, by Victor Hugo. Slowly she read the familiar lines:

Demain, dès l'aube, à l'heure où blanchit la campagne, Je partirai.

"'Tomorrow at dawn, when the countryside brightens, I will depart.'"

Liane nearly jumped out of her skin as she heard Alessandro huskily quote the poem, his voice seeming to caress every syllable. He'd come into the room without her even realising, close enough to see the page she was reading, and, embarrassed, she realised she was snooping and he knew it.

'You know the poem?' she asked, clumsily closing the book and putting it back on the shelf.

'Very well.' He paused and then continued softly,

'"Vois-tu, je sais que tu m'attends. J'irai par la forêt, j'irai par la montagne."'

'"*You see,*"' Liane translated, her voice as soft as his, '"*I know you will wait for me. I will go through the wood, I will go past the mountains.*"' She shook her head slowly. 'You speak French?'

The smile that quirked his mouth seemed almost tender as his gaze swept over her, leaving a heated, tingling awareness in its wake. *'Mais oui.'*

She laughed a bit unevenly, shocked at how a single look turned her weak at the knees, filled her with a yearning she was afraid to name. He gave a playful grimace of acknowledgement. 'Actually, I only have schoolboy French. I can't speak or write it, really. But it's a beautiful language.' The observation felt strangely intimate, as if he were complimenting her and not her French. When she dared look at him his gaze was pensive, lingering. Something in her trembled and ached.

'Yet you're able to quote Hugo?' she managed as she clasped her hands together in front of her in an attempt to calm her fluttering nerves. 'I'm impressed.'

'I always liked that poem.'

'But it's so sad,' Liane protested, even though she liked it as well. It captured something of the grief she'd felt when her father had embroiled himself in scandal and their lives had changed so drastically—leaving the little house in Lyon, moving to Paris and then to New York, only to have her father die soon after, so they were catapulted into a new life that had felt unfamiliar and even hostile. It was a loss that ran right through her, like silk shot with silver thread, tingeing everything with sorrow, making her stay in the shadows.

'Hugo wrote it for his daughter,' Alessandro remarked, 'who drowned in the Seine when she was newly married.'

Liane nodded, knowing the story. 'Her skirts were too heavy and weighed her down, and her husband died trying to save her. She was only nineteen.'

'Not so much of a fairy tale.'

'But then fairy tales aren't real, are they?' she felt forced to return. She tried to give him a teasing smile but she didn't quite manage it.

He cocked his head, his gaze sweeping slowly over her, making her feel strangely revealed—not as if he were stripping away her clothes but her very soul, plumbing depths that she'd hidden from everyone. Goodness, but she was being fanciful, thinking this man saw something in her that no one else did—of course he didn't. He barely saw her at all. But right now she was in the spotlight of his gaze and it made her burn in ways that were both welcome and uncomfortable. *Oh, to be seen, truly seen*...and yet how utterly terrifying.

'Is that what you think?' he asked.

She was hardly about to admit that she longed to believe in the fairy tale, at least for herself. She wasn't about to spout about true love and the happily-ever-after she yearned for when she already suspected him to be a cynic about such matters, and in any case she didn't have any evidence to substantiate her dreams, just a deep-seated belief, or maybe just hope, that true love did exist somewhere, that it could blossom into something big and wonderful.

'It's what I've seen so far,' she replied as pragmatically as she could. 'Here you are, making up a fairy tale for public consumption.' She'd meant to sound light but her voice came out a bit sharper than she intended.

He arched one eyebrow. 'So you really are disapproving.'

'I'm not disapproving so much as…dubious,' she allowed. 'As to the efficacy or morality of such a scheme.'

'Morality?' He folded his arms so his biceps bulged against the crisp cotton of his shirt, his lush mouth hardened into a frown. 'What is immoral about posting a few images of the Rossi hotels on social media?'

Liane shrugged, discomfited. She wasn't as disapproving, she thought with a pang, as she was jealous, something she would never, ever admit to Alessandro. 'You're bringing Ella along to generate gossip and speculation,' she hedged.

'I'm bringing Ella along,' he corrected, 'to raise the profile of the hotels on social media.'

'But you know she'll make up some silly story through her posts. The Prince and the Princess, et cetera.' She hoped she didn't sound jealous.

Alessandro cocked an eyebrow. 'Will she? I have to sign off on them, remember.' That steely gaze swept over her yet again, creating a wash of awareness in its wake, making everything prickle and heat. 'In any case, you are allowing your sister to take part in it.'

'She's twenty-two,' Liane returned with a hint of acerbity. 'I can't make her decisions for her.'

'Too true.' He propped one shoulder against the bookcase, close enough that Liane could feel the heat of his powerful body, breathe in the citrusy scent of his aftershave that made her senses swim. If she took a step towards him they'd be touching. She imagined the feel of the crisp cotton of his shirt under her hand, the warm skin underneath, even as she strove to stay still and unmoved. Her body, though, felt like swaying towards him, the way a plant might tilt to the sun. So ridiculous. So shaming, especially when she doubted he was feeling anything remotely similar. 'So you'd rather she hadn't agreed?' he pressed. 'That I hadn't suggested such a plan?'

She shook her head, not wanting to be drawn. 'It's not for me to say.'

'But you must have an opinion on the matter,' he observed silkily.

She glanced up at him from beneath her lashes, uneasy to offer an opinion when she—and Ella—were both so dependent on his generosity for the next week. And, she realised, she didn't want him to think her prudish or stern. Schoolmarmish, even, although she knew that was what she was. 'Everyone will think the two of you are falling in love,' she said after a moment, her voice the tiniest bit unsteady.

'They'll wonder,' Alessandro agreed with a shrug. 'What is that to me?'

'Nothing, I suppose.' He obviously didn't care what other people thought about him. 'I suppose I don't like deceiving people,' she stated finally. Although would it really be deception if they did end up falling in love?

'Neither do I,' he replied equably.

She frowned, glancing at him in uneasy confusion. 'But then why…?'

'This is hardly deception,' Alessandro informed her mildly. He angled his body so his shoulder was practically brushing hers, causing every sense to twang to life. She didn't dare move away, and in truth she didn't want to. The citrusy scent of him was making her head spin. 'All marketing is spin, you know. Showing whatever it is in the way you want to. That's all this is.'

Liane nodded slowly. She knew she wasn't actually bothered so much by any seeming element of deception, rather than the simple fact of Alessandro and Ella posing as a couple together. Although he'd implied yesterday that he intended them to be no such thing and even right now seemed to think himself immune to her sister's enviable charms, she still feared it would be inevitable. Ella was gorgeous, charming, funny and always willing to tumble into love. How would a man like Alessandro resist her? He wouldn't, she thought, unable to keep from feeling despondent, even try.

Her eyes, Alessandro thought, were marvellous—the colour of pansies, or perhaps a bruise. A deep, damaged violet, fringed by silvery lashes that swept her pale cheeks every time she blinked, which had been quite a lot. He made her nervous—something that gave him a sense of both remorse and satisfaction. He realised he enjoyed the ability to affect her, to *matter*. It was an alarming thought because normally he didn't want to matter to anyone. Mattering allowed you to hurt and be hurt, to use and be used. He wanted no part of any of that, not even a little bit. Life, he'd long ago determined, needed to be a solitary affair; emotions were not to be engaged.

And yet…he liked the way her eyes widened and her breathing turned uneven when he moved closer to her. He breathed in the flowery scent of her perfume, something subtle and not too sweet. A grown-up fragrance—understated, sophisticated. He felt there was something fragile and vulnerable about her, yet also tensile and strong. A woman of complexities, enigmas, perhaps without her even realising it.

He found her far more fascinating, and even alluring, than her charismatic yet fundamentally insipid sister, who couldn't look up from her phone for more than thirty seconds, and then only to tease or flirt. There were depths to Liane that he hadn't sensed in Ella. But why should he compare the two women? Liane was in her own category altogether.

Not, he reminded himself, that it made a bit of difference to anything. He had no intention of taking this burgeoning attraction between them anywhere, as enjoyable as this moment was, as much as he was now wondering what it would be like to lean forward just a little bit, breathe in her fragrance, slide his fingers along the silkiness of her skin, draw her to him…

'How do you know that poem?' he asked, easing back slightly. He was curious to learn more about her—and direct the conversation away from the social media scheme he was already beginning to regret. It had been a rather recklessly impetuous decision, so unlike him, and if he was honest with himself he feared it had little to do with the state of the Rossi hotels and everything with the woman before him.

'It is taught in school in France. It was one of my favourites. I teach it as well.'

'You grew up in France, then?'

'Yes, in Lyon and then Paris, but we moved to New York when I was eleven.'

'How come?'

'All these questions.' She laughed lightly as she moved away from him with a whisper of fabric over skin, her plain, pale blue cotton sundress swishing about her slender legs. 'My father was a minor diplomat. He was posted to New York.' She turned back to him, a teasing glint entering her eyes although there was still something sombre about her manner. 'Apparently he was a great friend of your father's.'

'Was he?' Alessandro asked, his tone decidedly neutral.

The friendship was not, he thought, anything to recommend the man to him. His father had been for his whole life a reckless, thoughtless and louche dilettante, embarking on one affair after another, never caring whom he hurt in the process.

'Well, that is perhaps a matter of some debate,' Liane conceded. 'But it was how we were invited to your ball. My father lent yours a hundred francs at the baccarat table in Monte Carlo. Apparently he never forgot it. He put my family on the invitation list for several occasions over the years, although this is the first one we have been able to attend.'

'Ah.' He couldn't keep his lips from twisting cynically and Liane nodded slowly in understanding, or perhaps admission.

'My father was a gambler,' she stated quietly. 'He lost all his money at those tables and we moved to Paris and then New York to escape the disgrace. He died soon after.'

He heard the throb of pain in her voice and found it touched him, more than he wanted it to. 'I'm sorry.'

'So am I. If he hadn't lost all his money, he might not have drunk himself to death and then died of liver failure just a year later.' She let out a little sigh, the sound no more than a breath, as she looked away.

'I'm sorry for that as well.' He paused. 'I'm afraid my father shares many of your father's traits. He's still alive, though, living what he sees as the high life in Ibiza, but he has behaved in a similarly feckless manner all his life.'

She turned back to regard him seriously, her eyes wide and unblinking. 'You're not like him.'

'I thank God for that.'

'That was a deliberate choice you made? To be different?'

Her insight, appreciated only a few moments ago, now caused him a frisson of unease. 'Yes, it was.' He would never be led, the way his father had been, by his lust, or like his mother had been, by her emotions. One had caused his father's dissipation, the other his mother's death. He preferred to remain apart.

'The tabloids are so curious about you, you know.' A smile flirted with her mouth and lightened her eyes to lavender. 'You seem to be something of a recluse, which makes this whirlwind of parties all the more surprising.'

He took a step towards her. 'You've been reading up on me?'

A blush pinked her cheeks as she held his gaze. 'It would be rather remiss of me not to, considering my sister and I are travelling with you for the week.'

'True enough. Well, don't believe all you read in the tabloids.'

Her eyebrows arched. 'So you're not a recluse?'

'Recluse might be too strong a word. I like my own company, certainly, and I often find others' tedious.'

'Then these parties really will be torture for you,' she teased with a small smile.

Right now he was experiencing an entirely different kind of torture, breathing in her scent, watching her eyes turn different shades of twilight, the way her chest rose and fell with each breath. Why was he so affected by her? It was both alarming and annoying, to feel such an instant and overwhelming attraction for someone he barely knew. Even now his palms itched with the desire to reach for her, draw her to him slowly, so slowly...

'I only intend to stay long enough at each one to generate the publicity needed,' he stated, banishing the provocative images from his mind.

'You do sound like a cynic.'

'That's because I am one.' His voice came out rougher than he expected and she blinked, startled. Alessandro was not sorry. As entertaining as it could be to chat and to flirt, he wanted Liane to have no misapprehensions about who he was. What he was. Like she claimed—although he didn't know whether to take her at her word—he didn't believe in the fairy tale. At all. And he refused to give her or anyone else a moment's hope about it, no matter what attraction was springing to life between them.

She held his gaze a moment longer, as if weighing the truth of his words, and then she moved away from him, towards the door that led to the adjoining room. 'What's in here?'

Alessandro came to stand behind her as she opened the door. 'The bedroom,' he said and she shivered slightly, as if she'd felt his breath ripple over her skin. She stood there for a moment, surveying the wide double bed piled high with pillows in varying shades of gold and cream silk. Alessandro stood behind her, close enough that if he bent his head he could have brushed a kiss to the nape of her neck. He eased back.

'What a lovely room,' she remarked after a moment, her voice low and husky, and he wondered if she too were imagining the scene that could be so pleasurably played out there. She started to close the door.

Alessandro caught it with his hand, his fingers brushing hers so she stilled, her body tense, practically vibrating. For a second Alessandro remained with his hand touching hers, the air seeming hushed, expectant. It would be so easy to turn and take her in his arms...

But, no. He was mad to think this way. He *didn't* think this way. He never let himself be led by his emotions or desires. Restraint was his watch word. He couldn't let Liane Blanchard change who he was.

'You should see the bathroom,' he told her, drawing his hand back from hers. 'It's even more luxurious.'

'Oh?' She glanced back at him, her expression veiled, and he enjoyed the way her eyes both widened and darkened, the slight parting of her lush lips—he noticed every reaction, no matter how tiny, and felt the answering flare of both need and desire in himself. Did she feel it too? He thought she must, but her face was as blank and lovely as a marble Madonna's. What was she hiding—and how much?

'Come and see,' he murmured and placed his palm near the small of her back, letting it hover questioningly for a moment, which she answered as she moved forward, slow enough that he was able to keep his hand there, and he was almost fiercely glad. He felt the warmth of her skin through the thin cotton of her sundress, burning his palm, firing his senses. Surely she felt the same pull of attraction. He wanted her to, even though he knew he wouldn't act on it. But this couldn't be in his own mind, his own body. She felt it as well, no matter how carefully veiled her expression.

Slowly, savouring every moment, he guided her towards the bathroom and with an unsteady hand she opened the door.

'Oh, my.' Her voice came out in a breathy rush as she surveyed the room—the sunken whirlpool tub for two, the gilded mirrors on the wall, the pillar candles, the crystal chandelier winking above. 'How…decadent.'

'Isn't it, though.'

He hadn't meant to sound sour, but she noted it and it clearly broke the mood as she stepped away from his hand with a questioning look. Just as well, he told himself.

'Did you not design it yourself?'

'No, this jet belonged to my father. I usually prefer to travel by regular aeroplane but, considering the nature of our travels, it seemed both more sensible and ecological to use a private jet on this one occasion.'

'Your father was a man of decadent tastes?' Her gaze swept slowly over him, seeking, finding.

'You could say that.'

'Another way you're not like him then, I think.'

'I'll thank you for the compliment, although I'm not sure how you've discerned so much.'

'Everything about you is restrained.' He blinked, startled and a bit unnerved by her assessment. 'As if you're always keeping yourself in check. As if you have to, as a matter of principle.'

He managed a laugh, although he was shaken by her perceptiveness. That was exactly how he felt. Never give in to the yearning he sometimes felt because it was weakness. Never let himself be used. 'I'm not sure that's a compliment.'

'I admire a certain amount of restraint.' She paused. 'My father certainly didn't have it, more was the pity for him.'

'And you're not like your father either, are you?' he returned.

'Well, I'm not a gambler.' She let out a small, sad laugh. 'But to be honest I wouldn't mind being like him in other ways—a bit more fun and carefree, able to enjoy life. People loved being around him. I did.' She paused. 'He was a bit like Ella, and she's not even related to him.'

Alessandro didn't reply for a moment; he knew he didn't fully understand the grief she felt for a man who had clearly wasted so much of his life. He refused to feel such emotion for either of his parents. 'So Ella was the daughter of your mother's second husband?' he surmised.

'Yes, Robert Ash. They married when my sister Manon and I were in our early teens.'

'Ella mentioned she doesn't get along with your mother.'

'That would be putting it mildly.' Liane looked away. 'That's not Ella's fault, though.'

'Then is it your mother's?' he asked, curious as to what was making her look so sorrowfully pensive.

'She can be a difficult, prickly sort of person.' She turned back to face him. 'What about your mother?'

Briefly he thought of the woman he'd called mother for a handful of years; his blurry memories were of her drunk or passed out, shrieking or weeping or causing a scene, certainly nothing to dwell on—or to miss. And yet, shamefully, he had. He thought of the last time he'd seen her…throwing clothes into a suitcase, barely looking at him. He'd been eight years old, tearful, begging… *Please, Mamma, please…*

'She left when I was eight,' he told Liane in a clipped voice. 'I don't remember much about her.'

'Left?' Pity flickered in her eyes and he tensed, hating that he was its object. Why had he said as much as he had? It was an odd sharing of confidences they were having, secrets drawn from them almost reluctantly, as if they were compelled to share their souls with each other. Now he really was being fanciful. He had no idea why he was talking like this with Liane Blanchard. Why she affected him so much, both physically and emotionally. It was alarming. It was intoxicating. It needed to stop.

'Yes,' he confirmed dismissively, deciding it was time to put an end to the conversation. 'And then she died when I was eleven.'

'I'm so sorry.'

He shrugged. 'I moved past it.'

'Does anyone move past that sort of thing?' she mused. 'My father was a gambler and a wastrel, but he was fun and he loved me. He…accepted me as I am. I still miss him.'

'Then you have finer feelings than I do.' And, judging by the even more sorrowful look on her face, that pithy remark had revealed more about him than he'd meant it to.

'I'm still sorry,' she said quietly. 'As I would be for any little boy who lost his mother. Ella lost her mother when she was a baby—did you know?'

'It didn't come up in conversation.' They'd kept their chat light and easy, which was how he suspected both of them liked it. Yet here he was, spilling secrets with Liane. It didn't make *sense*…and yet it did.

'Well, it's something you have in common.' She spoke as if she were reminding herself of something, and Alessandro wasn't sure he liked it. He realised he didn't particularly want to be thinking of Ella just now. Liane slipped past him, back into the bedroom, her slender figure moving gracefully past the bed piled high with pillows and silken sheets—and for a second Alessandro could picture her there, lying languidly among the pillows, the spill of her white-gold hair like spun silk against the smooth sheets, her eyes at half mast, her body…

At the door she turned back to him, her expression carefully blank. 'Ella will be wondering where we are,' she said, and it seemed almost as if there was a warning in her words.

Shaking his head as if he had to wake himself from a dream, Alessandro followed her.

CHAPTER FIVE

'ISN'T THIS *AMAZING*?'

Ella held her arms out as she twirled around the centre of their hotel suite, her hair flying out all around her. 'I've never, ever seen a room like this before.'

'Well, Rossi Hotels are meant to be the epitome in elegance and luxury,' Liane reminded her with a laugh. Even though she wasn't twirling around the room like a ballerina, she was similarly impressed, even stunned, by the sumptuous suite they'd been given—a living room with a wraparound terrace, a dining room and kitchen and two enormous bedrooms with en suite bathrooms that were the most luxurious Liane had ever seen—sunken tubs, waterfall showers and more marble and crystal than she'd ever seen outside of Versailles.

'I feel like I'm living in a dream.' Ella flung out one lithe golden arm. 'Pinch me.'

'Very well,' Liane replied with a laugh and gave her sister a light pinch that had her squealing melodramatically.

'Ouch!'

'You know that didn't hurt.' Liane moved past her to the French windows overlooking the terrace, the palm tree-lined boulevards of Los Angeles spread out before them, the Pacific Ocean a blue crescent in the distance. She stepped outside, resting her hands on the wrought iron railing of the balcony as she breathed in the hot, dry air, so different from New York's summer mugginess.

'You aren't angry with me, are you?' Ella asked as she joined her on the terrace.

'Angry?' Liane repeated in surprise. 'No, of course not. Why would you think such a thing?' She was never angry with Ella; it would be like being angry with a kitten. Still, she could see her sister looked worried as she studied her face.

'I don't know,' Ella told her. 'You've seemed a bit distant since we got off the plane.'

Had she? Liane forced a reassuring smile. 'I'm just tired. This has all happened so fast, my head is spinning.' Which was true enough, even if there were other reasons for her quiet. That conversation with Alessandro on the plane had left her feeling unsettled, as if someone had, very gently, pushed her off balance and she was struggling to right herself again.

She didn't know why he'd spent so much time talking to her, or if she'd been imagining the sensual currents she'd felt flowing between them. When he'd put his hand on the small of her back all her senses had sprung to life, her whole body twanging with awareness and need. It had been shocking, to feel so much from one little touch. To *yearn* so much.

But there was no way, she told herself, that he could feel the same. If he was flirting with her at all, and she wasn't even sure he was, then that was all it had been— just for fun, a light amusement to while away the journey. Except he didn't seem that sort of man, to amuse himself with other people's emotions. By his own admission, he was restrained, even a recluse, someone who eschewed parties and socialising for hard work and solitude. Why would he tease her like that?

Or had she really been imagining all of it, and his gestures had been born of nothing but mere solicitude? But why seek her out, why ask her about herself, her family? It had almost been as if he wanted to get to know her, even to care. Her ever circling thoughts were making her head ache. She had to stop thinking about him, second-guessing every look, every remark…

'Yes, I know what you mean,' Ella agreed, bringing Liane back to the present. 'But it's an adventure, isn't it?' Her smile was playful but her eyes were still full of worry. 'You're not sorry I asked you along, are you, Liane? You know I couldn't do this without you.'

'I'm not sorry, but are you?' Liane asked, managing to bring another smile to her lips. 'I don't want to cramp your style with Alessandro.'

'Oh, yes, Alessandro.' Ella rolled her eyes. 'He's almost *too* handsome, isn't he? So dark and brooding.' She gave a little shiver. 'I don't know whether he scares me or bores me, to tell you the truth. A little of both, I think. The two of you were gone for quite a long time on the journey.' Her eyes narrowed speculatively. 'What was that about?'

'He was just showing me the plane.' Liane heard how nervous she sounded. How silly she was, to think it meant anything. 'Being a gracious host, I suppose.'

'A gracious host,' Ella mused. 'Or something.' She slid her phone from her pocket. 'I thought for today's post I'd do a little video story of our trip—I took a photo on the plane, looking out the window, and then I'll do another one getting ready for the party. And then a shot of the ballroom at its most elegant, with Alessandro brooding away in the background—I don't want to give away too much at the start, keep everyone guessing. What do you think?'

Liane glanced down at the artful shot of the blue sky from the plane window, sunlight on clouds, and then another of Alessandro, gazing down at his pile of papers. Brooding indeed. 'I think it looks wonderful,' she managed, doing her best to squash that absurd pang of jealousy—and over what? 'But it's what Alessandro thinks that matters.'

'Unfortunately.' Ella sighed. 'I can't believe he doesn't even have any social media accounts.'

'I don't have any social media accounts,' Liane reminded her. As a teacher, it had been advised for her not to have any, and she wasn't interested in what seemed like a rather shallow world anyway.

'You guys are actually perfect for each other,' Ella told her with a speculative little look. 'Both of you old-fashioned stick-in-the-muds.'

'So that's how you see me.' Liane tried to sound laughingly wry, but she feared a little hurt came through. Did Ella really think she was that boring, that old? *Was* she? As for her and Alessandro being perfect for each other... Ella had clearly meant that as a joke.

'Oh, you know it isn't, not really,' Ella assured her. 'Come on, let's pick out our dresses for tonight. Alonso has a designer friend who lives in LA and he's sent half a dozen dresses for us to choose from. We're both going to look stunning, I promise. Alessandro won't take his eyes off either of us.'

Forcing a smile, Liane let herself be carried away on

her sister's enthusiasm and forced the pinpricks of hurt she'd felt at her offhand comments from her mind.

The dresses had been delivered to Ella's bedroom and she unzipped them from their garment bags one after the other, oohing and ahhing over each creation. 'Aren't they stunning?' she exclaimed. 'You'd look amazing in the emerald, Liane. Try it on.'

'I don't think so.' Ella could carry off a gown that was slashed down to the navel and up to the thigh, but she certainly couldn't and she had no intention of trying.

'Come on,' Ella pleaded. 'You'll look amazing, Liane. You have a lovely figure when you choose to highlight it. Don't be such a fuddy-duddy all the time.'

So she was a fuddy-duddy as well as an old-fashioned stick-in-the-mud, Liane thought wryly. Well, what did it matter? She could never be like Ella—fun and carefree, traipsing happily through life, drawing people to her like bees to honey. She'd always known that, and so why should she even try?

'I'll stick with the dress I brought with me, thank you very much,' she told her sister firmly. 'It's perfectly suitable.'

'You don't mean that blue monstrosity of your mother's?' Ella exclaimed in horror. 'Liane, you *can't*. You'd look like…like my maiden aunt or something. We're at a party in *LA*, for heaven's sake—'

'So?' She hadn't really wanted to wear that old dress—she'd only brought it as a desperate backup—but some stubborn streak made Liane tilt her chin, decided now. She *was* a stick-in-the-mud after all. 'It's the only one I have.'

'What about the purple dress that I lent you—?'

'It had to be returned, as you know.' None of these

fabulous gowns were theirs to keep. All of this life, she thought, was a mirage, disappearing in mere days. It would be good for her to remember that. 'I'll be fine in that dress, Ella. I'm not the one here for the publicity photos, remember. I don't really need to go to the ball at all.'

'Not go?' Ella's jaw dropped and she snapped it shut. 'Of course you're going. I need you there.'

'You didn't need me last time,' Liane reminded her. 'I barely saw you the whole evening.'

'Still, this is different,' Ella insisted. 'People will be taking photos…they'll be watching more now. I might do something stupid. You know how I can be.' She reached for her hand. 'I need you, Liane. Please.'

Liane couldn't help but soften. 'Don't worry, I'll go,' she promised, squeezing her sister's hand. She'd go even if she didn't want to, not any more, and she wasn't even sure why. Was it just because of how Ella's thoughtless remarks had rankled, or because she was tired of her supporting role? Ella would naturally be by Alessandro's side, chatting and laughing, flirting and making him fall in love with her, and where would she be? Standing in the corner as usual, but at least it wouldn't be in one of these fabulous dresses that would surely make her seem as if she were trying to be the belle of the ball who absolutely wasn't. The last thing she wanted was anyone's pity, the ugly stepsister who tried too hard. If she had to be a wallflower, Liane thought resolutely, then she might as well look the part.

Another evening, another event. There was no point checking his watch because the party hadn't even begun yet. And if he wanted the publicity to work, he was going to have to stay more than his usual fifteen minutes. Alessandro took a sip of champagne as he glanced towards the doors of the mirrored ballroom of Rossi's Los Angeles Hotel, a modern building of glass and steel, but one that still promised old world luxury and elegance. Where was Ella? And, he wondered with an even greater impatience, where was Liane?

He hadn't seen either of them since they'd arrived at the hotel, when they'd gone to their suite while he'd checked in with the local management. He'd done his best to focus on the work at hand but, irritatingly, his mind had kept drifting—not to Ella, who had kept up a steady stream of chatter all the way from the airport to the hotel, exclaiming about the blue sky and the palm trees and the YouTubers who apparently lurked on every corner, but to Liane, who had been quiet and withdrawn, her face turned to the tinted window of the limo.

She hadn't looked at him once and he'd found it annoyed him, a fact that then caused him even more annoyance. He didn't want to be affected by anyone, and certainly not a little mouse like Liane Blanchard. Except she *wasn't* a mouse, even if sometimes she seemed as if she liked to act like one. Why—and how—did she slip under his skin the way she seemed to, without even trying? Why did he care what she thought, what she was feeling? Why, even now, could he remember the exact shade of her eyes, the tiny freckle at the corner of her mouth?

It was all so ridiculous. He was here to do a job, perform a function, and then return to Rome and the more important business he had there. The last thing he needed was a distraction—or a temptation in the form of a woman whose lavender eyes he couldn't get out of his mind.

'Alessandro!'

He turned at the sound of Ella's musical trill. She

looked stunning, and yet his gaze was already moving past her, searching the empty corridor.

'Where's Liane?'

'She's still getting ready, but I didn't want to be late. I wanted to take some shots of the ballroom—look.' She brandished her phone, but Alessandro could barely be bothered to scroll through the photos she'd taken.

'So you approve the post?' Ella asked as she slipped her phone back into her tiny beaded bag. 'Or do you even care?' There was a hint of amusement in her voice that had Alessandro's gaze snapping back to her laughing one.

'Yes, I approve.'

'Oh, good. And here I was, worried that you'd be sticking your nose in too much, telling me how to do my job.' She raised her eyebrows as she eyed him thoughtfully. 'Right now I get the feeling you couldn't care less about any of this. Or me.'

'I leave the social media expertise to you, naturally.' He smiled tightly. 'Wasn't that the arrangement?' His gaze moved past her yet again, to the doors. Guests were beginning to trickle in, waiters circulating with trays of champagne and canapés, the music starting up. *Where was Liane?*

'Now I do believe it's time for you to sparkle,' he told Ella. He took her arm, smiling in greeting at an online entrepreneur he'd met in passing a few months ago along with his latest girlfriend, a Hollywood starlet, who was already starting to gush. He could already tell this evening was going to feel like for ever, every minute ticking by like an hour. And where the hell, he wondered again, was Liane?

An hour passed, every minute feeling endless, just as he'd known it would. Ella, at least, was in fine form, chatting and laughing and tossing her curls for the camera, while Alessandro did his best not to look as distracted and bored as he felt. He still hadn't seen Liane and Ella must have noticed, for as she plucked a second glass of champagne from a passing tray she remarked dryly, 'I saw her slip out to the terrace a little while ago, if you're looking for her.'

'Looking for who?' Alessandro asked, and Ella rolled her eyes.

'Liane, of course. You've been scanning the ballroom all evening searching for her. Fortunately I'm not offended.' Her smile was playful although the expression in her eyes was dangerously speculative. 'Like I said, she's out on the terrace.'

'I wasn't looking for her,' Alessandro replied stiffly. 'I just wondered where she was.'

'Well, now you know,' Ella returned flippantly, toasting him with her glass. 'So you can find her if you want to. You seem to be very curious about her whereabouts, at any rate. And now I'm going to go sparkle some more.' She started off, tossing over her shoulder, 'Good luck with your search.'

He told himself he wasn't going to go out on the terrace; there was no need for him to look for Liane, never mind actually find her. He'd mingle for a few minutes more and then he'd call it a night and do some work up in his penthouse suite. He continued to tell himself that as he walked towards the doors that led out to the wide terrace overlooking Beverly Hills, now shadowed in darkness, and then stepped through them. He scanned the clusters of chatting guests but he didn't see Liane among them. He wasn't actually *looking* for her, he told himself as he wandered amidst the groups of people, greeting and chatting as necessary. He was just mingling, as required.

And then, as he rounded the last corner, he found her, in an alcove off by herself, her hands on the balustrade as she gazed out at the city, her blonde hair blowing in the breeze.

'Why are you hiding?' he demanded, and she turned to him, no doubt startled by his aggressive tone.

'I'm not hiding. I don't particularly like parties, and two in quick succession are quite enough for me. I just wanted some air.' There was a defensiveness to her tone that both rankled and touched him. He didn't like the thought of her spending the whole evening hiding out here, and why? To get out of Ella's way?

'You've been out here for some time, I should think. I haven't seen you in the ballroom at all.'

Her chin tilted, her eyes flashing. 'Have you been looking for me?' she asked, her tone rather disdainfully incredulous, and he stiffened.

'I merely wondered where you were.'

She shrugged. 'Now you know.'

He stared at her, and she glared back. Why were they arguing? Somehow they'd both been put on the defensive and he wasn't sure how or why, only that he felt off balance, unsettled by her very presence affecting him in all sorts of ways. He should just turn around and walk away, but for some reason he didn't.

'Were you hiding out here for a reason?' he asked and she shrugged, still defensive. 'You belong at this party as much as Ella does,' he said, feeling his way through the words, and Liane gave him a sceptical look.

'No, I don't, and in any case I don't want to be.' She hesitated, and then said with an attempt at a laugh, 'Never mind ridiculous shoes, you must realise this dress is even more ridiculous.' Her lips turned up in a forced smile. 'In fact, it's ugly.'

He glanced down at the dress and had to concede that, even though he hadn't noticed before, the dress left something to be desired.

'It may not be the latest fashion,' he allowed, 'but if you don't like it, why are you wearing it?'

She let out a huff of weary laughter as she turned back to the view, her slender hands resting on the railing. 'I'm not really sure.'

'Was there something else? Ella assured me that your wardrobe was taken care of—'

'*Her* wardrobe. I could have worn one of her fashion designer friends' dresses, it's true, but they didn't suit me, and I'd just look silly wearing something plunging to my navel and slashed to my thigh.'

Alessandro's blood heated at the thought of her wearing such an outfit, but he kept his expression neutral as he answered, 'If you cannot find a gown to suit you, then we must buy one. We'll go shopping tomorrow, before our flight leaves for London.'

She turned to him, her eyes widening in surprise. 'What? No.'

'Why not?' Alessandro was baffled by her resistance. 'There's time, and you need to be suitably attired.' And, he knew, he wanted to spend time with her. Buy lovely things for her. *See her in them...*

'Fine,' Liane countered, her chin tilting up. 'I can pick out my own dress, then.'

Alessandro found he didn't particularly care for that notion. 'Nonsense. You don't know the city or its boutiques, and as I'm the one who invited you on this trip it is my responsibility to make sure you have all that you require. We'll go together.'

She stared at him for a long moment, her eyes dark and troubled, her body stiff with tension. 'Don't feel sorry for me,' she warned him at last.

'Feel sorry for you?' he repeated, his eyebrows rising in surprise. 'Why would I feel sorry for you?'

Liane simply shook her head. 'I might not be as glamorous or beautiful as Ella, but I don't need to be your pity project.' She started to move past him and he caught her arm.

'Liane, that is not what this is about. I don't pity you. If anything...' He hesitated, not wanting to reveal too much about what he felt. Hell, he didn't even *know* what he felt, and he certainly didn't want to think about it too much. But he did want to take her shopping tomorrow, he realised. Quite a lot. 'Ella is starting to give me a headache,' he said at last. 'All that chatting and laughing and tossing her hair. It's exhausting. To tell you the truth, I'd rather be out here on the terrace as well.' *With you.* He swallowed down the words. He had no intention of admitting that much, even to himself. It wasn't as if he *needed* her...or anyone.

A small smile flirted with her mouth and then slipped away. 'You made a rod for your own back with all these parties.'

'I suppose I did.' He let go of her arm, even though he didn't particularly want to. 'Now, tomorrow. Meet me in the lobby at ten o'clock in the morning. That will give us a few hours before we have to leave for London.'

'And Ella? Should she come too?' she asked, and he realised how little he wanted Ella to accompany them.

He'd been envisioning a day spent together, just the two of them, Ella nowhere to be found.

'If she needs some new dresses, she's welcome to come along, of course,' he replied after a moment. How could he say anything else? And really, perhaps it was better if Ella did come along. His feelings for Liane Blanchard already felt too complicated, too much. He'd been acting decidedly out of character, doing and saying and thinking things he didn't normally, and all because of this beguiling woman. It unsettled him for all sorts of reasons, and yet he didn't need any distractions from the business at hand and he certainly had no intention of taking this fascination he felt for her anywhere.

And yet he still found he was looking forward to tomorrow.

CHAPTER SIX

'WHERE'S ELLA?'

The abrupt question had Liane pausing mid-stride as she headed towards the doors of the hotel lobby, where Alessandro was waiting, looking as devastating as always in a navy-blue suit, his close-cropped hair still damp from a shower, his brows drawn together in a frown as he surveyed her.

'She said ten o'clock was too early for her, so she's sleeping in.' Liane tried to keep her voice light as she stood in front of him, her insides wobbling like a bowl full of jelly. She'd been fully expecting Ella to come along for this excursion and serve as some sort of protective barrier between her and Alessandro. With Ella chatting and laughing, Liane wouldn't have to talk to Alessandro, or feel like a fool in his presence—the way she had last night, when she'd admitted she had nothing to wear, or at least nothing she was brave enough to wear. All right, perhaps it had been a silly, stubborn thing to do, to wear that ugly old dress, but it had felt like a strange sort of protection at the time. Easier to be a wallflower than to try to step into the spotlight, but she had no intention of explaining that to Alessandro.

And now here he was, staring at her with that same

sort of critical assessment he had last night, as if she were nothing more than a problem to solve. It made her want to shrink right inside herself and disappear. The fizzy flirtation she'd felt on the plane, when they'd chatted alone together, when she'd felt his interest like a warm balm on her skin, now seemed like a surreal step out of time. Clearly she'd been imagining those so-called currents flowing between them. She'd *thought* she had been, she'd certainly feared it, but she knew the leaden certainty of it now. Everything had been in her mind—her silly schoolgirl hopes as ridiculous as those stupid shoes.

Now, standing in front of him, trying not to fidget as he scowled down at her, she felt the full weight of his disapproval, or perhaps just his indifference. His face was expressionless, his eyes shuttered.

'Very well,' he said after a pause, his voice clipped. 'My car is waiting.'

Silently Liane followed him outside to the waiting limo. Ever the gentleman, Alessandro opened the door for her first and with murmured thanks she slipped inside, sliding along the sumptuous leather. Alessandro joined her, closing the door and taking out his phone to text a few messages. Liane turned to look out of the window at the palm trees and pink stucco buildings blurring by as they rode in silence for the few minutes it took to arrive at what looked like one of Beverly Hills's most exclusive boutiques, its frosted glass window hiding the elegance within.

'Why is no one else here?' she asked, instinctively letting her voice fall to a whisper as a sophisticated woman in a silk blouse and pencil skirt ushered them inside the empty boutique. The place had remarkably few clothes, just a few curated outfits draped on blank-faced mannequins or padded hangers, the walls papered in silk and a few velvet chaises and sofas scattered tastefully around. Even the air smelled expensive, a subtle scent of bergamot and vanilla.

'Because I arranged for us to have the place to ourselves.' Alessandro spoke as if this were a normal thing to do. Liane couldn't help but be struck by how different their lives were, their whole *selves*. It made her even more certain that she'd been imagining any spark between them. Why would a man who could commandeer shops and fly by private jet have any interest in a poor plain Jane like her? As Alessandro positioned himself on a divan of grey velvet, scrolling through his messages, Liane couldn't help but feel he'd already dismissed her from his mind.

'She needs at least three evening gowns,' he told the woman who was hovering nearby.

'I don't!' Liane protested. Three…! She'd never had so many dresses.

Alessandro lifted his head to give her a questioning look. 'There are three more evening events. You need a dress for each one.'

'I can wear the same one—'

'Your stepsister's social media is already starting to do what it was meant to do. You're likely to find yourself on the front page of something, and you don't want to be wearing the same dress.' He shrugged and then turned back to the assistant. 'Three, please.'

'What it was meant to do?' Liane repeated, excitement warring with unease at the thought of finding herself on the front page of anything. 'What do you mean?'

'Some newspapers have picked up the story. There has already been a request to feature the New York hotel in a lifestyle magazine, and the concierge there has told me reservations are on the increase.'

'That's…that's wonderful.' She studied his face, all harsh planes and angles, his gaze trained on his phone. 'Isn't it?'

'Of course.' Another shrug, barely a twist of one powerful shoulder. 'Now, are you going to try some things on?' He gave the sales assistant a pointed look and she immediately sprang to attention.

'Yes, of course, Mr Rossi. I have already selected several outfits for Miss—'

'Blanchard.' Her name came out in something like a snap. He gestured to the dressing room, which was almost as big as Liane's bedroom back in New York. 'Then let's get going.'

Liane retreated into the dressing room, closing the door behind her with a firm click. Why was he being so terribly terse? She'd told him last night that she didn't need a dress, or if she did, he didn't need to come with her to shop for it. So why was he now acting as if this was the hassle to end all hassles? This had been his idea, not hers. She'd almost, for a second, thought he might enjoy it, but she realised now how ridiculous a notion that was. How ridiculous all her silly romantic notions had been.

Her fingers trembled as she unbuttoned her blouse, the sales assistant waiting with a gown in aquamarine silk that flowed like water over her arm. She wasn't just annoyed or even angry, Liane realised as she slipped on the dress, although admittedly she was both of those. She was *hurt.* When they'd been on the plane she'd known their conversation—and those delicious currents—hadn't *meant* anything, but some stupid part of her had still believed, or at least hoped, that Alessandro was interested

in her, if only a tiny, tiny bit. Now she knew he wasn't.
She was nothing but an inconvenience to be dealt with,
and impatiently at that. Everything had been in her imagination or, worse, she realised as a new, awful possibility occurred to her, done out of pity. What if he'd given
her attention simply because he felt sorry for her? A pity
project, indeed, just as she'd said last night. The thought
made her stomach roil unpleasantly. She might be mousy
but she didn't want to be pitied for it. She wouldn't let
herself be.

'Well?' Alessandro called out. 'Let's see.'

Liane barely glanced at her reflection in the mirror.
'It's fine. You don't need to see it.' She had no desire to
parade herself in front of him. This whole morning was
excruciating enough.

'I want to see what I'm buying,' Alessandro replied
mildly enough, but Liane still gritted her teeth.

'Fine.' She yanked open the dressing room door to
glare at him, her hands on her hips, wanting him to see
the extent of her ire. 'Satisfied?' Her breath came out in
an unsteady rush as her angry gaze met his—and then
saw the heat flaring there.

'I wouldn't say I'm *satisfied*,' he replied slowly, and
Liane's toes curled, everything in her clenching at the
innuendo. Was this yet more pity? Throwing her a bone?
She couldn't bear it.

'But it suits?' she asked, striving to keep her voice
steady. The gown was Grecian in style and covered her
from neck to ankles in gently pleated folds, but underneath his considering gaze she felt nearly naked. It wasn't
an unpleasant feeling—far from it. As he continued to
look at her she felt achingly aware of her own body, his
sweeping gaze seeming to burn everywhere it lingered.

Senses stirred. Nerves tingled. And heat flowed through her in a molten, honeyed stream. Why was he looking at her this way? Was he teasing her? Toying with her—or did he mean it? The man was *impossible*.

'Yes, it suits. Certainly.' He held her gaze and she had to turn away with effort.

'Fine. Then I will get this one, and thank you for it, but nothing else.'

'But—'

'No.' She spoke firmly, more firmly than perhaps he'd ever heard from her before. She had her limits. 'Only this.' She turned back to him and saw his heated gaze had turned narrowed and considering. 'I don't need you to buy me things,' she told him. 'And I don't want to be your pity project.'

His eyebrows rose towards his hairline. 'Not that again—'

'Only this,' she said again, fiercely this time. Then, as the sales assistant murmured that she would go ring it up, she turned back into the dressing room, her heart thudding at having forced a confrontation. If his attentions had been born of pity then she wanted no more of them. At least she'd made that clear.

She reached for the zip on the back of her dress—and realised she couldn't reach it. She arched her back, stretching her arm till her shoulder socket felt as if it would be dislocated, and still she couldn't manage to grasp the tip of the zip. *Damn.*

Reluctantly she opened the dressing room door. Alessandro looked up from his phone, eyebrows snapping together. 'Where has the sales assistant gone?' Liane asked.

'She went to ring up the dress. Why?'

Even more reluctantly, she admitted, 'I can't undo the zip on my dress. I was hoping she could help.'

Alessandro rose from the sofa in one fluid movement. 'I can help.'

Which was what she didn't want. *Couldn't* want. Him touching her. Her melting—and making a fool of herself. She took a quick breath and then nodded, determined not to show her reluctance *or* her desire. 'Thank you.'

She turned around and caught her breath as she felt his fingers at the nape of her neck, gentle, caressing. She stayed completely still, willing herself not to respond— and reveal. She held her breath, not wanting to breathe in the subtle male scent of him, knowing it would affect her. She couldn't bear the thought that he would know how much she responded to him—and that it would amuse him.

His fingers took hold of the zip and gently tugged. Liane remained rigid as he pulled the zip slowly, so slowly, down her back, stopping midway, the fabric whispering against her bare skin, his fingers so tantalisingly close to her flesh.

'Is that enough?' His breath fanned against the nape of her neck and she had to keep from shuddering in response as a molten longing spread through her veins and she nearly swayed.

'Yes, I think so.' Unsteadily she stepped away, turning around, only to have the dress begin to slide off her shoulders. Panicked, she slapped her hands against her chest to keep it from falling off completely.

She glanced up at Alessandro, and now there could be no mistaking the heat in his eyes. He took a step closer and her breath came out in a shuddery rush as his heated gaze remained trained on her. His hand moved to her hip, fingers barely skimming the dip of her waist as if to help her balance, anchor her there. A shudder of longing escaped her as he bent his head and she closed her eyes, her face tilted to his as she breathed in his citrusy male scent.

Was he actually going to kiss her?

Then the sound of clacking heels.

'Mr Rossi…?' the sales assistant called, and then stopped at the sight of them, frozen there together, so close to a kiss. 'Oh.'

Horrified, Liane bolted back into the dressing room and slammed the door in both Alessandro and the woman's faces.

What had just happened?

What had just happened?

Murmuring his thanks to the assistant, Alessandro stepped back towards the sofa, running his hands through his hair as he tried to tamp down on the heated desire raging through his body. His fingers tingled where they'd touched Liane. His lips burned as if they'd already tasted her sweetness and fire. The moment when she'd turned, his hand near her waist, his head bent as he'd breathed in her feminine, flowery scent…

He'd been so close to kissing her.

Ever since he'd first laid eyes on her, he acknowledged, he'd been fighting this relentless attraction. Today he'd been trying to hide his desire with a pragmatic terseness. Last night he'd called himself all kinds of a fool for seeking her out, insisting he take her *shopping*, of all things…

What was happening to him? Why did this slip of a woman affect him so much, make him say and do things he normally never would? He was a man who prized control, restraint, caution—all the things his own father hadn't. The last thing he wanted to do was lose his head over a woman, any woman. And he wasn't even going to *think* about his heart.

The door to the dressing room opened and Liane stood there, dressed in the plain top and skirt she'd worn before, her cheeks flushed but her expression composed. Just.

'Thank you for the gown,' she said stiffly as the sales assistant came forward with the dress swathed in a garment bag, draped over her arm. 'I suppose we should be heading back to the hotel.'

'We need to have lunch.' The words popped out before he could think them through, surprising them both. He glanced at the sales assistant. 'Thank you,' he said and took the dress.

'I can eat lunch in my room.'

'There's a little bistro near here where I've eaten before, on business. I'm sure they'll have a spare table.'

Liane didn't reply and Alessandro sent a quick text to secure the reservation. It wasn't until they were back in the limo that she spoke, her face angled to the window so he could see her profile—the porcelain curve of her cheek, the delicate line of her jaw. 'I don't understand you,' she said quietly.

'What is there to understand? We're hungry, so we'll eat.' He slid his phone into his pocket, determined to make things simple and not think about the welter of emotions churning inside him.

'You know that's not what I mean.' She turned to face him, her expression grave, her chin tilted at that determined angle. 'Don't you?'

Alessandro stilled, doing his best to keep his expression neutral. He did not want to have the kind of discussion Liane seemed to be angling for, and yet even so he admired her courage in pursuing it. He could tell it cost her, and yet still he couldn't make himself be honest. 'I don't know what you're talking about.'

'You blow hot and cold,' she stated with quiet dignity. 'At first I thought I was imagining it. I was sure I was, because I thought you would never even look at me, especially with Ella around.'

'What does this have to do with Ella?' he asked sharply.

Liane gave a little shrug. 'She's beautiful, charming, funny, charismatic. Everything I'm not.'

'That's not true.'

'I'm not looking for compliments—' she cut across him '—I'm just telling you I don't know how to play these games, if that's what they are.'

He was annoyed, even though already he knew he had to acknowledge the truth of her words. But he didn't play games. That wasn't who he was. 'I'm not—' he began, only to fall silent as she shook her head.

'Whatever it is. You sought me out on the plane, spoke to me as if...' She bit her lip. 'And then in the dressing room, for a moment I... I thought you were going to kiss me.' A rosy blush touched her cheeks but to her credit she held his gaze. 'But last night you seemed annoyed, and this morning you seem angry. I know I'm probably naïve, but you're making my head spin, and not in a good way. I don't know if you're giving me attention as some sort of...of pity but, whatever it is, I don't want it.' She turned back to the window. 'So, if you don't mind, could you please just go back to ignoring me all the time? It's much easier.'

Alessandro was silent, shocked and more than a little

shamed by her dignified speech. He *had* been sending mixed signals, he knew, mainly because he felt so conflicted within himself. He didn't want to feel anything for her…and yet he did. That fact was as undeniable as it was irritating. He barely knew her. He didn't need the distraction. He didn't want the temptation. *The risk.*

The limo had pulled up to the discreet bistro Alessandro had texted and neither of them spoke as he helped her out of the limo and then they walked into the restaurant.

'You're right,' he finally said when they were seated at a secluded table in the corner, menus to hand. She deserved his honesty, at the very least. 'I'm sorry. I have been feeling…conflicted.'

'About me?' Her lips twisted. 'Funny, that doesn't really make me feel any better.'

'I am attracted to you,' he stated baldly. Her eyes widened, her lips parting soundlessly. He found he enjoyed the colour that flared into her face. 'But I don't want to be. And that has nothing to do with you.'

She glanced down at her menu, mainly, he suspected, to hide her expression. 'Doesn't it?' she asked quietly.

'How could you think it did?'

She shrugged, her gaze remaining downcast. 'I'm not exactly about to set the world on fire, am I?' She looked up, trying to smile, determined to be pragmatic, and Alessandro's heart twisted with sympathy. Why did she hold herself in such low esteem? Had she lived in Ella's laughing shadow for too long, or was there something else that had made her doubt herself? He hated the idea that she saw herself like that, but he surely wasn't the man to help her in that regard. 'I never thought I was, you know,' she said softly.

'Falling for someone who sets the world on fire hardly

holds any appeal for me,' he told her, keeping his tone wry. 'But this is not about your lack of anything, Liane, but rather a…a discernment in me. I have no interest in pursuing a romantic relationship with anyone. So if I've been sending mixed signals, that's why.'

She stared at him for a moment, her head cocked to one side, her gaze considering, her cheeks still pink. 'Why don't you?'

'Because I've seen the damage romantic attachments can do. Broken hearts and ruined lives hold no appeal for me, and happily-ever-afters only belong in fairy tales. You said you didn't believe in the fairy tale,' he reminded her, 'although I suspect that you really do. But I don't. Not at all.' If he hoped that to be the end of the conversation, he was to be disappointed.

'You don't have to believe in fairy tales to pursue a romantic relationship,' Liane pointed out. 'Not,' she added quickly, 'that that's what I'm suggesting. I'm just making a point. You're taking it to extremes, surely—'

'By romantic I mean falling in love,' he stated. Better to get it all out in the open. 'I am not at all interested in loving someone or being loved back.' Risking hurting or being hurt. He'd seen it all with his parents, the endless cycle of despair and futility, with him at the centre. He had no desire to experience the like again. 'Shall we order?'

'But…' Liane stared at him for a moment, confusion clouding her eyes until realisation dawned and her mouth twisted. 'Ah, of course. You have…other…relationships, don't you? Affairs?' She flung the word at him, her face turning fiery.

Alessandro inclined his head in the briefest of nods. 'I've had certain agreeable arrangements in the past,' he admitted. 'But, returning to my main point, I apologise for sending out mixed signals, and I'm grateful for the opportunity to clear the air. We can now consider the matter settled.' And he would, he vowed, steer clear of her from now on. He'd been foolish to seek her out so much as it was. He was aggrieved to realise he didn't possess the self-control to remain sensible in her presence. Better not to seek her out at all, to ignore her completely, just as she'd said.

The waiter returned and they gave their orders, lapsing into silence as soon as he'd left. The air, Alessandro thought ruefully, didn't feel very clear at all.

'Why not me?' Liane asked finally, a quaver in her voice, and Alessandro blinked at her.

'Why not you?' he repeated, raising his eyebrows. 'Why not you what?'

'Why not consider me for one of your *arrangements*?' Her chin tilted up. 'I never asked for you or anyone to fall in love with me. I told you I don't believe in the fairy tale, even if you doubt me. You have no-strings affairs,' she stated, her voice so very matter-of-fact, even if it possessed a tremble, 'so why not consider me?'

CHAPTER SEVEN

LIANE HELD ALESSANDRO'S gaze as he gaped at her, but only just. She couldn't believe how brazen she was being, but even so she was glad she'd forced the issue. Ever since laying eyes on the man she'd been lambasting herself for thinking about him at all. For indulging a schoolgirl crush and allowing the man to affect her so much, to make her senses spin and her nerves tingle.

She'd had a crisis of confidence, thinking she'd been imagining his response to her, and then an even worse one, fearing he pitied her. Now she was beginning to glimpse the truth, or at least some of it. He simply didn't want to have a casual affair with her. Well, why not?

'Why…why not you?' he practically sputtered, shaking his head as if the answer were too obvious to state.

'It's a reasonable question.' To her credit, her voice didn't tremble any longer, even though her hands did. She hid them in her lap. She could hardly believe she was talking about this—having an affair. *Sex*. And she with virtually no experience of such matters at all. 'So tell me why not.'

'Because.' He reached for his glass and took a sip of water. 'Because you're not the kind of woman a man has affairs with.'

Ouch. She kept her expression bland with effort, her hands still clenched in her lap. 'I'm not?'

'Would you even want such an…an arrangement?' he demanded, turning the tables on her neatly. 'A casual affair with absolutely no future in it? No-strings sex, merely a physical transaction, admittedly pleasurable, that ends when I say it does?' The heat in his eyes as he stared at her in challenge made her lower her gaze.

She'd challenged him out of pique, a momentary boldness that had allowed her to fling the question at him like throwing down a gauntlet, but now she found herself having to consider the matter seriously, a prospect that filled her with both deep unease and utter yearning.

She closed her eyes as she remembered that charged moment in the dressing room when he'd dipped his head, his hand near her waist, the promise of a kiss hovering between them—it had been so little and yet she'd felt so much. How much more would she feel if he'd actually kissed her? If he—

'Liane.' Her name came out sharply. 'Answer me.'

She looked up and saw colour on the slashes of his cheekbones, his eyes glittering fiercely—why? Because of her? *Could he actually desire her?* The knowledge was incredible, wondrous. Powerful. A knowing, cat-like smile curved her mouth as a new, dizzying delight raced through her veins. She'd never, ever felt this way before. Never known she could feel it.

'Answer you?' she asked innocently. 'But I'm still considering the matter.' She could hardly believe she was saying the words. She wasn't really considering such a thing, was she? No-strings sex, a soulless, emotionless affair? And yet…*such pleasure.* To feel wanted, to finally, fully step into the spotlight…

Alessandro let out a sound that was close to a groan. 'The question was meant to be *rhetorical*. Of course you don't.'

'Don't I? Why not? I already told you I don't believe in the fairy tale.' She spoke the words with insistence, even though they seemed to ring hollow. She *did* believe in the fairy tale, absolutely, she always had, but in this moment she almost didn't want to. She wanted to flirt. To feel wanted. To have this fiery longing racing through her veins and know, or at least hope, it was racing through his as well. That they could both stoke the flames higher and then finally, wonderfully, sate them…

She glanced at him, eyebrows lifted, meaning to look flirtatious, provocative, but the sudden sober look in his shuttered gaze made her falter, the feminine confidence she'd been enjoying for a few brief seconds trickling away, leaving her feeling empty and embarrassed. The real Liane, looking for a fairy tale that didn't exist, the happily-ever-after that was not for the likes of her.

'But you do,' he said quietly. 'I know you must, no matter what you just said. You're a woman who…who was made for the fairy tale.'

Her lips parted but no sound came out. Was that meant to be a compliment? It sounded like one, and yet…it was also a rejection, she realised with a sudden, stinging shame. Even if she had practically just said out loud that she'd happily jump into bed with him, Alessandro was telling her he didn't want to. He *wouldn't*.

How could she have been so stupid? How could she have believed for a moment that a man like him wanted a woman like her, someone mousy and shy and uninteresting? She stared down at the table, willing herself not to blush or, worse, cry.

'I believe this conversation has got a little bit out of hand,' he continued lightly, a kindness in his tone that Liane couldn't bear. 'Shall we draw a line under it all and move on—as friends?' He gave her a smile that was full of gentle whimsy and it made her feel like bursting into tears. This was worse than being his pity project. Far worse.

Wordlessly, her throat too tight to speak, Liane nodded. She forced herself to look up to meet his all too compassionate gaze, nodding again as she managed to force out, 'Yes, I think that sounds like a good idea.'

Alessandro hesitated, his grey gaze scanning her face, looking for clues, and Liane prayed she wouldn't give him any. The last thing she wanted was for him to feel sorrier for her than he already did. Somehow she made her lips turn upwards as she leaned back in her seat, eyebrows raised, as if this had all been nothing more than an interesting, theoretical discussion.

'Good,' he finally said, and thankfully the waiter came then with their main courses and Liane could concentrate on her food instead of the awful look of naked pity she'd seen on Alessandro's face.

Somehow he didn't feel that conversation had gone quite as he might have wanted it to. It had been entirely surprising, shocking even, as well as unsettling, to have Liane ask him so directly. *Why not me?*

Why not, indeed?

The truth was, he could imagine all too easily how she would feel in his arms. Her lips on his, her body pliant against his as he plundered her softness, as she yielded it up to him…yes, he could imagine it very well indeed. But the truth was, he'd meant what he'd said. All his affairs had been conducted in an almost businesslike fashion: two people agreeing to use each other's bodies for pleasure. It was cold-hearted, yes, but it had worked. No emotions engaged, no possibility of feeling exposed or hurt, of sending wrong signals, of making it more than it was.

But the thought of having such an affair with Liane was...*wrong*, on a fundamental level. Wrong and distasteful and definitely not something he wanted, strangely enough, considering the desire currently racing through his veins, setting his blood on fire.

She wasn't a woman to be trifled with, to use as he felt like and then dispense with when he was done, even if she agreed with what he already knew would be the undoubtedly, overwhelmingly pleasurable using.

You're a woman who was made for the fairy tale.

What a cringingly sentimental notion, and yet he'd meant it, absolutely. Even if she didn't believe she did, Liane deserved the fairy tale, complete with the bow-wrapped happily-ever-after ending, and that was something he knew he could never, ever give. He refused to try.

Looking at her closed expression now, her eyes veiled as she focused on her meal, he suspected that she didn't believe he'd meant what he'd said. She persisted in clinging to the exasperating idea that he felt sorry for her, simply because she wasn't like her stepsister. As if anyone needed more Ellas in the world!

Even so, Alessandro was hesitant to disabuse her of the notion. Better they simply move on, as friends as he'd said, and never discuss this again. Because if Liane was meant for the fairy tale, he wasn't. And he had no intention of hurting her by letting her think even for a second that fairy tales were real when it came to him…no matter what her sister was able to show on social media.

He thought they managed, more or less, to recover their equilibrium over the course of the lunch; Alessandro asked her if she'd ever been to London, which she had, and then told her he wanted her to show him some of the sights in Paris.

'I'm sure you've seen Paris dozens of times,' she replied, and he smiled at her, longing to get back some of the connection he'd felt before, if not quite all of it.

'Not by a true Parisienne.'

'I grew up more in Lyon than Paris, but very well.' She shrugged, managed a smile that didn't quite reach her eyes. 'If there is time, I'd be happy to show you some sights, but this trip does seem like a whirlwind.'

'I'm sure we can spare an afternoon.' He would make sure of it. Really, Alessandro told himself, this had all worked out for the best. They could spend time together without any miscommunication or uneasiness, knowing exactly where they stood. He could count her as a friend, and maybe even help her believe in herself a bit more. He told himself he was glad they'd had that conversation, uncomfortable as it had been. It really had made everything easier.

'Where's Liane?'

Alessandro glanced behind Ella, where waiters were prepping trays of champagne for yet another gala, this one at the Rossi Hotel in Mayfair. He was so very tired of these parties, and yet he'd been looking forward to seeing Liane in the gown he'd bought her tonight. Looking forward to it quite a lot, in fact, no matter what he'd told himself about them being *friends*.

'She decided not to attend,' Ella replied with a careless shrug. 'The flight tired her out, apparently.'

'She's had all day to recover.' They'd taken a redeye from LA to London, and he'd offered the jet's bedroom to Liane and Ella, preferring to work through the night and then doze in a reclining chair. There had been very little opportunity to talk during the eleven hours from LA to London and yet now he realised that, even so, Liane had been rather pensive and quiet. Had she been avoiding him after their discussion yesterday? Why, when they'd finally cleared the air? Unless, of course, they hadn't.

Ella raised her eyebrows. 'What does it matter? Unless you want her to feature in today's posts? I could take a photo of her, lying in bed with a cloth to her head, you hovering by her bedside...' The smile she gave him was disconcertingly knowing.

'No, of course not.' It was a ridiculous idea, and in any case he couldn't care less about the stupid social media posts, even if they were achieving exactly what he'd intended them to. 'I simply expected her to be here.' Wearing the gown he'd bought for her, that made her look like a Greek goddess come to life—Persephone, perhaps, or the nymphs Echo or Thetis... Good grief, but he needed to get a hold of himself. 'Is she unwell?'

'I think she might have a bit of headache.' Ella cocked her head, looking at him speculatively, one hand planted on her hip. 'If you want, you could go check on her before the party starts. Make sure she's okay.' Her eyes danced. 'I think she'd appreciate it.'

'I'm sure there's no need,' Alessandro muttered, turning away. He needed to stop thinking about Liane. He'd thought they'd reached an understanding, an equilibrium, yesterday afternoon, when he'd made it clear they would not be taking their relationship anywhere, if they even had a relationship, which they didn't, but clearly his brain hadn't got the memo because he'd been thinking of nothing *but* her all day.

Still, he realised as he began to circulate among the arriving guests, he was annoyed and even worried that she'd decided to be a no-show. What was really going on? Was she hiding again, or what if something was wrong? What if she was ill? He frowned, considering the matter. Ella had said she had only a bit of a headache, but what if it was something more? What if she was upset? He'd been a bit brusque yesterday, perhaps. He hadn't meant to hurt her feelings, but neither had he wanted to give her any hope.

The most expedient thing to do, he decided, was to check on her. Five, ten minutes, max, and then he'd be back at the party. He strode through the hotel, mindless of the guests glancing his way. Soared upwards in the lift to the top floor where Liane and Ella were staying in one of the two royal suites, a sudden sense of urgency firing his long strides, the thudding of his heart. Hammered on the door.

'Liane?' he called. There was no answer and he rapped again sharply. 'Liane! Answer the door!'

'I'm coming, I'm *coming*.' Sounding harassed as well as a bit alarmed, Liane flung open the door and stood there, chest heaving, face flushed, as she stared at Alessandro in irritated confusion. She was wearing a soft jersey T-shirt that clung to her slight curves and a pair of tracksuit bottoms that hung loosely from her hips. A single white-gold plait lay over one shoulder and her eyes sparkled like amethysts. She looked, Alessandro thought, irresistible.

'What on earth is wrong?' she exclaimed, at the same time he cut across her,

'Why didn't you come to the ball?'

'Because I'm not Cinderella,' she shot back, 'and I had a headache.'

'But the gown—'

'I'll wear it in Paris. You didn't want me to wear the same thing at each party, anyway.' She shook her head slowly, her expression caught between exasperation and weariness. 'Why are you looking so furious? Just because I'm not downstairs to do your bidding?'

He stared at her for a moment, completely discomfited. He was acting like a *madman*. Why had he raced up here? Why was he so angry? Not with her, he realised, not with her at all, but with *himself*. She drove him crazy...and that was his fault. He was allowing his emotions to be engaged, to be overwhelmed, by this slip of a woman. No matter how they'd allegedly cleared the air in LA, he couldn't get her out of his mind.

'I... I don't know,' he said, his tone wondering, incredulous. This was so unlike him, so unlike everything he prided himself on being. Restrained. Controlled. Level-headed...

'You don't *know*?'

No, he realised, the problem was he *did* know. He knew all too well. And as Liane stood there, gazing at him in confusion, he closed the space between them, taking her into his arms, feeling the rightness of her body against his, slender and supple and pliant. He bent his head, his lips a fraction of an inch from hers, and heard her inhale sharply. Then, with a tiny sigh, she softened against him. And he kissed her.

CHAPTER EIGHT

ALESSANDRO'S LIPS HOVERED over hers for a moment in a silent question that Liane answered as she relaxed into him, revelling in the feeling of his hard, muscular body against hers. His lips brushed hers softly, once, twice, and then settled on them firmly, with deliberate, delicious intent. The fluttering sensation inside Liane's middle exploded into fireworks through her whole body. Her mind reeled. Her nerves twanged. Her senses sprang to life as his arms came around her and her body melted into his.

It was a kiss like no other, although in truth she had precious few to compare it to. Still, it blew them all away, left her reeling and longing for more. One large, warm hand cupped her cheek, another spanned the dip of her waist, fingers sliding up under her T-shirt, warm and seeking on her skin, and still the kiss went on, until Liane felt she saw stars—or maybe she'd swallowed them. Every inch of her was alive, sparkling, incandescent.

She pulled him towards her, revelling in the feel of his powerful shoulders beneath her questing hands, his lips moving from hers to the pulse beating at her throat, her hands now lost in his hair, her mind reeling, reeling…

And then Alessandro, with something like a groan, stepped away, his absence reverberating emptily through every atom. As Liane did her best to straighten her clothes and blink the world back into focus, she saw the colour slashing his cheekbones, the way his eyes glittered. He'd been affected as much as she'd been, or almost. Of that she was sure. She might be naïve, but that kiss, at least, had *not* been motivated by pity, and the knowledge made her fiercely glad.

'Well.' His breath came out in a rush as he squared his shoulders. 'At least we got that out of the way.'

What? For a few seconds Liane could only keep blinking as she fought an urge to laugh in incredulity. *Out of the way?* She felt as if Alessandro Rossi had very much got *in* the way. In her system, her blood, her brain. That kiss had affected her in every way possible; need was still thrumming through her insistently. And now he thought they could move on as if it, along with yesterday's conversation, had *cleared the air?* Was he actually serious? Or was he just trying to convince himself that could happen, because he wanted it to?

She pressed her fingers to her stinging, swollen lips. 'How do you reckon that?' she managed shakily.

Alessandro glanced around the empty hallway and then gestured into the suite. 'May I come in?'

'Yes, of course.'

She watched, everything in her still pulsing with desire and life, as he stepped through the doorway and strode into the suite's luxurious living space, with its velvet sofas and antique art. She closed the door after him and then followed him into the room, standing in the doorway as she watched him warily. He prowled through the space like something caged and restless, before he gave a brisk nod and turned to her, his mind clearly made up, a hard certainty sparking in his steely eyes.

'I'm sorry if I seemed unreasonable. I know I've acted…out of character. But now that we've kissed, perhaps we could see it as breaking the tension. We can put this behind us and move on…' He paused, his words turning weighted. 'If that's what you want.'

If that was what she wanted? Was it her choice, then? Liane gazed at him, nonplussed, wishing she felt more certain about what *he* wanted. The memory of that kiss would stay with her for ever, seared onto her memory, her body, her heart. And it had only been a kiss. How much more would she have been affected if that kiss had gone on and turned into something else? If he'd drawn her by the hand into the suite, into the bedroom, with that wide bed piled with silk pillows, and laid her down gently there, joining her, covering her body with his own…

'You're not interested in an affair, and I'm not interested in anything else,' he stated flatly. 'And, in any case, a few more days and you'll be back in New York, and I need to return to Rome.' He held her gaze, a hint of challenge in his eyes, his voice. 'That's all true, isn't it, Liane?'

She hesitated, a dozen different scenarios unspooling in her mind. She longed to be the kind of woman who could sashay over to Alessandro right now, grab him by his rumpled bow tie and pull him towards her. *That's not quite true*, she'd murmur against his lips, before she kissed him.

He'd take her to bed, and then they'd spend the next few days—or however long it lasted—enjoying each other in every way, ways she didn't even know existed but could heatedly imagine…

And then what?

He'd walk away, just as he'd promised, when he decided. And she'd return to New York with a loved-up body and a broken heart, sick with regret, feeling sad and used, because she knew she would. She wouldn't be able to help it.

'Liane?' Alessandro's voice was low and insistent as he took a step towards her. Her heart clenched, turned over at the intensity of his expression, the planes and angles of his face seeming even harder than usual, more unyielding, more demanding. 'That *is* all true, isn't it?'

'What are you saying? That if I wanted an affair, you'd have one?' She forced the words out through lips that felt strangely numb. She could hardly believe she was asking the question. She was imagining the answer, her body tingling and flaring with desire, aching with the need to cross the small space between them and show him just what she wanted. Or why didn't he make it easy for her and sweep her up in his arms, seduce her so she felt as if she had no choice?

But, no, he was giving her control, and she wasn't sure she even wanted it.

'I'd certainly find it hard to resist you.' His voice was low, thrumming through her, thrilling her, and yet… 'But that's all it would be. A handful of days, and some very memorable nights. I can promise you that, but I can't offer you more. Ever.' He sounded resolute, the words a warning. Clearly he wanted to make sure she would know absolutely how little she was getting. *And yet how much.*

'Yesterday,' she couldn't help but remind him, 'you weren't even offering me that.' He inclined his head in acknowledgement, saying nothing. 'What happened to me being a woman who was made for the fairy tale?' she asked, her voice possessing a ragged, mocking edge. Had he ever truly meant it? Or had he simply not wanted to hurt her, by admitting he could never fall in love with someone like her? Maybe the problem wasn't him, it was her, just as she'd always feared. She wasn't noticeable enough; she wasn't *lovable*.

It was a fear that was rooted in the depths of her, yet one she'd never truly wanted to face. If she was, her mother wouldn't have been so disappointed in her. She'd have found someone by now, twenty-seven years old and no one had even spared her a look…and the one man who had the power to capture her heart didn't want it. She swallowed hard.

Alessandro hesitated, his iron gaze burning into hers. 'The truth is, I want you too much,' he finally said, the words emerging with obvious reluctance. 'If you were willing to take what I can offer, then yes, I would offer it. In a heartbeat. But I want to make sure you understand what I am offering.'

'Yes, I understand that perfectly well,' she assured him shakily. 'You've made it very clear, trust me. A few days and then you're gone. Message received loud and clear.' She tried not to sound hurt, but she could tell that she did by the way his mouth hardened.

'All right, then. You can decide.' He held her gaze, the heat in it both thrilling her and scaring her. No one had ever looked at her that way, with such desire, such naked need. It made her feel strange—powerful and yet helpless at the same time.

'Why me?' she whispered.

'Why not you? Why do you keep acting surprised that I might desire you?'

'Because no one else has before.' She tried for a laugh and didn't quite manage it. 'Because no one else has even noticed me before. Not when Ella is around, anyway, and not really ever. I'm…forgettable.' It hurt to say the words.

'You're not forgettable to me,' Alessandro assured her,

his voice a low thrum. 'I haven't been able to stop thinking about you since I first stepped on your toes.'

She shook her head in instinctive denial. 'You don't have to say that—'

'Why don't you believe me? It's true.' He took a step towards her. 'You have this ridiculous insistence on believing that you're not worthy of my attention or desire. Or anyone's. That's simply not true.'

Worthy of his attention and desire, Liane thought, but not worthy of his love. And while Alessandro would tell her that was because of who he was, she couldn't help but think it had to have something to do with her. If she were different, *better*, she would be. Wouldn't she?

Liane took a deep breath. 'And if,' she asked slowly, 'I said I wanted what you were offering?'

His blazing gaze slid to the bedroom and then back to her, making her mouth tingle again in memory. Making her whole body tingle. 'I think you know what would happen next.'

She stared at him for a long moment, so very tempted as well as impossibly torn—but not, she realised with a sinking sensation that was a cross between utter disappointment and weak-kneed relief, torn enough. She wasn't that woman. She never had been. She couldn't offer her body without risking her heart. She couldn't agree to his terms, as much as she longed to.

Already she could imagine it—his fingers threaded through hers as he drew her gently to the bedroom. The heavy-lidded gaze he gave her as he slipped her T-shirt over her head before sliding his large, warm hands down her body, cupping her breasts, spanning her waist, slipping lower...

Her body pulsed with need at the mere thought. How much more intense would the reality be?

And yet she already knew she would refuse. She had to. Alessandro had been right, in a way. She might not be made for the fairy tale, but she still wanted it, and she held herself in enough esteem not to settle for less. And, she acknowledged, just as he did, she didn't want to get hurt, and she knew, she absolutely knew, if she said yes to his offer, she would. She would give him her heart along with her body. She wouldn't be able to stop herself.

He'd walk away without a backward glance, his cold heart completely intact, whereas she would, she knew, be left broken and reeling. Why let that happen, for the sake of a few days' fleeting pleasure, a pleasure that, no matter how incredible, would always be tinted with pain, with loss?

And yet it still hurt, almost unbearably, to force the words she knew she needed to say. 'I guess we got it out of our system, then,' she told him, and she saw his expression become shuttered, like a curtain coming down, veiling all that heat and desire. 'Because you won't risk more, and I won't settle for less.'

'Fine.' His voice was clipped as he gave one terse nod. 'That was what I expected.'

'I'm sorry.' She didn't know why she said it, except that was how she felt. Sorry that it ended here, that he wasn't willing at least to explore the possibility of more. That he had already decided she wasn't worth it. In some ways they barely knew each other, and yet she already knew she could have fallen in love with him if he'd let her. She would have tumbled as hard and fast as Ella ever had, if not harder. Faster. And that, she knew, was the danger she had to avoid. Because a few days would break her heart right in two.

'Don't be sorry,' he told her brusquely. 'It's better this

way, really. And in any case, there's only a few more days left of this trip. After that we'll never see each other again.'

Was that supposed to make her feel better? She nodded jerkily. 'Right.'

A silence stretched between them, heavy with the possibilities of what could have been. Candlelight burnishing bare skin, the sensuous slide of silk, of lips and limbs, bodies tangled, joining...

No. It was better this way. It had to be.

'Goodnight,' Alessandro said, and then he turned on his heel and was gone.

There was no need to feel as disappointed as he did, Alessandro told himself as he headed back to the ball. As devastated. He hadn't actually expected Liane to agree to his offer of a brief, no-strings affair. Hell, he hadn't really been expecting to offer. It had taken him by surprise, just as that kiss had taken him by surprise. The intensity of it, as well as the sweetness. The aching need, along with the sense of completion. *At last.*

No. It hadn't been like that at all. It had been a kiss, nothing more. One simple kiss with a woman who happened to set his body on fire. Fine. Sexual chemistry was a proven fact. He could get over it because now, just as he'd said, and Liane had agreed, they'd got it out of their system.

Yeah, right.

He was going to have to believe that, or at least act like he did, if he was going to get through the next few days. Part of him was already longing for the moment when he'd never have to see Liane again and deal with the irresistible temptation she provided, while another, greater, part shied away from such a thought.

Focus.

As he stepped out of the elevator he heard the tinkling of laughter, the clink of crystal, and knew he should go back into the party. Smile, chat, pose. He couldn't think of anything he wanted to do less.

He was a man of determination, he reminded himself, never tossed about or led by his emotions or desires. He'd seen his father run after every woman who caught his fancy, throwing himself into one relationship after another with a passion that bordered on obsession. He'd near ruined his business in the process and even now, at sixty-five years old, living with another mistress whom he insisted was 'the one', he was restless, unhappy, always looking for more. Alessandro had never seen him any other way. He wouldn't be like that. Not for Liane, not for anyone.

Setting his jaw, he turned and walked into the ballroom.

The next morning, under a bright summer sky, they boarded the jet for Paris. If he'd been apprehensive about seeing Liane after their kiss, he shouldn't have been, Alessandro soon saw, she'd smiled at him coolly and taken her usual seat, diagonal to him, opening a book without a care in the world. It seemed as if that kiss *had* got him out of her system.

Why did that thought annoy him to the extreme?

'An American news channel wants me on their breakfast programme,' Ella announced as they took off, waving her phone in excitement. 'Can you believe it? They'll conduct it by video—they're calling it "The Prince of Manhattan's Mystery Princess"!'

'That's a ridiculous title,' Alessandro dismissed. 'I'm descended from a duke, not a prince.'

'Surely you're not much of a mystery?' Liane interjected as she looked up from her book. 'They must know exactly who you are, Ella, from your social media profile, as well as the publicity photos that have been taken during the parties.'

Ella's eyes danced. 'You haven't looked at the posts at all, have you? Either of you.'

Alessandro glanced at Liane, who was looking as uneasy as he now felt. He'd looked at them a little, he conceded, sparing a glance for Ella's phone once in a while when she showed it to him. All he'd seen were artful shots of ballrooms and dresses, champagne glasses and shoes.

'What are you talking about?' he asked, an edge to his voice. 'What is the big mystery?'

Silently, a catlike smile curving her mouth, Ella handed him the phone.

The first thing he saw was the social media account was anonymous—its name was simply *The Glass Slipper*, the profile pic a close-up of the original shoe, lying on the steps. All the photos, he saw as he scrolled through, were artful, mysterious—a tray of glasses, light from a chandelier glinting off crystal. A shot of Ella's reflection as she looked in the mirror, but so the viewer only had a glimpse of blonde hair, a diamond earring, the smooth curve of her cheek. The balcony of the London hotel, one slender, pink-tipped hand on the balustrade.

The captions were intriguing, as well as admirably smooth advertising for each Rossi hotel:

Who has captured the Prince's heart in the heart of LA?

Pining for the Prince with a view of Mayfair...

She'd even included some shots of the suites, captioning each one with something provocative yet whimsical. Each post had garnered thousands of likes, hundreds of comments. And, it seemed, an interview on American television. As silly as it could seem, Alessandro had to admit there was a certain artistry to it all.

'You're a talented photographer,' he told her as he handed back the phone, 'as well as marketing consultant. I might hire you in that capacity, if your social media career turns out to be unsatisfying.'

'Oh, I doubt it will,' Ella told him.

'Still,' Alessandro continued with a frown, 'they must know it's you, considering the photos we've had taken together.'

Ella shrugged, that catlike smile still playing about her lips. 'We'll see,' she said.

It was less than an hour to Paris and Liane immersed herself in her book the whole time, so Alessandro kept to work. As Paris came into view, Liane put down her book and looked out of the window, a faint smile touching her lips. This was her home, Alessandro couldn't help but think. Had she missed it?

As they were exiting the plane, he laid one hand on her arm and she turned to him, eyebrows raised in query.

'I'm still looking forward to you showing me the sights,' he said, and her smile, when it came, was like a starburst of sunshine.

'Of course. I'll be happy to.' Still smiling, she moved past him, down the ramp, leaving Alessandro feeling strangely unsettled. Yes, he thought rather moodily, they had certainly cleared the air.

CHAPTER NINE

'So WHERE SHALL we go first?' Alessandro asked as he joined Liane in the lobby the next morning for a day of sightseeing. 'Or are you going to surprise me?'

'I'm afraid you might be disappointed,' she told him with a little laugh. 'The sights I'm showing you are, I fear, somewhat ordinary.'

'But it's still Paris,' he said, smiling as he took her arm. Liane tried not to react to the feel of his strong forearm twined with hers. Since she'd turned down Alessandro's offer, she was doing her best to act unfazed. Cheerful, even, and certainly unaffected, although it felt like the performance of a lifetime. Still, they both knew where they stood. That had to be a good thing. She kept telling herself it was, even as she'd lain awake all night, staring at the ceiling and trying not to imagine Alessandro taking her into her arms, his mouth on hers, his hands on her body…

At least this felt like a good thing, to walk out into the summer sunshine of her favourite city in the world, the pavements sparkling with dew, the sky a fresh, breezy blue, the Eiffel Tower piercing its brightness in the distance.

'I've become rather used to spending my nights in a penthouse suite,' she remarked teasingly as they headed down the Champ de Mars. Alessandro had offered the use of his limo and chauffeur but Liane had insisted they walk, in order to experience the city better. 'It's going to be a shock when I return home.'

'You live with Ella in New York, yes?'

'Yes, in a townhouse by Central Park. It's lovely, so I can't really complain.'

'But?' Alessandro filled in, his crinkled gaze scanning her face with a half-smile.

'But it's not mine. Ella's father, my stepfather, left it to her, with the proviso that my mother and sister and I could all live there as long as we wanted.' She shrugged. 'And considering the astronomical rents in Manhattan, it makes sense to stay there, especially on my teacher's salary. But one day…' She paused, embarrassed, unsure whether to continue, but then Alessandro prompted her again.

'One day?'

Why shouldn't she tell him? She'd made it clear, and so had he, where they both stood. That could give them a certain freedom to be honest, to be real, and she suddenly found that she wanted to be so. 'One day I'd like a house in the country,' she told him with a smile and a purposeful swing in her step. 'It would need to be old, a rambling kind of place with hidden corners and twisting stairs and funny, poky rooms.'

'Poky rooms?' He raised his eyebrows and she laughed.

'Not in a bad way. Just…the kind of house that has a personality, feels alive. One that keeps surprising you with its secrets.' They'd turned onto the wide, sunny avenue of Rue de l'Université, the chestnut trees that lined the boulevard providing some welcome shade from the bright summer sun.

'And what would you do in this house?' Alessandro

asked, and once again Liane hesitated. Did she really want to share her dreams, private and precious as they were? But why shouldn't she? They were friends, after all. They'd both made that so abundantly clear. Surely that freed her to tell him her fairy tale, the one she'd dreamed of since she'd been a little girl, the one she was still waiting for. She knew, with a deep, certain instinct, that he wouldn't laugh at her for it.

'I'd have cats and dogs and children,' she informed him with blithe determination. 'Several of each, preferably. And a garden. A big vegetable garden, and pots of herbs, lavender and thyme and sage, and flowers too. Big, blowsy roses and lilac bushes… I love the smell of lilac. It was at the house where I lived as a child, in Lyon—it makes me feel sad and happy at the same time, somehow. I want a house that smells of lilac the whole spring long.' She glanced at him uncertainly, realising she was babbling, but Alessandro, gratifyingly, looked arrested.

'Tell me more,' he said.

'And there'll be a big kitchen, but cosy too, with a range and a big, square oak table and a sofa somewhere, the squashy kind you curl up on with a dog or a cat or…or a lovely little toddler.' She looked away, blushing, because she realised she was imagining a serious, dark-eyed boy a lot like Alessandro, one who had that same glinting smile. 'And it would have a wood burner too, for winter nights or frosty mornings…'

'It sounds as if you've imagined this house in detail,' he remarked dryly.

'Oh, I have.' She let out a wobbly little laugh. Embroidering her dream house, her dream life, with all of its wonderful threads had been a very pleasant pastime over the sometimes lonely years, from when she'd been a little girl to far more recently.

'And what about the man in this scenario?' Alessandro asked mildly, his hands in the pockets of his trousers as he sauntered along. 'I assume, with the children you mentioned, there is a man of some description?'

'Oh, yes.' Her cheeks warmed and she kept her gaze straight ahead. 'There's a man.'

'And what is he like?'

Alessandro's tone was neutral, but Liane's skin still prickled and her lips tingled as she remembered their kiss. The house was one thing, but did she really want to talk about this with him? The man she hoped she would love one day. Well, she thought with sudden, heady recklessness, why not? He'd made it clear it would never be him. That didn't mean her fairy tale prince wasn't real, or at least wouldn't be one day.

'I don't have as many preconceived notions about him,' she told him. 'I don't mind what he looks like or does for a job, or anything like that. What matters is that he is kind, and honest, and loyal. And he must have a sense of humour. That's very important.'

'And like cats and dogs, I presume. And children.'

She gave a little laugh. 'Well, yes.'

'And of course he must want to live in this pastoral paradise with you.'

'That, too.' She slid him a sideways glance, uncertain of his dry tone. Was he mocking her? Or merely cataloguing her rather ridiculously long list of requirements? 'It is just a dream,' she reminded him quietly, and he stopped right there on the street, laying a warm, sure hand on her arm.

'Dreams are important.' His silvery gaze blazed down

at her as his hand tightened briefly on her arm. 'Don't give up your dream, Liane.'

Why, she wondered, did that feel like some sort of warning? 'What about you?' she asked. 'What are your dreams?'

He removed his hand, shaking his head as he kept walking. 'I don't have dreams. Not like that, anyway.'

'Too jaded?' she teased softly, although his words made her feel sad. 'Too cynical for daydreams?'

He gave a small, rueful laugh of acknowledgement. 'Perhaps.'

'And what made you so?' she asked as she fell into step alongside him. 'Was it your parents, their difficult marriage?'

'That was certainly the start of it.'

'Tell me about them.' She longed to know more about him, but she also wondered if, for Alessandro, speaking of them would be similar to lancing a wound. That prized restraint, that all-important self-control, she suspected, hid a depth of emotion he was afraid to feel or even acknowledge to himself. Perhaps she was being fanciful, but she felt it all the same.

Alessandro didn't speak for a long moment, and Liane began to wonder if she'd pushed too hard. Maybe they should have stuck to daydreams. Then, finally, the words emerged slowly, chosen with care, offered with reluctance.

'They were the fairy tale, at the start. Italian nobility and a movie starlet, their wedding was covered by all the European newspapers. Everyone thought they were perfect together.' He paused, his mouth tightening. 'All I remember is the fighting—and the tears.'

'Oh, Alessandro…'

He shook his head, as if to stay her words. 'My father had affairs. He couldn't resist a woman, still can't. My mother was beside herself with jealousy, and in her misery she drank and wept and raged. And fought him, doing her best to make him hurt, the way she was. They were always at each other, doing their best to draw blood, metaphorically speaking, but sometimes literally as well.' He paused, his gaze distant. 'I remember lots of shouting and tears, broken glass, slammed doors.' A short sigh escaped him. 'They loved each other, and that love caused them only pain.'

'It doesn't have to be that way for everyone,' Liane felt compelled to remark quietly. 'Surely you can see that, Alessandro?'

'I haven't seen many, if any, examples of a relationship that worked,' he replied brusquely. 'And I have no desire to try myself.' He gave her a fulminating glance. 'Don't make this about that, Liane.'

Chastened, she nodded. 'I'm sorry. Tell me more.'

He shrugged. 'What more is there to say? They made both their lives a misery, and mine as well. Sometimes they'd trot me out at parties, proof for whoever was wondering that their marriage wasn't the disaster it really was, a point of pride, I think, considering their celebrated start. They wanted to present a united front, and I was the only way they knew how to do that.'

Liane's heart twisted hard with sympathy. She'd had her own childhood challenges, with her mother's critical sternness and her father's tragic death, but she'd never had to deal with the kind of confusion and heartache Alessandro clearly had. 'That must have been awful,' she said quietly.

'It was. One of the reasons I don't like parties.'

'And it ended when you were eight, you said? Your mother...?'

His expression became shuttered and he angled his head away from her. 'She finally left. I suppose she'd had enough of my father's affairs.' He paused, as if he were going to say something else, but then he merely looked away, his lips compressed.

'You're an only child?' she asked gently.

'Yes, of my parents. I have a younger half-sister, the child of my father's third wife—or is it fourth?' He glanced back at her, wryly this time, although there was a grim set to his mouth. 'She lives in Umbria. I'm planning to see her after all these parties.'

'You're close?'

'I wouldn't say close, but I want to make sure she has a childhood that's better than mine was. She's only fourteen.'

'And what about your father? You told me he's in Ibiza. Why is he not with her?'

'Because he's hopeless with any sort of responsibility. She lives with her mother, Christina. As far as my father's wives go, she's not so bad. Better than some. Better than my mother's second husband, anyway.'

'What was he like?'

Alessandro shrugged. 'I only met him once, when she was leaving m…my father.' The slight hesitation made her think he'd been going to say *me*, and her heart ached for him, for the small boy he'd been. 'He was quite a bit younger than her, clearly with an eye for the main chance. He lasted all of nine months before he left her, taking most of her money. She tripped from man to man after that, and died in a car crash when her latest lover was at the wheel, and over the limit.'

'Oh, Alessandro.' Liane couldn't keep the dismay and compassion from her voice. 'I'm so sorry.'

He shrugged again, looking away. 'She was out of my life by then. I could barely remember her.'

'But still…' Liane hesitated, and then said quietly, 'I'm not surprised you're cynical about love, considering. I suspect I would be too, if my parents had been like that. If I'd encountered so much heartbreak and tragedy along the way.'

'Perhaps.' He quickened his step, giving her a smile that didn't quite reach his eyes. 'But why are we talking about such a gloomy subject? It's a beautiful day, and we're in Paris. Let's enjoy it, and not lose ourselves in the past.'

Why had he told her all that? Alessandro wondered. He normally didn't talk about his parents; he hated even thinking about them. Remembering their regrettable marriage took him back to his own lamentable childhood—hiding upstairs, wincing at the sound of screaming, only to have one of the house staff appear at the door.

'You're wanted downstairs, Master Alessandro.'

And he'd go, he'd always go, filled with dread and, worse, that tiny, treacherous flicker of hope.

Maybe this time it will be different. Maybe I'll be able to get them to stop fighting…

No, he certainly didn't want to think about those days.

And yet, he acknowledged, Liane drew the past out of him, all his secrets and hurts, the way a doctor drew poison. He felt unsettled for having said all that, but he also felt, in a strange way, better. It had been something of a relief, or perhaps an emotional bloodletting. Either way, he was ready to move on.

'So you haven't actually told me where we're going,' he said, and Liane gave him a glinting smile.

'My favourite museum in Paris, the Musée d'Orsay.

It has the best collection of Impressionist paintings. And then afterwards I thought we could stop by the Orangerie, where Monet's water lilies were installed. You step inside a curved room and feel as if they're completely surrounding you.' She paused, a small, sad smile touching her lips. 'My father used to take me there.'

'Did he?' Alessandro couldn't help but sound diffident, although he realised he might be biased, when he considered his own father and all his shortcomings. 'You told me before you've missed him.' Although he'd wanted to stop talking about the past, he'd much rather talk about hers than his.

'Yes, I do. I know he was both a gambler and a drinker, and my mother despaired of him, but…' She sighed, a soft breath of sound. 'He was so *fun*. He could make you feel like you were the centre of his world, and whenever I was with him I felt as if I could have an adventure. Now that I'm older, I recognise how destructive some of his behaviours could be. But as a child…he felt magical to me. After he died, I retreated a bit, I suppose.'

'It must have been hard.'

She nodded. 'Yes, we'd only been in New York a short time, we hardly knew anyone and I didn't actually speak English very well.' She grimaced. 'There were some challenging years.'

'Why didn't you move back to France?'

'Because my mother had already met Ella's father, Robert Ash, and there was nothing to go back to in France, anyway. My mother's parents were dead and my father had lost all their money.' She sighed. 'It all sounds terribly tragic, but it wasn't so bad, especially after Ella came to live with us.'

Had Ella been someone to love, Alessandro wondered,

in a life that seemed sadly devoid of it, since her father's death? He wasn't normally one to overanalyse emotions, but he sensed a similar kind of loss in Liane that he felt in himself. They just happened to have reacted to it very differently, with her insisting on the happily-ever-after dream and him refusing to believe in it.

They reached the museum and by mutual, silent accord they both stopped talking about the past and instead focused on the present, touring the museum's incredible offerings, although Alessandro enjoyed watching Liane's face light up as she looked at a painting more than seeing the actual art on the walls—Monet, Cezanne, Van Gogh—such masters had nothing on the play of emotions in Liane's violet eyes, her porcelain skin. The pink flush that came onto her cheeks, the sparkle in her eyes, the way she cocked her head to one side as she considered a painting or sculpture—Alessandro felt as if he could have watched her for ever.

And it was risk-free, he reminded himself, since they'd both made their positions clear. Strange, how that thought did not comfort him very much.

After the Musée d'Orsay, they went to the Orangerie, Liane leading Alessandro by the hand into the centre of the room where the massive canvases of Monet's water lilies hung all around, laughingly insisting he close his eyes.

She guided him to a bench, her hand soft and slender in his, and then whispered, like it was Christmas, like it was magic, 'Open your eyes.'

He did, and for a second all he saw was a blur of colour—lavender and green, flower and water and sky, all of it surrounding him. For a second, fancifully, he imagined he was in Liane's fairy tale garden, with the blowsy roses and the lilac bush. He could almost smell their sweetly haunting scent. The dogs were in the distance, there was a child toddling on chubby legs, Liane's laughter floating on the breeze. He felt...*happy*, a joy springing up in him that made a smile come to his lips.

Then he blinked the paintings into focus and found that the smeary beauty of Monet's lilies in their endless misty garden was nothing compared to the vision that, for a second, he'd conjured from the yearning depths of his own mind.

'Well?' she asked, squeezing his hand. 'What do you think?'

'I... I think it's beautiful.' He felt strangely emotional, and he suspected it had nothing to do with Monet. She was still holding his hand, as if she'd forgotten, and he didn't want her to let go. He certainly wouldn't. He turned to her and for a second he longed to cup her face in his hands, draw her to him. Forget all his stupid resolutions. He cleared his throat. 'Thank you for showing them to me.'

They had lunch at a little café near the Tuileries Garden, washing mussels and crusty French bread down with a carafe of white wine, and then walking slowly through the gardens, resplendent in sunshine, drinking in the day.

'So what will you do when you return to New York?' Alessandro asked as they wandered along, past the placid pond of the Grand Carré.

'Nothing much, I suppose.' Liane gave a little laugh that somehow sounded resigned. 'School doesn't start back up till September, and I don't have any holidays planned. I'm working on a translation of Rimbaud's poetry for a text-book. If I can, I'll finish that.'

She spoke pragmatically, but Alessandro thought it sounded rather lonely—and sad. 'And what about your farmhouse in the country?' he asked, and she gave him a startled, uncertain look.

'What about it?'

'How are you going to find it, languishing in the city, translating poems?'

'I'm not expecting to find it,' she said after a moment. 'Not like that. I won't stumble upon it like…like the Prince did the bewitched castle in *Sleeping Beauty*, to name another fairy tale.' She let out a laugh that held a note of longing.

'You won't? How, then?' He wasn't sure why he was pressing the point; did it matter to him if Liane found her fairy tale? The answer came instantly, absolutely. *Yes.* Yes, it did.

'I suppose… I suppose it will find me. Somehow. Some day…' Self-conscious now, she gave him a wry yet troubled look. 'Don't worry, I'm well aware life doesn't actually work like that and I should probably go out and find it myself, hack down the thorns and storm the castle, as it were. But I've never been particularly adventurous.'

No, she'd simply supported her stepsister in *her* adventures. Of course he was entirely the wrong person to tell her to go have her adventures. Cut down the thorns, storm the castle, find the Prince and kiss him senseless. How could he tell her any of that when he hadn't done it himself? When he'd told her, and convinced himself, that he didn't believe in fairy tales, that love was nothing but pain and trouble and not worth even finding, never mind fighting for?

And yet, as they started back towards the hotel, he still wanted the fairy tale for Liane. Even though the thought caused him an almost agonising twist of jealousy and longing, he hoped she found her happily-ever-after…even if it could never be with him.

CHAPTER TEN

'WHERE HAVE YOU *BEEN*?'

Ella clucked and shook her head, her hands on her hips, as Liane came into the hotel suite. She'd just left Alessandro down in the lobby, with a bittersweet smile and a promise to wear the dress—his dress—tonight. She'd had the most marvellous day, she thought, full of laughter and fun, of both companionable silences and enjoyable conversation, of strolling through Paris on the arm of the most beautiful man…yes, it had been wonderful, but it had filled her with an impossible longing too. Alessandro was *not* part of the fairy tale. She had to keep reminding herself of that again and again, because the more time she spent with him, the more it felt as if it could be possible—if only in her own head. Her own heart.

'I told you I was going sightseeing with Alessandro,' Liane replied as mildly as she could.

'I didn't think you'd be gone for so long—'

'It's only four in the afternoon. The party's not till seven.' Liane gazed at her sister in concern. 'Is something wrong?'

'No, far from it. Something's *right*.' Ella looked as if she were bubbling inside. 'Something's really right. I had that online interview this afternoon—'

'Oh, yes, how was it?' Liane exclaimed, a pang of guilt assailing her at the realisation that she hadn't even remembered that was happening; she'd been too wrapped up in her day with Alessandro.

'Oh, it was fine.' Ella waved a hand in airy dismissal. 'It's so easy online, you just open your laptop. They wanted to know how I met Alessandro, whether I really was "his Princess", as the tabloids are saying.' She grinned and rolled her eyes as jealousy made Liane's stomach clench. She knew it was all smoke and mirrors, pretence and presumption, but it still rankled. She hadn't let herself look at any of the online speculation, hadn't wanted to see the photos of Ella on Alessandro's arm, knowing how the media would play it, the Prince and the Princess. The fairy tale and the happily-ever-after.

'And what did you say?'

'Oh, I let them wonder, of course,' Ella replied with one of her rich, throaty laughs. 'Can't give the game away! I said I thought there was definitely someone he was interested in, but whether it was me…' she took on a look of wide-eyed innocence as she gave Liane a slow blink '…that I really couldn't say.'

'And they bought that?' Liane returned with a laugh that came out just a bit too forced. 'When you've been in all the magazines, draped on his arm?'

'How many magazines do you think I've been in?' Ella exclaimed. 'It's the *hotel* that's being featured, Liane, not me. I might be in a shot or two, but that's all. I'm hardly a celebrity.'

Liane stared at her in surprise. 'But the whole reason Alessandro asked you to go along was to give the hotels some publicity—'

'Yes, the *hotels*. And I have, through my social media. But no one even knows it's my account.'

'What?' Liane blinked at her in confusion. 'Why? I mean…you want to be an influencer, Ella! Why would you make it anonymous?' She realised she'd been imagining Ella in every shot, arm snugly woven through Alessandro's, her head on his shoulder as they danced the night away…

Had it not been like that? Had her own tortured imaginings been worse, and far more painful, than the reality?

'Did you not hear me talking to Alessandro about it on the plane?' Ella's eyes danced as, mutely, Liane shook her head. No, she'd tuned out their conversation because she hated how unsettled and, yes, *jealous* it made her feel. She knew their so-called relationship was fake, and she felt relatively certain that Alessandro wasn't interested in Ella, but it still made her feel small and mousy and forgettable to see them together, circulating among the crowds, dazzling everyone. She didn't want to think about it more than she had to.

'Well, the point isn't to make me famous,' Ella explained with a smile and a toss of her head. 'It's to make the hotel famous. Keep people intrigued as well as guessing—'

'Guessing what?'

'Who Alessandro is in love with, of course!'

Liane tried not to flinch.

He isn't in love with anyone, she wanted to tell her sister. *He refuses to be, because he thinks love is somehow damaging, or maybe even dangerous, and he's never, ever going to risk it.*

'And how are you doing that?' she asked, and with a canary-eating grin Ella handed her her phone.

Silently Liane swiped through the images—the artful shots of crystal and candlelight, the glimpse of Ella in the mirror, so it could—almost—be any woman. *The Prince of Manhattan's Mystery Princess.*

'They're wonderfully done,' she told her as she handed back the phone, 'but everyone must know it's you. You're the Instagrammer, after all, and you posted the first shot with that glass shoe—'

'Oh, I keep them guessing,' Ella replied with a smile that bordered on smug. 'Trust me on that.' She slid her phone into her pocket. 'But now onto more practical matters! I can't go to the party tonight, so you have to go in my place.'

Liane's jaw dropped as terror and delight twined tightly together, flared low in her belly. 'What? I can't possibly—'

'Oh, but you can, and you have to. After my interview this morning some French YouTubers got in touch with me. They follow fashion and they want me to feature in some of their videos, wearing some of Alonso's designs. They've only got this evening free, though, so I have to go.'

'But Ella,' Liane protested as a growing feeling of alarm took hold of her, 'you have a contract with Alessandro.'

'Did I sign anything?' Ella challenged blithely. 'No. And to be honest I think I'm doing him a favour. I've been at every party so far. It's becoming boring. People expect me to be there—the presenter on the TV show who interviewed me thought I was his PA.' She rolled her eyes, pretending to look affronted. 'Far better to focus on you, this new, mysterious woman.'

'Me?' Liane squeaked. She could hardly believe it.

She could never be like Ella, basking in the limelight. Everyone would laugh at her, they would think she was being ridiculous… 'No. I can't.'

Ella's baby blue eyes sparkled with challenge. 'Why not?'

'Because…because I'm not the sort of person who steps into the spotlight. Who enjoys it.'

'Then maybe I have to give you a push.'

'No.' Liane shook her head, her hands pressed to her hot cheeks. She hated the thought of being not just Alessandro's object of pity but the whole world's and worse, of scorn. 'No, no, I couldn't, Ella, really.'

Ella stared at her for a moment while Liane kept shaking her head. 'Don't you want to?' she asked finally. 'At least a little? Aren't you tired of standing on the sidelines—not just of a party, but of life?'

'Ella.' Liane couldn't keep the hurt from her voice.

'I'm serious, Liane. You live so quietly, never attracting attention, never putting yourself forward for anything or, more importantly, for anyone. When's the last time you even had a date?'

'I'm not like you,' Liane protested. 'I never want to be the centre of attention.'

'I'm not saying you have to be the centre,' Ella replied with a laugh, 'the way you know I love to! But you deserve more than the shadows. I know you think your mother makes my life miserable, and she definitely tries, but she does for you as well. You don't even see it, the way she asks you to fetch and carry for her, how she's always criticising, acting as if you're never quite good enough. In some ways she's harder on you than on me. At least I know she doesn't like me. She's meant to love you.'

Liane opened her mouth and closed it again, shocked by Ella's clear-eyed assessment.

'And I know I'm as much to blame as anyone,' Ella continued frankly. 'I know I take advantage of you without even meaning to. It's so easy to do, Liane, because you're so wonderfully kind and supportive. You're always thinking of other people…'

'Then don't take advantage of me by dropping me in it this evening,' Liane interjected a bit desperately. 'Please.'

Ella planted her hands on her hips, her eyes narrowed. 'Why not?'

'Because!' Liane cried. 'Because I can't do this. I don't know how to sparkle and chat the way you do. Alessandro will be furious—'

'Somehow I don't think he will,' Ella murmured. 'And I'm afraid this is going to be a bit of tough love. I'm going, Liane, and you're doing it. But don't worry, I won't drop you in it.' She glanced at the time on her phone. 'We've got two and a half hours to get you ready and, trust me, we're going to use every minute.'

Liane couldn't believe how ruthless her stepsister could be—not just about insisting she attend the ball on Alessandro's arm, but in preparing her for the privilege. Liane had always known Ella loved her spa days and beauty treatments—some of them rather ridiculous—but she'd never subjected her to them, the way she was now.

'Fortunately I brought my supplies,' she told Liane as she opened a suitcase that was devoted entirely to a vast array of beauty products. 'We'll start with an exfoliating face mask, and then a soothing one, so you won't look like a tomato tonight! I'll do your nails too—goodness, you clip them short!'

'It's sensible,' Liane murmured.

'Oh, let's forget all about sensible, shall we?' Ella replied with a wicked glint in her eye. 'For tonight, at least.'

At some point Liane gave up trying to put up a fight; she'd always known what a whirling dervish her sister could be, although her attentions had never been so singularly focused on her before. She let herself submit to not one but two face masks, a manicure and pedicure, a body scrub and then a host of hair treatments before Ella led her out of the huge, sumptuous bathroom to the bedroom, covering her eyes with one hand as she insisted she did not look in a single mirror.

'Wait till you see the finished product,' she instructed severely. 'I want you to get the full impact.'

'I do have a dress, you know,' Liane told her.

'Oh, yes, I know,' Ella purred. 'Alessandro bought it himself, didn't he? Thank goodness we won't have that blue bag of a dress to worry about.'

'It wasn't that bad...' Liane protested feebly.

'It was *worse*. Absolutely horrendous. Now come here, because I'm going to do your make-up.'

Obediently Liane came, sitting down on a stool and closing her eyes while Ella got out her bag of tricks. 'I don't want to look *painted*,' she began nervously.

'You sound like Belle-Mère,' Ella scoffed as she began to rub some sort of lotion into Liane's face. 'Painted, indeed. What is this? The Victorian age? Pinch your cheeks for a bit of colour? You can wear make-up, Liane, and not look like some sort of wicked woman.'

'I know that,' Liane said quickly. Perhaps she was acting at least a little ridiculous, still stung by old memories.

She did her best to relax as Ella continued with her ministrations and then helped her into her dress and heels, adding some tasteful costume jewellery from her own collection and a final generous spritz of perfume. She placed her hands on Liane's shoulders, steering her towards the mirror, insisting her eyes remain closed.

'I'm afraid to look,' Liane admitted with a shaky laugh as Ella positioned her in front of the full-length mirror.

'Don't be, you're amazing!' Ella squeezed her shoulders. 'Now open your eyes.'

Alessandro glanced at his watch, his mouth tightening. All around him waiters circulated, guests were arriving and a headache was banding his temples. After he'd left Liane he'd gone straight to work, dealing with various matters on both the investment and hospitality fronts, lambasting himself for taking a day off, even though he couldn't make himself regret it. The day with Liane, he knew, would be one that would stay in his memory for a long time to come. One that would bring a smile to his lips and a poignant sorrow to his heart. A day out of time.

He glanced at his watch again and then looked up, his breath catching in his throat as he caught sight of Liane coming into the ballroom.

She was a vision, enough to make everyone's heads turn, although she hardly seemed aware of the attention, her lovely, tremulous gaze focused on him. Just as he was focused on her, the whole world falling away as he drank in the sight of her.

Her hair was piled on top of her head, a few white-gold curls trailing over her bare, silky shoulders. Her eyes looked luminous, a deep, velvety purple, her lips lush, her skin like the creamiest porcelain, touched with a blushing pink. And as for her figure—swathed in the Grecian-style gown, the fabric rippling like crystalline water over her slender, supple curves. A single sapphire nestled in the hollow of her throat, matched by diamond-encrusted ones at her ears. Her toes peeped out as she walked—silver-spangled heels, another pair of ridiculous shoes. He realised he was grinning as he stretched out one hand.

Her fingers whispered against his as he drew her closer. 'Ella…' she began, and he had to blink because for the last minute at least he'd completely forgotten Ella even existed. 'Ella can't come tonight. I'm so sorry.'

'I'm not,' he said simply, and a smile of incredulous wonder bloomed across her face like the most precious of flowers. 'I'm not at all.'

He heard the murmurs of speculation ripple around the room; no doubt people were noticing his change of escort, his reception of her, and yet he hardly cared. Gossip, rumour, speculation, publicity—none of it mattered a whit in this moment. This evening was for him and Liane.

Was he imagining how the music swelled, a crescendo within him as he took her in his arms and they started to dance, moving together in perfect harmony and rhythm?

'I have two left feet,' Liane warned him, and he shook his head. He wouldn't hear her disparage herself, not tonight.

'You dance beautifully. And you're dancing with me. That's all I care about.'

Her eyes widened as confusion clouded their violet depths, and he knew why she was confused, because he felt it in himself, even as something in him crystallised and became wonderfully clear. Tonight, he decided, was magic. Tonight was a moment out of time, out of reality. Tonight was for them, and neither of them needed to think about the future.

The song finished on a crescendo of strings and Alessandro fetched them both glasses of champagne before they joined some of the other guests. If he'd had any concern that Liane would somehow not be able to handle the endless chitchat—and he realised quite quickly that he hadn't—then they would have been put to rest as soon as she spoke. She wasn't all sparkle and glitter the way Ella was, commandeering a conversation with her energy and wit. No, Liane was quieter, deeper, listening with an intensity that made people feel important, asking questions that were pertinent and interesting. Her French flowed easily, her voice light and musical, and Alessandro's heart swelled with pride and something more. Something like possession.

Halfway through the evening he'd had enough of the crowds and he drew her out onto the balcony, the perfumed night air as soft as silk, the Eiffel Tower a beacon of light in the distance.

'This all feels so unreal,' she said quietly as she grasped the railing, as if she needed to anchor herself to reality. 'I feel as if I need to pinch myself.'

'I assure you, you don't. It's real.' His voice was a low thrum and she turned to him suddenly, an urgent light coming into her eyes.

'Is it?' she asked softly. 'You've been so attentive, Alessandro, so…enchanting. And acting as if you're… you're almost enchanted with me.'

'I am—'

She shook her head, a quick movement. 'Don't,' she whispered. 'If this is for Ella's social media, or the press, or—'

'Do you honestly think that?' Alessandro demanded in a raw voice. He gestured to the balcony, the empty darkened space. 'Do you see any cameras? Any paparazzi?'

'No…'

'I am not doing this for show. This isn't about any of that, Liane. I couldn't care less about any of it. All of it. I never have.' The words came from deep inside him, a place he hardly ever accessed, where his yearnings had lain dormant for so long. He could hardly believe he was confessing to having them at all, and yet he could not ignore them now. He wanted her. He *needed* her. And he didn't care if she knew it.

'Then why…'

'You've got into my blood,' he said simply. 'My mind. My…' *Heart.* He couldn't say it. Even caught up in the moment, drunk on both her beauty and sweetness, he couldn't let himself go that far. 'I need you,' he said instead, and her lips parted softly in surprise.

It felt like an invitation, and slowly he wrapped his hand around the nape of her neck, his fingers sliding through the silk of her hair. A shudder escaped her in a breath of acceptance. He took a step towards her and she let her head fall back so he was cradling it, her eyes heavy-lidded, her lips lush and waiting.

The kiss, when it came, was soft and slow and languorous, as if they had all the time in the world when he knew they only had this evening. This moment. And still it went on as he traced the outline of her lips, tasted the honeyed sweetness of her mouth, and her arms came around him as she returned his passion, firing his senses and his blood, making him crave even more.

He broke the kiss to press another to her cheek, her ear, her throat…he couldn't get enough. He wondered if he ever would. Her breath came out in another shudder as she sagged against him as if her legs couldn't carry her any more, her fingers driving through his hair.

Alessandro had a primal urge to sweep her up in his arms, carry her through the ballroom like a prince of old with his bride. Somehow he managed to claw back some sanity.

'Stay the night with me,' he whispered against her throat, her mouth. 'Stay the night.'

Her fingers stilled in his hair, her body tensing beneath his. 'Just the night,' she said slowly, carefully, and of course he knew what she was asking.

'I don't know how long it would last,' he admitted in a voice ragged with wanting. 'But I know what I feel for you now and it overwhelms me.' He lifted his head to gaze into her eyes, cradling her lovely face in his hands. 'Please, Liane.' He'd never begged before, yet it felt like that was what he was doing now. He, a man who never asked for anything, who made sure he never needed anyone, was *begging*. It was shaming and freeing all at once, to admit to this need. To need someone this much, when for so long he hadn't let himself.

Liane stared at him, her eyes full of torment, her lips trembling. 'You told me I was made for the fairy tale,' she said after a moment, a catch in her voice, her face cradled in his hands. 'You're the only person who has said such a thing to me, who let me believe that I was. That I could be.'

'Liane…' Already he felt the moment slipping away; what had, seconds ago, felt beautiful and precious now felt sordid and wrong. Had he really been begging her to sleep with him? Had he fallen that low, become that craven? He dropped his hands from her face and took a step away.

'I'm sorry, Alessandro.' She pressed one hand to his cheek and he closed his eyes, resisting the urge to turn

his head and press a kiss to her palm. 'It's taking everything I have to say no to you, and the only reason I'm
doing it is because I know you have the power to break
my heart.' He swallowed hard, humbled by her honest
admission, horrified by his own. He'd done the one thing
he'd said he never would—been led by his emotions. Let
them bring him to this awful place of loss and rejection
and *hurt*. How could he have been so stupid?

'I could fall in love with you,' Liane confessed, an
ache in her voice as Alessandro struggled to school his
features into something cool and implacable. 'I think part
of me already has, without wanting to, without meaning
to. I'm sorry, for your sake as much as mine. I know it's
not what you want. This has happened so suddenly, so
intensely. For me, anyway.' She let out a wobbly laugh
that held more than a hint of sadness as well as an ache
of longing, and it made Alessandro want to take her in
his arms again, but he didn't. He wouldn't, now that it
was so obvious where he stood. 'I'm not trying to pressure you into offering more than you can give. I hope
you believe me on that. I just… I just can't give myself
to you knowing what you are willing to offer in return.
How little. I… I can't let myself be hurt like that, and
I know I would be. I'm sorry.' Her voice choked on the
last words and before he could reply she hurried from the
balcony, moving quickly through the crowded ballroom,
just as Ella had a week ago, except this time, Alessandro
knew with a leaden certainty, it was no publicity stunt.

Liane was running away—from him.

CHAPTER ELEVEN

LIANE STARED DOWN at the note, written in Ella's loopy scrawl, with complete incredulity. Her head ached from too much champagne and too many tears. Last night, after the most magical evening she'd ever experienced, she'd come home to the unhappily-ever-after she knew would be waiting for her. Never mind the glass slipper, she'd turned into a pumpkin, or the carriage had, however the old story went. She was back to being hide-in-the-shadows Liane, and she wished she wasn't.

She wished she'd had the courage to say yes to Alessandro, to take what he had to give. Who even knew if it might lead to something else, something so wonderfully more? And, even if it didn't, it would have been more than she'd ever been offered before. Why not risk it?

And yet she hadn't, because she was cautious and careful and *scared*. She didn't leap into life, she didn't have adventures, and she certainly didn't tumble into bed—or into love. She'd managed to escape with her heart intact, but in the cold, dull light of morning she bleakly wondered if it was worth it. She wished she had the courage to act differently...

She gazed down at Ella's note again and slowly shook her head. How could she have done this? A quick, impatient tap on the door had her slipping the note into her pocket. *Alessandro.* She wasn't ready to see him again, not after she'd fled so melodramatically from the ballroom, and after he'd admitted to so much. *Why* couldn't she have said yes? Why couldn't she have taken what he was willing to offer? Could she still? Another tap on the door.

With a quivering sigh, Liane went to answer it.

'You look tired,' Alessandro remarked critically as he stepped into the suite.

Liane let out a shaky laugh. 'I am tired,' she told him, trying for tart and feeling she missed it by a mile. 'Thank you, though, for pointing it out.'

Alessandro gazed at her coolly, completely unapologetic for his criticism. He didn't look tired, she thought bitterly. Freshly shaven, dressed in a three-piece charcoal-grey suit, smelling of citrus, he was as devastatingly attractive as always, powerful and remote, needing nothing and no one. *Utterly unaffected.* This was not the same man who had held her in his arms and pleaded with her to spend the night with him. Liane was already half wondering if that had actually happened, doubting her own recollection in light of this new, hard reality. Perhaps it had been too much champagne and wishful thinking...

'Where's Ella?' Alessandro glanced around the empty suite, Liane's suitcase by the door.

'She's gone,' she replied wearily. 'She left with the You-Tubers early this morning, before I woke up.'

'What?' His dark brows snapped together as he stared at her. 'What do you mean, she *left*?'

Liane shrugged, spreading her hands helplessly. 'They're doing some video thing in the south of France. She didn't give me the details, just said she was sorry that she had to go and she thought she'd done enough already, in terms of the hotel's social media.'

You can take care of the rest yourself, she'd written, but Liane wasn't about to say that to Alessandro. She couldn't take Ella's place. She hadn't managed it for a single evening. 'I'm sorry,' she told Alessandro.

'You don't need to apologise,' he replied. 'You are not your sister's keeper.'

Liane remained silent, knowing there was nothing more she could say. Ella should have explained to Alessandro herself, but she'd left that unfortunate task to Liane. Briefly she thought of the playful postscript to Ella's note—*And have fun!!!*

As if.

Right now Alessandro was looking more than a little annoyed, and colder than she'd ever seen him. Last night seemed like nothing more than a dream, a figment of her desperate imagination. And to think she'd been wondering if she should reconsider…!

'What shall we do?' she asked uncertainly while Alessandro gazed dispassionately around the empty room. The last of the Rossi Hotel balls was tonight, in Rome. But without Ella…

'We'll go without her,' he stated flatly, as if the matter was both settled and of little interest. 'After last night's performance, she's not even needed.'

Liane's cheeks heated as she held his cool unaffected gaze. 'What do you mean, last night's *performance*?'

In response Alessandro pulled a tightly rolled magazine out of his pocket and dropped it, without ceremony, on the coffee table where Liane had found Ella's note. She blinked in disbelief as the magazine unrolled and the cover page was revealed—the photo was unmistakably of *her*.

Her fleeing the ball last night, the blue folds of her gown streaming out behind her, the crowds parting as she ran towards the double doors like a deer being hunted. Colour touched her cheeks. She looked ridiculous—foolish and frightened, as if she'd had the very devil at her heels.

'But…' Her lips formed the word numbly. 'How did they…'

'We had invited the press there, of course,' he remarked dispassionately. 'And it seemed this was the perfect photo op.'

'Photo op…!' Her head jerked up from the sight of the photo as she stared at him in shocked dismay. 'You can't think…'

'I can't think?' He arched one eyebrow coolly.

'You can't think I left the ballroom for some sort of publicity shot,' she forced herself to say. It seemed laughable as well as horrible—she, mousy little Liane, looking for publicity the way Ella did? And yet Alessandro was looking at her so coolly. 'Do you?' she burst out.

'No,' he answered after a moment, his voice toneless. 'And in any case, this is the kind of publicity we want, isn't it?' He didn't sound particularly enthused. 'Everyone buzzing about who the mystery woman who ran out of the ballroom is. Apparently Rossi Hotels is trending on Twitter.' He sounded bored rather than pleased by this fact.

'Oh…' Liane's mind whirled unhappily. She didn't want to be on the cover of a magazine, or trending on Twitter. There was a reason, she realised, why she'd avoided the limelight. She didn't like it. And right now she wished, quite desperately, that none of this had happened.

'As it is,' Alessandro continued, 'now that you've made the covers of these tabloids, you can finish the job and accompany me to Rome. You were going to anyway, so the matter, really, is negligible.'

He started to turn away and she burst out, 'Is that really what you want?'

'It's just one more day,' he replied with a shrug. 'The day after tomorrow you can fly back to New York and translate your Rimbaud.' He didn't look at her as he strode to the door. 'I'll meet you in the lobby in fifteen minutes.'

As the door clicked shut behind him, Liane sank onto the sofa, her knees watery, her mind spinning. She'd lain awake half the night, her body aching, her lips stinging from when he'd kissed her, wondering if she could possibly be bold enough to tell Alessandro this morning that she'd changed her mind. That she'd take however little he had to give, and be glad. Be ridiculously happy, as a matter of fact.

Thank goodness she hadn't blurted that out the moment he'd come in! He clearly had moved on from last night's tender moment. But why was he acting so cold? The idea that she'd run from the ballroom in order to catch something on camera…why, it was completely absurd. And even if she'd done it, wasn't that what he wanted? It was what he'd hired Ella for, after all. If for Ella, then why not her? Why act as if she'd…she'd *betrayed* him?

And then the penny dropped, a flicker of realisation unfurling inside her, along with a cautious wonder, a tentative hope. Was his irritation over the photo, his remoteness with her, a cover for his hurt? Because she'd run away? He'd asked her to stay the night. He'd kissed her with unashamed passion and framed her face with his hands and he'd practically *pleaded*. That had not been her wishful thinking.

Liane knew he was a proud man, one who did not allow

himself to be guided or controlled by his emotions. Who hated the thought of being vulnerable. Was that what was behind his icy demeanour this morning? Or was she ridiculous to hope she'd affected him that much? To hope that he actually cared, if just a little.

With a start Liane realised she'd wasted ten minutes in pointless reflection. She was due in the hotel lobby in just five minutes, and she didn't want to add to Alessandro's ire. Quickly she jumped up and packed the last of her things, throwing tissues, a lip balm and her phone into her bag before she hurried to the door.

'You're late,' Alessandro said shortly as she came breathlessly into the lobby.

'I'm sorry—'

He'd already turned away, walking briskly out of the hotel to the waiting limo. As soon as Liane slid into the sumptuous interior, Alessandro took out his phone and started scrolling.

'Checking the publicity for the hotel?' she enquired tartly and he glanced up at her, the look in his steely eyes veiled.

'Answering work emails, as it happens. I couldn't care less about the publicity.'

'Really? Then why were you so annoyed that I was on the cover of that magazine?' His jaw tightened and she continued, unable to keep both the hurt and hope from her voice, 'I thought you *wanted* publicity. I thought that was the whole point of this—this exercise!'

'It is.' He turned to look out of the window as the Paris traffic streamed, a steel-grey glimpse of the Eiffel Tower visible in the distance. He was closing her out, Liane realised hopelessly, and why should she be surprised? Even if he was acting angry in order to hide his hurt, what did it matter?

Even if he felt something, he didn't want to feel it. The end result was still the same. She turned to look out of her own window, blinking back sudden tears. She'd refused him last night because she hadn't wanted to get her heart broken, so why was she feeling so miserable now? It seemed the end result had been the same for her too, no matter what she'd chosen.

They didn't speak until they were settled on Alessandro's jet, he with his work laid out in front of him and Liane feeling as uncertain as ever. She gazed around at the luxury that had left her speechless just a week ago, and now she was already becoming tired of it. She wanted to go home, to return to what was familiar and safe, and yet at the same time she knew she didn't want that at all. When she finally had to say goodbye to Alessandro, she knew she would be devastated. No matter how hard she'd tried to protect her heart, it clearly hadn't worked.

Alessandro gazed at Liane from the corner of his eye as he did his best to focus on his work. She looked bereft, and he couldn't blame her. He'd been acting like an ass. He should apologise, and he kept meaning to, but somehow he could never find the words. He couldn't bear to admit that he'd been acting this way because her rejection of him last night still stung.

He hadn't meant to plead with her. He never begged, and yet last night he'd wanted her so much he hadn't been able to keep the words from spilling from his lips. *Stay... Please, Liane.* He cringed at the memory, and yet he knew he'd meant it, even if he wished he hadn't.

He'd promised himself a long, long time ago that he'd

never beg for someone's attention, their love. He'd never even want to. At least, he told himself, it had been clear that all he'd wanted was her body in his bed. Not her heart. Not her love.

No, never that.

Impulsively Alessandro checked Ella's account to see if she'd posted anything about last night, and he saw, with something he decided was irritation and nothing deeper, that she'd posted the photo of Liane fleeing from the ball. From him. She'd captioned it *Can the Prince find his Princess again?* There were already thousands of views, hundreds of comments.

From the angle of the shot, no one could tell it was Liane. No one, Alessandro realised, even knew who Liane was. Ella was certainly playing up the mystery angle, and the world's media had captured the spirit of the thing. He should be glad, he knew; this was what he'd wanted, a controlled narrative that brought publicity for the hotels. As it was, he was starting to find the whole thing both tedious and distasteful. He didn't want any more of it—not for himself, and not for Liane.

He glanced at her again, taking in the ivory curve of her cheek as she looked out of the window at the azure sky, her gaze shuttered, the downward turn of her lips desolate.

'What are you thinking about?' he asked suddenly.

She glanced at him, startled but also weary. 'That I don't want to go to yet another wretched party,' she replied on a sigh.

'Neither do I.'

Something flickered in her eyes and then was gone. 'For someone who says he hates parties, you've gone to rather a lot of them.'

'An astute assessment.' A faint smile flickered about her mouth and he leaned forward. 'Why don't you want to go?'

'Because I'm tired of parties. Tired of pretending.'

'Were you pretending last night?' The words slipped out before he could bite them back. At least his tone was cool, repressive rather than pleading.

She gazed at him for a long moment, her eyes as dark and soft as pansies. 'No,' she whispered. 'No… In fact, this morning I was…' She took a breath, let out a little uncertain laugh. 'I was reconsidering my answer.'

His breath caught as he gazed at her, a pulse hammering in his throat as hope unfurled, then soared. 'Were you?'

'Yes, I was. I…' She moistened her lips, lifted her chin. 'I want to be with you, Alessandro. For…for however long you're offering.'

He sat back, his mind whirling, his blood roaring. *She wanted him.*

She nibbled her lip as she regarded him uncertainly. 'You…you haven't changed your mind?'

'Changed my mind?' He swallowed a hoarse laugh. 'No.'

'Then…'

Why, when he finally had her surrender and his victory, did he feel…not disappointed, no, never that, but something almost like…sorrow? It was so strange. He should be expectant, exultant, and instead he was…confused. He couldn't understand it at all.

'Alessandro?' she prompted, a waver in her voice.

'What made you change your mind?'

'I'm tired of being cautious and careful,' she replied, again with the tilt of her chin. 'I want to live. I want to… experience things. Ella has always been telling me to have fun, to be in the moment—well, that's what I'm choosing now.' She met his gaze defiantly, and Alessandro couldn't help but think it was all a far cry from what she'd said she wanted. The fairy tale in all its glory.

Yet who was he to decry her choice, especially when it dovetailed so neatly with what he wanted?

Or at least what he'd thought he did…

'If you haven't changed your mind,' Liane asked with a nervous laugh, 'why are you glaring at me?'

'I'm not glaring.' He gave her a quick smile as realisation unfurled within him. Niceties be damned, Liane had made her choice…and he would make his. 'I was just thinking about what you said. What it meant.'

A blush touched her cheeks, turning them to rose-tinted porcelain. 'Then you…agree?'

'Oh, yes.'

Her smile was both shy and lovely, filled with hope and longing, and it made Alessandro certain, his flickering doubts finally quenched.

'Wait.' He rose from his seat and walked swiftly to the cockpit, issuing instructions to the pilot before returning to Liane. His blood was roaring in his veins, his heart singing with joy. He knew he'd never felt this way about a woman, an affair, just as he knew, already, that it was so much more than that. Even if he'd tried for it not to be. Already, before they'd even touched, it was…whether Liane knew it or not.

She twisted around as he came back into the main cabin. 'What were you doing?'

'Telling the pilot to redirect the flight to Perugia.'

'What…?'

'We'll skip the party in Rome. We've both had enough of these ridiculous charades, the stares and suggestions. We'll go to my villa in Umbria instead.' He realised he couldn't wait to show it to her—the gardens, the spacious rooms, the sense of home. He wanted to share it all.

'But people are expecting you,' Liane protested. 'They'll wonder why you haven't shown up.'

'Then let them wonder. After last night's photo, they'll think we've run away together.' His blood heated at the thought.

'And do you really want them to think that?' Liane asked in surprise.

'I don't care what they think.'

Her gaze flitted away from his, and then resolutely back again, heat shimmering like gold in their violet depths. 'What now?' she whispered unsteadily.

He chuckled softly as he felt the answering flare of need fire through his body. 'We enjoy the expectation,' he murmured. 'And we drink champagne.'

'Champagne?' She sounded endearingly scandalised. 'It's ten in the morning!'

'So?' One of his staff silently appeared and Alessandro asked for a bottle of Cristal. 'We're celebrating.'

Her mouth kicked up at the corner. 'I suppose we are.'

He sat down opposite her and reached for her slender hand, taking it in his. It felt small and cold as he pressed it between his palms. 'Are you regretting your decision?'

She shook her head, the movement almost vehement. 'No, not at all.'

'You're sure?' He desperately wanted her to be.

'Yes,' she said firmly. 'I'm just nervous.'

'You don't need to be.'

Her mouth quirked wryly. 'You can say that because you've probably wined and dined thousands of women before taking them to your bed.'

'Hardly thousands.' And they faded to insignificance in light of this moment.

'Yes, but this isn't new for you, the way it is for me.'

'It's new for you?' He kept himself from admitting just how new it all felt to him.

'Yes. Newer than…well, newer than anything.' She flushed as she let out a little embarrassed laugh. 'If you know what I mean.'

Alessandro hesitated, startled but, he realised, not entirely shocked by her admission. She had to be in her late twenties, and yet… 'Liane, are you saying you're…you're a virgin?'

'That's exactly what I'm saying,' she replied with an attempt at flippancy that made his lips twitch and his heart ache. 'So you might be regretting your decision, as I'm probably going to be very clumsy and gauche about it all.'

'Somehow I doubt that very much.' No, he realised, he wasn't regretting anything. Rather he felt hugely gratified. *She'd chosen him.* The steward came back with a bottle of champagne, popping the cork neatly before pouring two flutes. Alessandro murmured his thanks while Liane waited, watching him apprehensively.

'Let us toast each other,' he said softly, after the steward had gone. He handed her a glass and then clinked his with hers. 'To us,' he said, and a smile flitted across her face, curved her lips.

'To us,' she agreed, 'and to now.'

Was that a warning to herself—or to him? Or was she just letting him know that she understood the rules? The trouble being, he realised, that he was somehow managing to forget them all. He took a sip of champagne and then put his glass on the coffee table, realising he could not go a moment more without touching her.

'Come here,' he said, his voice a low thrum, and then, as she fumbled to put her glass down, he reached for her hand and drew her slowly, willingly, from her seat, her lips parting in expectation, her eyes going dark with desire.

'You're so beautiful,' he said softly as she stood in front

of him, her body slender and supple and *his*, even before he'd touched her.

'You're the beautiful one.' Gently, but with daring, she rested her hand against his cheek. He closed his eyes, savouring the simple touch. 'I feel as if I'm dreaming,' she whispered.

He put his hands on her slender waist and then drew her down to his lap. A little clumsily, with a breathless laugh, she put her arms around him.

'I don't even...'

'You do.' He cupped her face in his hands as he drew her towards him for a long, lingering kiss. She tasted like champagne, but infinitely sweeter. Already he knew he could never get enough. 'Oh, you do.'

She let out another breathless laugh of wonder as his lips moved to her throat. 'Do you know what you do to me?' he murmured as he kissed the hollow of her throat, one hand cupping the slight fullness of her breast. She was perfect. Perfect in every way.

'No.' Her body arched against his hand. 'What do I do to you?'

'You drive me mad. Make me ache.' He settled her more firmly on his lap and her eyes widened. 'You never have to doubt yourself about that.' He wanted her to know how beautiful she was, how desirable. She never need doubt herself, her allure, again. He could give her that much at least. 'You've been driving me crazy since I first stepped on your foot.'

Her surprised laugh morphed into a gasp as he undid a button of her blouse, revealing the lacy silk of her bra. His lips moved over the ridges and seams and she arched against his mouth. '*Oh*...but...you were annoyed with me then.' She drove one hand through his hair to anchor herself as he continued his explorations, tasting her sweet skin, enjoying her little gasps of pleasure.

'Annoyed at how affected I was.'

'Even then…' Her breath came out in a sigh as he nudged the lace aside, tasted the silky sweetness of her skin.

'Even then.'

Her eyes were dazed, her face flushed as he undid another button, his fingers dancing across her heated skin, daring to go lower. 'Alessandro…'

They'd barely begun and yet already he was aching for her in every way possible. He'd wanted to give her a delectable taste of what was to come, but this sweet, slow torture would be the undoing of him. He settled her more firmly on his lap, pressing into her, feeling her yield.

'*Oh…*' Her eyes widened as she braced her hands on his shoulders and tentatively pressed back against him, gasping softly as pleasure flared hotly through him at the feel of her so intimately against him. Her breasts were pressed to his chest, her thighs splayed across his. He knew he was precariously close to losing control, and he could not have that happen here. He wanted to give her much more than a quick, desperate fumble.

Slowly, regretfully, he eased back. 'That,' he told her huskily, 'was a promise of things to come.'

She let out a breathy laugh as she rested her forehead on his shoulder. 'I feel as if I'm singing inside,' she whispered shakily.

He laughed softly and pressed a kiss to her bare shoulder. Tonight, he thought, would be an opera, an endless aria of pleasure as he made her body sing…and sing…and sing.

A discreet knock sounded on the door of the cabin.

'Signor Rossi?' the steward called. 'We are approaching Perugia.'

CHAPTER TWELVE

LIANE FELT AS if she were walking through a dream. The plane landed and they emerged into the sun-baked heat of an Umbrian afternoon, an SUV waiting to take them to Villa Rossi, tucked among the rolling green hills, while she existed in a daze of remembered pleasure.

Her body was thrumming, all the secret parts of her twanging to life, uncovered and aching, yet with a pleasurable ache as she thought, with a frisson of thrilled wonder, of how Alessandro had touched her…and how he would touch her still.

He looked unaffected as he chatted to the driver who greeted them, yet Liane caught the slight flush still on the hard planes of his face, remembered the throb of his body against hers, and it made her blood heat and her heart race all over again. There had been no doubting his desire for her, of that she was sure.

And is desire enough?

She ignored that small, panicky voice inside her. It would be, she told herself. She would make sure it was. She'd made her choice and she would enjoy every very pleasurable moment of it.

They drove down winding roads through ancient hill towns and sleepy villages until they came to a pair of impressive stone pillars topped with lions and a long sweeping drive that led to a sprawling whitewashed villa with a red-tiled roof, perched on its own hillside, surrounded by vineyards and olive groves.

'Alessandro!' An elegant yet relaxed-looking woman in her fifties with long, curly greying hair came out onto the steps as the car pulled up. 'I thought you weren't coming till tomorrow.'

'Change of plan.' Alessandro stepped out of the car and then extended a hand to Liane, keeping hold of it as he approached the woman and kissed her on both cheeks. '*Ciao*, Christina. Where's Sophia?'

'On her phone as usual, I'm sure,' Christina answered with a laugh. 'She'll be down in a second.' She glanced in curiosity at Liane. 'But who is this?'

Alessandro laced his fingers with hers as he drew Liane to his side. 'This,' he said firmly, 'is Liane.'

Liane didn't miss the note of possessive pride in his voice and she thought Christina didn't either, as a speculative gleam entered the older woman's eyes.

'I'm glad to meet you,' she said as a teenager tumbled out of the front door.

'Alessandro!' she exclaimed, and hurled herself into her half-brother's arms.

Liane took a step away, watching in poignant bemusement as Alessandro hugged the smiling, dark-haired girl. Here, she thought, was someone who loved him and wasn't afraid to show it. And he had to love her back, judging by the way he hugged her before he set her on her feet.

If he was capable of that kind of love...

No. She couldn't let herself think that way. Hope that much. She'd known what she was agreeing to when she'd said yes to Alessandro. Yes to a night, maybe two, perhaps even three, and no more. As long as she kept reminding herself of that, she'd be fine.

'Come inside,' Alessandro said, reaching for her hand once again. As he took it, Sophia's gaze narrowed and she glanced at Liane in unabashed curiosity, although without any hostility. Liane smiled, and Sophia smiled back.

Inside, the villa was an eclectic and tasteful mix of old world antiques and comfortable modern pieces. Christina led the way into a sprawling living room, its louvred doors open to an inner courtyard with orange trees and a tinkling fountain. A staff member brought iced coffees and a selection of Italian pastries.

'So…we've been watching your story unfold on social media,' Christina told them with a laugh as they sat down. 'Everyone's buzzing with it, wondering who your Princess is, Alessandro.' She gave him a teasing look. 'And now we know.' There was a slight questioning lilt to her voice and Liane forced herself to rush in.

'Oh, no. That was just a…a stunt, for publicity.'

'A stunt?' Christina glanced at Alessandro. 'That's not like you. You hate publicity.'

He shrugged, reaching for a pastry. 'The hotels had the publicity, not me.'

'So you don't mind that everyone is wondering what lovely young woman has caught your eye?'

'It was you, wasn't it,' Sophia interjected eagerly, 'running out of the ball last night? I saw it on YouTube this morning!'

She was on YouTube? Liane's stomach cramped. She wasn't ready to be famous, not even for fifteen minutes, and she definitely wasn't ready for her romance with Alessandro to be offered for public consumption. Except of course it wasn't a romance; it was an *arrangement*.

She wasn't having second thoughts, she told herself

fiercely. She absolutely wasn't. She was looking forward to tonight; she was practically counting the minutes. Her body was still humming. And yet despite all that she still felt she had to brace herself for the hurt she knew would come after, no matter how hard she tried to avoid it.

'We came here to get away from all that,' Alessandro told his sister and former stepmother. 'We'd had enough of the speculation.'

'Our lips are sealed, then,' Christina replied, her eyes dancing. 'I'm glad you brought someone to meet me, at least.' She turned to Liane. 'He never has before, you know.'

'Oh…' Liane couldn't think of anything to say. She didn't want another reason to hope. 'I'm only staying for a day or two.' She glanced at Alessandro, whose bland gaze gave nothing away. 'Actually, I should call my sister, let her know where I am. Do you mind…?'

Christina gestured to the hall. 'Of course not. Please.'

Liane murmured her apologies as she rose from her seat and stepped out into the hall, wondering if Ella would even answer her call, yet feeling a sudden, desperate need to talk to her sister. To hear her advice, even if she'd never been brave enough before to follow it.

'Liane?' To her surprise, Ella picked up after the first ring. 'How are you?'

'Good. I think.'

'You think? What's going on with Alessandro? You guys didn't fight, did you? I saw the photo of you running out of the ballroom. I posted it this morning. People are going crazy.'

'You didn't!' Liane exclaimed. 'Has absolutely everyone seen that wretched photo?'

'About three hundred thousand people, last time I checked. What's going on?' Ella sounded surprisingly interested, even avid. 'Where are you?'

'I…that is, we…we decided not to go to Rome. I'm in Umbria, at Alessandro's family's villa.'

'Oh, I *see*.' Ella sounded delighted, and Liane let out an uncertain little laugh.

'Yes, I guess you do.'

'So you *are* having fun.'

'Well…' Liane did her best to ignore the fluttery panic taking up residence in her stomach. 'I hope to.'

'Ah, Liane!' Ella let out a throaty chuckle. 'That's the spirit! He's crazy about you, you know. Don't doubt it.'

'You drive me mad.'

But how had Ella been able to see that? 'Crazy about me for the moment,' she agreed, 'but that's all.'

'Then enjoy the moment,' Ella advised. 'And see what happens. Is it just the two of you?'

'No, his father's ex-wife and her daughter are here. Sophia. She's fourteen, and clearly adores her brother.'

'Sophia, hmm? I'm sure they'll both be eager to give you some privacy. Anyway, he adores *you*.'

'Ella! He doesn't.' Liane's face flushed and she lowered her voice, not wanting anyone to overhear. 'It's…it's not like that.'

'I wouldn't be so sure.'

'Trust me—'

'Oh, he might be fighting it, and you might be as well, but I know what I see.' She let out a peal of laughter. 'Social media doesn't lie.'

'Don't be ridiculous,' Liane protested. The last thing she wanted to think about was wretched social media. 'Anyway, I just called to tell you where I am.'

'Right. Well, I could have guessed that,' Ella told her loftily. 'Or at least who you were with. Keep me posted. And I mean that literally.'

'You seem happy, Alessandro.'

Alessandro turned to see his former stepmother glancing at him in gentle speculation. She'd been married to his father for only a handful of years before she'd left him because of his unfaithfulness, but she'd been pragmatic about the relationship, and grateful she'd got a daughter out of it. Even though she'd divorced his father over ten years ago, because of Sophia they'd remained close.

'I am,' he replied equably. Christina had shown Liane her room, with Sophia in tow, before returning downstairs to him.

'Because of her?' she asked, and he gave her a quelling look, or at least the approximation of one. In truth he was feeling too light and easy inside to get seriously annoyed with his stepmother's curious questions.

'Don't read more into it than there is,' he warned her. Even if he already felt the *more* in himself. His feelings for Liane went beyond the physical, he knew that much. 'We've only known each other a week, after all.' Could it really be such a short amount of time?

'Sometimes that's all it takes. I fell for your father in a single night.'

Alessandro's stomach tightened. He was *not* going to be like his father. 'And look how that turned out.'

'That may be, but I still loved him. Love doesn't follow rules, Alessandro.'

'This isn't love.'

'Are you sure?'

'Give it a rest, Christina.' He spoke good-naturedly although he was starting to feel tense. 'And don't push.'

'I won't,' she promised with a laugh. 'But it's nice to see you happy, with a woman. Sophia will be the one ringing the wedding bells for you. She can't wait to have a little niece or nephew.'

'Good Lord.' Alessandro shuddered, but there was more theatricality in it than conviction. He found himself picturing Liane's fairy tale garden, with the dogs and the cats and, yes, the children. 'I think I'll go see how Liane is settling in.'

His stepmother's laughter followed him out of the room. 'You do that,' she said.

Upstairs he found Liane perched on the window seat of her bedroom, with Sophia sprawled on her bed, her chin planted in her hands. Liane, he saw, was looking bemused, Sophia eager.

'So you've been to four balls together?'

'Well, not exactly together…' She glanced at Alessandro, who flicked his fingers at his half-sister.

'Out, scamp. I want to talk to Liane alone.'

Far from looking injured at being so dismissed, Sophia's face lit up. 'Of course you do,' she said as she scrambled off the bed.

Alessandro turned to Liane. Sophia hesitated by the doorway and he let out a good-natured groan. *'Sophia.'*

With a laugh she scampered from the room.

'It seems we haven't escaped the speculation here,' Liane said lightly as she turned to look out of the window.

'Naturally they're curious.'

'Your gardens are beautiful.'

He took a step towards her, his hands in his pockets. 'There's even lilac.'

She closed her eyes briefly. 'Don't, Alessandro.'

Surprised by her reaction, he put his hand on her shoulder. 'Don't what?'

'Don't… I don't even know…don't tease. Or warn. Or whatever it is you're doing. I know what this is. I'm perfectly fine with it, trust me.'

He pressed her shoulder gently to turn her towards him. 'And what is this?'

'An affair. One of your arrangements.' She drew an unsteady breath. 'I just want to be clear with you that I understand, so you don't have to keep giving me reminders. I'm not going to hope for or even think about more than… than what we have. I promise you I won't.'

Her words should have given him great relief, but he only felt disquiet. 'Is that supposed to reassure me?'

'Yes, of course it is.' A flash of something almost like ire was in her eyes. 'Why shouldn't it?' Indeed, that was the question, wasn't it? 'Anyway,' she dismissed, 'enough about that.'

Alessandro continued to gaze at her, noting the steely glint in her eye, the determined tilt of her chin. She'd made up her mind, without any regrets. He should be thrilled, he thought wryly. He had everything he'd wanted—Liane with him, agreeing to an affair, no strings, no complications. No possibility of either of them getting hurt.

So why did he feel so…strange?

'Why don't we go explore the garden?' he suggested. 'I want to show you the property.'

'All right.' The smile she gave him was both bright and determined. 'Let me just change.'

Fifteen minutes later they were strolling through the extensive gardens, past tinkling fountains and tumbling miniature waterfalls, climbing clematis and beds of sweet-smelling lavender. Liane had changed into a sundress in pale green linen, her hair in a single plait over one shoulder.

'So whose villa is this, anyway?' she asked as she bent to breathe in the fragrance of a deep pink overblown rose.

'Mine. I bought it while I was working in Rome, as a bolthole, I suppose. Christina and Sophia were living in Milan then. Christina's British, as you might have guessed, but she was translating Italian textbooks for a living while she raised Sophia singlehandedly. When the rent got too expensive in the city, I offered for them to live here.'

Liane turned to him in surprise. 'Too expensive?'

'My father is perpetually broke,' Alessandro explained with a shrug. 'My grandfather knew him for a wastrel and so kept most of his assets in trust. He has enough to live in Ibiza, but not much to give to Christina, and so I've helped. Sophia is my sister, after all.'

'She's very sweet. Asking me all sorts of questions, though.'

Alessandro nodded in acknowledgement, a small smile tugging at his mouth. He'd always had a soft spot for his half-sister, wanting her to have the stability and love he hadn't known, even with her parents having divorced. 'She's a good kid.'

'She's lucky to have you. And this.' They'd strolled up to a lilac bush, its purple blossoms drooping nearly to the ground. With a small smile, Alessandro broke off a stem and handed it to her. Liane closed her eyes as she breathed in the scent. 'It smells like memory to me. There was a lilac bush outside our house in Lyon when I was growing up, during happier days.'

'Do you miss it?' Alessandro asked quietly.

'I miss the idea of it more than anything. A happy home. Two parents. My father wasn't gambling then. My mother wasn't quite so stern. We had a little dog, Bisou. It felt… simpler. It all changed when we moved to Paris for a bit, and then on to New York. After my father started gambling, he was never the same.' She sighed as she twirled the flower by its stem. 'Sometimes I wonder if the daydreams I've had are nothing more than me trying to get back what was lost. Maybe it's better, wiser, just to let it all go.'

'Don't say that.' He realised he couldn't stand the thought of her giving up on her dream—the garden, the cat and the dog, the children. 'It will happen for you.'

'Maybe,' she replied with a shrug, 'but what if it doesn't? Shouldn't I at least accept that might be the case?' Liane twirled the lilac blossom by its stem once more and then flung it onto a small pond nearby, where it floated, slightly bedraggled, on the water. 'Surely it's better to grab what you can of life, enjoy it while it lasts, than wait for a silly dream. That's why I'm here, after all.' She met his gaze with a playful smile.

'And I'm very glad you are.' He reached for her hand, drawing her to him.

As she came closer, her eyes fluttered closed and his lips brushed hers. 'I am too,' she whispered. 'Truly.'

He deepened the kiss, let it take them over. Liane wrapped her arms around him as she lost herself to the moment, just as he was—a moment that was as sweet as it was passionate, as innocent as it was sensual, her soft body yielding to his, promising so much.

As they drew apart, that was when it hit him.

All along he'd been insisting to himself that he would never be weak like his father, or needy like his mother. He wouldn't beg someone to stay; he wouldn't even want them to. He'd keep himself from dreams, from love, from hurt, taking each moment and enjoying life just as Liane had said...*except he hadn't.* All the while he'd been searching, longing, hoping. Feeling empty inside...until Liane.

And now, Alessandro thought as he stared down at her, the fairy tale had found him.

CHAPTER THIRTEEN

LIANE GAZED OUT at the violet night, the first stars beginning to twinkle in the night sky, and a shiver of expectation went through her as the cool breeze from the open shutters whispered over her skin.

She and Alessandro had spent the afternoon going through the garden and then playing a rollicking game of lawn boules with Sophia. Then they'd gathered in the drawing room for drinks, followed by a dinner that was both delicious and enjoyable, as Liane had seen how relaxed Alessandro was with the people he loved, smiling and joking in a way he had so rarely during their travels together.

And yet through it all an exquisite tension had been building inside her as well as between them. Every time she'd caught Alessandro's glance her body burned. When, during dinner, he'd casually brushed her fingers with his own everything in her had ached with desire. She'd enjoyed the towering sense of expectation, even as it had frightened her.

This was really happening...

As soon as dessert had been cleared, Christina and Sophia had both made their excuses; Liane didn't miss the fact that her bedroom suite was in a guest wing, far from any others. Ella had been right; they were certainly giving her—them—privacy.

She'd returned to her room, showered and changed, feeling a bit self-conscious and even silly as she'd slipped on the thick terrycloth robe provided. Almost like a bride on her wedding night…except of course that wasn't how it was at all. And she didn't even know if or when Alessandro would arrive. Arrangement this might be, but they'd made no *actual* arrangements about how it was all supposed to go.

Should she go to his room? He to hers? How was this actually going to *work*?

She'd been standing at the window, trying not to let her nerves overwhelm her, for fifteen minutes before she heard the gentle tap at the door, and in the next moment Alessandro slipped into the room, regarded her with eyes that blazed silver with intensity—and desire.

He wore a white button-down shirt, open at his bronzed throat, and a pair of dark grey trousers. He looked so potently virile that Liane's heart turned over and a flush broke out over her skin. She felt, quite suddenly, nearly naked in her dressing gown and she fumbled with the sash to, rather ridiculously, tighten it.

'I didn't know if you were coming.'

He took a step towards her, a tiny, tender smile quirking his mouth. 'Why would you doubt it?'

'I don't know. Lack of experience, I suppose.'

'I've been thinking about this all day. For quite a few days, in fact.' Another step and another, and then he was there in front of her, gazing down at her with both tenderness and need. 'Surely you need no more convincing of how much I want you?'

'No…' she whispered. 'Although, to tell the truth, it does boggle my mind.'

He laughed softly. 'As it does mine.' He tugged gently on the end of her sash. 'Is there a reason why you were tightening that? You haven't changed your mind?'

'No.' She gulped. 'I was tightening it because right now you're wearing a few more clothes than I am,' she explained a bit tartly. 'And I'm nervous.' He smiled as he toyed with the end of her sash.

'The clothing situation can be remedied, you know. Quite quickly, as a matter of fact.'

'Okay.' She waited for him to unbutton his shirt, shrug out of it—*something*. But he merely looked at her. 'Would you do the honours?' he asked softly, and a nervous excitement skittered along her skin.

Could she…? Would she? Was that how this was going to work? Oh, yes, she realised, it was, and she would. Her fingers trembled at the first button, but by the third they were steady, and by the fourth they were lingering. His skin felt like burnished satin, the crisp hairs tickling her fingers, the muscles of his chest and abdomen tautening under her lightly skimming touch. Pleasure flared low in her belly as she undid the last button and then slid the shirt off his powerful shoulders.

He was so beautiful, every muscle sculpted in bronze, his taut belly quivering as she trailed her fingertips over it, and a low groan escaped him as he captured her fingers with his own.

'First let me look at you.'

With one slow tug he undid her robe and the heavy folds swung apart. Liane tried not to shiver, both from the cool air and the inevitable sense of apprehension as Alessandro regarded her naked body. She was too pale,

too slight, Liane thought, even as she registered the gleam
of deep masculine approval in his eyes.

He reached out one hand to cup her breast, his palm
warm and sure, making her whole body tingle. 'You're
perfect,' he told her. 'Absolutely perfect.'

And, amazingly, she *felt* perfect, in his eyes, in a
way she never, ever had before. She finally felt seen and
accepted and loved...yes, loved, even if she knew she
wasn't, not like that. What she saw in his eyes, what she
felt in herself, was, in that moment, enough. It was more
than enough.

Her self-consciousness faded away as he slid the robe
from her shoulders and it fell in a soft, silent pool at her
feet. He took another step towards her so her breasts
brushed his chest and everything in her quivered. A kiss,
slow and deep, plumbing the very depths of her, and already she felt her mind start to blur and the last of her
nervousness burned away in the heat of his gaze, as well
as that of her desire, their bodies brushing each other at
the most exquisitely aching points.

Boldly now, sure of his need as well as of her own,
she reached for his belt buckle. Her fingers didn't tremble as she undid it and then the button on his trousers,
her palm skimming the length and heat of him, thrilling
to that touch, feeling him strain against her with desire
and need. A slight smile of acknowledgement curved
his mouth, the colour high on his cheekbones, his glittering gaze pinned on her. She didn't look away as, taking a steadying breath, she tugged his trousers down
his muscular legs and then in one abrupt movement he
kicked them off.

'And the rest?' he murmured and, taking a deep

breath, she pulled his boxer shorts down, thrilling to the sight of his body, glorious and naked, ready for her.

In an instant they fell upon one another, bodies glimmering in moonlight, grasping, seeking, finding, hands and mouths, limbs tangled, a laugh escaping along with a groan, and Liane didn't even know who it was. It didn't even matter; she felt as if they were moving as one, a tangle and a blur as they stumbled their way to the bed, until, with a muttered oath, in one easy movement Alessandro swooped her into his arms and laid her down on it like a treasure, a precious pearl.

She gazed at him with nothing but trust in her eyes, her body utterly open to him, revelling in the desire and appreciation she saw in his heated gaze. Here she was, exposed, vulnerable, and yet not afraid. Not ashamed.

Then he stretched out beside her, one hand slowly skimming her body as if it learned its lines, from the curve of her ankle to the dip of her waist to the swell of her breast. A new country, explored by his hand—and then by his mouth as, with leisurely languor, he followed that route with his lips, seeming to memorise every hidden swell or dip until Liane was writhing beneath his questing touch, and wanting to explore his body in just the same way. To know him the way he was knowing her, for that was what it felt like—an intimacy beyond any other, a communion of bodies if not souls.

And yet already she knew her soul was touched, that no matter how she'd tried to separate it all in her mind, in reality the two were entwined for ever. She couldn't possibly separate her body from her heart; they were innately, intensely joined, just as their bodies were joining—Alessandro's leg between hers, his hands in her hair, his lips on her navel, making her gasp, dipping lower.

How could this be anything but a total offering of self, of soul—and a joining with his? Whether he knew it or not, whether she admitted it to him or not, Liane knew what this was—a total surrender, not just to him, but to what she felt for him. No matter how hard she'd tried to guard her heart, to keep it safe, she knew then that she'd offered it along with her body. She loved him and could not keep herself from loving him...whether or not he loved her back.

Had he ever felt this way before? Already Alessandro knew he had not. The physical transactions that had counted for his arrangements in the past, merely to satiate a physical need, had been nothing like this. They'd been nothing, full stop, forgotten in an instant, while Liane—her perfect body, her open, trusting gaze—would be seared on his memory for ever.

She lay supine beneath him, her expression dazed as she gazed up at him in both wonder and need. A gasp escaped her as his mouth moved lower, testing, tasting. A shaky laugh as her fingers drove into his hair.

'Alessandro...'

He loved the way she said his name, with both wonder and need. He kissed his way lower, along her belly to her thighs, longing for her to say it again.

'Alessandro...'

The ache in her voice, the throb of her body...had he known anything sweeter? Deeper? She arched against him as he tasted her sweetness, his mouth hot and sure on her most intimate place, exploring the very depths of her, making her moan out as his own body throbbed with longing.

'Please…' she gasped as she thrust her hips up in instinctive demand. 'Please…'

He braced himself on his forearms as he gazed down at her flushed face. 'I'm trying to go slowly…' he told her, his teeth gritted from the effort of holding back, when all he wanted to do was plunge deep inside her and lose himself completely.

'Don't.' She let out an unsteady laugh as he reached for a condom. '*Don't.* I'll go mad…please… I want you inside me…completely.'

And then he was, a gasp escaping him as he felt her warmth enfold him, *accept* him. Accepting him completely. She folded her body around his, drew him even more deeply into herself, giving him all that she had.

'Oh…' she whispered, and then thrust up against him, her arms clasping him to her as her body instinctively began to move in that ancient rhythm, that beautiful dance. '*Oh*… I never knew…'

Neither had he. The sense of completion was far more than physical in that moment, as if they'd joined everything, and not just their bodies. Alessandro matched her pace, watched with a deep, primal satisfaction as her eyes widened and her lips parted and pleasure sang through their veins, united them in its joyous melody, taking them higher and higher, each note more beautiful than the last…

And then they arced on a crescendo of pleasure, their bodies trembling in the aftershocks as he clasped her against him, rolling onto his back and bringing her with him, never wanting to let her go. Ever.

He felt both broken open and made whole, as if it was in the breaking, the revealing, that he'd found something even more. It was as if his world had shifted on its axis and then righted, and he now saw it all so much more clearly than ever before.

Was this, then, what he'd been afraid of for so long? This startling clarity, as if the entire world had been brought into dazzling focus, and a deep, settled happiness thrummed through his veins. Was this what he'd been running away from?

Sex, for him, had always been about using—a pleasurable mutual using, but a using just the same. A transaction, a trade-off. This felt completely different, utterly more…instead of a deal, it had been a surrender. Instead of using, he had given.

It both humbled and amazed him, and horrified him too, because this was so new, so strange, and even with Liane clasped in his arms he wasn't entirely sure he welcomed it.

Liane's body was boneless against his as she pressed her damp forehead against his shoulder.

'We are definitely doing that again before I go,' she told him, and Alessandro let out a huff of startled laughter before her words trickled through him.

Before I go? Her words sounded like a warning, and perhaps one he needed. She'd said such things before, but he'd thought they'd been for her own sake. Now he wondered if they were actually for his. Why should he assume that what he felt in this moment was real, or more than infatuation? Liane had no trouble making clear what she thought. She knew the rules—and so should he, because he'd made them. How could he let his judgement be so clouded?

He was acting like a lovesick fool, he realised with a burning twist of shame. Doing the exact thing he'd warned Liane against—reading so much more into a physical transaction that had been mind-blowingly plea-surable…and no more.

And yet it *had* felt like more…for him. And the thought was as terrifying as it was wonderful. He didn't want this—the risk, the pain, the rejection, the fear. *The joy.* He didn't want to love Liane—and yet he was afraid he did.

The fairy tale might have come for him after all, but had it for her?

The question was still thudding through him as she slipped out of his arms, off the bed, and disappeared into the bathroom. Alessandro felt the yawning absence in his empty arms, the expanse of rumpled sheets. Quickly he disposed of the condom and moved to a seated position, raking a hand through his dampened hair. He'd felt as if he could have lain there for ever, sated and sleepy, but perhaps it was better this way. Get things back on the terms he was used to, the ones Liane had agreed to, and stop wondering if his world had changed when it hadn't.

It was another five minutes before she returned, look-ing cool and composed. She walked over to the crumpled heap of her dressing gown and shrugged it on.

'What now?' she asked with a small, rueful smile, or at least an attempt at one. 'I'm afraid I don't know the rules. Do we sit and chat? Do you go back to your room?'

He almost smiled at her practical tone, even as it stung. He didn't know the rules either, not any more, and though he knew he should remind himself of them, he didn't. He knew what he wanted—Liane in his bed, for the rest of the night.

'Now you take off that ridiculous dressing gown and come back to bed,' Alessandro told her. 'And we stay here till morning.'

Her playful smile turned cautious, surprised. 'Till morning?'

'Yes. Till morning. At the very least.' He held his arms out and with a little laugh she shrugged off the robe once again and scrambled across the bed towards him.

Laughing too, Alessandro snatched her up in his arms, rolled her under him as she squirmed breathlessly, looking up at him with both joy and wonder.

'I thought…' she began, and he silenced her with a kiss.

'No thinking,' he told her as his mouth moved lower. 'No thinking at all.'

He wasn't going to think about what this was, not now. There would be time later to worry, to wonder, because all he wanted now was the sweetness of Liane in his arms, looking up at him, giving herself to him. Again and again.

CHAPTER FOURTEEN

THE NEXT WEEK passed in a golden haze of happy moments. Not for the first time since meeting Alessandro Rossi, Liane wondered if she should pinch herself. It certainly felt as if she were dreaming.

They spent the days lazing in the garden or villa, walking through the hills or wandering through the sun-soaked towns, playing boules or cards or taking a dip in the pool. Sophia often accompanied them, developing a friendship with Liane as she watched her easy camaraderie with Alessandro. Christina worked from home during the day, although she joined them in the evenings for dinner, with laughter and conversation, sometimes long into the night, although never too long, leaving Alessandro and Liane plenty of time together.

'Sophia is thrilled to have Alessandro here for so long,' she told Liane one evening, while they were waiting for the others to join them in the drawing room. 'He usually only stays for a day or two, and it's been a whole week.'

'Has it?' Liane felt as if the days had flown, each one more precious than the last, for who knew when they would end? She'd told herself—and Ella, when she'd texted to check in—that she was simply enjoying letting it all happen, the moments as they came, and she was, oh, she *was*.

For beyond the fun-filled days there were the pleasure-filled nights…as night after night she and Alessandro explored each other's bodies, drove each other to new heights of both passion and intimacy, limbs tangled, hands seeking, hearts thudding as one.

Could you *do* those things with someone, Liane had wondered more than once, and not fall in love with them? She was already realising, more and more with each passing day, she couldn't. With every day she spent with Alessandro she fell deeper and deeper in love. She'd even stopped trying to keep herself from it, knowing there was no use, and understanding for the first time why Ella was so willing to tumble headlong into relationships.

It was *fun*. It was wonderful to look at someone and have your stomach fizz, your heart fill. To lie in someone's arms and listen to the thud of their heart, to roll over and see the smile playing on their lips as they drew you closer for a kiss. To feel that closely attuned, that dearly beloved.

Was there anything more wonderful, more magical, than falling in love?

Well, yes, Liane knew there was. It was knowing that person loved you back.

Sometimes, when she caught Alessandro looking at her, or when he held her in his arms and stroked her hair after they'd made love, both of their hearts still racing as the aftershocks of their climax shuddered through them, she could almost convince herself that he did. Or at least, perhaps, that he could, if he let himself. He was capable of it, surely; whether he was willing was another matter.

Sometimes, as they wandered through the market of

a nearby hill town, buying a jar of olives swimming in brine and a crusty loaf of bread for an impromptu picnic, she told herself it didn't matter if he loved her or not. This was enough—his attention, his affection, his body in her bed. Did she really need more than that? Wasn't she happy enough, at least for now?

Then she'd catch him looking pensive, a shadow coming over his face as he became remote, and it felt like the sun disappearing behind the clouds, a darkness coming over the whole earth. His answers would become clipped, his gaze distant, and her heart would thud an erratic beat as she wondered if he was thinking of ending it between them. She thought she saw it in the tightening of his mouth, the flicker in his eyes, and a few times she felt he'd been on the cusp of saying something. *It's been fun, but...*

It had been longer than she'd expected, she knew, longer than she'd even hoped. She shouldn't, she told herself, even be surprised. Really, she should be ready.

In those moments she knew she couldn't live in the balance, always wondering, worrying what would come next. She might not crave the spotlight, but she no longer wanted to live in the shadows. Not like that, anyway. If he couldn't love her, it would be better to end it, surely.

And yet...they'd only known each other a handful of weeks. Couldn't she give him time to develop the feelings she knew she already had? If he could just tell her he wanted to *try...*

But he never did.

Ten days into their idyll, seeming more remote than ever, he shut himself away in his study for most of the afternoon and Liane half wondered if she should pack her bags. She gazed out at the lemony sunlight spilling over the gardens and hated the thought of leaving this wonderful place where she'd briefly known so much happiness. But perhaps it would be better to leave before Alessandro told her to...if she had the strength. Was that what was going to happen?

Wouldn't she rather be the first to say, *It was fun, but...?* A sense of self-preservation told her she would, and yet even so she was reluctant. She wasn't ready to say goodbye...

Just then her phone buzzed with a call from Ella.

'So, it's been ten days,' she said by way of greeting. 'Are you guys engaged yet or what?'

'Ella!' Liane couldn't keep from sounding horrified. What if Alessandro overheard? Not, of course, that he would. He was still holed up in his study, ignoring her. 'Don't talk like that, please. As a matter of fact, I was just thinking about whether I should go home.'

'What?' Ella sounded shocked. 'Why?'

'To keep myself from getting hurt,' Liane stated flatly. *It was too late for that, though, wasn't it?* 'Alessandro said this would end when he said it would,' she told Ella. 'And I'd like to think I have a little more self-respect than to wait for him to tell me to go.'

'He's not going to end it,' Ella insisted. 'He loves you.'

'Ella, we've only known each other for a couple of weeks,' Liane reminded her painfully. 'And I'm not sure Alessandro even knows what love is, or, more importantly, if he wants to. He's told me he doesn't, as a matter of fact.'

'That may be true,' Ella answered slowly, 'but maybe he needs someone to point it out to him.'

'And you think I should?' The thought terrified her. If she told him she loved him and he rejected her, and he *would* reject her, surely… There was a reason why she stayed in the shadows, wasn't there? The spotlight was far too bright, too dangerous. 'I don't know if I can do that.'

'I'm not sure you should at this point,' Ella replied thoughtfully. 'I think he actually needs to see it for himself.'

'How?' Liane cried. If only it were simply a matter of *seeing*…

'I know how.' Ella sounded alarmingly certain.

'You do?' Liane exclaimed. 'Ella, don't even think of… I don't even know what. But don't.'

Ella only laughed. 'What could I really do from France?' she asked innocently.

'I don't know, but please—'

'Sometimes,' Ella cut across her, 'love needs a little helping hand. Or at least a mirror.'

And with that she hung up, leaving Liane both fuming and afraid, wondering what on earth Ella could be up to now. But did it really matter? Would Ella's interference, whatever it was and no matter how well meaning, make a difference to Alessandro's feelings? To his heart?

Liane glanced out at the gardens, now gilded in evening sunlight; from the open window she breathed in the faint fragrance of lilac. The flowers she loved so much, she'd seen earlier that day, were browning at the edges, their blooms already fading, releasing the last of their sweet, sweet scent, as the season turned and summer came on with its relentless heat and endless blue skies.

Maybe that was just how life happened; one season gave birth to another. She and Alessandro had had something special, but that was all it was—a season, a moment in time. Perhaps she was foolish in longing for it to be more. To wish for the fairy tale…

And yet why shouldn't she at least *try*? Perhaps she was stubborn, or merely hopeful, but she wanted to be brave enough to tell him how she felt, or at least how she *thought* she felt. It was all still so new, she could admit that, but it was still something... Maybe, just maybe, she could be brave enough to step into the spotlight once more.

The tap at the door had Alessandro looking up from his desk in weary irritation. He'd spent the last eight hours trying to put out the flames of a scandal that had been brewing while he'd been essentially asleep at the wheel.

One of their investors whose fund they managed had been caught with his hand in the cookie jar, to the tune of many millions, and there were those who were looking to implicate Rossi Enterprises as well.

'You know that saying, no publicity is bad publicity?' one of his staff had remarked tiredly. 'Well, that's certainly not the case.'

No, it wasn't. Alessandro hadn't paid any attention to the media in the last ten days, but now he saw that the financial scandal was splashed all over the newspapers and some smart aleck had decided to tie the breaking scandal to his appearance at the Rossi balls. *Is the Prince of Manhattan too busy playing with his Princess to pay attention?* ran one headline. Another one screamed *Notorious recluse has decided the party circuit is more fun than fusty numbers...*

For heaven's sake. Once upon a time such things would have coldly amused him, for he knew absolutely that they held no truth. Now, he wondered. Why had he allowed himself to get so distracted? He'd never been away from the office for this long. He'd never spent days ignoring the world around him for the woman right there. *What was happening to him?*

Was it love—a thought that admittedly terrified him—or merely infatuation? The prospect made him feel bleak. How could he know? How could he trust himself, never mind Liane? *And did he even want to?*

'Alessandro?' Liane's voice was soft, tentative.

Alessandro raked his hands through his hair as he pushed himself away from the desk. 'Come in.'

She opened the door cautiously, standing in the doorway as she regarded him with dark, uncertain eyes. 'You've been working?'

'Yes.' He paused. 'I'm sorry I haven't been available.'

'It's all right. I never expected…' She swallowed. 'I understand you have other obligations.'

She sounded so small and sad, and it filled Alessandro with both remorse and annoyance. He didn't want to care so much…and yet he did.

'I just…' She swallowed hard, her face flushing, her hands clasped together tightly. 'I know you're busy, and maybe…maybe you need to return to Rome or New York or wherever…'

'What are you saying?' His voice came out terse.

'I just wanted to tell you that I…that I've really…'

The *ping* from his mobile lying on the desk made her falter and Alessandro's gaze snapped to the screen, which was lighting up with message after message.

Ping. Ping. Ping.

He snatched up the phone, swiping the screen, his eyes first widening and then narrowing as he read all the alerts.

'Alessandro…' Liane's voice wavered. 'What is it?'

His stomach clenched and he felt as if he'd swallowed

a stone as he swiped through the images, one after the other: *The secret is out...the Prince of Manhattan is desperately in love!*

He looked up to see Liane, her face now deathly pale, biting her lips in nervousness. *I just wanted to tell you...*

'You did this?' he asked in a low voice.

She glanced nervously at the phone still clenched in his hand. 'Did what?'

'Put our...our *arrangement* up for public consumption.' He flung the word at her like a weapon, meant to wound. 'Were you hoping to force my hand? Did you actually think that would work?'

'I...' She shook her head slowly. 'What are you talking about?'

'You must know what I'm talking about.' No matter how innocent or confused she pretended to be. How else could these photos have been posted online? She must have been conspiring with Ella all along. The thought made him feel sick.

'Did Ella post something?' she asked, and he was reminded of the first night he'd seen her, when she'd come outside and recognised that damned shoe. He saw the flicker of recognition, resignation, in her eyes and he understood. She had known then, and she clearly knew now. Had their time together all been an act, a con? No, surely not. *And yet...*

'She might have posted it, but you provided the images.' Images of him that he'd never, ever want anyone to see.

'What images? Alessandro, I haven't seen anything—'

'Then go look on your phone,' he practically snarled. 'And then you can leave this house immediately.'

Even as he said the words he knew he didn't mean

them. He was angry but, more fundamentally, he was hurt, devastated by her betrayal, and he was lashing out because he couldn't bear her to see his vulnerability, not when he'd been so used. Used in a way he'd promised himself he never would be, trotted out to serve someone else's schemes. Hers or Ella's, did it even matter? She'd been party to it all.

Liane's face was white, her eyes wide and dark as she stared at him. For a second he thought she'd walk out without a word, turn and run, an admission of guilt. Then colour flared in her cheeks and her eyes narrowed, her lips parting.

'So that's it, is it?' she asked with a strangely lethal quiet. 'You act as judge and jury? This is you deciding when it ends?' Her voice remained quiet yet it held a razor-sharp mocking edge that made Alessandro blink.

'I decide,' he replied, 'because of what you did.'

'I don't even know what I'm supposed to have done, but it doesn't even matter. Ella posted something. I get it. Just like I get how angry you are, because it's easier to be angry than hurt, isn't it, Alessandro? Be outraged and then you have a reason for running away.' She lifted her chin, her eyes glittering. 'I came down here to tell you I loved you. Or at least that I could love, if we had more time. If we gave ourselves that chance. Even though I was terrified, I was going to be brave enough to do it, to risk my heart and my pride, because I thought we shared something that was worth that risk. I thought—I deluded myself, really—that I could make you see that. Because...' her voice wavered and she took a quick steadying breath '...you made me feel *seen*. And important. And...and loved, in a way no one else had before. And I believed in that. I believed in us. More fool me, clearly.'

Alessandro opened his mouth but no words came out. He was reeling and yet he was still angry. 'Then who took these photos, Liane?' he demanded, and it wasn't until he'd spoken that he realised that wasn't the question he'd wanted to ask at all. *Do you really love me?* was the one that burned on his lips.

'Oh, Alessandro.' Liane gave a sad little laugh as she shook her head. 'I haven't even seen the photos, so I couldn't tell you. But it doesn't really matter, does it? For you to jump to the conclusion that I took them…and then to ask me to leave…' She drew a hitched breath. 'Well, that says it all, doesn't it? Unfortunately.' She paused, her spine straightening, that poignant lift of her chin. 'Thank you for these last few weeks. I'll go pack my bags.'

And he watched her walk out of the room, her back straight and proud, her body bristling with dignity, while he stayed silent.

CHAPTER FIFTEEN

She made it back to her bedroom before the tears came in a hot, scalding rush as she closed the door behind her and crumpled into a heap right there on the floor. *Stupid,* she thought. *Stupid, stupid, stupid. You knew all along he wasn't going to love you.*

But to *accuse* her, and of something so absurd—as if she would have taken photos and posted them...! It was an excuse, it had to be, or maybe he really didn't know her at all, much less love her...

Either way, did it really matter? He still wanted her gone.

Drawing a shuddering breath, Liane stood and walked on shaky legs to the wardrobe, resolutely pulling her suitcase out as an unruly sob escaped her. She'd call for a taxi, she'd leave right away. She couldn't bear seeing him again, that haughty look of disdain on his face...

From the bedside table, her phone pinged. She didn't even want to look at the photos Ella must have posted, although she supposed she ought at least to know what had been the catalyst for her heartbreak. Sniffing, she pushed her tangled hair out of her face and went to grab her phone.

It only took a few swipes to get to Ella's profile and

then a shuddery breath escaped her as she slowly lowered herself onto the edge of the bed. Silently she began to swipe through the photos—about a dozen—together, all of them telling a story. *Revealing the truth?*

No, not the truth. The truth, Liane acknowledged hollowly, was Alessandro's icy rage of just a few moments ago as he'd told her, just as he'd said he would, when their *arrangement* would end. And yet…she'd always known Ella was a master of manipulation, capturing the perfect image, zooming in on a face, spinning a story, just as she'd promised when Alessandro had first suggested she accompany him to all the Rossi hotels.

The Prince finds his Princess, indeed.

And what happened next?

He booted her out.

And yet here was the love story Ella had been wanting to tell—Alessandro gazing at Liane across the ballroom, his forehead wrinkled with concern, a faraway look in his eyes, with the caption underneath, *Looking for his Princess…* And there he was dancing with her, except the camera had zoomed in on Alessandro's face, and the unmistakably tender look softening his eyes, his mouth.

Liane gulped. There was more, so much more. Alessandro and her chatting on the plane, but again the camera revealed something Liane hadn't seen. The blatant look of affection in his eyes, the smile tugging at his mouth, the way his arm was draped across the top of her seat…

A gasp escaped her as she saw the next photo—of them kissing in the garden here at the villa, in what she'd believed to be a completely private moment. Who on earth could have taken that one? And another, walking hand in hand as the sun set behind them, through an olive grove. Liane was laughing as she looked up at him and Alessandro was smiling. There were several more, all taken at the villa, all showing a man who looked so wonderfully in love, showing the most vulnerable part of himself—to the world.

So this was what Ella had meant about giving a helping hand! But where on earth had she got the photos from? And then realisation thudded through her—Sophia. *Of course.* Ella must have contacted her through social media, enlisted her help. Sophia had been so cheerful, always popping up to spend time with them, always with her phone, as any teenager was...

A choked laugh escaped Liane that ended in a wavery sigh. Her sister had meant well, and so had Sophia, of that she was sure, but their so-called help had had the utterly opposite effect. Alessandro was more determined than ever not to believe the truth in these photos and to convict her instead of some sort of cold-hearted manipulation.

With another shuddery sigh she put the phone down. She had more sympathy for him now that she'd seen the photos, and she realised how hard they must have hit him. It must have been extremely galling—humiliating, even—for Alessandro to see those photos of himself looking so vulnerable, so open, his emotions seemingly laid bare, and especially when they'd been taken here, where he'd assumed it was private. He'd thought he was safe. For him to believe he was being used, just as he had been as a child...well, for him it was proof that the fairy tale wasn't real, wasn't it?

And it *wasn't*. Because, as compelling as these photos were, they weren't the truth. The truth was Alessandro coldly telling her to get out of his house, refusing even to listen to her. She'd done all she could, Liane knew.

She'd told him she loved him. It might have been said in anger and hurt, but she'd meant it. All that was left now was to go.

And so she did, as quietly and unobtrusively as she did everything else—packing her single suitcase, calling a taxi, writing a note for Sophia and Christina thanking them for their hospitality, and then slipping out of the villa without anyone even noticing she had gone.

Half an hour later she was in Perugia; she took a connecting flight to Milan, spending the night in a cheap hotel, and then the next day flew back to New York, all in a state of numb, abject desolation.

By the time she arrived at the townhouse overlooking Central Park her eyes were gritty, her heart still aching. Twenty-four hours hadn't helped her feel the tiniest bit better. If anything, she felt worse, the loss of Alessandro reverberating emptily through her. She hadn't answered Ella's calls, simply texting her that she was going home. Then she'd turned off her phone because she knew she didn't want to deal with the media frenzy that had erupted with Ella's posts. If anything, she thought wearily as she lugged her suitcase up the steps of her home, she just wanted to go back to the way she had been before, safe in the shadows. The online world would forget her in a heartbeat, she knew. And so would Alessandro...

The front door opened and she glanced up, expecting to see her mother's stern face.

'I've been waiting for you.'

Liane's jaw dropped and her fingers slipped from the handle of her suitcase. *'Alessandro...'*

It had taken Alessandro about fifteen minutes to realise he was a complete idiot. He'd gazed at those photos, every single one, first in shock, then in shame, then in wonder. He hated, absolutely hated, feeling so exposed, his most private and personal emotions on display for everyone to see, and he hated even more the thought that Liane might have done it on purpose, aiding and abetting Ella in whatever publicity scheme they'd worked up.

He'd sat slumped in his chair for at least an hour, looking at those photos in turn as understanding had slowly crept up on him, like the dawn of a new morning. Of course Liane hadn't taken them on purpose. He doubted she'd even known they were being taken. He'd accused her out of anger and fear, not wanting to acknowledge the truth that was blazing out of each and every photo. The truth that he loved her.

He hadn't been able to deny it, even though his first instinct, as ever, had been to do just that. To accuse rather than admit. To lash out rather than love. When Sophia had come in tearfully a little while later, telling him Liane had already left and it was all her fault, Alessandro had been able to piece the story together. Ella had contacted Sophia, asked her to take some photos for her to use on her social media. Sophia had been thrilled, especially as she was so sure Alessandro and Liane were in love.

'But she's left and it's all my fault. I didn't realise how it would affect her…'

'It's not your fault, Sophia, *cara*,' Alessandro had told her grimly. 'It's mine.'

He was the prize idiot who could look love right in the face and pretend he wasn't seeing it. Love wasn't blind; *he* was. By the time he'd realised the truth Liane had already left. Alessandro had packed his bag within minutes and he'd been in a car to the private jet still idling in Perugia so fast his head spun.

'What are you doing here?' Liane asked now as he stood in the doorway of her house, shaking her head at him in weary wonder. 'And how did you get here before me?'

'Private jet, remember,' he replied with a little smile. His heart ached to see how tired and worn down she looked, how *sad*, sorrow shadowing her eyes and causing the corners of her mouth to droop. That was his fault. 'I arrived several hours ago.'

'I'm sorry about the photos,' Liane blurted. 'Ella must have arranged it all. She hinted to me that she was doing something, but I had no idea what. I could have guessed, I suppose, although I never thought she'd get Sophia involved...at least, I assume it was Sophia.'

'I don't care about the photos,' Alessandro assured her. Only to amend, 'Actually, I do care about the photos. Because they showed me something I should have been able to realise on my own—and I *did* realise it, but I fought against it because I was scared. Terrified, in fact.'

Hope started to spark in Liane's eyes and her lips trembled. 'Terrified...?' she whispered.

'Of love,' he stated starkly. His heart beat with painful thuds; as sure as he was, this still felt hard. Being vulnerable got easier, but perhaps it was never easy. Saying how you felt, admitting the truth. Being willing to be rejected. 'Of loving you. It wasn't until I saw those photos that I realised the truth of it. I couldn't deny it any longer, even though I tried, terribly. I'm so sorry for accusing you, Liane. For hurting you. I did it out of my own fear and hurt, but that is no excuse.' He reached for her hand, threading her fingers through his. 'Forgive me?'

Tears pooled in her eyes and she blinked them back rapidly. 'Oh, Alessandro...'

'I love you, Liane.' Instead of making him feel weak, as

he'd always thought, saying it aloud made him feel strong. Powerful. 'You've made me believe in the fairy tale. You *are* the fairy tale. Or at least we can be it, together. We can try…not for some absurd photo op. Not for online consumption. But for us.'

His fingers tightened on hers as she gazed at him in both wonder and hope. 'I can't believe…'

'I couldn't either. I didn't want to. Love, to me, was about using and being used. Being hurt, being disappointed, being out of control. I let my parents' terrible marriage influence me—not just how they treated each other, but how they treated me, stuck in the middle, being used for their ends. I promised myself I'd never let myself need or be needed like that because it only ended in tears and regret. And yet, since meeting you, I've realised that that is a terrible way to live. Empty.'

A shaky laugh escaped her as she clasped their joined hands with her other. 'Well, it's certainly a lonely way. But I… I don't need the fairy tale, Alessandro. I just want real life…with you. I spent too long waiting to be swept away, telling myself it would happen without me needing to try. Waiting for my Prince to come charging down on his steed—'

'And meanwhile he stepped on your toes.'

She laughed, a pure, joyous sound. 'And charmed me while doing it.' She shook her head slowly. 'I still can't believe you're actually here. That you're saying these things.'

'I am here, my *bella* Liane,' he told her as he gathered her in his arms. 'Telling you I love you, now and for ever… if you'll have me.'

'I will,' she answered with heartfelt fervour and finally, thankfully, he kissed her.

EPILOGUE

Three years later

THE VILLA WAS swarming with stylists, models and photographers, all determined to create the perfect photo opportunity for Ella Ash's new fashion line, Cinders. After deciding social influencing was a bit too much like playing fairy godmother, Ella had gone into designing her own clothes, a mixture of frivolous and fun. She was an up-and-coming designer, considered 'the one to watch' by many fashion magazines, and when she'd asked Liane if she could have her first photo shoot at the villa in Umbria, Liane had told Alessandro and he'd laughingly rolled his eyes.

'We have to say yes, don't we?'

'Considering she brought us together,' Liane replied diplomatically, her eyes sparkling, 'I think so.'

'As long as she doesn't turn Emilia's head—'

'Emilia is two years old,' Liane reminded him with a laugh. 'I think she's a little young to be influenced by fashion and celebrity, although she does like sparkles.'

'Just like her mother then, with her ridiculous shoes.'

Now, as they gazed out at the garden, Alessandro slipped an arm around her waist as Liane stood on her tiptoes for the kind of kiss she never tired of. The last three years had been the happiest of her life; they'd split their time between Paris, Rome and the villa in Umbria, until Emilia was born and they'd moved there permanently. Liane was attempting a new translation of Victor Hugo's poetry while also caring for their daughter—and now another baby on the way, just a gentle bump beneath her flowing dress, a promise in the making.

She glanced around the villa's gardens, various assistants and stylists scuttling here and there. They'd put the dogs in the kitchen—they had two—and their cat had just had kittens. On each of their anniversaries Alessandro had planted a lilac bush, until Liane had teased him that they would be overtaken—not that she minded. It was all she'd dreamed of and more, better than any fairy tale she could have dreamed up.

Not, she reflected as Emilia came running over to them and Alessandro scooped her up in his arms, hoisted her on his shoulders, that there hadn't been challenges along the way as they'd come to know each other better, love each other more, because there had, but they'd been ones they'd faced together.

The fairy tale *wasn't* a fairy tale, Liane reflected. It was real and messy and wonderful and hard, all at once. It was life…together.

'Hey,' Ella called as she practically bounced up to them, brandishing her phone. 'We're almost ready and you guys look so perfect…' Liane glanced at Alessandro while he grimaced good-naturedly, tickling Emilia to make her laugh, and Ella, grinning, held her phone aloft.

'Now smile!'

* * * * *

HER SECRET
ROYAL DILEMMA

CHANTELLE SHAW

MILLS & BOON

PROLOGUE

THE WAVE WAS MONSTROUS. In the gleam of his head torch, Prince Eirik saw a towering wall of water rise up in front of the yacht. The sea was wild, whipped up by a storm that had arrived earlier than forecast. But this was a rogue wave, spewing white foam as it curled over and began its descent.

Eirik's yacht, *The Mako*, had lost its mast when the storm had first struck an hour or so ago. The VHF antenna had snapped, leaving him without radio signal and unable to put out a Mayday call. Thick clouds prevented the satellite phone from working. He'd had no choice but to abandon the Around the Island of Ireland yacht race, or AII as it was known. The competitors had set sail from the marina at Penash on the south coast of Cornwall. When he had turned back, he'd managed to erect a temporary mast and sail and had been making good headway towards the shore. The craggy Cornish cliffs were close—but not close enough.

Night had brought impenetrable darkness. His head throbbed from where he'd been struck by the mast when it had come crashing down. He pushed his hair out of his eyes, and, in the torchlight, he noticed blood on his fingers from the gash on his brow. He watched the huge wave tumble as if in slow motion towards the deck. The noise filled his ears and reminded him of the roar of the avalanche as it had raced down the mountain.

Had Niels felt afraid? Eirik recalled that fateful day just over a year ago. He had been a few metres ahead of his brother and had managed to ski over to a cluster of pine trees that had given some protection from the avalanche. When he'd looked back at the white wave of snow thundering down the slope, he had known in his heart that Niels would not survive. Eirik's grief was mixed with guilt because he had persuaded his brother to go skiing. They had both loved the slopes when they were younger, but Niels had been the heir to the principality of Fjernland's throne and discouraged by their parents from taking risks.

The world spun, and the starless sky merged with the black sea as the powerful wave caused the yacht to roll one hundred and eighty degrees. After what felt like a lifetime of being churned inside a washing machine *The Mako* righted itself. Coughing and spluttering, Eirik snatched oxygen into his lungs and assessed the new damage. The temporary mast had been destroyed. Fortunately, the compartment where the flares were stored had remained watertight. Distress flares were only meant to be used where there was 'grave and imminent danger to life'. It was sobering to acknowledge that his situation had become so serious. Moments later he watched a trail of bright red smoke soar into the sky and hoped that someone on land would see the flare and alert the coastguard.

The sea had calmed a little after the freak wave had subsided. A glimmer of moonlight appeared when the clouds parted and showed Eirik that the yacht had drifted closer to the coast. But the bow of the boat was sitting low in the water, and he realised that *The Mako* was sinking. His only chance was to attempt to swim to the shore, but huge breakers crashed against the cliffs, and it was likely that he would be smashed onto the jagged rocks.

He unclipped the safety tether that attached him to the yacht and climbed onto the gunwale. In the moonlight he could just make out the cliffs in the distance. He grimaced. This was a crazy plan, but he was out of options.

It was then that he saw the tail. He knew that dolphins were regularly spotted in the sea around Cornwall. But it hadn't looked like a dolphin's tail. The huge tail broke the surface again, closer to the boat this time, before it disappeared beneath the waves.

Eirik froze and stared at the face that had appeared in the water, a few metres away from the boat. He must be hallucinating. Maybe he was suffering from concussion. He closed his eyes. When he opened them again the creature was still in the sea. A female figure—with a fish's tail? *What the hell?*

She raised her arm and waved to him. Eirik swore. He did not believe in mystical stories of sea sirens and mermaids, but at that moment he could not think of any other explanation.

'Follow me.' Her voice rose above the noise of the wind. She disappeared beneath the waves and the great tail made a splash.

Water lapped the gunwale. *The Mako* was sinking fast. There was nothing Eirik could do but jump into the sea and swim for his life. The water was bitterly cold, and his body reacted automatically with a gasp reflex that made him choke as his mouth filled with brine. He knew there was a danger that he could develop hypothermia. His chances of survival were slim.

The sea creature, mermaid—whatever she was—surfaced a few metres ahead and beckoned to him. Her skin looked silvery in the moonlight and her face, with its high cheekbones, was as exquisite as a pre-Raphaelite painting. Her long hair streamed behind her as she turned and swam away. Eirik struck out after her. He did not know who or even *what* she was, but she was his only hope.

He had lost his head torch, but the moon was bright now, allowing him to keep sight of the tail when it broke the surface. His chest heaved and his shoulders burned with the effort of swimming. His life jacket helped to keep him afloat, but he could feel the strong current dragging him towards rocks that had appeared, rising out of the sea like terrible, giant's teeth.

Eirik remembered the legends of beautiful sirens who had led men to their doom. He had been a fool to follow his mystical guide, but he'd never been able to resist a beautiful woman, he thought with grim humour. He was done for. The current was sweeping him closer to the rocks and his will to live was ebbing away as the cold seeped down to his bones.

He felt a hand touch his arm. The mermaid, for want of a better description, was beside him. Her eyes were huge and fathomless in the black night. It occurred to Eirik that perhaps he was already dead and had slipped into some strange underworld.

'Don't give up,' she urged. 'Stay close to me.'

'Who are you?' he shouted after her, but she was already swimming a little way ahead of him. He forced his aching muscles into action and struck out once more.

They seemed to be in a channel of calmer water flowing between the rocks. Waves crashed against the cliffs on either side, but Eirik saw a small cove and a strip of

beach in front of him. Dear God! His feet found the sea-
bed and he half crawled, half stumbled out of the waves.
His throat felt raw from the salt water he'd swallowed.
He sank down onto his knees, coughing and retching,
struggling to breathe.

He must have blacked out. When he regained consciousness, his cheek was resting on the wet sand. Someone rolled him over onto his back and supported his head.

'You'll be all right. Please be all right.'

The voice was a lilting melody that Eirik knew he
would never forget. His eyelids felt too heavy for him to
open them, and he was cold, so cold.

'Don't go. Don't give up.'

Her voice caught. There was urgency in her song, a
tenderness that curled around Eirik's frozen heart. He
felt her warm breath on his face, his lips. A hand gently stroked his jaw, and then her mouth covered his. Her
lips were soft and moist, easing his lips apart. Her breath
filled his mouth. The kiss of an angel, or in this case a
mermaid, brought Eirik back from the brink.

He wished he could stay in her embrace for ever. He
opened his eyes and stared into her fathomless dark gaze.
Instantly she snatched her mouth from his and lowered
his head onto the sand. By the time he'd propped himself
up onto one elbow, his saviour had returned to the sea
and was sitting on a partly submerged rock. It was impossible to make out the colour of her wet hair that rip-
pled over her shoulders. Her tail—yes, it was definitely
a *tail*—sparkled silver in the moonlight.

'Who are you?' he rasped.

'You are safe now. Help will come,' she told him in
her sweet voice before she dived into the waves.

'Wait.' Eirik stared after her, but she had gone. Had

he imagined her? His logical brain argued that he must have done. But without her guidance he would not have found his way to the cove.

He fell back against the sand and drifted in and out of consciousness. Some time later, it could have been minutes or hours, he heard the womp, womp of a helicopter's rotor blades in the sky above him. Shielding his eyes against the glare of the searchlight, he watched a medic being winched down to the beach.

'Your Royal Highness, your aides will be relieved that you are safe,' the medic told him. 'There was great concern after radio contact with you was lost. It was an incredible chance that you found your way to Pixie Cove. Only a few people who live in these parts know that the sea around the cove is more sheltered than the rest of the coastline.'

Pixie Cove! The name was apt, Eirik thought. He pushed his fingers through his hair that was matted with salt and blood. 'It wasn't luck,' he muttered. 'I know it sounds crazy, but I was guided by a…mermaid.'

It sounded ridiculous and he expected the medic to laugh or at least reassure him that he was suffering from concussion. But the man was surprisingly unsurprised.

'Ah, Cornwall's very own mermaid. I've not seen her myself, but I have heard of Arielle.'

•

CHAPTER ONE

'EVEN YOU MUST admit that Prince Eirik is lush.'

The jeering voice startled Arielle, and she flushed when she realised that she had been caught staring at the handsome hunk across the lawn who was attracting admiring looks from every female present. She glanced at the woman who had come to stand beside her.

'Even me?' She was automatically defensive. Tamara Bray was a prize bitch and had been the leader of the gang of bullies who'd made Arielle's school days hell.

'You have never shown an interest in any of the men who live around here, but none of them would want to get involved with the daughter of a convicted criminal. Do you really think a nobody like you would stand a chance with the Prince?' Tamara had a good reason to hate Arielle's father for what he had done. In his absence she had directed her spite at Arielle and the name-calling when they had been teenagers had turned into something much nastier. 'Mind you, none of the local guys look like *him*.'

Arielle followed Tamara's gaze back across the garden to where His Royal Highness, Prince Eirik of Fjernland was chatting to the commodore of the yacht club. Undoubtedly the Prince was *lush*—a West Country expression to describe a good-looking person. The Prince was a golden god with his tousled, dark blond hair and skin tanned to the colour of honey. The surgical dressing on his forehead did not detract from his handsome features.

In the past, photos of the dissolute, playboy prince had regularly appeared in the tabloids, although since his brother's death Prince Eirik had dropped out of the media spotlight. Arielle had developed a bit of a crush on him, to be honest. She'd cut out his picture from the pages of a celebrity magazine and stuck it on the fridge. Every time she opened the door, she noticed his mesmerising eyes, which were the same shade of bright blue as the Cornish sky on this crisp, spring day.

The breeze blowing off the sea tugged at Arielle's hair, which she'd piled on top of her head in an attempt to look respectable. An errant auburn curl brushed against her cheek, and she lifted her hand to tuck it behind her ear. Her eyes were still fixed on Prince Eirik.

He looked a lot better than he had done three nights ago when she'd guided him through the rough sea to Pixie Cove. She had been concerned for him when she'd left him on the beach and gone to get help. When she'd seen a news report that the Prince had been airlifted to hospital in Penzance after he'd nearly drowned at sea, she had felt relieved that he was safe.

Prince Eirik's tall and imposing presence made him stand out from the other guests at the yacht club who flocked around him. His impressive, muscular physique and the thick blond stubble on his jaw were an indication of his Viking ancestry.

'Where is Fjernland anyway?' Tamara muttered. 'I used to bunk off geography lessons.'

'It's an island in the North Sea between the Danish peninsular of Jutland and the coast of southern Norway,'

Arielle explained. 'Historically, Denmark made repeated attempts to control Fjernland, but Fjernlandic men were reputed to have been the most fearsome and pitiless of all the Norse warriors and the island became an independent principality some time in the tenth century. The current monarch is His Serene Highness, Prince Otto III, who rules with his wife and consort Princess Hulda. Prince Eirik is their only surviving son and heir after the death of his older brother, Prince Niels.'

'You always were a swot. But even though you've got a fancy degree, your dad is a murderer, and a lot of people around here think you should be in prison too,' Tamara said viciously.

'I knew nothing about my father's activities or what happened to your cousin.'

'Yeah, right.'

Tension twisted in a knot in the pit of Arielle's stomach at Tamara's mention of her father. She felt that she could never escape from her past. She looked towards the marina, where the yachts that had taken part in the famous Around the Island of Ireland sailing race were moored. All the boats had completed the race within forty-eight hours, with one notable exception. Prince Eirik's accident had made the international news headlines, but thankfully there had been no mention of Arielle's involvement. The last thing she wanted was to attract the attention of the press.

The clink of rigging carried on the breeze, and the boats bobbed on the swell. The salty tang of the sea made Arielle impatient to go swimming. She swam and free-dived wearing a monofin most days. The sea was her second home, and she was a strong swimmer, but the

confidence she felt in the ocean was non-existent in every
other area of her life.

The villagers thought she was as reclusive as her father
when he'd lived at the cliff-top cottage that had been Arielle's home all her life. It was hardly surprising she kept
herself to herself, she thought bitterly. Gerran Rowse's
reputation as a troublemaker had caused people to shun
Arielle, and her mother when she had been alive.

Arielle did not fit in anywhere, certainly not at the exclusive yacht club. The members were mostly wealthy, retired professionals who had swapped city life for a coastal
idyll and bemoaned the lack of a well-known coffee-shop
chain. None of the local fishermen who took their trawl-
ers out to sea to make a precarious living belonged to the
yacht club. But Arielle was not part of Penash's tight-knit
fishing community either. The men who had visited her
father in the middle of the night had moored their boats
further along the coast.

She had been surprised when the commodore of the
yacht club had turned up at her studio the previous day.

'The Prince of Fjernland has left hospital following his
ordeal at sea and he will present the prize to the winner
of the AII race,' Charles Daventry had told her. 'I have
been informed by Prince Eirik's private secretary that
His Royal Highness would like to meet you.'

Arielle's heart had given a jolt. 'Why does he want to
meet *me*?' She'd wondered if the Prince had found out
that she had helped him, although she had not told anyone. But then she'd had the sickening thought that he
might be curious about her father's notoriety. The press
had hounded her after Gerran Rowse's conviction and it
was one reason why Arielle had changed her surname.

'Prince Eirik is passionate about marine conservation,'

Charles had explained. 'He supports the International Clean Sea campaign, and he heard about your project to recycle plastic waste collected from the ocean and turn it into decorative items.'

Charles had picked up a coaster that Arielle had made from recycled plastic granules and studied it with a perplexed expression. 'The committee have decided to ask you to bring some of your products to the yacht club. If the Prince has time after the prize-giving ceremony he might want to take a look at them.'

Publicity for marine conservation was always a good thing, Arielle had reminded herself when she'd arrived at the clubhouse earlier. The guests had still been having lunch and a snooty steward had directed her outside to a table set up on the lawn where she could display her work. Some other local businesses had also been invited and Tamara was there to represent her father's company.

Tamara gave Arielle a dirty look before she walked over to a table bearing crates of beer labelled Bray's Brewery. 'Why don't you do everyone a favour and clear off? I don't know why you are even here.'

'Apparently the Prince is interested in my plastics recycling initiative.'

'The Prince is not going to be interested in anything you have to say. If his security team have discovered that your father is a convicted criminal, they probably won't let you near him.'

Arielle was stung by Tamara's comments. She had endured years of being made to feel worthless by her father. Anger and resentment bubbled up inside her. She had done nothing wrong but nevertheless she'd been ostracised by the villagers. Her conscience pricked that she should have tried harder to discover the truth about her father's shady business dealings. The smallholding where he'd kept mainly sheep had not been profitable, but once Arielle had found a holdall stuffed full of bank notes hidden behind some hay bales. When strangers had come to the cottage, she had locked herself in her bedroom as her father had told her to do.

Automatically she lifted her hand and traced her finger over the faint ridge of a scar on her cheek. Her father was serving a life sentence in prison, and she no longer had to fear him, but she was haunted by his scandalous crimes.

Tamara was right. Prince Eirik would not be interested in anything she had to say, Arielle thought bleakly. The Prince's jet-setting lifestyle was one long round of lavish parties, from what she'd read about him. He was feted and adored wherever he went, and his legendary charm attracted women like bees to honey. But not this woman, she told herself.

'Prince Eirik is walking this way,' Tamara said excitedly. 'I can't believe I'm going to meet a real prince.'

Arielle watched the Prince stride across the lawn. He ignored Tamara and made a beeline for her. His tall figure blocked out the sun and she had to tilt her head to look at his face. Her eyes crashed with his glittering gaze, and she saw a flash of recognition in their blue depths.

'*You!* You're the mermaid.' He sounded stunned. He stepped closer to her, his eyes searching her face intently. 'Who *are* you?' Before Arielle could answer, Prince Eirik glanced over his shoulder and cursed when he saw his retinue of aides hurrying across the lawn after him. 'I told myself that I had imagined you. But you are a real woman.' He ran his eyes over her, and something in the way he looked at her sent a rush of heat through Arielle's veins.

He was even more gorgeous than she remembered from three nights ago. She had cradled his head in her lap and there had been a vulnerability to him then that had tugged on her heart. Now he appeared to be fully recovered from his ordeal in the sea and his male potency stirred an age-old feminine response low in her pelvis.

She estimated that he was three or four inches over six feet tall. The pale blue shirt stretched across his torso was unbuttoned at the throat to show a sprinkling of blond chest hairs. Arielle lowered her gaze and made a quick inventory of his narrow hips and long legs encased in slim-fit navy blue trousers. His whipcord body exuded strength and power. She lifted her eyes to his face once more and the gleam in his eyes made her heart miss a beat.

'You saved my life.' He swore softly when he saw the commodore bearing down on them. 'I want to talk to you,' he told Arielle in a low tone. 'But not here. Is there somewhere where we can be alone?'

'I don't think so,' she murmured, thinking that the press photographers who were at the yacht club would be wildly curious if Prince Eirik took her off for a private conversation.

He hid his frustration with obvious effort when Charles Daventry halted next to Arielle's table and made introductions.

'Your Highness, this is Arielle Tremain, who is involved with the Clean Sea organisation.'

Arielle held out her hand to the Prince and murmured, 'I'm pleased to meet you, Your Royal Highness.'

Out of the corner of her eye she saw Charles frown and belatedly remembered that she had been instructed to curtsey to the Prince. But before she could attempt

the manoeuvre, Prince Eirik curled his strong fingers
around her hand and a sensation like an electrical current shot up her arm.

'Arielle…' His husky accent was spine-tinglingly sexy.
'You have a beautiful name. It suits you.'

His smile stole her breath, and the tingling sensation
spread to her breasts. Her nipples tightened and she was
conscious of her lacy bra scraping against the sensitive
tips. For once she was wearing a dress instead of jeans
and a shapeless sweatshirt, which were her usual choice
of clothes. She spent most days alone in her workshop,
but for her visit to the yacht club she had dug out the
only dress she owned. It was a bit tighter over her bust
than she'd remembered and a hasty downwards glance
revealed the faint outline of her nipples beneath the clingy
material.

Arielle wished she could cross her arms over her chest
to hide her body's unbidden response to Prince Eirik, but
her hand was still trapped in his firm grasp. Sensual heat
suffused her as he roamed his eyes over her figure. She
was surprised by her reaction to him. It was two years
since she'd finished with Jack and sworn off men.

The Prince was an exceptional man, and she could be
forgiven for being dazzled by his stunning good looks
and charisma, Arielle consoled herself. He was a notorious womaniser and flirting was second nature to him.

Their eyes met and she felt a jolt of awareness. It was
as though time were suspended, and the crowd of people
in the garden disappeared, leaving her and the Prince
beneath the wide blue sky. He was a work of art with
those sculpted cheekbones and a mouth that was bla-
tantly inviting.

She knew about his mouth; the sensual curve of his

lips and the way they had fitted against hers. He had been semi-conscious, and she had acted to revive him. It was unlikely he remembered, she reassured herself, but the wicked gleam in his laser blue eyes caused her heart to crash against her ribs.

A discreet cough from the commodore broke the spell that Prince Eirik had cast on Arielle and with a faint gasp she snatched her hand out of his. To her relief he released her from his mesmerising stare, and she quickly moved away to stand behind her table. The Prince looked down at the items on display.

'You made all these things from recycled plastic? I'm impressed,' he murmured when she nodded.

'I mostly make small items such as key fobs, coasters and jewellery.' She picked up a pair of cufflinks and offered them to him. 'It's hard to believe that these were once crisp packets or other unrecyclable plastic. The plastic waste is processed through a granulator into a fine aggregate, which is mixed with a plant-based resin binder before it can be cast into the products you see here.'

The Prince lifted a necklace from a display stand. It was one of Arielle's favourite pieces, and had an intricate chain interspersed with tiny teardrop resin pendants. 'Who is responsible for the silverwork on the jewellery?'

'Me.' Her face grew warm beneath his intent gaze. 'I taught myself silversmithing through trial and error. Mostly error at first,' she admitted ruefully.

Prince Eirik leaned across the table and stretched out his hand to touch the green glass earring dangling from Arielle's earlobe. 'Did you make the pair of earrings you are wearing? They match the colour of your eyes.'

His face was so close to hers that she felt his warm breath on her cheek. The spicy scent of his cologne teased her senses. 'Yes.' Her voice emerged as a smoky whisper. She cleared her throat. 'As well as plastic I collect sea glass from the beach and use it to make jewellery, which I sell online.'

'You are full of surprises, Arielle,' he drawled.

She tensed, wondering if he had heard the local gossip about her father's crimes. 'What do you mean?'

His eyes narrowed. 'I understand that you organise the collection of plastic and other rubbish from local beaches.'

'Oh.' She released her breath slowly. 'Yes, I take part in regular beach cleans and encourage other people to help out.'

'I have campaigned for a similar scheme to be adopted in Fjernland.' Prince Eirik gave Arielle a thoughtful look and she was sure she had not imagined the sizzle of attraction between them.

While they had been talking, Tamara had pushed her way to the front of the crowd of people standing near the Prince. She dipped into a sweeping curtsey while the commodore introduced her.

'Your Royal Highness, it is an honour to meet you. I am a close friend of Arielle and I'm deeply committed to saving our oceans from plastic waste,' Tamara told him earnestly. She managed to simultaneously smile at the Prince and shoot a warning look at Arielle.

Seriously! Arielle almost laughed out loud at Tamara's blatant lies. She had never helped out at a beach-clean event. More people had crowded around Prince Eirik and Tamara was fluttering her eyelashes at him like a demented moth.

The Prince looked back at Arielle. 'I would have liked the opportunity to discuss your work with the Clean Sea

project in more detail,' he murmured before he was ushered away by the commodore to greet other local business leaders.

Arielle packed up her products and drove home in a
strange mood. Meeting Prince Eirik had left her feeling
restless and dissatisfied with her life. Tamara's words
echoed inside her head. *Do you really think a nobody
like you would stand a chance with the Prince?'*

Well, no, Arielle hadn't expected that he would notice
her, and she certainly wouldn't admit to having a secret
fantasy where the handsome prince saved her from her
dead-end life. Prince Eirik had seemed genuinely interested in her plastics recycling initiative. He had treated
her as an equal and listened to what she had to say, which
was more than her father or the villagers of Penash had
ever done. Living here, she would always be tainted by
her father's crimes.

Something inside her had changed and she vowed not
to waste any more of her life waiting for a prince to rescue her. The cliff-top cottage held happy memories of her
mother. But there had been sadness and despair within
the cottage's thick walls and the spilled blood of an innocent man. For as long as she could remember, Arielle
had been under the influence of her father. He had been
in prison for the last three years, but she had been trapped
in a prison of her own making.

Meeting the Prince had given her a glimpse of a world
where she did not feel judged, and she was determined to
make a new life for herself far away from Penash.

CHAPTER TWO

THAT NEW DRESS FEELING! Arielle's doubts multiplied as she fiddled with the narrow shoulder straps on the black silk jersey dress. She frowned at her reflection in the mirror, dismayed by the amount of her flesh on display. The skirt was too short, and the neckline was more low-cut than she remembered from when she'd tried the dress on in the boutique.

She was tempted to change into her faithful navy blue dress that she'd bought four years ago for her graduation ceremony from university. Since then, it had lived at the back of her wardrobe. She'd worn it to a couple of job interviews and to the event at the yacht club earlier in the day when she had met Prince Eirik, hence the need for a new outfit.

An invitation to have dinner with the Prince had sent her hurrying off to Truro in search of something suitable to wear. Her aim had been to look sophisticated, but the dress screamed available and possibly even desperate.

She picked up the gold-edged card from the mantelpiece and her eyes followed the bold handwriting inviting her to dine with the Prince at his hotel. A handwritten note was unusual these days, when most people communicated electronically by email or text. It was signed informally Eirik, and the sight of his name set butterflies loose in Arielle's stomach.

Soon after she had returned home from the yacht club, a limousine with dark-tinted windows had stopped in front of her cottage, and a man who she did not recognise had got out and knocked on the front door. Arielle had hidden behind the curtains. Memories of strangers who had arrived in cars with blacked-out windows to do secret business with her father made her feel tense. She had learned at his trial that Gerran Rowse had been a major drugs dealer and the mastermind behind an operation to smuggle huge quantities of heroin and cocaine into Cornwall on fishing boats.

But her father would spend the rest of his life behind bars, and Arielle had resolved not to live in fear any more. She'd opened the front door, prepared to tell the stranger to clear off. The smartly dressed man, greying at his temples, had introduced himself as Gustav Koch, Private Secretary to His Royal Highness, Prince Eirik.

'It is the Prince's wish that I convey your answer to him,' he had told Arielle after she'd read the invitation. 'He very much hopes that you will accept.' Gustav's inscrutable expression had not altered, but Arielle had noticed him glance at her scruffy jeans and sweatshirt that she had changed into because she'd planned to spend the afternoon working in her studio. Perhaps the royal assistant did not think she was good enough to meet the Prince.

Her chin had come up. 'Dinner will be lovely,' she had heard herself say before she'd had time to think of an excuse to decline.

'Good. A car will collect you at seven thirty.'

It was nearly that now, and there was not enough time

to change her dress or make another attempt to gather her hair up in a chignon. Her curls were always especially rebellious after she'd just washed her hair. Car headlights shone through the window. Cinderella's coach had arrived. Arielle's heart gave a lurch of nervous excitement. She wrapped the green silk shawl that had belonged to her mother around her shoulders and picked up her evening purse.

She had bought her first pair of stiletto shoes to wear with the new dress and wished she had practised walking in high heels when she stepped outside and made her way gingerly across the cobblestones to the waiting car. The chauffeur held open the door and she slid onto the back seat. The interior of the car smelled of plush leather and the faint but distinctive scent of the Prince's aftershave.

Her stomach muscles involuntarily clenched at the prospect of seeing Prince Eirik again. But she reminded herself that he had said he wanted to discuss the Clean Sea campaign to rid the ocean of plastic waste. It was likely that he had invited other guests who were involved with the campaign to the dinner party.

The hotel a few miles along the coast from Penash was the most exclusive place to stay in Cornwall. The car turned onto the driveway but instead of stopping in front of the grand entrance, the chauffeur drove around to the back of the hotel. 'I was instructed to bring you this way,' he explained as he ushered Arielle through a door next to the kitchens. They walked along a corridor where there was a strong smell of cooking. 'Wait here,' the driver told her. 'I will tell Gustav that you have arrived.'

Had the Prince's private secretary been concerned that she might wear her old jeans, and that was the reason she been brought into the hotel unseen? Arielle wondered. The chauffeur had strolled further up the corridor and was holding his phone to his ear. The door to the kitchen swung open and a young man dressed in chef whites walked out.

'Well, if it isn't Arielle Rowse,' he said in an unpleasant voice when he saw her.

'Tremain,' she corrected him quickly. But Tamara Bray's brother, Danny, shook his head. 'You might have changed your name, but it doesn't change who your father is. Gerran killed my cousin Josh, and you did nothing to stop him.'

'I didn't know...' Arielle broke off. There was no point trying to defend herself. A few people in Penash thought she had been involved in her father's drug-dealing operation and Danny and his family believed she had known that Gerran had shot and killed a local police constable.

'What are you doing at the hotel all dolled up?' Danny ran his eyes over her dress.

'I'm having dinner here,' Arielle said abruptly. She wasn't going to reveal that she would be meeting Prince Eirik.

'I'm surprised you can afford the Belvedere's prices. But maybe you are up to your dad's old tricks. A fancy car was seen driving up to your place.' Danny shrugged. 'The police never found the last consignment of drugs that Gerran smuggled into Cornwall before he was arrested. I reckon you know where he hid the stuff and you've been waiting for interest in the story to fade before you could carry on his drug-dealing business. All that collecting plastic from the beach and recycling it to make table mats is just a front to hide what you're really doing.'

'None of that is true.' Arielle panicked when she spotted Gustav walking across the hotel foyer. She feared

Danny might make more vile accusations and be over-heard. 'Get lost, Danny,' she muttered before she hurried away from him.

'Miss Tremain, please come with me.' Gustav directed her into the service lift that was used by the staff. 'I apologise for the secrecy, but there are journalists outside the front of the hotel. Prince Eirik's yachting accident has unfortunately made the headlines around the world.' The lift stopped at the top floor, and they stepped directly into the penthouse suite. 'I'll let the Prince know you are here,' Gustav murmured before he disappeared through a door.

Arielle looked around the elegantly furnished sitting room. She had never been in such luxurious surroundings and felt out of her depth. The conversation with Danny had been a painful reminder of her father's crimes and she felt tainted by her association with him. She was tempted to leave before the Prince's other guests arrived. No one would notice if she slipped out of the hotel through the back door. But a stubborn voice inside her insisted that she had nothing to be ashamed of.

Her heels sank into the deep-pile carpet as she walked over to the huge window that gave wonderful views of the bay. In the moonlight, the sea was as calm as a pond.

'It looks benign, doesn't it?' The gravelly voice from behind Arielle sent a quiver along her spine. 'It's hard to believe that the sea was so wild the other night and my yacht was destroyed by powerful waves.'

'I love its unpredictability. Only a fool believes the oceans can be controlled,' Arielle said softly. Her heart was banging against her ribs, and she could not bring herself to turn around immediately. But then she remembered that he was a *prince*. She spun away from the window and almost overbalanced in her high heels before making a clumsy attempt at a curtsey. 'Your Highness.'

'Please, no formality.' Prince Eirik crossed the room in long strides and stopped in front of her. 'I recognised your voice. When you appeared among the waves the other night, I thought I was hallucinating.' His eyes were the brightest blue imaginable, and he was completely gorgeous. Arielle was unprepared for his devastating impact on her when he smiled. 'It sounds crazy,' he said ruefully, 'but when I saw that you had a tail and silvery skin, I half believed you were an actual mermaid.'

She laughed. 'I was wearing a silver wetsuit, and I swim with a monofin. I'd love to be a real mermaid, but I have legs.'

'I noticed,' the Prince said in a low tone that sent a spike of heat through Arielle. The brilliant gleam in his eyes made her catch her breath as he roamed his gaze over her and lingered on the swell of her breasts, before moving lower to make a leisurely appraisal of her legs.

She prayed there wasn't a snag in her ultra-fine stockings that she'd picked up by mistake when she'd meant to buy a pair of tights. She was conscious of the bare skin at the tops of her thighs above the wide bands of lace that held the stockings up. Shockingly she felt a slick dampness between her legs as she imagined the Prince lifting her dress and sliding his hand over her naked thighs.

Something raw and feral blazed in his eyes. Arielle was mortified that he might have read her mind. 'Forgive me, I am forgetting my manners,' he said abruptly. He shoved his hand through his dark blond hair and walked over to a table where there was a bottle in an ice bucket and two glasses. Arielle's gaze followed him. He looked incredibly attractive in tailored black trousers and a cream shirt made of a filmy material, through which she could faintly see his golden skin and the darker shadow of his chest hairs.

'Would you like some champagne?'

'That will be lovely.' At least she supposed it would. She'd never tried champagne before. The Prince popped the cork on the bottle and filled a long flute with pale golden bubbles.

'Unfortunately, I can't join you,' he said as he handed Arielle her drink before he poured himself a glass of sparkling water. 'My doctor is concerned that the wound on my head could become infected and has insisted I take a course of antibiotics.'

He was no longer wearing the surgical dressing. Her eyes flew to the red weal on his brow where the cut had obviously been stitched. 'I suppose you can't take risks with your health now you are the heir to Fjernland's throne.'

She could have kicked herself for being so blunt when his expression became shuttered. It was only just over a year since the tragic death of his older brother, she remembered.

'Quite so,' the Prince said drily. 'Only a few of my closest aides knew that I was competing in the AII race. The news that my yacht had sunk in treacherous sea conditions was not well received by Their Serene Highnesses.' He noticed Arielle's look of surprise that he had referred to his parents by their formal titles and raised a quizzical eyebrow. 'The Sovereign Prince and Princess are monarchs first and foremost. When I was growing up, parenting me was low down on their list of priorities.' There was faint bitterness in his voice.

Arielle took a sip of champagne and blinked as the

tiny bubbles exploded in her mouth. She'd read somewhere that you couldn't get drunk on champagne, but she did not intend to put the theory to the test. She hoped the Prince hadn't opened the bottle just for her. 'I expect your other guests will drink the champagne.'

'Other guests?' He shook his head. 'There are no other guests. I wanted to meet you privately and we will have dinner here in my suite. But if you prefer, we can go down to the public dining room.'

And risk being spotted by someone from the press or by Danny Bray? She quickly shook her head. 'Here is fine.' She hesitated. 'Should I address you as Your Highness or Prince Eirik?'

He smiled, showing a flash of brilliant white teeth in his tanned face, and her heart collided with her ribs again. 'Eirik will do nicely—Arielle.' His husky accent turned her name into a song. Her skin burned where he placed his hand at the base of her spine and escorted her into the private dining room. 'Allow me,' he murmured as he lifted her silk shawl from her shoulders.

His fingers lightly brushed against her skin, and she felt as though he had branded her. Get a grip, Arielle told herself sternly. Maybe the champagne would help her to relax, she thought, and took a gulp of her drink.

Eirik took his place opposite Arielle at the table. She had tensed when he'd pulled out her chair and waited for her to sit down and he wondered why she was wary of him. It was not a reaction he usually evoked in women. He found her intriguing and the sexual chemistry between them was almost tangible.

She took several sips of her champagne, reinforcing his idea that she was nervous. It was difficult to believe after she had demonstrated incredible bravery when she'd swum out to his sinking yacht and guided him to safety. But the fact that he was not only royal but the heir to the throne tended to create a distance between him and other people.

When he had been the spare heir, he'd largely been left to his own devices and had enjoyed more freedom than his brother. Sometimes he'd felt guilty that Niels had borne the burden of being Fjernland's future monarch with all the expectation and weight of history on his shoulders. It was not a role that Eirik had ever wanted, and he'd been able to avoid much of the pomp and ceremony of royal life and focus on establishing his yacht-manufacturing company.

All that had changed on the mountain. From now on his life would be dictated by protocol and ceremony and above all duty to the crown. The very existence of Fjernland as a principality rested on Eirik's shoulders. According to the laws of succession, if the monarch died without an heir, Fjernland would lose its independent status that it had won in bloody battles many centuries ago and would once again be ruled by Denmark.

Eirik accepted that he must marry. It was not a prospect that filled him with pleasure, but that hardly mattered. He had been responsible for his brother's death—certainly that was his mother's opinion. He was under pressure to choose a suitably aristocratic wife and produce an heir as soon as possible, in preparation for when he became ruler of Fjernland.

Tonight was his last opportunity to have dinner with a beautiful young woman who was not in any way a contender to be his wife. Thinking of the future made him want to numb his mind with champagne, or even better spend a few hours in the arms of the sexy redhead whose sea green eyes hinted at a sensuality he was eager to explore. Was one last night of pleasure with no strings attached too much to wish for?

He shifted position in his seat as his arousal pressed uncomfortably against the zip on his trousers. He had been instantly turned on when he'd walked into the sitting room and studied Arielle's toned figure in a dress that was no more than a wisp of black silk, which showed off her full breasts and long, slender legs. As for that hair! He longed to bury his fingers in her riotous red curls that tumbled to halfway down her back.

Silently cursing his libido that had inconveniently sprung into life after more than a year's absence, Eirik was relieved when there was a knock on the door and Gustav entered the suite, followed by a team of waiters who served dinner. One of them topped up Arielle's glass with champagne.

Eirik caught his private secretary's eye. 'See to it that we are not disturbed for the rest of the evening, will you?'

'Of course, sir,' Gustav replied smoothly.

Eirik heard faint disapproval in his chief aide's voice. He had lived like a monk for over a year, and he was aware that if the media learned of an indiscretion with a woman they might resurrect his reputation—not wholly undeserved of a playboy prince. Eirik trusted Gustav, whom he regarded as a friend as much as an employee. But his brush with death had left him feeling reckless.

After the staff had left, Arielle drank more champagne. There was a soft flush on her cheeks and Eirik noticed that her hand trembled when she put down her glass. Wanting to help her feel at ease, he kept the conversation light and told her a little about his country.

'The North Sea around Fjernland's coast is never very warm to swim in, even in summer. But the country is a volcanic island and has numerous hot springs. If you ever get the chance to visit, I think you would enjoy the lakes, which are heated by geothermal activity. There would be no need for you to wear a wetsuit for swimming.'

His gaze was drawn to the pale curves of her breasts above the low-cut bodice of her dress, and he imagined her wearing a skimpy bikini. The atmosphere in the room crackled with electricity. His body tightened as he watched a pink stain spread across Arielle's face and down her throat and décolletage. Eirik could not remember the last time he'd seen a woman blush. Arielle's unworldly air fired his curiosity, and her sexy curves fanned the flames of his desire.

'The sight of a mermaid swimming in the clear water of the Crystal Lagoon, which is Fjernland's most famous beauty spot, would definitely be a newsworthy story,' he murmured. 'In fact, I am surprised that you are not a celebrity here in Cornwall.'

An odd expression flickered on her face. 'Ah, but mermaids are shy and elusive creatures who prefer to stay out of the limelight.'

She put down her knife and fork even though she had barely touched her dinner. Eirik hadn't eaten much either, although the lobster gratin was exceptionally good. His appetite had disappeared, and he felt hunger of a different kind.

'How did you know my yacht was in trouble? It was astonishing that you were able to find me in the dark when the sea was so rough.'

'I didn't realise it was you who had let off a flare, I just knew that someone was in trouble. Earlier in the day the weather had been quite calm when I swam around the headland. I'd left my clothes and phone hidden in a cave on the main beach. Pixie Cove is only accessible from the sea as the cliffs are too steep to climb and I was trapped there for a few hours until the storm passed.'

Arielle paused and tucked an auburn curl behind her ear. 'When I saw the flare, I had no way of alerting the coastguard. I hoped that someone else had spotted it, but I didn't see the helicopter, so I decided to swim back to where I'd left my phone. But I saw a tiny light further out to sea and swam out to investigate.'

'I knew my only chance of survival was to try to swim to the shore, but I would never have made it without you to guide me,' Eirik said gruffly. 'The waves were huge, and I would have been thrown against the rocks. When I saw a woman with a fishtail swimming in the sea, I told myself I was imagining things.'

'As soon as you had made it to the cove and I knew you were safe, I swam back to where I'd left my phone and called the emergency services.'

'Why do you use a monofin?'

'It helps me to swim greater distances and enables me to free-dive deeper. I don't use scuba gear. The dolphin-kick motion when I am wearing a monofin is quite different from conventional swimming and allows me to conserve energy and swim more powerfully.'

'Do you compete at swimming events?'

'I don't care about winning races. I learned to swim before I could walk. My mother passed her love of the sea on to me. She died when I was a child, but I feel close to her when I am in the ocean.'

Eirik had heard a tremor in her voice. 'That must have

been tough. Who took care of you after your mother passed away?'

Arielle drained the last of the champagne from her glass. 'I lived with my father, but he is not around now.'

Eirik sensed that she did not want to talk about her family. She was young to have lost both her parents, and he knew that grief could be consuming.

'Would you like dessert?' He indicated the sweet trolley. The gateau oozing with cream looked sickly, and he wasn't surprised when she declined. 'Let's take our coffee outside,' he suggested. 'It's fairly warm this evening, and there is underfloor heating on the terrace.'

He carried the tray with a cafetière and cups out onto the balcony, set it down on the table and poured the coffee.

Arielle followed and looked at him uncertainly. 'Shouldn't I serve you, seeing as you are a prince?'

'I'm capable of pouring coffee,' he said drily. 'I was fortunate to escape the stifling court etiquette and go to university in America. It gave me the chance to live a normal life and learn to fend for myself. As a matter of fact, I'm not a bad cook.'

Rattan furniture was arranged around a low table on the balcony. Eirik sat down on the sofa and was amused when Arielle claimed the armchair furthest away from him. Most women would have taken the opportunity to sit beside him and perhaps lean in close or play with their hair. He was used to the flirtatious games that women played. He'd been aware of the glances Arielle had sent him across the dinner table when she'd thought he hadn't noticed. If her cool reserve was intended to fuel his interest it was working.

He leaned back against the cushions and stretched his

long legs out in front of him. It was a clear night, and the sky was studded with glittering stars that multiplied when you tried to count them. The sound of the waves rippling onto the shore should have been soothing, but Eirik had never felt less soothed in his life. He forced his thoughts away from the carnal impact of Arielle's mouth that had driven him to distraction throughout dinner.

'I suppose your love of the sea led to your support of the Clean Sea campaign to rid the oceans of plastic waste.'

She nodded. 'I always knew I wanted a career that involved the sea and I have a degree in ocean science and marine conservation. I was employed for a year on a local project that involved underwater clean-ups, mainly plastic litter, and discarded fishing equipment. But the money for the project ran out.'

She sighed. 'Marine conservation is underfunded and there is a lack of job opportunities in Cornwall. I started making products from unrecyclable plastic waste and I belong to a collective, trading under the name Plastic-Free Sea. Fifty per cent of our profits go towards marine conservation projects. Obviously, there are production costs to consider.' She gave a rueful smile. 'I'll never be rich. The work of PFS and similar organisations barely touches the mountain of plastic waste in the oceans, but it's better than nothing.'

Eirik found himself captivated by Arielle's enthusiasm for her work. Would she exhibit the same fire and passion in bed? he wondered. He swore silently, irritated by his apparently one-track mind.

'Have you thought about looking for a job in marine conservation further afield? Fjernland is an island, and a healthy ocean environment is important to all Fjernlanders. But, unfortunately, the focus on marine issues has, until recently, lagged behind other countries.'

One hundred years ago, the principality had changed from an absolute monarchy and adopted a constitution, but the Sovereign Prince was also Head of State and still retained much of the governing power, although there were some judicial and legislative branches of government. Eirik had often felt frustrated by his father's lack of foresight in a rapidly changing world. Niels had understood the ecological problems that Fjernland faced and had supported Eirik's efforts to promote the principality as a leader in conservation.

'Five years ago, my brother and I established the Fjernland Marine Research Institute. The organisation employs people with a range of knowledge and expertise. I am sure there must be opportunities around the world for someone with your qualifications and enthusiasm.'

'You're right,' Arielle said in a low voice. 'I have seen advertisements for marine conservation jobs abroad. I even began the application process for a couple of positions, but I always came up with an excuse to withdraw my CV.'

She stood up and walked over to the balcony rail, standing with her back towards Eirik as she stared at the moonlit sea. He admired her derrière where her dress clung to her shapely curves. She was a mystery that he wanted to solve.

He strolled over to stand beside her. 'Why didn't you apply for jobs in other parts of the world? Is there a reason you are reluctant to leave your village? A boyfriend perhaps?' He'd noted that she wasn't wearing a wedding ring, but she might have a long-term partner. It was an oddly unpalatable thought.

'No.' She gave him a wry look. 'Many of the people I was at school with have paired off and some have started families. The dating pool in Penash is very small, and anyway none of the local guys are interested in me.'

'I find that hard to believe.' He stared into her eyes that were sea green pools deep enough to drown in. As for her mouth, so lush and inviting. It was all Eirik could do to restrain himself from slanting his lips over hers and tasting her.

'It's true. No one wants to get involved with me because... I have crazy hair.' She ran her fingers through her riot of red curls and laughed, but it sounded strained, and he was sure she had been going to say something else.

'Your hair is incredible,' he murmured. Unable to resist, he lifted his hand and wound a silky curl around his finger. 'You are beautiful and intelligent. Courageous.' Eirik remembered the reason he had invited Arielle to meet him. One of the reasons, he mocked himself, conscious of the taut ache in his groin. 'Come inside,' he said softly. 'I have something for you.'

CHAPTER THREE

'IT'S VERY KIND of you, but I can't accept this,' Arielle said firmly. For a second when she'd opened the slim box Eirik had handed her, and seen the sparkle of diamonds, her heart had missed a beat. The bracelet was exquisite. Even though she did not know much about proper jewellery—as opposed to the eco-friendly trinkets that she made—she could tell the bracelet was valuable.

'If you don't like the style, I will ask Gustav to arrange for an alternative to be sent to you. Perhaps you would prefer a necklace or diamond earrings?' He frowned when she shook her head. 'You risked your life to save mine, and the least I can do is gift you a small token to show my gratitude.'

'It's unnecessary.' Arielle's throat felt tight. 'I didn't know you were a prince when I realised that you were in trouble in the sea. I would have helped anyone, and I certainly did not expect to be rewarded.'

She replaced the lid on the box. The bracelet must have cost a fortune, but she felt cheapened that Eirik had turned her act of compassion into a commodity. Even worse, she felt a fool. He had flirted with her all evening, and when they had been on the balcony she'd thought for a heart-stopping moment that he was going to kiss her.

She had wanted him to, she admitted. But the bracelet was a timely reminder that he wasn't interested in her, and his dinner invitation had simply been a polite gesture so that he could thank her for rescuing him.

He was a prince, and an inveterate womaniser by all accounts. No doubt he made every woman he met feel as though they'd stepped into the pages of a fairy tale. Arielle was annoyed with herself for being seduced by Eirik's charismatic personality. The truth was that she'd never met another man with his rampant sex appeal. Not even Jack, who she'd believed she was in love with, had made her feel so aware of her femininity.

But it was time for a reality check. She held out the box with the bracelet to Eirik. When he did not take it, she put it down on the table and said huskily, 'I should be going. It's late.'

Ten o'clock was hardly late, but she was impatient for the evening to be over. When she got home, she would hang her new dress in her wardrobe and look at it occasionally to remind herself that she had outgrown silly daydreams about handsome princes.

His frown deepened. 'I apologise if I have offended you. It was certainly not my intention.'

'You haven't,' she assured him in a too-bright voice. Her pulse quickened when he strolled towards her.

'Stay a little longer,' he said softly. 'I have enjoyed talking to you.'

There was temptation in the spicy scent of his aftershave mixed with something subtle but intrinsically male that made her stomach muscles clench. 'I really do have to leave. I've been working flat out to complete an order of recycled plastic jewellery for a London department store. It's a fantastic opportunity to showcase my products and publicise the Clean Sea campaign. I need to finish packing up the order tonight before it's collected by the courier tomorrow morning.'

'Your work is obviously important to you.' Was there a hint of pique in his cool voice? He probably did not get turned down by a woman very often, Arielle thought ruefully. Somehow it made her feel a bit better about her reaction to him. He was unfairly gorgeous, and she was not the first woman to be bowled over by him, nor would she be the last.

He picked up her shawl from the back of the chair and draped it around her shoulders. She felt the whisper of his warm breath on the side of her neck and her heart slammed against her ribcage.

'If I can't persuade you to change your mind I'll walk you down to the car,' he drawled.

Perversely she wished she hadn't decided to leave, but Eirik was striding over to the door and Arielle followed him out to the corridor. While the lift whisked them down to the lobby she avoided his curious gaze, but she was conscious of the prickling tension that filled the small space.

They left the hotel through the back door. Arielle held her breath when they passed the kitchens, but Danny Bray did not appear. She was surprised when Eirik led her across the staff car park to an old truck that looked the same as every other farm vehicle, with mud-spattered wheels and dents in the bodywork.

'The paparazzi who are camped outside the hotel do not take any notice of me when I drive past them in this,' he explained as he opened the passenger door and offered his hand to help her step up into the truck. He walked round to the driver's side, and Arielle's heart lurched when she realised that he intended to drive her home himself. She gave him directions to her cottage, and once they had left the main road, they were both silent while he concentrated on driving along the narrow lanes that wound up to the top of the cliffs.

'It's certainly remote,' he said when the truck rattled across the cattlegrid next to an old sign that said Rowse Farm. Arielle had been meaning to take the sign down, but few people visited her cottage. She tensed, wondering if Eirik had recognised the name of Cornwall's most notorious criminal. 'Do you keep livestock?' he asked.

'Not any more.'

The moon had disappeared behind clouds and the darkness was impenetrable. Eirik pulled up in the courtyard and switched off the engine. 'Do you ever feel spooked living out here on your own?'

'I'm not afraid of ghosts, if that's what you mean.' Arielle was sure she'd switched the porch light on before she'd left, but the wiring in the cottage was old and the light bulbs had a habit of blowing.

Eirik got out of the truck and came round to open the passenger door. Once again, his nearness made her pulse quicken. Feeling flustered, she ignored his hand and jumped down. Her heel caught on a cobblestone, and she would have unbalanced if he hadn't caught her.

'Let me help you. Your shoes are not ideal for the terrain.'

It would be churlish to refuse. His old-fashioned chivalry was something she'd never experienced before, and butterflies fluttered in her stomach when he slipped his arm around her waist to support her over the uneven cobbles. In the dark porch Eirik used the torch on his phone so that Arielle was able to fit her key in the lock.

She opened the front door that led directly into the living room and took a deep breath. 'Thank you for bringing me home.'

'It was my pleasure.' His face was all angles and planes in the shadows cast by the lamp just inside the door that she'd switched on. He did not move, and she could hardly close the door while he was standing there.

'Well, goodnight,' she murmured.

'You could invite me in for coffee.'

'I don't have coffee. I only buy tea because it's cheaper. Do you drink tea?'

'All the time.'

There was a gleam of mischief in his eyes as well as something else that caused her heart to miss a beat. With a faint sigh, Arielle admitted to herself that she did not want the evening to end yet. 'In that case would you like to come in?'

'Thank you.' His smile made her think of a wolf, and she wondered if he viewed her as prey.

'Mind your head on the beams,' she warned as she ushered him into the living room.

He looked round the room. 'How old is this place?'

'It was built about two hundred years ago.' She had no idea if he thought the cottage was quaint or pokey. Since her father had been sent to prison, she'd covered the ancient sofa with brightly coloured throws and hung some of her mother's paintings on the walls to make the house feel more homely. 'The kitchen used to be a piggery and the bedrooms are in the attic where hay was once stored. You had better sit down,' she said, noticing that Eirik's head brushed against the low ceiling.

He dominated the small room, but it wasn't just his height and athletic build. He possessed a magnetism that would make him stand out in a crowd. 'I'll put the kettle on,' she said a little breathlessly. But she did not move. Her heart was thudding painfully hard. 'You're not a tea drinker, are you?'

'No.' He crossed the room in two strides and stared down at her. His mouth lifted at the corners, but his gaze was watchful and intense.

She gave a helpless shrug that turned into a shiver of excitement. 'Then why are you here?'

'You kissed me,' he drawled. 'I can't get the memory of your lips pressed against mine out of my mind.' His husky accent made the tiny hairs on Arielle's skin stand on end.

She felt herself blush. 'It wasn't a kiss as such. You had almost drowned, and it was necessary for me to use mouth-to-mouth resuscitation on you.'

He laughed softly as he slid his hand beneath her chin and tilted her face up. 'Explain it to yourself that way if you want, but you kissed me, *skatta*, and I liked it, a lot. So much in fact that I think we should kiss properly. What do you say?'

Arielle tried to think of a flippant response, something that would ease the screaming sexual tension, but her mind was blank. The musk of male pheromones evoked a purely feminine reaction. Her breasts felt heavy and there was a dull ache between her legs. Shockingly, she imagined pressing her pelvis up against his and opening his zip while he shoved her dress out of the way and slipped his hand between her thighs. What was happening to her? She had never thrown herself at a man, but she had never met a man like Eirik.

His eyes glittered as he lowered his face towards hers, and she was powerless to stop him. His mouth was tantalisingly close. When his arms came around her, she allowed him to draw her against the solid wall of his chest. Her senses went wild as she was enveloped in his heat and his tantalising, male scent.

'You brought me back to life three nights ago,' he murmured. His breath whispered across her cheek. He grazed his lips over hers, once, twice, tasting her with leisurely sips that sent a quiver of anticipation through Arielle. Instinctively she knew that his light, almost playful kisses were a prelude to the passion building inexorably between them.

She moaned softly when he pushed his tongue between her lips, and he answered with a low groan, angling his mouth over hers and deepening the kiss until it was flagrantly erotic. Arielle melted against him, and reality faded.

'Du er smukke,' he murmured against her lips. He smiled at her puzzled expression. 'It's Fjernlandic for you are very beautiful.'

Where was her sanity when she needed it? 'I don't think…' *That this is a good idea.* But she did not finish her sentence for the good reason that he claimed her mouth in another breath-stealing kiss.

'Much better not to think. Instead, feel what you are doing to me.' He moved his hand down to her bottom and pulled her against his hard thighs. His groan of raw sexual need evoked a quiver of longing inside her. 'Why don't we continue this upstairs in your bedroom?' he asked thickly. 'I want to make love to you, and you want that too, don't you, my little mermaid?'

She did, heaven help her! Desire swept hot and urgent through her veins as Eirik's mouth sought hers once more. He kissed her with mounting hunger, and she responded with a wild abandon she'd never experienced before, a need that made her desperate to lead him upstairs to her bed.

Reality intruded as Arielle pictured her tiny bedroom with the narrow bed that she'd slept on since she was a little girl. There was still the mural on the wall of a princess in a castle that her mother had painted. The other bedroom along the landing was bigger than her room, but it was where her father had slept, and she never, ever went into that room.

She crashed back down to earth and stiffened in Eirik's arms. He lifted his mouth from hers and gave her a quizzical look.

'I think we should slow things down,' she said unsteadily. 'It's a big leap from dinner to bed.'

He released his breath slowly and dropped his hands down to his sides. 'Forgive my impatience, but I want you very badly and we only have tonight.'

Something cold and heavy replaced the fire he'd aroused in her. 'What happens after tonight?'

'I will return to Fjernland to accept the formal title of Hereditary Prince. The health of my father, the Sovereign Prince, is not good and, with the loss of my brother, it is my duty to prepare for the day when I will become monarch.' His gaze narrowed on her frozen expression. 'You and I can only ever be two shooting stars who briefly collide before continuing on our different trajectories.'

'In England we call it a one-night stand,' she said curtly. What a fool she was for thinking that Eirik was actually interested in her as a person when clearly all he wanted was sex.

He might not be so keen if she admitted that her sexual experience was limited to one disastrous relationship.

Arielle remembered how Jack had fallen asleep immediately after sex, leaving her feeling unfulfilled. She'd assumed it was her fault their lovemaking had been disappointing. Often when she had visited Jack at his flat, he'd left a mountain of washing up and dirty laundry for her to do. He had treated her more like a servant than a girlfriend, but he had been her first and only proper relationship and she'd had low expectations as a result of growing up with her surly father, who had demanded that she kept the cottage clean and cooked his meals after her mother died when Arielle was a child.

One reason why she had been attracted to Jack was because she'd believed he did not know about her father. But he had admitted that he'd only been interested in her after he'd discovered that she was Gerran Rowse's daughter. Jack had been convinced that Arielle knew where her father had hidden money from his drug-dealing operation. Finding out that Jack had pretended to be in love with her had been another blow to her shaky self-confidence. Would she ever meet a man who genuinely wanted to be with her?

'I think you should leave,' she told Eirik stiffly.

His eyes were no longer the warm blue of summer skies. He gave her a haughty look that served as a reminder, if she had needed it, that they were not only from different countries, but they were worlds apart.

'We both got carried away,' he growled. 'There is nothing wrong with two consenting adults spending a pleasurable night together.' His jaw hardened. 'What did you expect?'

'That's my problem. I never expect anything, but maybe it's time I did.' Arielle bit down on her lower lip that felt slightly puffy from where he had kissed her with masterful passion. 'I really want you to go.' Before she made even more of an idiot of herself and burst into tears or, worse, asked him to stay.

He stared at her as if he couldn't believe she was turfing him out. It had probably never happened to him before. But she felt no sense of triumph in the thought, just a heaviness in her heart when without another word he strode across the room and opened the front door.

The breeze had picked up and above the rattle of a loose roof tile and the creaking branches of the hawthorn tree that was bowed by years of the punishing wind Arielle heard the barn door slam. Eirik stepped into the porch and his feet crunched on something on the floor. He bent down and picked up a shard of glass.

'I hadn't noticed when we arrived at the cottage, but it looks as if the light bulb was deliberately smashed.' He stooped again and, when he straightened up, Arielle saw he was holding a pebble that he'd found on the doormat.

The barn door clattered. 'I know I locked my studio,' she muttered. She grabbed a torch from the dresser, kicked off her high heels and slipped her feet into her wellington boots that were standing next to the front door.

'Wait here, and I'll go and check it out.' Eirik held out his hand for the torch. His expression told her she would be wasting her breath if she argued. She gave him the torch but followed him across the courtyard to the barn. Arielle sucked in a breath when she saw in the torch's gleam that the padlock on the door had been broken.

'Someone has been busy,' Eirik said grimly as he picked up an iron bar from the ground. 'This must have been used to break the lock.'

He pushed open the door and Arielle quickly found the

light switch on the wall. The overhead strip light flickered and then became brighter.

'Oh, no.' Her brain took a few seconds to compute the
carnage in front of her. The first things she saw were the
ripped-open boxes that she'd packed, ready to be sent to
the London department store. The numerous pieces of
eco-friendly jewellery that she'd painstakingly created
had been destroyed.

Tears filled her eyes as she looked around at the dev-
astation in her studio. Her worktable had been upended
and her collection of sea glass had been smashed and
was scattered over the floor. She bent down and picked
up two halves of a piece of pink glass that had obviously
been hit with a hammer lying on the floor nearby. 'This
was the first piece of sea glass in my collection. I found
it when I was swimming in the sea with my mother,' she
told Eirik. 'Pink sea glass is rare, and after Mum died I
kept it because it reminded me of her.'

It was idiotic to cry over bits of broken glass, she told
herself. Even worse was how much her silly treasures
that she'd collected from the sea had meant to her. She
had been hiding from real life in her studio, haunted by
her past and afraid to face the future. 'Everything is ruined,' she choked out.

'Arielle...' The sympathy in Eirik's voice was too
much to bear.

'Just...leave me alone.'

He took out his phone. 'I'll call the police.'

'No.' She hurried over to him, praying he hadn't noticed the graffiti that had been sprayed in red paint on
the wall. *Blood on your hands.* It wasn't true, but some
of the villagers believed that she had lied to protect her

father when he had been charged with the murder of the young police constable, Josh Bray.

Arielle remembered Danny Bray's accusation that she had taken over running her father's drug-dealing business. Danny could not have known that the car with dark-tinted windows that had been seen outside her cottage had been driven by Prince Eirik's private secretary.

Eirik was frowning. 'Why don't you want to report the break-in and criminal damage done to your property to the police?'

'It will create more resentment,' she said in a low voice. 'Some of the local fishermen were angry when I supported a campaign for them to use more expensive biodegradable nets to reduce the amount of discarded plastic fishing equipment in the sea.' That much was true, although Arielle did not believe it was the reason her studio had been destroyed. 'I was planning to leave Penash anyway and now I have no reason to stay.'

'Where will you go?' Eirik frowned as Arielle avoided making eye contact with him. Something was going on that he did not understand. Her reluctance to involve the police about the break-in was odd, and he was not convinced by her explanation that her environmental campaigning had angered the villagers.

She hugged her arms around herself, and he sensed that her composure was on a knife-edge. 'I don't have any definite plans,' she admitted.

'Well, I suggest you make some quickly. In the meantime, is there somewhere you can go where you will be safe?' He thought of the smashed light bulb in the porch. 'Whoever destroyed your workshop might be planning to return and break into the cottage.'

'I'm sure that won't happen.' She bit her lip and Eirik was furious with himself when his gaze was drawn to her mouth, and he remembered how soft and moist her lips had felt beneath his. 'My best friend got married last year and moved to France with her husband. I'm not close to anyone else in the village. I'll do as you suggested and apply for a job abroad.'

'That will take time.' Eirik rubbed his hand over the stubble on his jaw. The idea that had come into his mind was admittedly not sensible. But his conscience would not allow him to leave Cornwall and abandon Arielle to the mercy of the thugs who had wrecked her studio. 'I have to fly back to Fjernland tomorrow and I want you to come with me.'

She stared at him. 'Why? You said that we are on different trajectories.'

Eirik glowered at her for reminding him of his crass behaviour. He'd come onto her like a teenager with an overload of hormones, and it wasn't his style at all. He blamed it on his libido, which had kicked into life after more than a year when he'd simply felt numb. Frustration was a nagging ache in his groin. But he had been honest with Arielle. He hadn't wanted her to think he could offer more, or indeed that he wanted more, than one night of mutual pleasure.

'Don't get the wrong idea. My offer to help you leave Penash has nothing to do with what happened, or didn't happen between us,' he said sardonically. 'I am indebted to you for saving my life. You want to pick up your career, and I can make it happen.'

Her green eyes flashed. 'You don't owe me anything and I am not your responsibility.'

His patience evaporated. 'Are you always so stubborn?

You said you want to work in another country, and I happen to know that a temporary position to cover maternity leave will be available at the Fjernland Marine Research Institute. The director is a friend of mine. His wife is involved in a research project studying the effects of microplastic pollution in the oceans. Frida is expecting their first child soon and she intends to take several months off to be with the baby. I will give your CV to Valdemar. Obviously you would have to go through a proper interview process, but with your qualifications and experience I think you stand a good chance of being offered the job.'

'But I don't speak Fjernlandic,' Arielle said.

'It won't be a problem. All Fjernlanders are taught English at school from the age of five. Our national language is important, but we are a small principality and have to be able to communicate with the wider world.'

Eirik broke off when his phone rang. He cursed beneath his breath when he saw the name on the screen. Her Serene Highness, Princess Hulda—Eirik had been a toddler before he'd understood that the woman who had occasionally visited him in the palace nursery was his mother—had been short on sympathy and highly critical of his decision to take part in the AII race, which had ended disastrously for his new yacht and nearly cost him his life. A late-night call from the Princess was unexpected. 'I must take this,' Eirik excused himself to Arielle.

'Why are you still in England?' Princess Hulda did not waste her breath greeting him. 'Gustav informed me that you did not experience any ill effects from your yachting accident. It would have been nice if you had bothered to tell me yourself.'

Eirik refrained from reminding his mother that she

CHAPTER FOUR

'Was it a wise decision to invite Miss Tremain along?' Gustav murmured.

Eirik followed his private secretary's gaze across the aisle of the private jet to where Arielle was curled up on a leather recliner. She was fast asleep, which was hardly surprising as it was one o'clock in the morning. Eirik felt too wired up to sleep. 'I gather you do not think it was a wise decision,' he snapped.

'I simply thought that in light of the situation with your father's health you would not want any...distractions.'

'I spoke to my mother a few minutes ago. It appears that His Serene Highness did not have a heart attack and has been diagnosed with a condition called pericarditis, which is inflammation around the heart caused by a viral infection. Prince Otto is expected to make a full recovery.'

'I am very glad to hear that.' Gustav sat down when Eirik waved him to a chair. 'You must be extremely relieved.'

'Of course.' The news that his father's life was not in danger felt as though a weight had been lifted from Eirik's shoulders. He was reprieved from becoming the ruling monarch of Fjernland, for the time being at least.

More surprising had been the rush of emotion he'd felt. For most of his life he had not had a close relationship with Prince Otto, who had only been interested in Niels, the oldest son and heir to the throne. But recently Eirik had spent more time with his father while he'd prepared for when he would rule the principality.

A tentative rapprochement had developed between them, helped by the fact that Prince Otto had mellowed since he had battled cancer for two years. He had been given the all-clear, but this latest health scare had renewed Princess Hulda's determination that her husband should abdicate in favour of the surviving heir. However, Prince Otto had stated that he would not stand aside until Eirik was married.

'It is imperative that you choose a bride and marry her as quickly as it can be arranged.' Eirik replayed his latest phone conversation with his mother in his head. 'Baron Lundberg's daughter is ideal in every respect. She comes from one of the oldest aristocratic families in Fjernland, and she is charming, gracious and—'

'Chilly,' he had cut in.

'Don't be absurd.' Princess Hulda's voice had bristled with impatience. 'What do you even mean?'

'It doesn't matter,' he'd murmured as he'd pictured Ida's cool, blonde beauty.

'If you have decided that you do not want Ida Lundberg to be your Princess Consort there are plenty of other suitable candidates on my list.'

'Seriously, you have a list?'

'Of course I have a list. You have had over a year to choose a wife, but you have made no effort to do that one simple thing.' The Princess's displeasure had been obvious. 'It would not have been necessary if your brother had lived,' she had reminded Eirik. 'Niels would have married Princess Catalina and ascended the throne on your father's abdication.'

If only you hadn't suggested the skiing trip.

His mother's unspoken accusation had evoked a familiar, eviscerating guilt in Eirik's gut.

The truth was that Ida Lundberg would make him a perfect wife and she had made it clear when they had met at society events in the past year that she was keen to be the Princess Consort. Keener on the title than on having him as her husband, Eirik suspected cynically. Ida was renowned in European high society for her elegance and sophistication. It was impossible to imagine her swimming in a wild sea wearing a mermaid's tail.

His gaze was drawn by some invisible force to Arielle. Her riotous red curls were constrained in a thick braid. Before leaving the cottage in Cornwall she had changed out of her sexy black dress into jeans and a fine wool jumper that moulded her firm breasts. Her dark green jumper was the same colour as her eyes, which right now were hidden behind her closed eyelids. Her long auburn eyelashes were fanned on her softly flushed cheeks and beneath her left eye was a small, barely noticeable scar.

Eirik wanted to know how she had got the scar. Hell, he wanted to know everything about her. That should have set an alarm bell ringing. He enjoyed women's company in the bedroom, but he never allowed himself to be pinned down in a relationship. He was perplexed by his desperate need to cover Arielle's lush red lips with his mouth and lose himself in the unguarded sensuality of her kiss. It was that word *need* that troubled him.

His mind flew back to when they had discovered that Arielle's studio had been ransacked. He had tried to persuade her to take the job opportunity in Fjernland, but then he'd received the phone call from his mother.

'Has something happened?' Arielle had been sweeping up the broken glass on the floor. She'd leaned the broom against the wall and hurried over to him. 'You look as if you have received bad news.'

'My father has collapsed, and I must return to Fjernland tonight.'

'How awful. I'm so sorry.' She had put her hand on his arm, and the gentle expression in her sea green eyes had tugged on something inside Eirik. Arielle's livelihood had been destroyed, but she had been more concerned for him, and her compassion had shaken him.

'I need you to come with me,' he'd blurted out. He did not know where the words had come from. For as long as he could remember he had only cared about his brother. Since Niels had gone, the warm place in Eirik's heart where his brother had resided had frozen over. Arielle had looked as shocked as Eirik had felt.

'You saved my life and now it is my turn to help you,' he'd told her. He had assured himself that obviously it was what he had meant. 'I don't feel responsible for you,' he'd insisted when he'd seen the storm brewing in her eyes. 'I will introduce you to the head of Fjernland's Marine Research Institute, and it will be for Valdemar to decide whether to offer you a job, and for you to accept or not. The likelihood is that you and I will not meet again when I am busy with royal duties.'

It was the truth, Eirik brooded as his mind returned to the present. The minute the plane landed in Fjernland his life would no longer be his own. He would go straight to the hospital to visit his father and then to the palace, where he might manage to snatch a couple of hours' sleep before a day of meetings with royal advisors and government ministers in his capacity as the Reigning Sovereign's deputy. He certainly would not have time to be distracted by a flame-haired siren.

Beside him Gustav cleared his throat. 'I was wondering what plans you have made for Miss Tremain when we arrive in Fjernland. Might I suggest that it would not be a good idea for you to be seen with her in public? No doubt there will be news reporters outside the hospital and at Sejrrig Palace.'

The private secretary was right. The information that Prince Otto was in hospital had been leaked to the press and it was likely that there would also be paparazzi photographers outside the building where Eirik owned a penthouse apartment. Not that he had considered taking Arielle there. Tempting though she was, he must put duty before his personal pleasure from now on. But she would have to stay somewhere until he could arrange for her to have an interview at the marine research institute. He could send her to a hotel, but his conscience pricked that it would be unfair to abandon her in a strange country.

He needed to take Arielle somewhere where she would not attract the attention of the press or cause gossip among the palace staff. A place that was out of the way, and with someone whose discretion he could rely on.

Catalina was the obvious solution. She understood him better than anyone and they had forged a strong bond through their shared grief for Niels. Eirik sent a text message on his phone. When he glanced at his private secretary, he saw that Gustav's head had drooped and his chin was resting on his chest.

He had been a surly sixteen-year-old when Gustav had been appointed as his equerry. Over the years the older man had become a loyal and trusted friend, and in many ways he had been a better father than Eirik's own father. He stood up and pressed the control panel to recline Gustav's chair before covering him with a blanket.

He looked over at Arielle and his heart banged against his ribs as his eyes met her sea green gaze. She stretched her arms above her head, and he felt a certain part of his anatomy jerk to attention when her jumper rose up to reveal a strip of bare stomach above the waistband of her jeans.

Faen! Eirik cursed beneath his breath. He could not remember ever being so fiercely attracted to a woman. After Niels had died, he had felt bereft, and he'd lost interest in everything, including sex. Arielle had reignited his urges, but, for a man who had always been in control of himself, it was disconcerting to find that his body had a will of its own.

'We will arrive in Fjernland in just over an hour,' he informed her in a cool voice that he hoped disguised the fire raging inside him.

She gave a tiny yawn. 'I don't think Gustav approves of me.'

'Possibly he doesn't. He thinks you could be trouble.'

Her eyes widened. 'What do you mean?'

'Gustav knows that I find you desirable.' Eirik decided that if he acknowledged the problem he would be able to deal with his inconvenient attraction and dismiss it.

Colour ran along Arielle's high cheekbones. 'You do?'

'Don't pretend you are unaware of what you do to me. We both feel an awareness, chemistry, whatever you want to call it.'

She nibbled her lower lip but did not deny the truth of his statement.

'Gustav's concern is unnecessary,' Eirik assured Arielle. 'Our stars briefly orbited each other, but from now on our lives are set on different paths. You want to kick-start your career and I will become the ruling sovereign of my country.'

But first there was the matter of his marriage, which would happen sooner rather than later if his mother had her way.

Arielle leaned back in her seat and closed her eyes again, but she had napped for a couple of hours and no longer felt sleepy. When she had boarded the private jet with Eirik, she'd been overwhelmed by tiredness, partly as a result of the shock of discovering that her studio had been destroyed. She was sure that Danny Bray had been responsible, but if she'd reported the break-in to the police, as Eirik had wanted her to do, there had been a chance that he would have learned of her father's crimes.

Through her half-closed eyelashes she studied the Prince, who was sprawled in a chair on the opposite side of the plane. He had opened his laptop and took no further notice of her. Eirik was an enigma, Arielle thought ruefully. In one breath he'd admitted that he desired her, but he'd gone on to say that when they arrived in Fjernland he would be busy with his royal duties, and they were unlikely to meet again. Clearly he would not find it difficult to dismiss her from his mind, but she doubted she would forget him so easily. It was silly to feel hurt that Eirik planned to abandon her once he had introduced her to the head of the marine research institute, but it emphasised that all he'd wanted was to have sex with her for one night.

Arielle remembered that Eirik had said he wanted to

help her leave Cornwall because he felt indebted to her for saving him when his yacht had sunk in the storm. It was hard to believe that she had finally left the cottage in Penash where she had felt trapped by her father's control over her, and, after he had been sent to prison, by her lack of confidence. She felt a mixture of trepidation and excitement as she tried to imagine herself living and working in Fjernland.

The only other time she had been abroad was when she'd gone to France for her best friend's wedding. Flora had been in Arielle's class at school and had also been bullied by some of the other girls because her mother had a reputation in the village for having numerous lovers. Now Flora was happily married to Jean-Luc, who owned a vineyard in Provence. Arielle was glad for her friend, and a little envious. Would she ever meet a man who would love and cherish her? She had often wondered if her mother had loved her father when she had married him. It was hard to imagine that Gerran had ever been kind or loving. Falling in love required a leap of faith, and Arielle's childhood had left her with trust issues. It was odd then, she thought with a jolt, that she trusted Eirik enough to leave Cornwall to start a new life in his country.

She must have dozed, and she woke to the sound of her name. Eirik was leaning over her and dropped his hand from her shoulder when she stirred. Her gaze meshed with his and she recognised the flare of sexual interest in his bright blue eyes before he straightened up abruptly as if he'd felt as burned by their momentary closeness as she did.

'We are about to land,' he told her. 'I must go to the

hospital to see my father, but first I'll take you to stay with a friend of mine for the remainder of the night.'

'I can go to a hotel rather than disturb your friend.'

'Catalina is expecting you. Fasten your seat belt,' he instructed, giving her no chance to ask further questions as he returned to his seat in preparation for the landing.

A car was waiting for them at the side of the runway. Eirik had explained that Fjernland's main airport was near the capital city Ved Floden, but they had come to a private airfield. He ushered Arielle into the back of the car and slid in beside her. Gustav got into the front, next to the driver. Arielle felt a definite vibe of disapproval from Eirik's private secretary. She stared out of the window, but in the darkness she could not make out much, especially when the road wound through thick woodland. Eventually they came to a clearing where there was a large house. The chauffeur opened the door and she followed Eirik across the driveway to the front door, which was opened by a butler.

As they stepped inside, a woman walked towards them. She was exotically beautiful, with long, lustrous black hair. She carried herself with a curiously regal bearing and her kaftan-style dress whispered around her ankles so that she appeared to glide across the floor. The many gold bangles on her wrists gleamed in the light from the chandelier.

'*Caro,*' she greeted Eirik warmly and kissed him on both cheeks. 'It is good to see you.'

'Lina,' he murmured softly. 'I did not expect you to wait up.'

The woman gave a heavy sigh. 'You know how it is. I do not sleep well.'

'This is Arielle Tremain.' Eirik turned to Arielle. 'May I introduce Princess Catalina of San Sabinus?'

Princess! Arielle had a vague idea that San Sabinus was a principality somewhere off the coast of southern Italy. She remembered her manners and quickly curtseyed to the Princess.

Princess Catalina's faint smile did not reach her eyes. 'Gerado will show you to your room, Miss Tremain.'

The butler took Arielle's bag that Eirik had carried from the car. She hesitated and her heart sank as she wondered if this was the last time she would see him. She wanted to ask him about his friendship with the beautiful princess.

'I'll be in contact tomorrow to let you know about your interview at the marine research institute.' Eirik's handsome face showed no emotion, and his dismissive tone suggested that he had quashed the spark of desire he'd felt for her.

'Thank you.' Arielle kept her tone as cool as his had been. As she followed the butler across the entrance hall, she heard Princess Catalina speak to Eirik.

'Is there any news on your father?'

'His condition is not as serious as was first thought.'

'Thank God you are spared another tragedy, *caro*.' There was raw emotion in the Princess's voice.

The following morning, when Arielle woke up, she was disorientated for a few moments before she remembered where she was. It had been a disturbed night, and she did not function well without a solid eight hours of sleep. A shower revived her somewhat. She had thrown clean underwear and a few other essentials into an overnight bag before she'd left the cottage with Eirik. After pulling on jeans and sweater, she ventured out of her room and went downstairs.

The house was large and rather gloomy, surrounded by thick forest that blocked the light coming through the windows. In the distance Arielle saw the gleam of water. The sound of someone weeping drew her towards the dining room. The table was laid for breakfast, but Princess Catalina was not eating. She had buried her face in her hands and her sobs were heart-wrenching.

Arielle was torn between the need to respect the Princess's privacy and a deep sense of compassion. 'Forgive me for intruding,' she murmured as she stepped into the room. 'Is there anything I can do to help you?'

'I am afraid not.' Princess Catalina lowered her hands from her face. Her eyes were red and puffy from crying. She indicated that Arielle should sit down. 'So you are the mermaid. Eirik told me how you saved his life,' she explained, noticing Arielle's start of surprise.

'He told me that you are a close friend of his,' she said stiffly.

The Princess nodded. 'I was engaged to Eirik's brother, Prince Niels.'

Of course. Arielle remembered why Princess Catalina's name had seemed familiar. When Prince Niels had been killed just over a year ago, it had been reported that his fiancée was distraught. 'I'm so sorry.'

'Eirik loved his brother as deeply as I adored Niels. Since the accident we have grieved together.' Catalina sighed. 'Both our lives have been changed for ever. I would have become the Princess Consort on my marriage to Niels, who was to have become the Reigning Sovereign. Prince Otto wishes to abdicate and pass the responsibilities of being the monarch to his remaining son, but he is insistent that Eirik must choose a bride and marry to produce an heir.'

A heavy weight dropped into the pit of Arielle's stomach. 'Does Eirik have someone in mind?' she asked, trying to sound casual, but she saw Princess Catalina give her a speculative look.

'It is expected that he will soon make a formal announcement of his betrothal to the daughter of Fjernland's second most important family. Ida Lundberg is entirely suitable to be the Princess Consort, and Eirik will be involved with the preparations for a royal wedding.'

The Princess rose to her feet and gathered her silk robe around her. 'Please sit and enjoy your breakfast,' she said when Arielle made to stand up. 'I understand that Eirik's staff packed up your belongings at your house in England and your luggage arrived early this morning. If you want to swim, the lake is heated by geothermal activity and I am told it is as warm as a bath, although I have not swum in it myself.'

Princess Catalina walked across the room and paused in the doorway. 'One more thing. I do not recommend that you fall in love with the Prince. He has assured his parents that he will devote himself to duty and the monarchy, and there will be no room in his life for…distractions.'

Arielle was reeling from the news that Eirik intended to marry. No wonder he had said he could only spend one night with her when he'd kissed her at the cottage, she thought dismally. She felt her face grow warm. 'I definitely won't fall for him,' she said staunchly. But she couldn't promise not to boil Eirik in oil if she got the chance.

Princess Catalina studied her for a few moments.

'Love is the greatest beauty and tragedy of our lives,' she told Arielle softly before she swept out of the room.

The mountains in the distance were snow-capped, and this far north of the equator the spring sunshine did not have much heat, but the temperature of the geothermal lake was warm enough for Arielle to swim without a wetsuit. Swimming was usually her stress release. The water was crystal clear, and she dived deep, propelled by her monofin tail that she'd found with the rest of her luggage. Rising to the surface again, she floated on her back and stared up at the cloudless sky.

When she had left Cornwall last night, she'd felt excited about coming to Fjernland. But today she was apprehensive about her future in a strange country where she had only a vague suggestion of a possible job, and she did not know anyone apart from the Prince, who had made it clear he would not have any time for her. For once in her life, she had acted impulsively, but now she was beset by doubts.

Although it was foolish, she was disappointed that there was no chance of the attraction between her and Eirik developing into…what? Arielle asked herself. He had been honest with her and said they could not have more than a one-night stand. It was entirely her fault that her heart had longed for a fairy-tale romance with a handsome prince. But the stark reality was that Eirik must marry, and he certainly would not choose a woman with her background to be his princess. Arielle had searched on the Internet for information about Eirik's possible future wife and discovered that the houses of Sorensen and Lundberg could be traced back to when Viking warriors had fought bloody battles to claim independence for

Fjernland. And then there was Ida herself. Photographs showed her to be classically beautiful and the epitome of elegance and refinement. She was highly regarded in court circles and would be a popular choice with the Fjernlandic people when Eirik made her his Princess Consort.

So why had he flirted with her? Arielle knew the answer. He had shown her a glimpse of heaven when he'd held her in his arms, and she had convinced herself that there had been tenderness in his kiss. But all Eirik had wanted was to scratch an itch. She was glad she hadn't succumbed to his potent charm. At her cottage in Cornwall it had been Eirik's last night of freedom before returning to Fjernland and the life of duty that awaited him, and presumably he had decided that she would be a convenient bed-mate. It was ridiculous how badly the truth hurt. *She* was ridiculous. Angry with herself for being such a fool, Arielle ducked beneath the surface and swam to the far end of the lake.

When she looked back towards the house, she saw a boat being rowed across the lake. The bright sunshine turned Eirik into a gilded god, and he had the physique of a top athlete as he powered the oars through the water. Arielle's pulse quickened. She had not expected to see him again and she'd assumed he would be busy with royal duties. He had told her on the plane that Prince Otto hadn't suffered a heart attack but would need time to recover from an illness.

Reluctant to face Eirik while her emotions were in turmoil, Arielle dived down to the bottom of the lake and hoped he would row back to the shore. Looking up through the clear water, she could see the dark shape of the underside of the boat. Eventually a need for air meant she had to swim to the surface.

'There you are,' he said softly when he saw her. His smile drove the breath that she'd just snatched into her lungs out again in a whoosh. He was *so* handsome and, despite herself, Arielle felt her treacherous body respond to his potency.

'Aren't you a bit overdressed for boating?' she murmured, eyeing his exquisitely tailored three-piece suit. He had taken the jacket off and draped it over the seat in the boat. His shirt sleeves were rolled up to his elbows and his blue silk waistcoat emphasised the broadness of his chest.

'I had breakfast with the Foreign Minister, and I was in meetings for the rest of the morning. There are a lot of arrangements to be made for a big event that will take place soon.'

He must mean his wedding. Arielle hated how her heart dropped into the pit of her stomach. Eirik meant nothing to her, she reminded herself. He leaned over the side of the boat and stretched out his hand to trace the edge of her sparkly green bikini top. She held her breath when his knuckles brushed against the slopes of her breasts, above the triangles of stretchy material. 'You are certainly not overdressed,' he said roughly. 'You are a siren, and you have cast a spell on me, *skatta*. I can't stop thinking about you.'

Time stopped, and her foolish heart leapt. She tilted her face up and her eyes locked with his brilliant blue gaze. Eirik's lips were centimetres away from hers and Arielle shivered in anticipation of his kiss. A cloud blotted out the warmth of the sun, and she shivered again as cold disgust replaced the heat in her veins. Eirik was as good as engaged to be married, and in Arielle's opinion he had no right to say that he could not stop thinking about her, much less to be about to kiss her. She snatched her mouth away from the temptation of his and, with a flick of her monofin tail, dived beneath the boat and surfaced again on the other side.

He grinned. 'Give me a minute to strip off and I'll join you in the water.'

'What a good idea.' She was furious with him and with herself for being so fiercely attracted to him. Arielle told herself that she deserved better than to be a brief distraction for a prince before he settled to married life. She placed her hands on the edge of the boat and used all her strength to pull down, just as Eirik stood up and started to undo the belt on his trousers. The boat rocked dangerously.

'Hey, what are you doing?' He tried to balance himself, but she held onto the gunwale and gave a hard, downwards tug. Her tail gave her extra momentum, and as the boat tipped over Eirik was catapulted into the lake. Arielle heard him swear before there was a splash. She did not wait around and started to swim towards the shore, kicking her tail to propel herself in a sinuous motion through the water.

The stony beach where she had left her clothes was farther away than she'd realised. She was breathing hard by the time she reached the shallows. When she glanced over her shoulder, she panicked when she saw that Eirik had hauled himself back into the boat and was rowing after her.

The monofin had allowed Arielle to swim fast, but now she was stranded on the beach. She frantically attempted to wriggle out of the mermaid costume that had moulded itself to her lower body. In normal circumstances she could slip the tail on and off in a few minutes, but she was flustered and sweating. She cursed as she tried to tug the clingy material over her hips while keeping an eye on the boat as it came nearer.

'Goddammit!' Her situation was laughably ridiculous, but Eirik's furious expression warned her that he was not amused.

He jumped out of the boat and dragged it onto the pebbles. 'What the hell did you do that for? Thanks to your juvenile actions, my suit is ruined, and my jacket is at the bottom of the lake with my credit cards and phone.'

His trousers were soaked and plastered to his hard thighs. Through his wet shirt clinging to his chest Arielle could see the outline of his impressive pectoral muscles. Her heart missed a beat when he unfastened the buttons and slipped his shirt off so that he could ring the water out of it. She tore her gaze from his tanned chest covered with whorls of golden hairs and vainly tried to shift herself across the stones, but she was hampered by her tail.

Eirik gave a triumphant laugh. 'I've heard of a fish out of water, but never a mermaid. You are well and truly trapped, my beauty.'

CHAPTER FIVE

ARIELLE MADE ANOTHER attempt to shuffle away from Eirik, but it was futile when the lower half of her body was tightly wrapped in a tube of silicone rubber—recycled of course.

'Not so fast,' he mocked her. He dropped to his knees and straddled her with his thighs on either side of her body. She caught her breath when she realised that the angry gleam in his eyes was mixed with something more dangerous. The air around them simmered with sexual tension, but she was determined to resist her treacherous body's desire for him.

'Leave me alone.' She pushed against his chest, but he captured her wrists in his hands and held them above her head.

'I thought the point of the game was for me to chase, and for you to capitulate, *skatta*.'

'We are not playing a game.' To her horror, the idea of capitulating to Eirik's sensual demands made her breathing quicken. 'I don't know what *skatta* means,' she muttered, hoping to distract his attention from the swift rise and fall of her breasts.

He shrugged. 'In English I suppose it means honey or sweetheart.' His eyes were still on her breasts and

Arielle was mortified when she felt her nipples swell, and she knew the hard points must be visible through her bikini top.

'I am not your sweetheart. How could you put me in such a humiliating position? I don't mean the one I'm in now,' she snapped when his brows rose. She was pinned beneath him and totally at his mercy.

She bit her lip. 'You should not have brought me here to Princess Catalina's house. I feel awkward that I have invaded her privacy while she is grieving for her fiancé, your brother, Niels.'

Eirik lifted himself off Arielle and sat beside her on the pebbles. He raked his hand through his wet hair. 'I did not want to abandon you at a hotel, and it was only for last night. I rushed through my meetings this morning so I could come to collect you and take you to your interview with the director of the marine institute.'

He sighed heavily. 'Catalina was devastated when Niels was killed a week before their wedding, and she could not bear to return to San Sabinus. Instead, she came here to the holiday home they had bought as a place to escape to, away from the spotlight of royal life. In the past year she and I have grown close. Lina would have been my sister-in-law and she loved Niels as much as I did,' he said gruffly.

Arielle had finally managed to peel her mermaid's tail down her legs and slipped her feet out of the moulded foot compartment of the monofin. Beneath the costume she was wearing tiny bikini bottoms. She flushed when Eirik roved his bold gaze over her skimpily clad figure. The warmth of feminine arousal between her legs made her despise her body for its weakness for him.

'Princess Catalina told me that you are going to marry

an aristocratic woman, Ida Lundberg.' She glared at Eirik. 'You had no right to kiss me and ask me to sleep with you when you had already promised to make another woman your bride.'

He frowned. 'You're wrong—'

'Don't tell me I'm wrong.' Arielle's temper blazed. She had spent most of her life feeling voiceless, too afraid of her father to speak out against him. She hadn't complained when Jack had treated her badly because she'd felt worthless and been grateful that he was her boyfriend.

She stood up and marched over to where she had left her clothes, trying not to wince as the pebbles dug into the soles of her feet. She thrust one leg into her jeans and hopped inelegantly while she stepped into the other leg. Her heart crashed into her ribs when she turned her head and discovered that Eirik had followed her up the beach. His close proximity and raw masculinity made her feel dizzy.

She yanked her jeans up her legs with such force that the denim scraped over her thighs. 'You made a fool of me when you kissed me knowing that you have a fiancée.'

'I am not engaged to Ida Lundberg,' he bit out. 'I haven't promised her or any other woman that I will marry them.'

'But Princess Catalina said that everyone expects you will formally announce your betrothal to Ida. And you told me that you had spent this morning planning a big event. I assumed you meant your wedding.' Arielle searched Eirik's face for any signs that he had lied. He held her gaze steadily, and she was the first to break eye contact.

He exhaled heavily. 'I am under pressure to marry a woman from an aristocratic background who will be my

Princess Consort when I become ruler of Fjernland. My mother has let it be known publicly that she believes Ida Lundberg is the ideal candidate for the role, but I have not formally discussed the matter with Ida.'

Yet. Arielle mentally filled in the space when Eirik hesitated. She had always known he was out of her league, she reminded herself. But she felt a little happier knowing that, when he'd kissed her, he hadn't been cheating on a woman who had hopes of marrying him.

He stepped closer to her and took her sweater, which she was clutching tightly as if it were a security blanket, out of her fingers. 'For now, I am a bachelor and free to kiss whoever I desire,' he drawled.

Did he mean that he desired her? The sun was in her eyes, and she could not read his expression, but she hadn't imagined the hunger that thickened his voice. A shiver of longing ran through her. She did not move and could barely breathe as he lowered his face towards hers.

'Tell me you don't feel the same way and I'll end this madness now,' he said rawly.

The sensible thing would be to walk away from him. But Arielle did not want to be sensible. She could not lie and so she said nothing. Her lips parted in an unconscious invitation and Eirik's eyes narrowed to gleaming slits as he slanted his mouth over hers. He made her wait a fraction longer, and she trembled, every nerve ending on her body so acutely aware of him that it *hurt*.

She heard a low moan and realised as he closed the tiny gap between their mouths that the husky plea had come from her. But then her mind went blank as Eirik claimed her lips in a kiss that was thrillingly possessive. It was different from when he'd kissed her at the cottage. Then he had taken his time and teased her with light, almost playful caresses. But now there was nothing teasing in the way he ground his mouth down on hers and pushed his tongue between her lips.

Now there was heat and flame as her body caught light. The stubble on his jaw felt abrasive against her cheek when he kissed his way up to the sensitive place behind her ear before he nipped her earlobe with his teeth. She pressed herself closer to him and felt the play of hard muscles beneath her palms when she placed her hands on his chest. His skin felt like satin, overlaid with soft hairs that were springy beneath her fingertips.

Eirik tightened his arm around her waist and pushed his other hand between their bodies to cup her breast. He rubbed his thumb over her nipple and sensation shivered through her. The thin material of her bikini was a frustrating barrier. She wanted his hands on her naked skin and she must have spoken out loud because he laughed softly and brought his other hand up her back to release the clasp on her bikini top.

It fell away and he closed his fingers around her bare breast, playing with her nipple and making her gasp with pleasure. Reality faded, and Arielle was aware of nothing but this golden prince who seemed to understand her body better than she did herself. He seemed to know of the insistent ache between her thighs and clamped his hand on her bottom, hauling her against him so that her pelvis was flush to his and her bones turned to liquid when she felt the hard proof of his arousal.

It had been a mistake to kiss Arielle. Eirik knew it the moment his lips met hers, but the taste of her was more intoxicating than a fine wine and he wanted more. She was so damned responsive, pressing herself up against him and winding her arms around his neck as she opened her mouth beneath his and held nothing back.

Her soft breast filled his palm, and he liked the way she moaned when he rolled her nipple between his thumb and forefinger. He liked it way too much. It was as if he had never done this before. He felt as excited as a teenager exploring a woman's body for the first time. But Eirik had done a lot of exploring and he'd slept with more women than he could remember. This was different, this insane need to strip Arielle naked and possess her with fast, hard strokes.

Where could he do it? Here? He tore his mouth from hers and glanced around him. The lake was some distance from the house, and they were unlikely to be disturbed by Princess Catalina or the household staff. But the pebbly beach would be an uncomfortable place to have sex. He thought of carrying Arielle up to the grassy bank and making love to her there. But he did not have a condom, and she might not use any sort of contraceptive.

Finally, Eirik's brain kicked into gear. He could not risk having unprotected sex with Arielle. And definitely not in a place that had been special to his brother. He remembered when he and Niels had sat beside the lake and talked of the future.

'I will bring my children here and teach them to swim. Catalina and I are planning to try for a baby as soon as we are married,' Niels had said.

'You need an heir.' Eirik had thanked his lucky stars that he was not the future Sovereign and did not have to bother with marriage or babies.

'I want a baby with Lina because I love her more than I knew it was possible to love someone. Wait until it happens to you,' Niels had told Eirik with a smile.

'Love creeps up on you when you are not expecting it, and then—*pow*!'

But Niels's life had been obliterated by an avalanche and the crown would pass to Prince Otto's second-born son. The second-best son, Eirik thought grimly. It was how his parents had always made him feel. He had told himself he didn't care and had built a life and career away from the stifling royal court. He had made a fortune and was a multimillionaire in his own right. That achievement at least had impressed his father. But now his future would be very different from the freedom and independence he had once enjoyed.

He had begun the process of selling his business, Sorensen Yachts,, and he was preparing to devote his life to duty. It was up to him to prove he was worthy of the role that should have been his brother's. So what was he doing, instigating casual sex with a beautiful siren who could never be his Princess Consort? Arielle would lure him to his doom unless he resisted her sensual witchery.

Eirik stared into her sea green eyes and knew for sure that she had cast a spell on him when she reached up and pressed her lips to his. Her sweet breath filled his mouth and he kissed her because he simply could not stop himself. She was heat and flame and he was burning up. He had never felt so out of control.

The sobering thought made him wrench his mouth from hers and set her away from him. Her hair was drying into titian curls and her bare breasts were creamy globes tipped with dusky rose nipples that he ached to suck on.

'This can't lead anywhere,' he told Arielle. His voice rasped in his throat.

'I don't care.' Her eyes were glazed and there was a

hectic flush on her cheeks. She put her hands on his chest and he wondered if she could feel the erratic thud of his heart. 'I know that our lives are on different paths, but I want this one time with you before we go our separate ways. I want you to teach me everything, Eirik.'

He understood then just how much of a threat she was. The temptation to pull her back into his arms and take what she was offering was an insistent drumbeat in his blood. His arousal was uncomfortably hard. But an alarm bell rang inside his head.

'Teach you? Are you saying that you are a virgin?' He must have sounded as appalled as he felt.

Arielle bit her lip. 'No, of course I'm not. I had a boy-friend for a while. Not a very nice one as it happens. It… sex…wasn't great, and, if you must know, he didn't… satisfy me.'

Faen! Eirik swore silently. Arielle's face was scarlet. Her vulnerability was the most dangerous thing of all. He suspected that, for her, sex and emotions were inex-tricably linked. But he did not do emotions.

He captured her hands and pulled them away from his chest before he stepped back from her. 'This was a mistake.' He forced himself to sound coolly dismissive, despite the thunderous desire still pounding inside him. He could not risk having sex with Arielle and for her to think that he might develop feelings for her. There was no chance of that happening.

Impossibly her face turned even redder, and the blush spread down her throat and décolletage. Eirik wondered if her pale breasts would flush so prettily pink with the heat of sexual desire. But he would never find out.

'You started this,' she said in a low voice that held the suspicion of tears.

'And now I'm finishing it.' He stooped to pick up her jumper and held it out to her. 'Get dressed.' Eirik hoped he would feel more in control of himself when he was not faced with the tantalising sight of Arielle's naked breasts.

'I told you the truth when I said I have not promised marriage to any woman. But the event I have been involved in organising is a masquerade ball, which will take place two weeks from now, at my official residence, the Winter Palace. The ball is to celebrate my birthday.' He grimaced. 'My mother has decided that it is an ideal opportunity to invite every woman who she deems suitable to be my future Princess Consort, and there is an expectation that I will announce I have chosen my bride.'

'You make it sound so businesslike. How can you be sure you will fall in love with a woman who has your mother's approval?'

'I have no intention of falling in love. Nor do I want a wife who might fall in love with me. In that respect Ida Lundberg is ideal. Since childhood, her goal has been to become the Princess Consort. Her father hoped she would marry my brother, but Niels met Princess Catalina and it was love at first sight. Now Baron Lundberg sees another opportunity to link our two families.'

'How romantic,' Arielle said drily. 'Why is your mother in such a rush for you to get married?'

'Two years ago, my father was diagnosed with a malignant tumour. While he underwent treatment, he gave in to my mother's pleas for him to abdicate and allow Niels to become ruler of Fjernland with Princess Catalina as Consort after their wedding. Obviously that did not happen,' Eirik said gruffly. 'Prince Otto has made a full recovery from cancer, but my mother is desperate for him to retire from public life. My father has agreed to stand down in favour of me, but only when I have a wife who will hopefully give me an heir.'

Eirik looked away from Arielle's wide-eyed stare. He was royalty and this was how these things were arranged. That was what he had been taught. Love played no part in the begetting of heirs who would ensure the House of Sorensen's bloodline as rulers of the principality that few people outside Fjernland had heard of.

By lucky chance his brother had fallen in love with a princess, who would have been his bride. But Eirik knew there was a dark side to love. Jealousy, despair, rejection; he understood that his mother had suffered those things in her marriage to his father, and he had experienced them himself when he'd been hurt by his parents' indifference before he had learned to detach from his emotions.

He glanced at his watch. 'We should get back.' He waited while Arielle rolled up her mermaid's tail, and she followed him as he strode up the beach. The path through the woods was just wide enough for them to walk side by side. The tall trees all around made the air feel close, or perhaps it was his intense awareness of the woman beside him that constricted his lungs.

'My mother was in her early twenties when she fell in love with my father. Prince Otto was nearly forty and enjoyed a playboy lifestyle before and after they were married.'

Eirik was aware of the surprised look Arielle gave him. He had no idea why he was telling her about his dysfunctional family. 'My parents were civil towards each other, but I never saw affection between them. I was about thirteen when I heard a rumour circulating at the palace that Prince Otto's dalliance with a kitchen maid was not his first affair, nor likely to be his last.' He shrugged. 'My father married because he needed a son, and Princess Hulda duly provided an heir and a spare. She showered her love that her husband had spurned on my brother.'

'What about you? Surely your mother loved you as much as your brother.'

'I was only ever an afterthought, an insurance policy if something happened to Niels. I'm not telling you this because I want sympathy,' he growled. 'I am my father's son, and for me marriage is an unavoidable duty. I cannot promise the woman I will marry love and romance. All I can offer is a crown.'

'You still haven't explained the urgency for you to get married.'

'My mother nursed my father when he had cancer, and after thirty-six years of marriage Prince Otto fell in love with his wife. Finally, my mother has what she has always wanted—her husband's full attention. But my father will not retire from royal duties until I marry.'

The weight of his guilt and his mother's expectations were a burden that Eirik would always carry. 'I can't deny my mother her chance of happiness with my father in retirement. Niels would have become the Reigning Sovereign a year ago. It's my fault that my brother died.'

Arielle halted and turned to face him. 'I remember a news report that Prince Niels had lost his life in a skiing accident. How can it have been your fault?'

'The skiing trip was my idea. It was meant to be an opportunity for us to spend a few days chilling out together before Niels took on the responsibilities of a husband and the ruler of Fjernland.'

'You didn't make the avalanche happen,' Arielle said

gently. She put her hand on his arm. 'Eirik, you can't blame yourself.'

He did not deserve her compassion. 'My mother blames me and rightly so. When we were growing up, my brother was the serious one and I was the clown. I felt it was my role to make sure he had some fun before he devoted the rest of his life to duty. My parents believed I was a bad influence, and so it proved. If I hadn't suggested the skiing holiday Niels would still be here. I will have to live with that for the rest of my life. I am the replacement heir to the throne, and I will choose as my bride a woman who is best suited to be the future Princess Consort.'

Arielle opened the car window and took a deep breath of sea air. Eirik had driven through the busy centre of Fjernland's capital city, Ved Floden. Now they had left the city behind and were on a road that ran parallel to the coast. The sky and sea were forget-me-not blue, but the snow-topped mountains across the bay were a reminder that, despite the spring sunshine, the temperature was in single digits.

She darted a glance at Eirik. Before they had left Princess Catalina's house by the lake, he had changed out of his wet clothes into jeans and a raincloud-grey cashmere sweater, and he looked divine. Conversation between them during the hour and a half journey to the city had been limited to Eirik pointing out places of interest and her mumbling a response.

Arielle shuddered with embarrassment when she remembered how she had practically begged him to make love to her. She did not understand what had come over her. Eirik had revealed a sensual side to her nature that she'd been unaware of, and she had been eager to explore the feelings he aroused in her. To cap it all she had blurted out that her only sexual relationship had been a disaster.

It was not surprising that he had rejected her clumsy advances. And he had made it very clear that she was nothing like the kind of woman he would choose for a wife. But she'd already known that. She did not have a drop of blue blood in her body. Giving a deep sigh, Arielle stared out of the window, glad of the distraction of the stunning scenery.

'The mountains remind me of white meringues,' she murmured. 'Do they always have snow on them?'

'The ice on the summits never melts, unless there is an eruption of course.' Eirik laughed when he glanced at Arielle's startled expression. 'There are several glacier-covered volcanos in Fjernland and two that are currently active. The last time one erupted was twenty years ago.'

His smile made her heart thump madly, and she quickly turned her head to look out of the window again. The buildings next to the coast were mostly single-storey wooden houses. Whereas the city skyline had been dominated by tall office blocks. Eirik had explained that much of Fjernland's wealth came from banking and technology, and tourism was a thriving industry.

'The volcanos are a draw for tourists,' he said now. 'Visitors come hoping to see the aurora borealis, and there are many health spas, which advertise treatments in the natural hot springs. It's a fine balance between the income generated by tourism, and the importance of protecting Fjernland's unique and beautiful landscape.'

Arielle's gaze was drawn to his handsome profile. 'You obviously love your country, but you don't want to rule it.'

'I never said I do not want to be the Sovereign,' he muttered. 'I did not expect that the role would be mine— and I'm not sure I will be any good.' The hint of vulnerability in this strong man tugged on Arielle's heart. 'My brother was taught practically from birth the protocols and duties of being the monarch,' Eirik continued. 'Niels was better suited to royal life than me. He accepted that things have been done the same way for centuries, but I find many of the old ways stuffy and archaic in the twenty-first century.'

'Why don't you change the old ways? I mean, you will be the Reigning Sovereign and you can make the rules. Maybe instead of trying to emulate your brother, you should do things your way.'

He snorted. 'You make it sound simple, but the traditions of the monarchy have stayed the same for hundreds of years.'

'Making changes isn't easy,' Arielle agreed. Her lack of self-confidence stemmed from growing up with her controlling father. Even when she'd become an adult, she had studied for her degree at a university in Cornwall because she'd lacked the courage to move to a different part of the country to escape her father's influence.

Since Gerran Rowse had been sent to prison, she had been a virtual recluse at her studio, fearful of pushing herself out into the wider world where she might be judged by people who had heard of her father's appalling crimes. But thanks to Eirik, she had the chance of working in marine conservation again, and she hoped that her father's notoriety had not reached remote Fjernland. Without Eirik's help, she might never have found the courage to leave Penash.

Arielle surfaced from her thoughts when Eirik drove

through a gateway with a sign above it that read Fjern-land Marine Research Institute. He parked the car in front of a large building that was a striking mix of old and new architecture.

'The site used to be owned by Fjernland's biggest brewery,' he explained. 'After a century of beer produc-tion here, the company moved to new premises. I saw the potential of the building when I decided to establish the marine research institute. The close proximity to the sea makes it an ideal location, and the laboratories and test-ing facilities are among the best in the world.'

'Well, I guess this is it,' Arielle said huskily. She pushed a stray curl that had escaped from her chignon, behind her ear, and smoothed an imagined crease from her blue dress.

'There is no need to feel nervous,' Eirik told her. 'Valdemar is impressed with your CV.'

She let him think she was uptight about her interview, but the truth was it had occurred to her that she would probably never meet Eirik again. Soon his father would abdicate and Eirik would become the Reigning Sover-eign, and he would be assisted by the woman he chose to be his Princess Consort.

He got out of the car and came round to open her door. His chivalry made her feel like a queen. Arielle forced a bright smile and held out her hand to him. 'Happy birthday in a couple of weeks. And good luck with wife hunting.'

Her heart gave an annoying flutter when Eirik clasped her hand in his strong grasp and lifted her fingers up to his lips to press a light kiss against her knuckles. Arielle knew the gesture was common etiquette in many Euro-pean countries, including Fjernland apparently, but that did not stop a sizzle of electricity shooting through her. She unconsciously flicked her tongue over her lower lip to moisten it and froze when Eirik's blue eyes blazed.

They were two shooting stars on different trajectories, she reminded herself. But right now, they seemed to be on a collision course as he moved closer to her. She breathed in the sandalwood scent of his cologne and then forgot to breathe at all when he lowered his face towards hers.

'Prince Eirik, it's good to see you.' The voice from behind Arielle shattered the sexual tension. Eirik swore softly and stepped away from her, running a hand through his hair.

'Valdemar, how are you?'

Arielle turned and saw a thick-set man sporting a bushy beard. She felt her colour rise when his curious gaze moved from Eirik to her and back again.

'This is Professor Valdemar Oskarsson,' Eirik told her. 'Valdemar, I'd like you to meet Arielle Tremain.'

'Welcome to Fjernland's Marine Research Institute, Arielle.'

'I'll catch up with you another time,' Eirik said to Valdemar. 'I must leave. My mother is hosting a tea party at the palace, and I promised I would be there.' He nodded to Arielle and shook hands with Valdemar before he strode over to the car.

Moments later he drove away, and a lump formed in Arielle's throat when the car disappeared from view. She wondered if Ida Lundberg had been invited to tea at the palace. Perhaps Eirik would decide to marry the beautiful blonde and announce their engagement at his birthday ball.

She realised that Valdemar was looking at her curiously. A job at the marine institute was the chance of a

CHAPTER SIX

EIRIK GLANCED AROUND the Red Drawing Room at Sejrrig Place where twenty or so guests, mainly young women who had been selected by his mother for their grace, sophistication, and suitability to be his wife, were conversing with each other in well-modulated voices while trying to catch his eye.

He considered drowning himself in the punch bowl. It might liven up the interminably tedious evening, he brooded. But he guessed that the liveried footman whose job was to serve the cocktail, made with fruit, alcohol and spices and known as *glogg* in Fjernland, would rush to pull his head out of the antique, silver-gilt bowl. Besides it would be a waste of good vodka, he decided, taking his fourth—or was it fifth?—glass from the tray.

Drinking himself into a coma was a more inviting option. The buffet supper was the third social event in the past week that his mother had arranged in her self-appointed role of matchmaker. Eirik knew there was no escaping his destiny as Fjernland's Reigning Sovereign, or Princess Hulda's determination that he would marry—tomorrow if she had her way. He had a sense of a tsunami racing towards him that would sweep away his old life and leave him drowning in duty and responsibility.

Where was a mermaid when he needed one?

Need. That irritating word again. He assured himself that he did not need Arielle. It was just that he could not stop thinking about her. And until he had got over his fascination, obsession—neither word felt comfortable— with a green-eyed siren, he could not concentrate on the task of choosing a wife.

All evening he had been aware of Princess Hulda's beady eyes on him. And he *had* tried. He'd worked the room, made small talk, and smiled until his face ached. But after two minutes of conversation with the daughter of a French duc, Eirik had known that he was not going to marry Madelaine Blanchet. There was no logical reason why he should not make her his bride. Mademoiselle Blanchet was charming, well educated and her father was a descendant of the brother of Louis XVI, the unfortunate last King of France.

'Madelaine has three brothers,' his mother had informed him before the party, when she had listed the attributes of each female guest. 'It is likely that she would give you a son. I don't know what more you could want.'

Eirik could guess what his mother's reaction would be if he admitted that he wanted a woman with a mermaid's tail and a tangle of russet curls. Aphrodite with voluptuous curves and eyes the colour of a stormy sea.

'I do wish you would make the effort to be more agreeable.' Princess Hulda's terse voice forced Eirik's mind from the image of Arielle naked in his bed, her riotous hair spread across the pillows.

'How am I not being agreeable?' His tone was curter than he'd intended. He forced a smile in an attempt to lighten the atmosphere between him and his mother, which was frosty at the best of times. 'I have spoken to each of your guests.'

'You have spent the evening pacing around the room like a caged tiger,' Princess Hulda told him waspishly. 'I am devoting all my time and energy in assisting you to find a wife. Is it too much to ask for your cooperation? You practically ignored Ida Lundberg, and the French girl did not hold your attention for long. With your brother gone, it is vital that you have a legitimate heir.'

'Let me reassure you that I am fully aware of what is expected of me,' Eirik gritted. As ever, the reference to Niels evoked a stab of guilt in his gut.

'I am glad to hear it,' his mother said crisply. 'I don't know what has been wrong with you since you returned from England, but you need to deal with it, and quickly.'

'Indeed,' Eirik muttered to himself when Princess Hulda swept away with a rustle of her black taffeta gown. He accepted that it was his duty to marry for the sake of the monarchy. But he realised he must have Arielle first. He had told himself that she was forbidden fruit. But wasn't it always the way that you wanted most what you could not have?

Arielle had said she wanted to make love with him before their lives went in different directions. He would spend a perfect night with her, Eirik decided. He did not doubt that the sex would be incredible. The chemistry between them was white-hot. But in his experience, sexual attraction was transitory, and he was confident that his fascination with Arielle would fade once he had slept with her.

Arielle switched off her laptop and stretched her arms above her head. Her neck and shoulders ached as a result of her sitting at her desk for too long. People often thought that marine conservation work meant spending every day on the beach or diving in the sea, but the truth was that a lot of time was spent in front of a computer. Not that she was complaining. It was wonderful to be doing the job she loved again.

After her interview ten days ago, the head of the marine research institute had offered her a temporary position for six months. Valdemar Oskarsson had said there was a good chance that her role could be made permanent when Prince Eirik became the Reigning Sovereign of Fjernland.

'The Prince donates money to the institute from his personal wealth. When he becomes the Sovereign, he hopes to persuade the principality's National Council to increase funding for marine conservation,' Valdemar had explained. 'Protecting the oceans is something Prince Eirik feels passionate about.'

Arielle had felt herself blush at the memory of Eirik's passion. Fortunately, Valdemar had not seemed to notice her pink cheeks when he had ushered her into one of the laboratories and introduced her to his heavily pregnant wife, Frida. Since then Arielle had been shadowing Frida in preparation for when she took charge of a project to measure microplastic pollution in the North Sea. The work was fascinating and left little time for her to daydream about Eirik.

The other scientists working at the institute were friendly and had invited her for a drink at one of the many lively bars in the area. The nearby coastal town attracted a community of artists, and surfers and divers flocked to the glorious beach. She had moved into an apartment in the same building as the marine institute. Accommodation on the upper floors was for visiting students and researchers, but a flat had been vacant and Valdemar had suggested she could live there while she settled into her new job in a new country. Although small, the apartment was bright and modern, and Arielle loved it.

Her life would be perfect, if only she could forget about Eirik and stop following the daily news coverage about him on social media. It was no secret in Fjernland that His Serene Highness, Prince Otto was prepared to abdicate in favour of his remaining son as soon as Prince Eirik had become betrothed. The media were in a frenzy, trying to guess who his bride and future Princess Consort would be. While his father was recuperating after a recent health scare, Prince Eirik had stood in for Prince Otto at several royal functions and had been accompanied by his mother.

Every photo and news film clip had shown Ida Lundberg in the background. In all probability Eirik would reveal at his birthday ball that he was going to marry the elegant blonde, Arielle thought dismally. And she would be there to witness him make the announcement.

At the beginning of the week Valdemar had handed Arielle an envelope bearing the royal coat of arms. Inside she'd found an invitation to attend the masquerade ball at the Winter Palace.

'Frida and I received our invitations a few weeks ago,' Valdemar explained. 'Representatives from the many organisations, societies and charities that Prince Eirik supports will attend the ball. I spoke to the Prince after I'd offered you a job, and he thought it would be a nice idea to invite the marine institute's newest recruit to the ball. He will send a car for us, and we have been allocated rooms at the palace for the night. The Winter Palace is high up in the mountains, and the journey home would be too much for Frida after the party.'

'I don't own a ball gown,' Arielle had said lamely. It was the only excuse she could think of. She couldn't admit that the idea of going to the ball and seeing Eirik with his future bride would be torture.

'I'm sure you will find something suitable to wear in one of the boutiques in Ved Floden,' Frida had suggested. 'I bought a dress for the ball a few weeks ago. But I've got huge.' She patted her pregnancy bump. 'I'll look like a whale.'

'You will be the most beautiful woman in the ballroom,' Valdemar had assured his wife. The tender look between the couple had caused Arielle a pang of envy. Since her disastrous relationship with Jack, she hadn't dated anyone else. Falling in love seemed a scary prospect. But seeing how happy Valdemar and Frida were had made her realise that loving the right person and being loved in return could be wonderful.

Not that she had any intention of falling in love with Eirik, Arielle told herself sternly. Setting her hopes on an unobtainable prince was a certain route to heartbreak. But at least the problem of a ball gown had been resolved. The previous day, after she'd finished work, the concierge of the apartments had handed her a parcel that had been delivered for her.

She had hurried up to her flat to open the box with the name of a Paris couture house on the front, and gasped when she'd lifted the dress out. It was dark green velvet, with a fitted bodice, low cut at the front and plunging almost to her waist at the back. The skirt clung to her hips before flaring out in a fishtail design to the floor. Arielle had discovered that she could not wear a bra beneath the daring dress. A pair of green velvet, high-heeled shoes and a matching clutch bag completed the outfit, and there was also a beautiful green and gold mask. A note in the box simply bore Eirik's name, and the sight of his bold handwriting had made her heart skip a beat.

The ball was on Thursday evening, and for the whole day Arielle's emotions lurched between excitement and dread. She had never been inside a royal palace and was never likely to get the opportunity again. As for Eirik, she guessed he had sent her the ball gown as a thank you for saving him after his yacht had sunk. It would be foolish to read anything more into his kind gesture, she told herself. He had probably asked one of his staff to choose a dress for her.

She spent the afternoon in the lab with Frida, analysing samples of microplastics using an infrared imaging machine. Discovering what types of plastics were in the oceans was an important step in the fight to stop the pollution.

'I'll finish typing up the report,' Arielle said when she saw Frida rubbing her back. 'Why don't you put your feet up for a while?'

'I will, if you don't mind. It feels like the baby is playing football inside me.'

'You only have a few more weeks to go, don't you?' Arielle murmured sympathetically.

Frida gave a weary smile. 'To tell you the truth I'm a bit anxious about the birth. Valdemar and I tried to get pregnant for six years before we struck lucky. This baby means everything to us.'

Arielle remembered that Eirik had told her he must marry in order to provide a legitimate heir to the throne. He had stated that love would not be a feature of his marriage, but would he love his child? She hoped so, for she knew what it was like to grow up without loving parents.

Her mother had loved her, but after she had died Arielle had had no one to praise her when she'd done well at school or comfort her when she was unwell. Her father had only noticed her if she'd forgotten to prepare the fire or failed to have his dinner ready when he wanted it. Children needed to feel loved, and so did adults. The loveless marriage that Eirik insisted he wanted sounded like a recipe for disaster.

She smiled at Frida. 'Go home and rest, and I'll see you tonight. The car will be here at six thirty to take us to the palace.'

Hair straighteners were a godsend, Arielle decided later when she studied her reflection in the mirror. Instead of her usual riot of curls, her hair fell in sleek waves to halfway down her back. The dramatic dress required her to wear more make-up than usual. She always used concealer to cover the small scar on her cheek, and for the party she'd emphasised her eyes with a smoky shadow and added a slick of dusky rose gloss to her lips.

The velvet gown moulded her curvy figure, and she hoped it wasn't too obvious that she was braless. The dress managed to be both sexy and sophisticated. It was hard to believe that the woman in the mirror was ordinary Arielle Tremain who had been teased by her classmates for wearing a threadbare school uniform several sizes too small. One of the teachers had taken pity on her and sorted out some second-hand skirts and blouses and a winter coat when she'd explained that her father did not give her money for clothes.

Her old insecurities flooded back. Why had she thought that she could go to a royal ball? She did not belong in Prince Eirik's world. But perhaps experiencing his luxurious lifestyle for one evening would make her accept that she did not stand a chance with him.

Hearing a knock on the door of the apartment, she grabbed her purse and overnight bag and found Valdemar in the corridor. He was wearing jeans rather than a dinner suit as Arielle had expected, and his expression was strained.

'I have to take Frida to the hospital right away. She was feeling unwell, and I asked the midwife to visit. Her blood pressure is too high, and it could be dangerous for her and the baby.' He stared at Arielle's dress. 'Obviously we can't go to the ball.'

'Of course not.' Arielle quashed the selfish stab of disappointment she felt. 'Hospital is the best place for Frida, and I'm sure everything will be all right,' she said gently.

'I hope so.' Valdemar's voice was gruff. 'It is too late to ask any of the other staff from the institute to accompany you to the palace, but you will be a great representative for our work in marine conservation. I sent a message to Prince Eirik explaining that you will be on your own this evening.'

'Oh, I thought…' Butterflies leapt in Arielle's stomach when she realised that Valdemar expected her to attend the ball alone.

He was already striding down the corridor and called over his shoulder, 'The car to take you to the palace is waiting outside. I must get back to Frida.'

The tall white towers of the Winter Place reached towards an indigo night sky that was scattered with thousands of glittering stars. Beyond the fairy-tale castle loomed craggy mountains with snow-covered peaks. A crescent moon was reflected in the still, black water of the lake in front of the palace.

Arielle wished she had more time to take in the beauty of her surroundings. But the car swept up the gravel driveway, past the line of limousines queuing to deposit party guests at the grand front entrance of the palace. The chauffeur drove on and turned into a small court-yard at the back of the building. He jumped out to open the rear door and when Arielle alighted from the car, she was met by Eirik's private secretary.

'Miss Tremain, please come this way.'

Had she imagined there was disapproval in Gustav's voice? Arielle followed him through a door that she guessed was used by staff and tradesmen and wondered why she had been escorted into the palace secretly, in-stead of entering through the main door with the other guests. Gustav led her through a maze of corridors be-fore he stopped and ushered her into a room.

Her heart leapt at the idea that Eirik might want to see her in private before the ball got under way. But there was no one in the study. A fire was crackling in the hearth, and the biggest dog she had ever seen stood up and pad-ded over to her.

'He belongs to Prince Eirik,' Gustav told her. 'Maks is devoted to the Prince and takes little interest in any-one else.'

'Hello, boy,' Arielle said softly. She loved all animals and had been heartbroken when Bess, the old border col-lie that her father had kept as a sheepdog, had died. 'I'm sure you guard your master well.'

The huge dog could have put his paws on her shoul-ders if he'd wanted to. Arielle held out her hand and patted his smooth golden coat, and after a moment Maks pushed his damp nose into her palm.

'You seem to have won Maks over.' Gustav sounded surprised. He crossed the room and took a flat leather box from the bureau. 'Prince Eirik would like you to have these,' he told Arielle, showing her an exquisite emerald and diamond necklace, and matching earrings.

For a few seconds she was too shocked to speak. Sending her a ball gown was one thing, although she intended to pay Eirik for the dress. But the jewellery must be worth a fortune. She shook her head. 'Please tell the Prince I can't accept such an expensive gift from him.'

'Yes, he anticipated that would be your reaction.' Gustav's voice was marginally warmer. 'However, His Royal Highness insists that you wear the jewellery this evening. You can return the items after the ball if you wish.' He lifted the necklace from the box and held it out to Arielle. 'All the aristocratic young ladies will be wearing tiaras, necklaces and other precious jewels that in many cases are family heirlooms. The Prince hopes that wearing the jewellery will help you to blend in with the other guests,' Gustav said drily.

Feeling that she had to comply, Arielle took the necklace from Gustav. It was heavier than she'd expected, and when she fastened it around her neck, the emeralds and diamonds felt cold against her skin. She removed her faux gold studs, and her hands shook as she attached the emerald drop earrings to her ear lobes. 'I'll be terrified of losing one. Even if I wore the Crown Jewels of England, I still wouldn't be an aristocratic lady,' she said flatly.

'At a masquerade ball you can be whoever you want to be.' Gustav gave something approaching a smile. He helped her to fit her mask over the top part of her face and turned her towards the mirror.

Arielle stared at the reflection of an elegant and exotic woman wearing a couture gown and fabulous jewels and did not recognise herself. None of the other guests at the ball would know that her father was a murderer, or that her integrity had been questioned at his trial, she reassured herself. The judge had believed her testimony that she'd been unaware of Gerran Rowse's crimes. But the Bray family had accused her of lying to try to stop her father from being sent to prison. It wasn't true. Arielle was ashamed of her father and hoped he would rot in jail.

Wearing the masquerade mask gave her anonymity. Gustav was right—tonight she could be someone different from her usual reserved self. At the ball she could be the self-confident woman she wished she were. Her mask would also hide her reaction if Eirik announced his engagement to his future wife. Of course, she *knew* she wasn't princess material, and he would never choose her, but that hadn't stopped her wishing for the moon.

The ballroom was vast and even more opulent than the other rooms Arielle had glimpsed when Gustav had escorted her through the palace. The polished parquet floor gleamed beneath the lights blazing from many chandeliers. Elegant marble columns rose up to meet the frescoed ceiling, and the vibrant blue silk wall panels were edged with gilded mouldings.

She was directed to join the line of female guests standing on one side of the ballroom opposite the men who had formed another line. The young woman next to Arielle looked towards the doorway and said excitedly, 'They'll be here any minute.'

'Who?'

'The royal family. They will make an entrance when all the guests are assembled. Is this your first ball?' Without waiting for Arielle to reply, the woman explained, 'Prince Otto has been ill, and he is not here tonight, so Prince Eirik will escort his mother. As they walk down the room, the women will curtsey to the Prince and the men will bow to Princess Hulda. Then Prince Eirik will choose a partner for the first dance. It's rumoured that he will dance with the woman he intends to marry. Naturally, everyone will try to guess her identity behind her mask. Although his most likely choice of bride is Baron Lundberg's daughter. Ida is easy to spot with her pale blonde hair, and she is wearing a white dress and mask. Perhaps a hint that she will soon be wearing a wedding dress,' the woman said with a heavy sigh.

Arielle's gaze was drawn to the set of doors as they were flung open by footmen and Prince Eirik, with Princess Hulda on his arm, entered the ballroom to a fanfare of trumpets. They walked slowly between the two lines of guests and each woman in turn bobbed a curtsey as Eirik passed by.

He looked breathtaking in a superbly tailored tuxedo that emphasised the broadness of his shoulders. His dark blond hair was swept back from his brow, and a black and gold mask drew attention to his sculpted cheekbones, but of course it could not disguise his identity. He possessed an aura of power and pre-eminence that set him apart from other men.

Arielle's heart thumped as Eirik drew nearer to where she was standing in the line. Her eyes met his intense gaze and she saw something flare in those blue depths that heated her blood. She was conscious of his smouldering scrutiny as he roved his eyes over her velvet gown and sleek hairstyle before lingering on the emeralds and diamonds at her throat. Her breath was trapped in her lungs, and she felt as though only she and Eirik existed.

The strange sense that they belonged to each other body and soul lasted mere seconds before she became aware that Princess Hulda had turned her head and was looking at her. Eirik's mother's coldly assessing stare sent a shiver through Arielle, and she released a shaky breath when the Prince and Princess walked on.

When they reached the far end of the room, Eirik led his mother to a chair and waited for her to be seated. There was a tangible air of expectation in the ballroom as he strode over to the line of women.

'Oh! That's a surprise. Prince Eirik has chosen Princess Matilda for the first dance,' the woman beside Arielle murmured.

'Does that mean she is the woman he intends to marry?' Arielle craned her neck to see Eirik's dance partner. There were so many beautiful young women at the ball, and she supposed that Princess Matilda was one of them.

'I shouldn't think so. Princess Matilda is Prince Eirik's elderly aunt and Prince Otto's sister. It seems that the Prince intends to keep everyone guessing who his bride will be for a while longer.'

Eirik and his aunt began a slow waltz. The male guests stepped forward to claim the women opposite them for the dance. Gustav offered Arielle his hand. 'May I have the pleasure of this dance, Miss Tremain? Prince Eirik asked me to look after you at the ball,' he said when she looked uncertain.

'I've never done ballroom dancing before,' Arielle admitted as the private secretary led her around the dance floor, and she accidentally trod on his foot.

'My bruised toes are testament to that fact,' Gustav replied in his dry voice. 'I will attempt to teach you the rudiments of a simple box step. When I take a step forward with my right foot, you step backwards with your left, then we both step to the side and finally bring the feet together to the count of three.'

She got the hang of it after a while. A brief interlude in the music played by the orchestra was a cue for the dancers to change partners for the next dance. As Arielle moved around the ballroom with a number of different dance partners she was determined not to look for Eirik, but his height and sheer physical presence drew her gaze to him.

Her heart sank when she saw him dancing with a tall, willowy woman with pale blonde hair piled on top of her head in an elaborate chignon. The woman was wearing an exquisite white ball gown and a mask decorated with white feathers. Ida Lundberg was as elegant as a swan, and her regal bearing would make her a perfect wife and Princess Consort for Prince Eirik. That seemed to be the opinion of the other guests when Arielle had overheard snippets of their conversations.

At that moment Eirik looked across the ballroom directly at her. He must have seen her as clearly as she saw him, but he gave no sign of recognition and turned his head away. His dismissal made it clear that he had no personal interest in her and had invited her to the ball simply because she was a representative of the marine research institute that he supported.

'Would you like some champagne?' asked the young man Arielle was dancing with.

She smiled at him and ignored the thought that she would like to escape to her room in the guest wing of the palace, crawl under the duvet and have a good cry. 'I'd love some.' Tonight was her one and only chance to attend a royal ball, and she was going to enjoy every minute of it, Arielle told herself sternly. Life was about embracing new experiences, not moping over a prince who she had known from the outset could never be hers.

The champagne helped, and after a couple of glasses of fizz, and finding there was no shortage of men who wanted to dance with her, she discovered that she was genuinely having a good time. She even had the confidence to flirt a little with her dance partners, and a few times when there was a lull in the music the sound of her laughter turned heads in her direction.

'You seem to be having fun.' Eirik's deep voice was close to her ear. Arielle's stomach muscles clenched when she turned her head and found him beside her. With effortless grace and a gleam of determination in his eyes, he drew her away from the man she had been dancing with. Spinning her round to face him, he captured her hand in his and placed his other hand on her waist.

'Isn't having fun the point of a party?' she asked breathlessly as she rested her free hand on his shoulder and tried to remember what to do with her feet.

'You call this evening fun?' Eirik demanded tersely. 'Every move I make is watched by three hundred and fifty guests, and my mother is in one of her sulks because I refuse to allow her to interfere in my life.'

'I suppose your mother is annoyed because you haven't made an announcement of your betrothal.' Arielle tensed when Eirik's thigh brushed against hers.

Even through his trousers and her velvet dress she was aware of the ripple of his hard muscles. The contact felt shockingly intimate. 'Ida Lundberg must be disappointed. Everyone expects that you will choose her to be your bride after she was seen with you at royal events in the past two weeks.'

'I attended a number of functions with Princess Hulda, and Ida was there because my mother recently appointed her as a lady-in-waiting.'

'Are you sure that was the only reason?' Arielle muttered. 'I saw you dancing with Ida this evening and the two of you looked perfect together.'

'Ida was not the only woman I danced with. Were you jealous, my green-eyed mermaid?'

She looked away from his speculative gaze. 'I had no right to feel jealous,' she said stiffly.

'I had no right to wish I could tear you away from every man I watched you dance with,' Eirik growled. 'As for the men who have undressed you with their eyes, I would take great delight in rearranging their features with my fist.'

She flushed. 'No one has undressed me with their eyes…have they?'

'Do you have any idea how beautiful you are? Or how incredibly sexy you look in that dress? I chose it from the designer's website because I knew it would be perfect for you. But you exceeded all my expectations. When I walked into the ballroom you blew my mind.'

Eirik's huskily spoken words sent a quiver of response through Arielle. She stumbled and he tightened his hand on her waist. He winced when her stiletto heel came down on his foot.

'Sorry. One back, two to the side, three together,' she said under her breath.'

His brows lifted. 'What are you doing?'

'Gustav showed me how to waltz. But I forget the steps if I am distracted.'

He laughed softly. 'Do I distract you, *skatta*?'

The sensual musk of his aftershave was all around her. The ballroom was full of people, but Arielle only saw him. She nodded, and his eyes glittered as he slid his arm around her waist and placed his hand on her bare back where her dress was cut away. His touch burned her, and she did not try to resist when he drew her closer so that they were hip to hip. 'Dancing is easy,' he murmured. 'Let me show you.'

The orchestra had struck up a fairly quick waltz and Arielle's feet flew over the floor as Eirik whisked her around the ballroom. She had wanted to be in his arms all evening, and she stopped telling herself the reasons why this was a bad idea and melted against his hard body.

'You're a good dancer,' she said breathlessly.

'My mother insisted that my brother and I took ballroom-dancing lessons every Saturday morning when we were younger. I would much rather have gone sailing, so I learned the steps quickly.'

'I suppose you attend a lot of parties and being able to dance must be a useful skill to have.'

His sexy smile stole Arielle's breath. 'I have many skills,' he whispered into her ear. The stubble on his jaw scraped over her cheek, and she knew that if she turned her head a fraction their mouths would meet. She would not have believed it was possible to make love on a crowded dance floor, but when Eirik slid his hand down to her bottom and hauled her even closer to him, so that her breasts were pressed against his chest and she felt the hard ridge of his arousal nudge her thigh, Arielle realised that he was seducing her, and she did not want him to stop.

CHAPTER SEVEN

ARIELLE COULD HAVE danced with Eirik all night, but, as the strains of the 'Blue Danube' faded away, the spell he had cast on her shattered when she saw Princess Hulda standing at the edge of the dance floor, watching them. The Princess beckoned imperiously to her son. Eirik gave a deep sigh and lowered his arms down to his sides.

'My mother wishes to meet you.' His unemotional voice gave no clue to his thoughts. He rested his hand lightly on the base of Arielle's spine and ushered her across the ballroom.

'Mama, I would like to introduce Miss Arielle Tremain from Cornwall in England.'

Arielle remembered that she was supposed to curtsey. She managed an inelegant bob but was hampered by her figure-hugging dress. 'Your Highness,' she mumbled.

Princess Hulda was wearing a black satin ball gown with a voluminous skirt made up of layers of ruffles, which had the unfortunate effect of emphasising her rather dumpy figure. Her silver hair was swept off her face in a severe style, and around her throat was a necklace of blood-red rubies.

The Princess gave Arielle an assessing look. 'Do your family own land in Cornwall, Miss Tremain?'

'Er…no, ma'am. We had a smallholding and kept a few sheep, but the land and cottage were rented.'

'Is your father successful in business?'

Arielle froze. 'My father?' She pictured Gerran Rowse the last time she had seen him as he had been led away from the court to begin a life sentence in prison. He had not looked at her once during the trial, but he'd never been interested in his daughter.

'Arielle does not have any family,' Eirik said, breaking the awkward silence that had fallen while she'd tried to think of something to say.

'How sad.' Princess Hulda's eyes were light grey, almost colourless, and cold. 'That is a very beautiful necklace you are wearing. A family heirloom, perhaps?'

'Um…no.' Arielle could not explain to herself why she was reluctant to tell the Princess that Eirik had lent her the emeralds to wear to the ball. She was relieved when Princess Hulda turned her gaze on her son. The dismissal was subtle, but Arielle felt as unimportant as the Princess had obviously intended her to feel.

'Eirik, I am feeling a little weary. I would like you to escort me to my private sitting room and ask my lady-in-waiting to come to me. I believe you will find Ida with Baron Lundberg in the orangery.'

'Of course, Mama.' Eirik's expression was unreadable. He turned to Arielle and said coolly, 'I hope you enjoy the rest of the ball, Miss Tremain.'

Princess Hulda took her son's arm and did not glance at Arielle. She might as well have been invisible, she thought as she watched Eirik escort his mother out of the ballroom. There were several hundred guests at the ball, but Arielle had never felt more alone. She touched the emerald necklace that Eirik had arranged for her to wear so that she fitted in with the high-society guests. Why had she thought she could belong in his rarefied world for even a few hours?

No one took any notice of her when she walked out of the ballroom. She looked for Gustav, hoping to return the necklace and earrings to him, but there was no sign of him, and she soon lost her way when she tried to find the study, thinking she could replace the jewellery in the bureau.

A damp nose nudged her hand. Eirik's dog, Maks, trotted down the corridor and Arielle followed him. 'You want to go outside, do you?' she said as the dog scratched on a door. Through the window she could see a dark garden. An icy blast of air struck her when she opened the door. Maks nudged her again as if he wanted her to follow him. 'Can you just get on and do what you need to do?' she told him. 'It's freezing out here.'

The frost on the lawn sparkled in the starlight. Arielle hugged her arms around her as the big dog gently pushed her along the path. In the pearly glimmer of the moon, she saw a wooden arbour and Eirik sprawled on the bench seat. Her heart hammered as she walked towards him and felt his intense blue gaze on her.

He had removed his masquerade mask, and the moonlight danced over his sculpted cheekbones. His bow tie was hanging open and he'd unfastened the top buttons of his shirt. Arielle recalled photos in celebrity magazines of a dissolute, playboy prince who had often been snapped by the paparazzi on a superyacht in St Tropez or at a nightclub in some European hotspot or other, invariably with a supermodel on his arm. But she had glimpsed another side to Eirik. He was not just a handsome hunk with a surfeit of charisma. He was trying to come to terms with his brother's death and the role that had been thrust on him as the future monarch.

He stood up and patted the dog's head. 'Well done, Maks. You can go now.'

Arielle watched the dog trot back up the path towards the palace. 'How did he know to bring me here?'

'I told him to.' Noticing her look of surprise, Eirik murmured, 'Animals understand more than humans think they do. But Maks is exceptional. I've had him since he was a few days old. He was the runt of a litter. The gamekeeper wanted pups who would grow into strong hunting dogs, and he was going to let Maks die. But I thought he deserved a chance, so I kept him. I had to feed him from a bottle at first. The funny thing is that Maks grew up to be bigger and stronger than his siblings.'

She could very easily lose her heart to this man, Arielle thought ruefully.

Eirik frowned when he noticed her shiver. 'You are cold. Here, wear this.' He slipped his jacket off and draped it around her shoulders. The silk lining carried the heat of his body and the heady scent of his cologne.

'I shouldn't be here...with you,' she said huskily.

He lifted his hand and wound a lock of her hair around his finger. 'I like your hair like this, but I miss your curls.'

She gave a breathless laugh. 'Oh, they'll bounce back. You should see my crazy hair first thing in the morning.'

'I would like to.' His voice was deeper than Arielle had ever heard it, and, despite the warmth of his jacket, she shivered again. 'I have imagined you naked in my bed, *skatta*. Your red curls spread across my pillows.'

'You shouldn't say things like that.' She clung to her sanity as if it were a life raft and she were adrift in a stormy sea.

'It's the truth.' He moved closer, and Arielle's eyes were drawn to where his shirt was open at his throat. She longed to undo the rest of the buttons and run her hands over his bare chest. 'For the past two weeks I have tried to forget you,' he growled, not disguising his frustration. 'But tonight at the ball it was hopeless. The only woman I saw was you.'

Eirik moved his other hand behind her head and untied the ribbons that secured her mask. It slipped to the ground, but neither of them noticed. His warm breath formed a gossamer cloud in the cold air, and Arielle's lips parted of their own volition in anticipation of his kiss.

'You are the only woman I want,' he said in a low voice that sent another tremor through her.

Whatever was happening, whatever was about to happen, would only be for tonight. She accepted that she could never be part of Eirik's world. But she desired him with every fibre of her body. Need made her breasts ache and evoked a deeper, more insistent throb low in her pelvis. Arielle knew she would regret it for ever if she turned down this chance to make love with the most fascinating man she'd ever met.

Eirik's arms came round her—at last. He pulled her against his whipcord body, and he felt so good, so male and strong. Safe. Arielle tilted her face up to his in mute surrender and watched his eyes blaze.

'Let me warm you,' he whispered against her lips.

'Yes.' Her answer was lost as he covered her mouth with his and kissed her beneath the stars.

Eirik lifted Arielle into his arms and carried her through the frosty garden. She rested her head on his shoulder and he breathed in her seductive perfume. Soon she would be his. The thought caused his pulse to accelerate, and he quickened his steps.

He had left a side door unlocked and there were no guards on duty, meaning that he could enter the palace unseen. This was not how he'd anticipated the evening would end, although in truth he had fantasised about making love to Arielle. He felt a stab of guilt as he acknowledged his failure to do what was expected of him by the Crown Prince and Princess, and by the entire population of Fjernland, it seemed. He was no closer to deciding who to marry, but he'd been aware that there would be fevered speculation at the ball about who might be his future bride.

Unfortunately, he'd taken one look at a green-eyed siren, as sexy as hell in a gown that showed off her gorgeous curves, and his blood had rushed to his groin. He had been certain that he could control his lust for Arielle, but he'd failed spectacularly, and he did not care.

No doubt tomorrow, in the cold light of day, he would question what it was about this woman that made him desperate to strip her naked and explore every inch of her creamy skin with his hands and mouth until she begged for his possession. Not that she would have to beg very hard, Eirik thought self-derisively. The truth was that he needed to be inside Arielle as quickly as possible.

He took the back staircase and corridors up to his private suite of rooms. There was no risk of being spotted by the staff, who would all be downstairs to begin clearing up after the ball had finished and assisting the guests to their cars.

'I can walk,' Arielle protested. 'I'm too heavy for you to carry me up the stairs.'

'Nonsense.' His heart was thundering, but not from

physical exertion. He could have carried Arielle to the top of the highest mountain in Fjernland. Desire pulsed in his blood and in his sex. He was descended from Vikings, and he was impatient to claim his shield maiden. Shouldering the door to his apartment, he carried her through to the bedroom and set her down on her feet next to the bed.

'Wow, this is amazing.' Arielle's eyes widened when she looked around the room that was as ornate as the rest of the Winter Palace. The four-poster bed with its gold brocade drapes was not to Eirik's taste, but he had inherited the palace and soon he would inherit the crown and, somehow, he would have to make his peace with the life that awaited him.

But tonight he would not think about the future. The huge bed was a perfect playground for what he had in mind, and he felt his body tauten as he pictured Arielle sprawled on the satin sheets.

'I did not bring you here to admire the decor,' he muttered against her mouth before he kissed her again and again. Her eager response as she parted her lips and kissed him back stoked the fire in his belly. 'I want to see you naked.'

He eased away from her a fraction and stared at the soft flush on her lovely face and those sea green eyes, which right now were glazed with desire. The sirens of ancient legends had sung an intoxicating song that lured men to their doom. Arielle's soft moans of delight as he cradled her breasts in his hands might well be the end of him, Eirik thought. But he did not care, and that in itself should trouble him. With other women he had always remained in control of his sexual urges, but his hunger for Arielle was a voracious beast that demanded to be appeased.

He stood behind her and pushed her glossy hair over her shoulder to expose the slender column of her neck. She tasted of honey and roses when he pressed his lips to her spine and kissed his way down her bare back. His fingers deftly unzipped her dress before he turned her to face him and slid the velvet gown from her shoulders.

Eirik had spent an unseemly amount of time during the ball wondering if Arielle could have worn some sort of bra beneath the backless dress. Now he had his answer and his body clenched.

Her breasts were perfect, round handfuls, tipped with dusky pink nipples that swelled against his tongue when he closed his lips around one taut peak and then the other. The sound of her swiftly indrawn breath delighted him, for it told him that Arielle was as much at the mercy of this inconvenient desire as he was.

With increasing urgency, he tugged the clingy velvet over her hips, and the dress fell to the floor, leaving her in a pair of tiny knickers and gossamer-fine stockings with bands of lace around her thighs.

'Have you any idea what you do to me?' he growled, enjoying her reaction when he traced the top of one stocking before moving his fingers higher to caress the creamy skin of her inner thigh.

'Eirik?' She whispered his name and he laughed softly at her husky plea.

'Tell me what you want, *skatta.*'

'I can't.' She blushed and seemed suddenly vulnerable, dropping her gaze from his. 'I told you that I'm not very good at this.'

He remembered the ex-boyfriend who Arielle had said

hadn't satisfied her. She had told him she wasn't a virgin, but Eirik suspected she was not very experienced.

He slid his hand beneath her chin and tilted her face up, forcing her to meet his gaze. 'I am very good at sex,' he murmured. It was not a boast—he had a high sex drive and enjoyed giving his lovers pleasure as much as he enjoyed receiving it. The idea that her ex had not taken the time to ensure that sex was good for Arielle, and from the sound of it had made her feel that it was her failure, made Eirik determined to show her how pleasurable lovemaking could be. They had all night, and he intended to satiate his damnable desire for her by the morning.

'Why don't we begin with me touching you, and you tell me if you like what I am doing, or if you want me to stop? Does that sound okay?'

She nodded but still looked uncertain. He could not resist kissing the tense line of her mouth until her lips softened beneath his. At the same time, he cradled her breast in his palm and rubbed his thumb across her nipple, eliciting a husky moan from Arielle.

'Do you like it when I do that?'

'Y-yes.'

'What about when I do this?' His other hand was still resting on her stocking top. He felt her thigh quiver when he skimmed his fingers over her sensitive flesh, higher and higher until he pressed his thumb against the moist panel of her panties.

'Yes,' she said in a breathy whisper that made Eirik even harder. 'I…like that.'

'And now?' He slipped his fingers beneath her knickers and his heart gave a kick when he discovered that she was wet down there. Wet for him. The sweet scent of her feminine arousal inflamed his desire. He gently parted her and pushed a finger between her silken folds. 'Do you like what I am doing to you now, *skatta*?'

'Yes. Oh, don't stop.' She pressed herself closer to him, inviting him to continue caressing her. The frantic jerk of her pelvis against his hand melted his frozen heart a little when it occurred to him that perhaps she had never been pleasured in this way before. *Faen.* She was so innocent, and he wanted to teach her everything.

'I have no intention of stopping,' Eirik promised. 'But we will be more comfortable on the bed.' He lifted her onto the mattress, removed her shoes and panties and rolled her sheer stockings down her legs. 'This is how I pictured you when I chose the jewellery for you to wear to the ball,' he said hoarsely. 'Naked in my bed and adorned with emeralds that match the colour of your eyes.'

The feral gleam in Eirik's eyes shocked and excited Arielle. No man had ever looked at her as he was doing, as if he wanted to devour her. Desire sharpened his features so that his skin seemed to be stretched tightly over his high cheekbones. He stared at her mouth as she flicked her tongue across her lower lip.

'I want to make love to you.' His voice was harsh with need and sent a thrill through her.

It hardly seemed possible that she—ordinary Arielle Tremain, who had changed her name to hide the dark secret in her past—could be responsible for Eirik's transformation from an urbane prince to a hungry wolf.

He knelt on the bed and straddled her with his knees on either side of her hips and his hands beside her head. 'You want me too, don't you, my beautiful siren?'

Oh, she did, with a desperation that stunned her. She had never felt this turned on with her ex. She'd only slept with Jack because he had expected her to. Her lack of confidence had made her believe that a dud boyfriend was better than no boyfriend. But Eirik was nothing like Jack, and her instincts told her that sex with him was not going to be a disappointing fumble under the duvet.

'How can I please you?' Eirik asked softly.

Arielle bit her lip, reluctant to admit her experience of sex was so limited that she did not know what she would enjoy. 'It seems unfair that I'm naked and you are still dressed,' she murmured.

He sat back on his heels and gave her a sexy grin. Taking her hands, he placed them on his shirt front. 'Feel free to undress me, *musaling*.'

Arielle had never undressed anyone other than herself. With unsteady fingers she undid a button on his shirt. 'What is *musaling*?'

'It means little mouse.'

She frowned. 'Mice are drab and unexciting.' Was that how Eirik saw her?

'I disagree. They are cute, timid creatures.'

'Nothing like me, then.' Was there a more unflattering description than *timid*? Determined to show him that she wasn't a nervous almost-novice—even though she was—she tore open the rest of the buttons and pushed the shirt off his shoulders.

His body was hot in every sense. She ran her hands over his golden skin and felt the soft abrasion of his chest hairs against her palms. The ridges of his abdominal muscles fascinated her as she skimmed her fingertips over the fuzz of blond hairs that arrowed down to the waistband of his trousers.

It was stupid to feel shy, Arielle told herself as she hesitated before undoing his belt. Her breath caught in her throat when she put her hand on his trouser zip and discovered the unmistakable proof of his arousal. He groaned as she tugged the zip down and her nails scraped over the bulge of his manhood.

'I'll take it from here,' Eirik growled. He levered himself off the bed and quickly stripped off the rest of his clothes. His eyes locked with Arielle's wide gaze as he pulled his boxers over his hips to reveal his impressive erection. Her heart missed a beat as she tried to imagine him sliding his swollen length inside her.

Naked, he was a work of art: long-limbed and lean-hipped, a washboard-flat stomach and that broad, muscular chest. A Viking prince with searing passion in his eyes. The air was thick with sexual tension. Arielle's breathing was shallow, and her heart was racing as Eirik stepped closer to the bed and put his hands on her thighs, gently pushing them apart. He dropped onto his knees, and she trembled when she realised his intention. Her secret sexual fantasy was for a lover to put his mouth on her, and she could hardly believe that it was going to happen.

With slow, deliberate movements that heightened her anticipation, he hooked her legs over his shoulders and slid his hands beneath her bottom to lift her towards him. And then he buried his head between her thighs and flicked his tongue lightly over her opening.

Arielle's whole body jolted in reaction. What Eirik was doing was shockingly intimate, especially as, really, she hardly knew him. But it did not matter. Nothing mattered except that he should continue his wicked caresses with his tongue. She felt utterly wanton with her legs spread wide open while he pleasured her, and it was better than she could ever have imagined.

He quickly took her to the brink, and she curled her fingers into the sheet, dimly aware that the husky moans that filled the room came from her. Eirik's hands were busy too, and the sensation of him sliding a finger inside her and gently stretching her, while simultaneously he closed his mouth over the sensitive nub of her clitoris, sent her over the edge. Her orgasm swept through her in rippling waves of pleasure.

When Arielle came back to earth, tears pricked her eyes. Eirik's consideration and patience as he'd brought her to a climax threatened to dismantle the barriers that she knew she must keep around her heart.

He stood up and rolled a condom over his thick length before he joined her on the bed. But even then, he did not rush her. Only his ragged voice as he muttered, 'You drive me insane, *skatta*,' reassured her that his need was as great as hers.

Propped up on one elbow, he was a golden god with his dark blond hair falling across his brow. He idly trailed his hand over her body, discovering the fragile line of her collarbone before moving down to cup her breast. He bent his head and took her tight nipple into his mouth. The sensation of him sucking hard sent a sharp tug of desire down to Arielle's feminine core. He transferred his mouth to her other breast, and she gasped when he slipped his hand between her legs.

'You are ready for me,' he said softly as he explored her slick heat with his fingers once more. 'I can't wait much longer.'

Nor could she. 'I don't want to wait. I want you,' she whispered. She moved her hand between their bodies and stroked her fingers along the length of his erection, eliciting a groan from him.

'Not this time,' he said, pushing her hand away. 'I'm

about to explode.' He positioned himself over her, and the hard gleam in his eyes made Arielle's tummy flip. 'Open your legs wider.'

She complied with his hoarse command and held her breath when he lowered his big body so that the tip of his shaft pressed against her opening. Slowly he eased forwards and entered her, filling her inch by incredible inch. She shifted her hips as the sensation of fullness intensified.

'Am I hurting you?'

'No.' She stared into his blue eyes, touched by his concern. But it was unnecessary. She was on fire for him, and more than anything she wanted him to reach the heights of sexual fulfilment that he had taken her to moments ago. When he withdrew a little way, she tilted her pelvis and slid her hands around his back, gripping his buttocks and urging him to thrust deeper inside her.

Eirik muttered something in Fjernlandic and rested his brow against hers. 'This is *so* good for me, but I need it to be good for you too.'

'It is, or it will be if you stop talking.'

His low rumble of laughter curled around her heart, and she felt a connection between them that was more than physical.

'No more talking,' he promised. He began to move, setting a devastating rhythm that Arielle found utterly addictive. She wrapped her legs around his hips as he drove into her faster, deeper. The orgasm he had given her with his mouth had been amazing, but now her body craved more. She sensed there was something even more intense, but it remained frustratingly beyond her reach.

'Relax, and it will happen,' Eirik murmured. He slipped his hand between their joined bodies and did something wickedly inventive with his fingers. At the same time he gave a hard thrust that drove the breath from her lungs and the world exploded. Her orgasm was so powerful, so pleasurable that Arielle lost all sense of time and place. Sensation after sensation tore through her as her vaginal muscles clenched and unclenched in the sweetest release.

Eirik was still plunging into her, faster, faster. She sensed his urgency and arched her hips to meet every vigorous thrust. He tensed and stared down at her. His eyes glittered, and his breath came in harsh pants, and then his face twisted, and he let out a savage groan as he gave one final, hard thrust. His big body shuddered with the force of his climax before he collapsed on top of her.

Arielle welcomed the weight of him pressing her into the mattress. She locked her arms around his back and turned her face into his neck. When she kissed his skin, she tasted the salt of his sweat. She wished they could stay there for ever, their limbs entwined and hearts thundering in unison. But wishes rarely came true, and after a while Eirik lifted himself off her and moved across the bed.

She missed the illusion of security when she had been in his arms and fought the temptation to snuggle up to him. 'That shouldn't have happened,' she said, getting in first before he told her that he regretted what they had done.

'Probably not,' he agreed. There was amusement in his voice. He rolled onto his side and leaned up on one elbow, stroking damp tendrils of hair off Arielle's face. She told herself that she must have imagined tenderness in his eyes. 'But it did happen,' he murmured. 'And very soon it will happen again.'

He grinned at her startled expression and caught hold of her hand, holding it against his burgeoning arousal. 'We have all night to enjoy each other, and I don't intend to waste a second, *min prinsessa.*'

as he remembered how in the throes of passion he had called Arielle his princess. Of course she never could be the Princess Consort. Even if the rules on who he could marry were changed, he would not choose Arielle to be his wife. Not because he cared about their perceived difference in social status. He firmly believed that all people were equal, and it was down to fate that he had been born a prince. But a tragic twist of fate had made him the future monarch. It was his fault that the only person he had ever truly loved was dead, and Eirik assured himself that he did not want or deserve love. The woman he married would have to understand that he expected the relationship to be uncluttered by emotions.

He acknowledged that he did not know Arielle very well, but he suspected she was highly emotional, romantic, and looking for love. He needed to make it clear that she would not find it with him. The way to do that was not to pull the sheet away from her body and settle himself between her thighs to arouse her with his tongue. Remembering how much she had enjoyed him caressing her in that way, and the husky moans she'd made when she'd climaxed against his mouth, made him instantly hard.

Swearing beneath his breath, Eirik slid out of bed and headed for the en suite bathroom to take a cold shower. Standing beneath the punishing spray, he tried to fathom why he was finding it hard to walk away from Arielle when he'd never had a problem compartmentalising his previous lovers in a file marked temporary. Possibly it was because Arielle had seen him at his most vulnerable when she'd saved him from the sea, he brooded. He felt a connection with her. He liked her and he was interested in her marine conservation work. Perhaps they could have been friends if he hadn't let his libido over-rule his common sense.

Who was he kidding? he mocked himself when he went into his dressing room and donned the uniform he was required to wear to a military ceremony he was to attend later. He did not want a platonic friendship with Arielle. He had hoped that sleeping with her would release him from her siren's spell. Surely, novelty had been part of her attraction. The thrill of the chase and her ultimate surrender.

But when he returned to the bedroom and saw Arielle still sprawled on the satin sheets, her red curls spilling over the pillow, Eirik was sorely tempted to wake Sleeping Beauty with a kiss that would quickly escalate into tumultuous passion, and he knew that he was in trouble.

'Arielle, wake up.' Eirik's curt voice pulled Arielle from an erotic dream in which she'd relived the many and varied ways he had made love to her throughout the night. But he did not sound like the sexy lover who had groaned her name when she'd wriggled down the bed and flicked her tongue along the length of his manhood.

Reluctantly, she opened her eyes and stared at a stranger. Eirik was resplendent in a dark blue suit decorated with gold buttons and epaulettes. A red silk sash was draped across one shoulder and tied around his waist. Attached to his jacket were several military medals. With his blond hair swept back from his brow and the stubble on his jaw neatly trimmed, he looked like the handsome Prince Charming beloved of fairy tales. But he was remote and unsmiling. Clearly he hadn't read the part of the story where he was meant to wake her with a kiss.

'You need to get up,' he told her.

'I gather that my presence in your bedchamber is no

longer required, Your Highness,' she said drily, determined not to let him see that she was hurt by his brusqueness. She sat up and snatched the sheet over her breasts.

A dull flush ran along his cheekbones. 'We both knew that we could only spend one night together.'

She nodded. It was true, but she hadn't expected him to dismiss her quite so brutally. 'Give me five minutes and I'll be out of your hair.' Her voice was as cool as his. She saw a pool of green velvet on the floor where her ball gown had landed when Eirik had undressed her the previous night. 'I left my overnight bag with a change of clothes in my room in the guest wing of the palace.'

'I had Gustav bring your things here to my private suite.' Eirik indicated her bag on a chair. 'I'll leave you to get dressed. I have an appointment this morning and Gustav will drive you back to the marine institute.'

But he continued to stand at the foot of the bed and his eyes narrowed when Arielle inched across the mattress and stood up, clutching the sheet around her to hide her nakedness. 'It's a bit late for modesty,' he drawled. 'Last night I kissed every inch of your body.'

'Last night we were lovers, but now we are not.' Tears threatened, and she wished he would go, before she suffered the humiliation of breaking down in front of him. 'I assume from your uniform and the impressive row of medals on your chest that you are going to a royal event.'

'A passing out parade at the naval college. It's an important day for the cadets and I will preside over the ceremony as the High Commander of Fjernland's Navy.'

'I didn't know that Fjernland had its own military.'

'We work in conjunction with the Danish armed forces. As a matter of fact, I earned the medals I'm wearing when I served as a naval officer for four years. For some of that time I was based on a patrol ship in the Arctic, and my unit was involved with monitoring pollutants including plastic waste on Arctic ecosystems. It was what led me to establish the Fjernland Marine Research Institute, to try to protect the oceans.'

'When you become the Reigning Sovereign you will be able to focus on issues that you believe are important and introduce changes if you deem them necessary for the good of the country.' Arielle wondered if Eirik was aware that there was pride in his voice whenever he mentioned Fjernland. He cared about the principality and the people he would rule. 'Maybe being the monarch won't be as bad as you think.'

He stared at her. 'Maybe not,' he said gruffly. 'Arielle...'

'We are two stars on different trajectories.' She remembered what he had said at the cottage in Penash, a lifetime ago it seemed. 'For what it's worth I think you will be a great Sovereign.'

He took a step towards her and swore when there was a knock on the outer door of the suite. Pulling back the sleeve of his jacket to check his watch, he said in a frustrated voice, 'I have to leave, or I will be late for the ceremony.' Eirik strode over to the door and halted. He turned around and even across the distance of the bedroom Arielle felt the heat of his gaze. 'I am not ready for this, us, to end,' he growled.

He was killing her. Arielle's heart missed a beat at *us*. But she reminded herself that all Eirik wanted was sex, while she was in imminent danger of falling in love with him. 'It must end,' she said quietly. 'You know it must. I can never be part of your world.'

'Good morning, Miss Tremain.' Gustav stood up when Arielle walked into the sitting room. He studied her skinny jeans and oversized jumper that had a habit of slipping off her shoulder and Arielle wondered if he was comparing her to elegant Ida Lundberg. She felt his sharp gaze on her pink-rimmed eyes and told herself she did not care what Eirik's private secretary thought of her.

'I'm ready to leave,' she said stiffly.

Gustav escorted her along numerous corridors that Arielle guessed were for the staff's use, and they left the palace unnoticed via a back door. Clearly Eirik did not want anyone other than his most trusted servant to know that he had spent the night with a commoner, she thought dismally.

Eirik's dog bounded up and pushed his nose into her hand. 'Goodbye, Maks,' she said in a choked voice, stroking his golden head. Gustav had put her bag in the boot of the car, and now he was talking on his phone. He spoke in Fjernlandic and glanced at Arielle a couple of times. She climbed onto the back seat and shook her head at Maks when he leapt into the car. 'I'd love to take you with me, but I'm afraid I can't.'

'Maks can come along for the ride,' Gustav said as he slid behind the wheel.

The big dog rested his head on Arielle's knee, and she was glad of his company. She closed her eyes as the smooth motion of the car had a soporific effect on her after her energetic night, memories of which brought a flush to her cheeks. Maybe she would get a dog when she settled somewhere, she mused. She had decided not to extend her contract at the Fjernland Marine Research Institute after her six months was up. Eirik would no doubt have married by then and seeing news coverage of him with his wife would be painful. But she had more confidence to look for another marine conservation job now. Valdemar was impressed with her work and would give her a good reference.

Arielle wondered if Frida had had the baby. The last message she'd received from Valdemar had said that it might be necessary to induce the birth earlier than Frida's due date. Hopefully she would find out more when she returned to the marine institute, Arielle thought. But when she looked out of the car window, she was surprised to see that the road was climbing higher, and the snow-capped mountains seemed closer.

Gustav drove along a track that ran beside a turquoise lake. The skyline was dominated by a towering mountain. The snow on the summit sparkled in the sunshine, but, lower down, the green meadows were filled with bright spring flowers. Standing on the shore of the lake was a picturesque wooden cabin and Gustav parked in front of it.

'Where are we? Why have you brought me here?' Arielle asked when he opened the door and she got out of the car, followed by Maks.

'Prince Eirik instructed me to drive you to his mountain lodge. It is his private retreat, and he will join you later.'

'But I don't want to stay here.' She followed Gustav inside and tried not to fall in love with the cabin's rustic charm. Colourful rugs on the floors and cosy throws and overstuffed cushions on the sofas gave a homely feel to the place. She poked her head round a door and discovered a bright kitchen with a sturdy-looking oak table.

'I follow the Prince's orders,' Gustav told her. 'The lodge is fully equipped with everything you might need, and there is food in the larder and freezer. Maks will stay with you.'

'I want to speak to Prince Eirik.' Arielle took her phone out of her bag. 'Will you give me his phone number?'

'The Prince cannot be disturbed while he is carrying

out royal duties.' Gustav sounded shocked. 'Unfortunately, the mobile phone signal is poor up here.'

Gustav was right, Arielle discovered when she walked around the cabin, trying to get a connection. She heard the car's engine and ran outside to see Eirik's private secretary driving away.

It was not the worst place to be stranded, she conceded when she wandered down to the lake, accompanied by the faithful Maks. The lake was not heated by geothermal activity and was too cold to swim in without a wetsuit. The mountain scenery was breathtaking, but the idea of Eirik spending time in this remote and tranquil place where there wasn't a nightclub or casino anywhere nearby did not fit with his image in the media of a playboy prince.

After a while, Arielle returned to the cabin and rooted through the well-stocked freezer for something to defrost for dinner. Although she hoped Eirik would arrive soon, and she'd insist that he took her back to her flat at the institute. She could not understand why he had sent her to the mountains. Recalling that he had said he wasn't ready to end whatever was between them made her wonder if he wanted to spend another night with her. She bit her lip. Sex with him had been earth-shattering, but while Eirik might not have a problem separating lust from deeper feelings, Arielle wasn't confident that she could do the same.

Lunch was crackers and dried apricots from the larder, and she opened a tin of dog food for Maks. Eirik kept a good selection of books at the cabin. She chose a thriller that had earned rave reviews and quickly became absorbed in the plot. When the sun slipped behind the mountain and the temperature dropped, she lit the log burner. Another hour passed and there was still no word from Eirik. Even if he had sent her a message, the lack of phone signal meant that she hadn't received it.

How dared he abandon her miles from civilisation? Arielle felt powerless, and it was a painful reminder of how she had felt growing up under her father's control. As a child and even when she'd become an adult, she had felt voiceless. Her father had treated her like a skivvy, and at school her shyness had meant that she had been mostly unnoticed by the teachers.

Now Eirik had taken control of her life. She had no way of leaving his mountain retreat and she was effectively a prisoner until he decided to release her. Even if she shouted at the top of her voice, there was no one around to hear her. Growing more furious by the minute, Arielle yanked open the front door and stepped outside. The moon was hidden behind clouds and the darkness was impenetrable.

'Can anyone hear me?' she yelled.

The silence reinforced her sense of unimportance. Blinking back tears, she went back inside. At least nobody had witnessed her being a self-pitying idiot, she told Maks when he nudged her with his damp nose.

Another few hours passed, and she guessed that Eirik was not going to arrive, and she would be spending the night in the cabin with only his dog for company. Deciding that she might as well try to sleep, she changed into her nightdress. The vintage cotton chemise was pretty but impractical on a chilly night, and she wrapped a soft woollen blanket around her before curling up on the sofa in front of the fire.

She must have dozed off, and stirred when Maks got up and padded over to the door. Arielle heard a noise from outside and was instantly on her guard. There had been many nights at the cliff-top cottage when she'd heard strangers' voices downstairs, and she had hidden beneath the bed covers. 'Keep your nose out of my business,' her father had told her, the only time she'd dared to ask him who the visitors were. Automatically she lifted her hand and traced the small scar beneath her left eye.

The door handle began to turn. Heart thumping with fear, she realised that she might need to defend herself and grabbed the fire tongs. The door opened and Maks gave a delighted bark when Eirik walked into the cabin. He smelled of frosty air and sandalwood cologne, and Arielle melted at the sight of him, looking utterly devastating in black jeans and a thick cream sweater.

She dropped the tongs so that she wasn't tempted to use them on him. Her pulse pounded with anger and adrenalin as Eirik strolled towards her. His lazy smile was the bitter end, as was his murmured greeting, 'Hey, baby.'

'You've got a nerve,' she told him heatedly.

His brows lifted. 'Is there a problem?'

'The fact that you have to ask if there's a problem makes the problem even worse.' The words tumbled from her lips as her temper exploded.

He held up his hand. 'If we are going to have a disagreement, can I just say that I will find it impossible to argue with you while you remind me of a fluffy chick?'

'Damn you, Eirik,' she choked out, fighting her way out of the cashmere blanket. 'You had no right to order your servant to dump me in the middle of nowhere.'

His eyes narrowed. 'I asked Gustav to bring you to the cabin—'

'But you didn't ask me if I wanted to visit your mountain retreat,' Arielle cut him off.

He frowned. 'I wasn't sure you would agree to come.'

'So you had me kidnapped and brought here against my will.'

'*Faen!* That's a little dramatic.' Eirik ran his fingers through his hair. 'Listen—'

'No.' She marched over to him and poked her finger in his chest. Hard. 'You listen to me.' She was determined never to be voiceless again, and she refused to be cowed by the angry glitter in Eirik's eyes.

'You made an arbitrary decision without consulting me, and without considering the impact on my career. It must look terrible that I failed to show up at the marine research institute today. I tried calling Valdemar to explain why I wasn't at work, but I couldn't get a phone signal.' She huffed out a breath. 'Valdemar has enough to worry about with Frida's pregnancy. He needs to know that he can rely on me to do my job.'

'He would not have expected you at work because today is a national holiday,' Eirik said calmly.

'Oh.' Arielle remembered that Valdemar had said the day after the masquerade ball was a national holiday, and she could enjoy a couple of glasses of champagne at the party as she wouldn't have to get up early for work.

'Tomorrow is the weekend, and Monday is also a national holiday. I managed to clear my diary so that we can spend a couple of days together.' Eirik grimaced. 'I'd intended to meet you at the cabin much earlier, but my mother had organised a surprise birthday dinner for me, and I couldn't get away.'

Arielle bit her lip. 'I'd forgotten about your birthday. But it doesn't change the fact that you took away my choice of if I wanted to see you again. You think you can do as you please because you are a prince, and I am nobody.'

He frowned. 'I don't think you are nobody.'

'It's how you make me feel. You had me smuggled out of the palace and brought to your remote mountain hideaway. I guess it's because you think I am only good enough for a secret romp. Was Ida Lundberg at your birthday dinner?' Jealousy twisted in Arielle's stomach.

Eirik strode over to a cabinet and took out a bottle of malt whisky. He half filled two glasses and came back to hand her one. Arielle took a sip of the drink and coughed as the fiery spirit hit the back of her throat.

'No, Ida wasn't there,' he said. 'My mother's latest selection of women who could be my wife included an English debutante. As a matter of fact, Lady Laura Hammett comes from your part of the world. Her father has a country house and estate near Truro.'

'Earl Hammett owns a large chunk of Cornwall,' Arielle muttered. 'I'm sure Lady Laura would be a perfect wife and Princess Consort for you.'

Eirik lifted his glass to his lips and gulped down the whisky as if he needed it. 'I'm not interested in Laura or any other woman.' His rough voice sent a prickle across Arielle's skin. Her heart started to pound when he took her glass out of her fingers and set it down next to his on the coffee table. 'I am only interested in you.'

He slid his hand round to her nape and pulled her towards him. Her sensible self knew she should try to resist his potency, but her body responded to him of its own accord and the tingle in her nipples arced down to the molten place between her thighs.

'I thought one night with you would be enough, but I was wrong.' There was frustration in his voice. 'We are highly sexually compatible. That's all this is.' He sounded as if he was trying to convince himself. 'But I can't look at another woman, let alone choose a wife, while I am hungry for you.'

Eirik's admission that he desired her more than any of the sophisticated socialites his mother had lined up as his prospective bride made Arielle's heart flip. He wanted to spend the weekend with her, and she couldn't deny it was what she wanted too. She could not stop thinking about how he had made love to her with fierce passion coupled with infinite patience that had allowed her to explore her sensuality.

When he lowered his head so that his mouth was centimetres away from hers, she waited in anticipation for his kiss. But he pulled back, and maybe her disappointment showed on her face because he said gruffly, 'Before we take this any further, I must warn you not to fall in love with me.'

Did he think she was that much of a fool? Arielle took a deep breath and counted to ten. 'You are going to need a bigger cabin for your ego.'

For a moment Eirik stared at her in a stunned silence, and then he thew back his head and laughed so hard that his shoulders shook. 'I've never met anyone like you,' he told her. 'You are not afraid to say what you think.' His expression became serious. 'That's the first time I've felt like laughing since my brother died.' He reached out and threaded his fingers through her curls. 'At the risk of being shot down in flames, I have to say that you are even more beautiful when you're angry.'

'I've never lost my temper before,' Arielle admitted. Fear of her father's unpredictable moods had meant that she'd supressed her emotions. Even when her mother had died, she'd cried alone in her room after Gerran had told her to stop snivelling. The only time she had stood up to her father had resulted in the scar on her face, and it had been a permanent reminder of his control.

But Arielle was not afraid of Eirik, and she knew he would never harm her physically. Her heart was another matter, but it was up to her to keep her emotions out of the sex-only relationship he wanted. Trusting him had allowed her to voice her anger for the first time in her life, and it felt liberating. What else could Eirik teach her about herself? Arielle wondered. She was eager to find out and gave a low moan when he dipped his head again and this time claimed her mouth in a searing kiss that turned her bones to liquid.

'I don't want to be accused of denying you your right to choose,' he murmured in her ear before he nipped her tender lobe with his teeth. 'You get to decide if you want to make love here on the rug in front of the fire, or in bed.'

'Here first, and then the bed.' She slid her hands beneath his sweater and explored the hard ridges of his abs before opening the zip on his jeans. 'And after that…' She hesitated.

Eirik's brows rose. 'Go on,' he prompted thickly.

'Well… I've fantasised about having sex on the kitchen table,' Arielle confessed, blushing hotly. But she felt emboldened by the gleam in Eirik's eyes to tell him what she wanted.

How the hell was he going to survive this woman? Eirik wondered. Arielle's intriguing mix of naivety and sensuality blew his mind. He was relieved that she understood sex was all there could be between them. Now that he'd established the necessary boundaries, he could relax and enjoy a brief fling with her. Although relaxed was the opposite of how he was feeling right now, he acknowledged, as he pulled his sweater over his head and hauled her close so that the hard points of her nipples pressed against his chest.

His heart thudded as he slid the straps of her lacy nightgown over her shoulders. The row of tiny buttons down the front tested his patience, but he resisted the urge to tear the gown off so that he could get his hands on her naked body. Instead, he concentrated on unwrapping the best birthday present he could have wished for. When the nightgown slid to the floor, he cupped Arielle's breasts in his hands and played with her nipples, eliciting husky moans from her.

Desire was a pagan drumbeat in his blood. He set her away from him and watched the firelight caress her gorgeous curves while he stripped off the rest of his clothes. He was already aroused, and Arielle's swiftly indrawn breath when she saw his proud erection heightened his anticipation.

Her lips parted beneath his as he kissed her deeply. 'Wrap your legs around me,' he bade her, and then he lowered her to the floor and came down beside her.

He knew her body so well, knew what she liked, and he pushed her legs apart and settled his shoulders between her thighs. He skimmed his fingers over the neat vee of red curls that hid her femininity and breathed in the erotic scent of her arousal. 'I want to taste you,' he said hoarsely before he flicked the tip of his tongue along her opening. With his finger he gently parted her, and then used his mouth to give her the most intimate caress of all.

'That feels so good.' Arielle gasped. She tilted her hips to offer herself to him. Eirik was tempted to give her an orgasm with his tongue, but the pressure was building inside him, and he knelt up to roll a condom over his erection and then slid his hands beneath her bottom. He entered her with a smooth thrust and groaned as he pushed deeper into her velvet heat.

'Does this feel good? It does for me. You drive me insane, *skatta*.' Sex had never been so intense with his previous lovers, and his self-control had never been threatened the way it was with Arielle. Eirik started to move, and everything got a whole lot worse, or better, as she matched his rhythm, and he knew he could not hold out for much longer. Their bodies had learned each other's secrets and they moved together in a synchronised dance as sensation built on sensation. His jaw clenched as he fought to hold back the tsunami and drove into her with powerful strokes.

'Eirik,' she cried out as she shuddered beneath him. He covered her mouth with his and kissed her hungrily, thrusting his tongue between her lips as simultaneously he thrust into her body and was overwhelmed by the strongest climax he'd ever experienced. The force of his release tore the breath from his lungs. He slumped on top of her and pressed his lips to her slender neck. After a few minutes he reluctantly lifted himself off her and rolled onto his back, waiting for his heart rate to return to normal.

It was just amazing sex, Eirik assured himself. The intense attraction he felt for Arielle couldn't last. It would burn out—at least he hoped it would. But until then…

He reached for her and drew her down on top of him, refusing to acknowledge the odd clench his heart gave when her body fitted against his as if she had been designed solely for him.

CHAPTER NINE

'Do you ski on the mountain in winter?'

Eirik stretched luxuriously and opened his eyes to see Arielle sitting up in bed. The window faced the mountain known locally as Kaempen—or Giant. In the gathering dusk, the mountain was a craggy, grey shadow with a dusting of snow on it topmost flanks.

'No, the terrain is not good. Fjernland's only ski resort is a few miles from here.'

'Is that where you and your brother were skiing when there was an avalanche?'

Eirik sat up and leaned back against the headboard. It was Sunday afternoon, and they had barely left the bedroom all weekend other than to raid the kitchen when the need for food had briefly topped their hunger for each other. Arielle had made pancakes served with lingonberry jam and they had fed each other the sweet treat before Eirik had lifted her onto the wooden table and pushed her legs apart to feast on her.

'We were in the French Alps,' he told her. 'Staying at a resort that we had visited years ago. Niels was keen to go back there when I'd suggested a skiing trip.' Eirik exhaled heavily. 'The conditions on the day of the accident were excellent for skiing and there were no indications that an avalanche might occur.'

His mind replayed the shocking moment when he'd glanced over his shoulder and seen a massive wave of snow thundering down the slope. Since then, he had only spoken about his brother with Niels's fiancée, Princess Catalina, when they had grieved together for the man they had both loved. But in the past two days, when he hadn't been having incredible sex with Arielle, they had talked about all manner of things, and he'd found himself opening up to her.

'Niels was the better skier out of the two of us,' he told her. 'From when we were teenagers, my passion was sailing, and I preferred to be on a boat than on the slopes.' His jaw clenched. 'It makes no sense that Niels was killed, and I survived. It should have been the other way round.'

'There was nothing you could have done to prevent the avalanche,' Arielle said quietly. 'Just as I couldn't have stopped my mum from being swept away by a freak wave. Fate can be cruel.'

Eirik reached out and wound a silky red curl around his finger. 'I assumed that your mother had been ill. I didn't realise she died in an accident. You were only young, weren't you?'

'Eleven. It was in the summer before I started secondary school. Mum and I had gone for a swim in the sea. She was a very good swimmer, and a qualified lifeguard. The weather had been calm when we'd swum round the headland to do some snorkelling. But the wind blew up suddenly and a huge wave rolled in. Mum pushed me up onto a ledge on the cliff, but as she tried to climb after me, the wave swept her away.'

Eirik cursed softly and shifted across the bed to draw Arielle against his chest. 'That must have been horrific.'

'It was so quick,' she said in a low voice. 'One second Mum was there, and in the next she had disappeared before my eyes.'

'I know what you mean. I watched my brother try to outrun the avalanche and then he was gone, buried beneath tons of snow. I prayed for the only time in my life,' Eirik admitted rawly. 'I prayed that Niels would be found alive. I couldn't accept that he was dead until his body was found three days later.'

He could only imagine how traumatised Arielle had been when she'd seen her mother swept away by a giant wave. He tightened his arms around her, wishing he could shield her from painful memories.

'I felt guilty that I hadn't jumped into the sea to help Mum. I suppose I was in a state of shock, and I clung to the rocks until I was spotted by some people on a boat, who rescued me.'

Eirik tilted Arielle's face up and felt a tug in his chest when he saw tears clinging to her eyelashes. 'There was nothing you could have done to save your mother. You must believe that.'

She nodded. 'Just as you could not have skied uphill and snatched your brother from the path of the avalanche.'

'I know,' he muttered. 'I felt so helpless. After Niels died, I felt guilty for being alive. My brother was not only the better skier, but he was also the better son, and he would have been a better Sovereign than me.'

'You can't think that. It's not true.' Arielle's voice was fierce, and she stared at him intently as if she was willing him to believe her. She laid her hand on his jaw, and Eirik turned his head and kissed her palm.

'Thank you,' he said gruffly. If he was fighting a battle, he would want Arielle by his side, he brooded.

'Sometimes things happen that are beyond our control,' she murmured.

Like getting more involved with Arielle than he had intended. Eirik's jaw tightened. He had lost count of how many times he had made love to her, and it was always, impossibly, better than the time before. Their sexual compatibility was off the scale. But there was more. He liked her, which was a first for him. In the past, personality had come at the bottom of the list of attributes he'd looked for in his lovers. Sexual attraction had invariably led to a brief affair, or more often a one-night stand before he'd moved on to the next pretty woman who had caught his eye.

This was different. For a start he wanted to know everything about Arielle, and he felt protective of her. He had brought her to Fjernland after her studio had been vandalised, but he could have sent a couple of his security team to her cottage to keep an eye on her. It was odd how she had been adamant that she did not want to report the break-in to the police, Eirik remembered.

Arielle rested her head on his shoulder. 'Mum's body was never found. Search and rescue teams looked for days, but it was likely that she had been swept out to sea by the strong current.'

'How is it that you love to swim in the sea after your mother drowned? You risked your life to save mine.' Her bravery was even more astonishing now he knew what she had witnessed as a child. 'I would have expected you to be scared of the power of the ocean.'

Her sweet smile made Eirik want to protect her from all of life's hurts. 'Mum believed that mermaids exist and maybe she was right,' she said softly. 'When I free-dive wearing my monofin I feel close to her.'

He brushed his lips over her hair. 'What about your father? You haven't mentioned him.'

She stiffened and pulled out of his arms. 'I'd rather not talk about him,' Arielle said abruptly. 'It's…difficult.'

Eirik vaguely recalled that she might have told him both of her parents were dead. Perhaps she had lost her father recently and found it too painful to speak about him.

He frowned. Why did he feel frustrated and hurt, dammit, because Arielle had shut him out? He moved down the bed and settled her on top of him. Framing her lovely face with his hands, he kissed the tip of her nose. Her skin was flawless apart from the tiny scar beneath her left eye. 'How did you get this?' he asked softly, brushing his thumb pad over the mark.

Once again, she tensed and avoided his gaze. 'Oh, it happened years ago. I…um…tripped and banged my face against the corner of the table.'

Arielle pushed herself upright so that she was sitting astride him and circled her pelvis against his. The effect was instantaneous, and Eirik felt himself harden. 'I can think of more enjoyable things to do in bed than talk,' she murmured seductively.

He let her take the lead and groaned when she guided herself down onto him, taking his throbbing erection deep insider her. With her fiery curls flying around her shoulders and her green eyes darkened to mysterious pools, she was utterly irresistible as she rode him to another mind-blowing climax. But afterwards, while their limbs were still tangled and their breathing was fractured, Eirik wondered why Arielle had lied about the scar on her cheek.

The weather, like Arielle's mood, had turned dismal. Rain lashed the promenade next to the beach, and the car splashed through puddles when Eirik turned into the courtyard in front of the Fjernland Marine Research Institute. It was Tuesday morning after the extended weekend, and they had left the mountain cabin early so that she could be at the institute in time for work. Conversation during the journey to the coast had been stilted. Eirik seemed to be absorbed in his own thoughts, and even Maks was subdued and lay on the back seat with his head between his paws.

'I have a feeling of déjà vu,' Arielle muttered when Eirik pulled into a parking bay, and they watched the rain beating against the windscreen. 'You dropped me off at the institute two and a half weeks ago, and I wished you luck in your search for a wife.'

He scowled at her flippant tone. Arielle refused to let him guess that her heart felt as fragile as spun glass. 'It is my duty to marry,' he said curtly.

'What would happen if you didn't get married and have a son and heir?' Her common sense told her to drop the subject and walk away from him with her dignity intact, but she seemed to be glued to the passenger seat.

'The heir to the throne does not have to be male,' he surprised her by saying. 'If my firstborn child is a daughter she will be the future Sovereign.'

Arielle pictured Eirik holding a little girl with blonde hair and blue eyes the colour of summer skies. If he married Ida Lundberg they would have beautiful children, she thought, feeling a pang of envy.

'To answer your question,' he continued. 'If I did not have a legitimate heir to ascend the throne after me, then, under the rules of the constitution, Fjernland would become a protectorate of Denmark. To put it simply, Fjernland would no longer be a principality and would lose its independent status that it gained in the tenth century.'

Eirik ran his hand over the stubble on his jaw. He hadn't trimmed his beard for a few days and looked rakishly handsome. 'A recent poll showed that ninety-eight per cent of the population want to be ruled by the monarchy. I will not let my parents down, or fail the Fjernlandic people,' he said tautly.

The rain had eased off a little, and Eirik retrieved Arielle's bag from the boot of the car before coming round to open her door. 'Wait there,' he told Maks. Arielle saw that he had left the window partly open for the dog's comfort.

The empty car park was a sign that the marine scientists and other staff who worked at the institute had not arrived yet. They walked over to the accommodation block and took the lift up to the third floor. Arielle's tension grew when Eirik followed her into her apartment. He was prolonging the inevitable when he would leave. It was unlikely she would meet him again, but no doubt his wedding to whichever aristocratic woman he decided to marry would be shown on TV and be headline news around the world.

She watched him prowl around her small but functional flat. 'I need to get ready for work,' she reminded him. 'Thanks for a nice weekend.'

His brows rose. 'Nice! Seriously, is that all it was for you?'

She glared at him. 'Do you want me to thank you for the most amazing sex I've ever had?'

'It was amazing for me too.' Eirik's soft tone made inroads on her heart. 'Come with me. I want to show you something. It won't take long.'

With a sigh, she followed him back to the lift and they went up to the top floor of the building.

'This is incredible,' Arielle murmured when Eirik ushered her into a huge open-plan apartment. Floor-to-ceiling windows along an entire wall gave a panoramic view of the beach, which even on a grey day was wild and beautiful. The décor in the apartment was Scandi style, with pale wood floors, and walls and furniture in neutral tones. Minimalism combined with comfort that probably cost a fortune, Arielle thought.

'I had the penthouse designed when I established the marine research institute,' Eirik told her. 'I lived here when I ran my yacht-building business, but now I've sold the business and I am busy with royal duties the penthouse is empty most of the time.' He strolled over to her and caught hold of her hand, linking his fingers through hers. 'You could move in here.'

Her eyes widened. 'Me? Why? I have an apartment. It's not as impressive as this, but I doubt I'd be able to afford the rent for the penthouse.'

Eirik pulled her towards him, and Arielle went unresistingly because it might be the last time she was in his arms. 'Don't worry about the rent,' he murmured. 'If you live at the penthouse I will be able to visit you without anyone knowing of our involvement.'

Arielle's heart dropped into the pit of her stomach. 'Are you suggesting that I could be your secret mistress?'

His eyes blazed. 'We are good together, *skatta*. You

admitted that it was the best sex you've ever had. And it's the same for me. I don't want to lose you.'

Her emotions see-sawed. Eirik seemed to be saying that he wanted her in his life, but she would be his grubby secret. They would not have a relationship, just an involvement, which was another way of saying he wanted to have sex with her when it was convenient for him to visit her at the penthouse. Arielle remembered Eirik had said that when he was growing up he hadn't had a close relationship with his parents, particularly his mother, who had largely ignored him while she'd desperately tried to win Prince Otto's love. Maybe being starved of affection in his childhood had hardened his heart and it was why he shunned emotional relationships.

'But you must marry soon so that your father can abdicate, and you will become the Reigning Sovereign with your Princess Consort to assist you.'

'I am not married at the moment. Even when I become engaged, a wedding will take time to arrange.' He shrugged. 'And afterwards I will retain my freedom.'

Arielle bit her lip. 'How can you ask a woman, perhaps Ida Lundberg, to spend the rest of her life with you when you are not prepared to offer her commitment and fidelity?'

Eirik's jaw tightened. 'I will make it clear to whoever I marry that in public we will give a show of unity, but in private we'll have separate lives, and lovers, as long as we are discreet.'

'That was what your parents' marriage was like, wasn't it? But you told me that your mother loved your father and was hurt by his affairs. What will you do if your wife falls in love with you?'

He swore. 'It won't happen. But if it did, why would it matter to you?'

'Because you have asked me to be your mistress. I'd be the third person in your marriage, and it would be unbearable to know that I was the reason for your wife's heartbreak.'

Eirik raked his hand through his hair. 'This is a crazy conversation. I don't have a wife.'

'Yet.' Arielle let out her breath slowly. 'You need to court the woman you intend to marry and who will be the mother of your children.' She tried to smile but failed. 'Who knows, you might fall in love with your bride.'

'I have neither the desire nor intention to fall in love,' Eirik said curtly. He tightened his arm around Arielle's waist so that she was plastered against his whipcord body, and threaded his other hand into her tangled curls, which she'd meant to style into a neat chignon before starting work in the marine laboratories. She should not be here in his penthouse, and her body should not be responding to the glitter in his eyes as he lowered his face towards hers. 'I want you, and you want me,' he insisted. 'That is all that matters for now.'

His warm breath grazed her lips, and she was so tempted to lose herself in the mastery of his kiss, but somehow she resisted. 'You want to keep me hidden,' Arielle muttered. 'Are you ashamed of me because I am a nobody?'

Eirik lifted his head and stared down at her. 'Of course I'm not ashamed of you. And you are not a nobody. Why do you put yourself down? You are beautiful, clever, passionate about marine conservation, and as sexy as hell.'

'But you wouldn't ask me out to a restaurant, or anywhere where we could be seen in public. I would be your invisible mistress.'

He frowned. 'Have you any idea what your life would be like if we were spotted together? If there was speculation that we were in a relationship, you would be hounded by the press. I have had to deal with media intrusion in my personal life for as long as I can remember, but you have never experienced the relentless attention you would receive.'

Oh, but she had, and it was an experience she never wanted to repeat. Arielle shuddered at the memory of the pack of journalists and press photographers who had been outside the court during her father's trial. The rumours that she had known about Gerran Rowse's drug-smuggling operation, and the murder of a policeman, had put her in the spotlight three years ago. Even before then, when she was a child, her surly father had been unpopular with the villagers in Penash because of his filthy temper and readiness to start a brawl in the pub when he was drunk. As a consequence, Arielle had been picked on by other children at school simply because she'd been seen as different. After Gerran had been sent to prison, she had been treated with suspicion by the villagers.

If the press in Fjernland discovered that the future monarch was having an affair with the daughter of a notorious criminal, the story would make headline news. Worst of all, Eirik would learn about her past. She had done nothing wrong, but she was deeply ashamed of her connection to her vile father.

Reality hit Arielle like a sledgehammer. She would never agree to be Eirik's mistress once he was married. But while he was still single, she had been tempted to have an affair with him in the hope that the chemistry between them would fizzle out. And if she was honest, she'd hoped that the fairy tale would come true, and the handsome prince would fall in love and want to marry her.

Eirik had made it clear there was no chance of that happening, but if a miracle occurred and he decided to conduct their relationship in the public eye, it would be a nightmare, Arielle realised sickly. The press would be certain to dig up the dirt on her father and she would be humiliated in front of Eirik. Worse still, Eirik would be embarrassed by his association with her, and perhaps his judgement would be questioned by the people of Fjernland. She simply could not allow that to happen.

He slid his hand beneath her chin and tilted her face up to his. 'When I arranged for you to be taken to the cabin without asking if you wanted to go, you accused me of denying you the right to make your own choices. I'm not asking you to decide right now where we go from here.' His eyes blazed. 'But you won't find this fire with anyone else, *skatta*.'

He bent his head and crushed her mouth beneath his in a kiss that startled Arielle with its urgency. She wound her arms around his neck and ran her fingers through the blond hair above his collar. When Eirik kissed her passionately as he was doing and stroked his finger gently over her cheek as if she were infinitely precious, she could almost believe that she meant something to him. But it was hopeless.

She broke the kiss and pulled out of his arms. He did not stop her, and his expression was unreadable. 'I…have to go,' she whispered before she walked quickly over to the door and out of the penthouse.

Valdemar arrived at the marine research institute in the afternoon. He looked as though he hadn't slept for days, but there was a wide grin on his face.

'How is Frida?' Arielle asked him. She really liked the couple and had enjoyed working with Frida on a report about microplastic pollution in the oceans and possible solutions to the problem.

'Mother and baby are doing well.' Valdemar showed her a picture on his phone of a tiny infant swaddled in blankets. 'Meet my son, Lars,' he said with obvious pride. 'The birth had to be induced because of Frida's danger-ously high blood pressure and Lars is small because he was a month early. But he has a healthy pair of lungs that he uses particularly well at night.'

'Congratulations.' Arielle felt an unexpected pull of maternal longing as she looked at the photo of the new-born baby. She'd vaguely hoped she would have a family one day, but she would want to be with a man who loved her and their children. Would Eirik love the heir he must produce to ensure that Fjernland continued to be an inde-pendent principality? She hoped so, for she knew what it was like to grow up without a loving father.

'Come into my office,' Valdemar said. He offered Ari-elle a seat. 'You may remember that Frida was meant to address the National Council and report on the effects of microplastics in the marine environment.'

Arielle nodded. 'We wrote the report together and our findings are based on sediment samples taken from the North Sea.'

'The assembly will take place on Saturday, but Frida is on maternity leave, and we are both agreed that you should address the National Council.'

'But there are other, more highly qualified marine bi-ologists than me who would be better to give the report,' Arielle stammered.

'You demonstrated when you gave a seminar to a

group of university students a week ago that you have a
gift for public speaking. Also, you wrote the report with
Frida, which makes you the ideal person to deliver the
speech.' Valdemar smiled. 'Please agree to take Frida's
place. A lot is riding on the report, and we are hoping
to persuade the National Council to increase the marine
research institute's funding.'

'Well… I am honoured that you have chosen me.'
Shocked was a better description of how she felt, Arielle thought. After a lifetime of feeling voiceless, she
was being encouraged to make a speech about a subject
close to her heart and hopefully bring more attention to
marine conservation. It was thanks to Eirik that she had
been given this chance. He had brought her to Fjernland
to work at the research institute. Why did everything
centre around him? she thought with a sigh.

For the rest of the week Arielle worked on polishing the
wording of the speech that she would give to the National
Council. Valdemar had explained that the fifteen members of the government were elected by the Fjernlandic
people every three years, and the ministers assisted the
hereditary Reigning Sovereign to rule the principality.
Crown Prince Otto was convalescing after his recent illness and Prince Eirik would deputise for his father at the
National Council's assembly.

At least worrying about speaking at such a prestigious
event had helped to keep her mind off Eirik during the
days, Arielle thought ruefully. But she was lonely in bed
without him. They had spent four nights together at his
cabin in the mountains and she had grown used to curling
up against his big body when they were in bed, which had
been most of the time. She felt a familiar tingle of longing

in her breasts and low in her pelvis as she remembered his skill as a lover. He had taken her to heaven with his thrilling caresses, but he'd coupled fierce passion with an unexpected tenderness that had captivated her heart.

On the first night back in her flat she had still been awake at midnight when her phone rang and Eirik's name flashed on the screen.

'I take it you can't sleep either,' he'd drawled when she'd answered on the second ring.

'No,' she'd admitted.

'I miss you.' His husky voice had made her toes curl.

'I miss you too.'

'Good. Tell me what you have been doing.'

She had told him about the report she'd been asked to give at the National Council's assembly. It had led to a wider discussion about marine conservation and Eirik's determination to protect Fjernland's seas and the island's unique natural environment when he became the Reigning Sovereign.

'You helped me to realise that when I am the monarch, I will be able to introduce changes to some of the policies that are outdated and hopefully bring a new energy to how Fjernland is governed,' he'd told her. 'I have made my peace with the royal life and responsibilities that await me.'

'I'm glad,' Arielle had said. She'd wondered if Eirik had also accepted that marriage was a non-negotiable part of his royal life. He did not mention *their* relationship and perhaps he had decided to take her advice and court the woman he planned to make his bride.

He had phoned again last night, and they had chatted until two a.m. When her alarm had gone off at six, she had struggled to wake up. After work she visited Valdemar and Frida and admired baby Lars. Arielle had never held a tiny baby before, and when she walked back to her apartment block next to the institute, she thought wistfully of the Oskarssons' happy family unit.

The sight of a black limousine in the car park made her heart leap at the thought that Eirik was here and would invite her up to his penthouse. As she approached the car, the chauffeur held the rear door open. Eirik must be intending to take her somewhere, Arielle thought as she slid onto the back seat.

'Hi, gorgeous…' Her voice faltered as her eyes met Princess Hulda's icy gaze. 'G-good afternoon, Your Highness. I did not realise…'

'I assume you were expecting to see my son, Miss Tremain. Or should I address you as Miss Rowse? That is the name recorded on your birth certificate.'

Nausea churned in Arielle's stomach. 'I…'

'You changed your name to Tremain, which was your mother's maiden name, after your father, Gerran Rowse, was convicted of murder and sent to prison.'

'H-how did you find out?'

'At a dinner party I gave for Prince Eirik's birthday, I happened to mention you to one of the guests whose family are landowners in the south-west of England. Lady Laura Hammett recognised the name Arielle, but she thought your surname was Rowse. Your father had the dubious distinction of being Cornwall's most notorious drug dealer until his criminal activities were exposed when he shot and killed a police officer who had been investigating his illegal activities.'

'Does Eirik know?' Arielle whispered.

Princess Hulda arched her brows. 'So, you have not told my son about your family background. I rather

thought you would not have done. But it was possible
that you had convinced Eirik you were unaware of your
father's crimes.'

'I *was* unaware…'

The Princess held up her hand imperiously, and Arielle fell silent. 'It is Prince Eirik's duty to marry a high-
born woman who will be the Princess Consort. You mean
nothing to him.' She gave a humourless laugh. 'Eirik has
always allowed his urges to override his judgement. It
is time that his dalliance with you finished.' The Princess's curiously colourless eyes raked over Arielle's ashen
face. 'I suggest that you end your affair with the heir to
the throne and leave Fjernland, Miss Rowse. There is no
reason for you to remain here. Secrets rarely stay secret
for ever.' Princess Hulda's lethally soft voice felt like a
knife through Arielle's heart.

She swallowed. 'Are you blackmailing me?'

The cold eyes flicked towards her. 'I will do whatever is necessary to ensure the continuation of Fjernland's monarchy.'

'Even if it means pressurising Eirik into a loveless
marriage?'

'Ah, you are in love with the Prince.'

'N-no.' Arielle frantically denied it to the Princess
and herself.

'And you hope that my son might fall in love with you?
Let us suppose he did.' Princess Hulda tapped her fin-
gernails on the leather armrest. 'The Fjernlandic people
would not accept a criminal's daughter as the Princess
Consort. If you had a child with Eirik, the future heir
to the throne would share the bloodline of a murderer.'

Arielle drew a sharp breath. She felt tainted by her father's crimes, but far worse was the realisation that any

children she might have would carry the same burden of shame. Eirik's mother had said that secrets rarely stayed secret for ever, and it was true. The story was bound to crop up from time to time, or feature on one of those true crime programmes that were so popular. She would never escape her association with a cold-blooded killer.

Princess Hulda tapped on the privacy screen, and the chauffeur got out of the car and opened the rear door for Arielle. 'Goodbye, Miss Rowse,' the Princess said briskly. 'I do not anticipate that we will meet again.'

As Arielle let herself into her flat, her phone rang. She stared at Eirik's name before she dropped the phone and ran to the bathroom to be violently sick. Staggering into the living room, she shoved her phone under a pile of cushions when it rang again. The third time Eirik called, she switched her phone off and curled up in a ball on the sofa. Her body was icy cold and hot tears streamed down her face.

CHAPTER TEN

Eirik knotted his grey silk tie before he slipped his waist-coat on. His valet held out his suit jacket for him to slide his arms into the sleeves. 'That will be all, thank you, Mikkel,' he murmured.

His phone was on the table in his dressing room and the ping of a new message arriving had him stride across the room and snatch up the device. Disappointment left a bitter taste in his mouth when he saw that the text was not from Arielle. Since they had returned from his cabin in the mountains three days ago, he had not been free to see her, but he'd looked forward to their nightly phone conversations. However, when he'd called her yesterday she had not answered. He'd left numerous messages, asking her to get in touch, but she hadn't responded. He looked at the last text he had sent her.

Miss you. Please call me.

Eirik swore and shoved his phone into his pocket. He was behaving like a lovesick teenager, but he couldn't stop thinking about Arielle and wondering why she had cut off communication with him. Guiltily, he remembered how in the past he'd stopped taking calls from his ex-lovers when they hadn't wanted to accept that the affair was over.

He reminded himself that the speech Arielle was due to give to the National Council tomorrow was a big deal to her, and it was likely she wanted to focus on preparing her report.

His private secretary was pacing up and down the carpet when Eirik walked into the sitting room of his private apartment in Sejrrig Palace.

'Sir, you need to see this.' Gustav's usually calm demeanour was missing, and he looked rattled as he held out a newspaper.

Without a word Eirik took it and stared in shock and mounting fury at the picture on the front page, of him and Ida Lundberg in what looked to be a close embrace. In the photograph, Eirik had his arm around Ida's waist, and her body was turned into his. Her head was tilted towards him while his cheek rested against hers. It was difficult to tell from the angle of the shot, but they appeared to be kissing. The headline on the paper said *Royal Betrothal Announcement Expected Within Hours!*

Eirik's first thought was that the photo was a fake. With modern technology it was easy to create an image that looked genuine. But as he studied the picture, he recognised that it had been taken the previous day, outside an art gallery that he had visited in his role as Patron of the Arts. He was meant to have been accompanied by Princess Hulda, but at the last minute she had suffered a migraine and had sent her lady-in-waiting to take her place.

'As you can imagine, the picture is all over social media sites,' Gustav told him.

There had been literally hundreds of messages on Ei-

rik's phone, but he hadn't bothered to look at them when
he'd seen that none were from Arielle. Now he remembered that when he had emerged from the art gallery Ida
had been beside him. She had stumbled as she'd walked
down the steps, and Eirik had reacted automatically and
wrapped his arm around her waist to prevent her from
falling. For a few seconds as Ida had regained her balance, her body had been plastered against his, and he'd
felt nothing. She was an attractive young woman, but his
libido had not shown the slightest interest.

The incident had been so brief that he had forgotten it.
Camera flashbulbs had been going off, but he hadn't considered how damaging a photo of him and Ida would look.
Had it been a genuine accident when she'd tripped on
the steps? Eirik swore. He suspected that his mother and
Ida had hatched the plan, which they'd believed would
force him into marriage. His mother did not suffer from
migraine attacks. And if she had actually been unwell,
surely she would have kept her lady-in-waiting at the
palace to attend to her.

'I was set up,' he muttered.

'Princess Hulda is in her sitting room and wishes to
see you urgently,' Gustav informed him.

'I bet she does.' Eirik gritted his teeth. 'I've played
right into my mother's hands.'

He wondered if Arielle had seen the newspaper picture or the frenzied rumours on social media that his engagement to Ida was imminent. Would she think that he
had taken her advice to court Ida before marrying her?
He frowned. Arielle had stopped taking his phone calls
before the photograph had been published.

The one thing Eirik was absolutely certain of was that
he could not marry Ida Lundberg. He had told Arielle

that love would not be a requirement when he married, and he'd meant it. But Arielle had reminded him that his wife would be the mother of his children. He realised that he wanted friendship and even affection between him and the woman he married. Otherwise, their children would grow up in a tense and unhappy family as he and his brother had done.

'Tell Princess Hulda that I will be with her in half an hour,' he instructed Gustav. 'And ask Miss Lundberg to meet me in the library immediately.'

'I have arranged a press briefing this morning so that you can make a formal announcement of your engagement to Ida. What do you think about holding the wedding in early July? It will give enough time for all the arrangements to be made. Your father is preparing to abdicate as monarch at the beginning of September when you will succeed him with your Princess Consort by your side.' Princess Hulda finally ran out of steam and looked expectantly at her son. 'Why are you glowering at me, Eirik? Do you have nothing to say?'

'Oh, I have plenty to say, Mama, but I will spare your sensitivities.' Eirik strode past the sofa where his mother was sitting in front of a low table that held a tea tray. He was not in the mood for a tea party. 'I will not be marrying Ida in July or any other time. At the press briefing I'll explain that there has been a misunderstanding and the rumours that we are engaged are untrue.'

The Princess slammed the teapot down. 'It is your duty to marry her now that a photograph of the two of you has appeared on the front page of every newspaper. Your behaviour has compromised Ida's reputation.'

'My behaviour? Your own behaviour does not bear

close scrutiny,' he grated. 'Ida admitted to me that you persuaded her to carry out her little stunt yesterday.'

Eirik pushed his hands into his trouser pockets. He felt restless and stifled in his mother's over-fussy sitting room. He thought longingly of his mountain cabin, the big skies and sense of freedom, and Arielle. She was always in his mind.

'I have told Ida that I have no intention of marrying her and apologised if I did anything that led her to believe I was considering making her my wife.' Eirik sighed when he saw his mother's pinched expression. 'I give you my word that I will marry, but you must allow me to choose my bride when I am ready.'

Arielle felt a nervous wreck whenever she remembered—and she was not likely to forget—that the National Council's assembly was tomorrow. She had edited her report to within an inch of its life, and Frida had read it and said that it was perfect. But the prospect of standing on a podium in front of government ministers, aides and goodness knew who else was terrifying. The knowledge that Eirik would also attend the assembly and perhaps be accompanied by his new fiancée made things even worse.

Ever since Arielle had seen the photo that was all over social media of Eirik and Ida wrapped around each other while they appeared to be kissing, she had switched off her phone and avoided watching TV. There were rumours of a summer royal wedding, but she would have left Fjernland long before then. She planned to give her resignation letter to Valdemar after she'd delivered her speech. He and Frida had become good friends and she'd miss them as much as she would miss working at the marine research institute.

Arielle sighed as she climbed out of the bath and dried herself on a towel before pulling on her fluffy pink dressing gown. Eirik's mother had been right to guess that she was in love with him. Deeply, madly in love. And feeling the way she did meant that it would be unbearable to remain in Fjernland. She hoped for Eirik's sake that his marriage to Ida would be happy. But he had said that he would retain his freedom after he married, and if he asked her to be his secret mistress, he would break her heart irreparably.

She frowned when there was a knock on the front door. Her neighbour in the apartment block often asked to borrow milk or coffee. But when she opened the door, her heart crashed into her ribs. Eirik lounged in the doorway, looking diabolically handsome in jeans and a black fine-knit sweater that moulded his muscular torso.

'Shouldn't you be with your fiancée?' Arielle muttered. 'I thought your mother would be over the moon about your engagement to Ida Lundberg and give a dinner party in honour of the happy couple.' She could not prevent a note of bitterness in her voice.

Eirik's eyes narrowed to gleaming blue slits. 'Evidently you have not kept up to speed with the news reports. I am not engaged. I have told Ida that there is no chance of us marrying.'

Arielle was so shocked that she simply stared at him. 'Was Ida upset?' she finally asked.

'Disappointed that she won't be a princess, but she acknowledged that if we had married, it would have been a disaster. There is no spark of attraction between us.' Eirik reached out and caught a handful of Arielle's curls. 'Unlike between you and me,' he murmured. 'Our sexual chemistry is more than a spark, it's a wildfire.'

Her breath was trapped in her lungs. 'You don't want to marry me,' she choked out, reminding herself that Eirik would never choose her to be his princess. But supposing he *had* decided to marry her instead of Ida…?

'Of course not,' he said smoothly. 'But we are good together. You know it's true, *skatta*.' He ran his other hand over the front of her dressing gown, and despite the thick material her nipples tautened. 'Even when you're dressed like a pink marshmallow you turn me on more than any woman ever has.' Eirik linked his fingers through hers and brought her hand up to his lips. 'Come up to the penthouse with me.'

'I can't.' Temptation and desire were a potent mix that she knew she must resist. A shiver ran through Arielle when she remembered Princess Hulda's threat to tell Eirik about her father. There was a chance that Eirik would feel sympathy for her. After all, she was not responsible for Gerran's crimes. But she still felt ashamed of her background. She dared not succumb to temptation and make love with Eirik when it would break her heart to do so.

'I want to practise reading my report aloud so there are no glitches tomorrow,' she told him.

He moved past her and stepped into the tiny sitting room. 'The conference suite where the National Council assembly is held is about ten times bigger than your entire flat. If you practise your speech in the penthouse it will give you a better idea of the level to pitch your voice. Is this the report?' He picked up the copy of her speech from the coffee table and walked back to the front door.

Arielle sighed as she gave in to her longing to spend one more hour with Eirik. 'I need to get dressed.'

He was already heading down the corridor towards the lift. 'You're fine as you are.'

'I feel ridiculous,' she told him a few minutes later. Eirik had directed her to stand at one end of the penthouse's open-plan living space and he was sitting on a chair at the opposite end of the room. 'Especially in my dressing gown.'

'Take it off,' he suggested.

'I'm not wearing anything beneath it.'

The low growl he made sounded as primitive as a lion's mating call, and molten heat pooled between Arielle's thighs. She cleared her throat and tried to concentrate on reading out her report. The sooner she got on with it, the quicker she could leave the penthouse before her resistance to Eirik's potency crumbled.

After a nervous start, she got into her stride and gave the speech. 'Did I sound okay?' she asked as Eirik stood up and walked towards her.

'You were brilliant. I mean it,' he said when she looked doubtful. 'Your enthusiasm for marine conservation is obvious.' He halted in front of her, and Arielle breathed in the intoxicating scent of his aftershave.

'I should go,' she mumbled. 'I want to get to bed early.'

'It's seven thirty.' His slow smile sent a tremor through her. 'But an early night is an excellent idea.'

'Eirik…' Her half-hearted protest was lost in his kiss as he angled his mouth over hers and teased her lips apart with his tongue. She would not deny herself this one final time to make love with him, Arielle decided, knowing that she was weak, but unable to resist him. Even though he was not going to marry Ida Lundberg, he must choose an aristocratic bride for the sake of the principality he would soon rule. But tonight he was hers.

She pushed his mother's threats to the back of her mind. Tonight she would show Eirik with her body what she could not tell him in words.

Eirik lifted her into his arms and carried her through to the bedroom. She rested her head on his shoulder and brushed her lips over his stubbled jaw. He turned his head and their mouths fused in a slow, sensual kiss that left them both breathless.

'You are so beautiful,' he said thickly.

'So are you.' She studied his face to imprint his chiselled cheekbones and the seductive curve of his mouth on her mind.

He set her down on her feet and untied the belt of her dressing gown before he pushed the robe off her shoulders and skimmed his hands over her naked body, finding each pleasure point with his fingers and then his mouth. She moaned when he closed his lips around one nipple and sucked the tender peak before he moved across to her other breast to do the same.

Desire swept hot and urgent through her veins when he slipped his hand between her legs and brushed his thumb over her sensitive upper thigh. Higher he went, until he found her wet heat and pushed his finger inside her. She rocked her hips against his hand, needing more, desperate for him to possess her fully.

Arielle reminded herself that she wanted their last night of lovemaking to be a memorable experience for Eirik. She did not belong in his world, but she was determined he would never forget her. He groaned when she slipped her hands beneath his sweater and roamed them over his chest. She felt the erratic thud of his heart beneath her fingertips and wished she could tell him that her heart belonged to him.

Sadness would come later. Now there was only the brush of skin against skin when he pulled his sweater over his head and drew her close to him. His chest hairs were silky beneath her cheek. She ran his zip down, and he kicked off his jeans and underwear to stand before her, naked and magnificently aroused. In the light from the bedside lamp he was a golden god, her prince. No other man would ever come close to him.

When he pulled her down onto the bed, she leaned over him and scattered kisses over his chest, following the arrowing of dark blond hairs down to his groin where his erection was jutting proudly.

'Do you have any idea what you do to me?' he growled, his thighs tensing as she ran her tongue along his swollen length before taking him into her mouth.

She loved to give him pleasure, and his unsteady breaths emboldened her to become even more inventive with her caresses. Eirik speared his fingers into her hair and shifted his hips restlessly. Having him completely at her mercy evoked a fierce tenderness in Arielle. He was so strong, this man, but she had glimpsed a vulnerability in him that made her love him even more.

Moving back up his body, she clasped his face in her hands and kissed his mouth before she took the condom he'd left on the bedside table and slid it over his manhood.

'Arielle.' He spoke her name like a prayer as he rolled them both over and settled himself between her spread thighs. His eyes blazed with an emotion she dared not try to define. With infinite care he entered her and sank deeper and deeper until he filled her, and they were one.

There was no need for words. Their bodies moved together in an age-old dance, and yet each touch and caress felt new and breathtaking. She arched her hips to meet his

thrusts as he set a devastating rhythm and every powerful stroke sent her closer to the edge. He held her there
and bent his head to claim her lips in a lingering kiss that
was utterly beguiling.

She sensed his urgency and locked her ankles around
his hips as he increased his pace and drove into her faster,
harder, until they both toppled over the edge. Eirik let out
a savage groan and Arielle pressed her lips to his throat
and tasted sweat on his skin.

How could something that felt so right be wrong? she
wondered. Princess Hulda's coldly condemning expression came into Arielle's mind and reminded her of why
she must leave Fjernland.

She looked good. Arielle did a slow twirl in front of the
mirror. The woman who looked back at her was dressed
in an elegant dark blue suit. Beneath the buttonless jacket
she was wearing a crisp white blouse. Three-quarter-
length trousers made the most of her long legs that were
further complemented by nude-coloured stiletto-heeled
shoes. Her curls had been tamed into a sleek style and
she looked professional and self-confident. The soft flush
on her cheeks was the only telltale sign that she was a
woman in love, and a closer inspection revealed shadows in her eyes.

But no one at the National Council's assembly would
guess that her heart was breaking, Arielle told herself
as she picked up her handbag and the report she was to
give and exited the cloakroom to make her way to the
conference suite. She walked to the front of the assembly room and sat on a chair at the side of the dais as an
official had instructed her to do. The rows of seats facing the dais quickly filled, and everyone stood up when

Prince Eirik strode into the room and walked down the central aisle to take his seat in the front row.

The last time Arielle had seen him, he had been naked and sprawled on the bed at the penthouse, his blond hair falling across his brow and an indolent smile on his lips after they'd enjoyed early morning sex. Now he was impeccably dressed in a light grey suit, and his expression was enigmatic.

Valdemar hurried over to the dais and sat down next to Arielle. 'The baby was sick on my jacket just before I left home,' he said under his breath. 'I wiped off most of it, but I thinks it's left a stain.'

'It's not too bad,' she whispered, trying not to giggle. The flash of normality eased her tension. Valdemar stood and walked to the centre of the dais to explain to the audience about the role of the marine research institute. When he introduced Arielle, she walked up to the lectern and arranged her notes in front of her. She glanced at Eirik, and her heart lifted when he winked at her. Without him, she would not have had the courage to speak in public. He had helped her to find her voice that her father had silenced. Taking a deep breath, she started to speak.

'In summary,' she told the assembly some twenty minutes later, 'the marine research institute needs your support to help in the fight against plastic pollution. Education, advocacy, and science will allow us to start to create changes in consumer and corporate behaviour that will benefit the world's oceans and ecosystems.'

Loud applause rang out in the assembly room when Arielle finished her report. She sensed that she had made a real connection with the audience and felt quietly proud of herself. Valdemar gave her a thumbs-up sign. She looked over at Eirik, but at that moment a commotion at the back of the room made everyone turn their heads.

The doors to the conference room were opened by two security guards and Princess Hulda walked into the room. A sense of foreboding snaked through Arielle when the Princess directed her haughty gaze at her.

'Arielle,' Valdemar said in a loud whisper from the side of the stage. 'It's time for you to answer questions from the audience.'

She blinked and turned her head to the front, struggling to regain her composure while she frantically wondered what Eirik's mother was doing here. Arielle shot a lightning glance at Eirik and guessed from his frown that he was surprised by his mother's appearance at the National Council's assembly.

One of the council members asked for more details about her proposal to encourage schools to organise beach-clean events for their students to take part in. Arielle explained about the beach-clean campaign she had been involved with in Cornwall and started to relax.

'Miss Tremain…' A journalist stood up and said that he was from *Fjernland Today*, the principality's most popular newspaper. 'What do you say about the allegations that you were aware that your father Gerran Rowse ran the biggest drug-smuggling operation in Cornwall? At his trial it was proved that millions of pounds' worth of class A drugs were brought in on fishing boats and stashed at the remote cottage where you lived with your father. Yet you stated that you knew nothing of your father's illegal activities.'

'I didn't know…' Arielle tried to defend herself, but no one heard. Her voice had disappeared. She felt faint and gripped the lectern to keep herself standing upright.

She could not bring herself to look at Eirik and see the disgust that he must feel for her.

'Furthermore,' the journalist continued, 'a young police constable called Josh Bray was shot and killed by Gerran Rowse, but you told the court that you had not heard the shot that was later proved to have been fired by your father. According to the constable's cousin, Danny Bray, you might not have pulled the trigger, but you were in the cottage when Josh died and as far as his family are concerned you are no better than your scumbag father.'

The room erupted in uproar. The other members of the press who had been invited to the National Council's assembly rushed towards the dais where Arielle was standing and thrust microphones at her. Camera flashbulbs popped. Dimly she heard Eirik yell to the guards. 'Clear the room, *now*.'

CHAPTER ELEVEN

EIRIK GRABBED ARIELLE and half carried her off the dais. He blinked in the glare of the cameras flashing all around them and knew that pictures of him holding his arm up to protect her from the rabble of journalists and photographers would add fuel to the firestorm that had just taken place. But he did not care. Nothing was more important than getting Arielle out of the assembly room.

'Why the hell didn't you tell me?' he gritted as he pushed her into an empty office and slammed the door shut. She was so pale that he thought she might faint. 'Sit down.' He guided her over to a chair. Her stricken expression evoked a pain beneath his breastbone. She looked *destroyed*.

He wanted to put his arms around her, hold her, but she looked as though she might shatter. He wanted to protect her from the journalist who had made vile accusations against her, from the rest of the goddamned press and their intrusive cameras, from anyone and anything that tried to hurt Arielle. She did not deserve any of it. There was no doubt in his mind. His little mermaid was the sweetest, bravest, most honest woman he had ever known.

His Arielle? When had he started to feel possessive as

well as protective of her? He shoved a hand through his hair. 'You had better tell me everything,' he said grimly. 'I can't believe you kept secrets from me.'

It felt like a knife in his chest to discover that Arielle had shut him out after he had opened up to her in a way that he'd never done with anyone else except his brother. Niels had been his best friend and confidant, and Eirik realised with a jolt of shock that Arielle was both of those and more to him. He pulled a chair round in front of her and sat down. 'I need answers.'

She swallowed. 'The journalist must have spoken to Danny Bray. There are several strands of the Bray family who have lived in Penash for generations. Josh was Danny's cousin.' Arielle would not look at Eirik. She twisted her fingers together. 'It's true that my father was a major drug dealer, and he…he killed Josh. But I swear I didn't know about the murder or what my father did.'

'I believe you.'

Her green eyes flew to his face. 'You do?' She let out a shaky breath when he nodded. 'People in the village, mainly members of the Bray family, were convinced that I was involved in my father's drug smuggling. I suspected that whatever he did was illegal, and I was sure the small-holding he ran was a cover to hide what he was up to. Strangers used to come to the cottage at night. Every few months my father would disappear for a while. He didn't tell me where he went, but at his trial it emerged that he used the money he made from drug dealing to fund a lavish lifestyle in Dubai. He'd invested in a nightclub there and owned a fleet of flashy cars. At home he always kept one of the outbuildings locked, but once I managed to break in and found a bag containing bank notes. There must have been thousands of pounds. When I asked him about the money he...'

'He what?' Eirik prompted her.

She touched the scar on her cheek. 'He hit me. The blow was so hard that I fell against the edge of the stone fireplace and must have cut my face on a piece of flint.'

Eirik bit back a savage curse. He was filled with murderous rage as he imagined Arielle lying on the floor after her father's blow had sent her flying. 'How old were you?' he asked tautly.

'Fifteen.' She brushed her hand across her eyes. 'He didn't care that he'd hurt me. There was blood everywhere, but he just stood over me and told me that if I ever interfered again, I would get worse than the back of his hand.'

'Where is your father now?' Eirik clenched his fist, wishing he could use it on Arielle's father.

'In prison. He was given a life sentence for murder. Josh Bray was the local police constable. He'd gone to the cottage to question my father about a minor driving offence. But Gerran...' she bit her lip '... I can't bear to call him Dad, had been expecting trouble from another drug dealer, and he shot Josh with his hunting rifle. It came out in the trial that he'd thrown the body over the cliffs, hoping, I guess, that it would be swept out to sea on the tide. But Josh was found, and the bullet mark was linked to my father's gun.'

Arielle stood up and hugged her arms around herself. 'At my father's trial I was questioned about what I knew. I admitted that I had heard a gun fired that night. I didn't go and investigate because I was scared of Gerran. Danny Bray is right,' she choked out. 'If I'd gone downstairs, perhaps I could have helped Josh. But I was too much of a coward to stand up to my father.'

Eirik looked furious, and she could hardly blame him, Arielle thought miserably. The fiasco that had taken place at the National Council's assembly was her fault. She shuddered as a new wave of humiliation swept over her. She was certain that Princess Hulda had arranged for her to be denounced in public and in front of Eirik. Arielle wanted to crawl under a stone.

Eirik had said he believed she had known nothing of her father's crimes, but it did not change the fact that she was the daughter of a murderer. If the media guessed that the future Sovereign of Fjernland was involved with her, especially now when Eirik had just announced that he was not going to marry aristocratic Ida Lundberg, it would not paint him in a good light.

'You shouldn't have been seen with me,' she muttered. 'There are bound to be pictures of us leaving the assembly room together, and people might wonder if there is something going on between us.'

'Don't worry, I'll deal with the press and deny any rumours about us.'

Of course he would. She had been his dirty secret and Eirik would make sure he was not tainted by his association with her. An association that must end immediately. He had been on his phone for the past five minutes, trying to limit the damage to his reputation, no doubt. She did not blame him. Eirik did not want his succession to the throne to be marred by scandal. Although she had not committed any crimes herself, Arielle knew she could never escape the shame of what her father had done.

Eirik finished his call and came over to her. 'How

did the journalist know to contact Danny Bray and ask about your past?'

'I suppose Princess Hulda tipped the journalist off,' Arielle mumbled half beneath her breath.

'My mother? Explain what you mean,' he ordered.

'I'd rather not. I don't want to cause trouble between you and your mother.'

Eirik swore. 'Tell me.'

She sighed. 'The Princess knew about our affair and disapproved of me, especially when she found out about my father. She…advised me to break off my relationship with you and leave Fjernland and threatened to tell you about my father if I didn't. She has your best interests at heart,' Arielle said hurriedly when Eirik's expression turned thunderous. 'It is your duty to marry a woman who is suitable to be your Princess Consort. I was only ever a distraction.'

He stared at her as if he was seeing her for the first time. Seeing her for what she was, Arielle thought bleakly. A nobody. There was a knock on the door, and Eirik's private secretary entered the room.

'Sir, I have made all the arrangements you asked for, and you are expected at Sejrrig Place for a meeting with His Serene Highness, Prince Otto. The helicopter is ready for you.'

'Gustav will drive you to the Winter Palace,' Eirik told her. 'I want you to stay there until I am free to come to you, and then we will talk about where we go from here. There are things I need to do first,' he said grimly.

He stepped closer to Arielle, and his eyes blazed into hers. 'Promise you will wait for me.'

She wanted to touch his face, kiss him one last time. Unable to lie to him, she gave a slight dip of her head.

Eirik seemed to want to say something else, but then he exhaled heavily and strode out of the room.

Gustav escorted her out of the building via a back door to avoid the press. 'I need to collect some things from my flat,' Arielle told him when he held the car door open for her.

At the marine research institute, she left her resignation letter on Valdemar's desk. She had packed before going to the National Council's assembly and when she emerged from the apartment block carrying her suitcase, Gustav frowned.

'You love Eirik, don't you?' Arielle asked him.

Gustav looked startled for a moment before he nodded. 'I have served the Prince since he was a youth.'

'I love him,' she said softly. 'That's why I need you to take me to the airport. Eirik will be better off without me.'

'I am not sure the Prince will agree.'

'But you know I am right. Eirik must fulfil his destiny for his sake as well as for the people of Fjernland.'

The story had made the international news sites and was the headline on most of Fjernland's newspapers. Leaning back in his seat in the helicopter that was taking him to the Winter Place, Eirik grimaced when he flicked through some advanced copies of the next day's publications. Most had reprinted accounts of Gerran Rowse's trial three years ago. The details of the murder of a young police constable were harrowing. Rowse was a vile individual. In an interview with a neighbour who lived in the Cornish village of Penash, Arielle's father was described as a cruel and violent man.

Eirik thought of the scar on Arielle's face and rage

swept through him. Nothing would ever hurt her again. It was his personal mission to make sure of it. She'd be upset if she saw the newspapers, but he would insist that no copies were brought into the Winter Palace. Better still he would take her to his cabin in the mountains, and he planned to keep her distracted in his bed until the story about her father had died down.

Anticipation tugged in his loins. When he made love to her it felt as if they were the only two people in the universe. He had stopped wondering when his desire for her would fade and accepted that he would always want her. And she wanted him too. His nostrils flared as he recalled in erotic detail how she had made love to him with sensual abandon the previous night at the penthouse.

Eirik frowned when he remembered that Arielle had said she was just a distraction for him. Maybe at first it had been true, he acknowledged. He had been under pressure to find a wife and Arielle had been a breath of fresh air compared to the refined young women with pedigrees a mile long his mother had thrown at him.

His eyes narrowed as he thought of his recent, tense conversation with Princess Hulda. He had made it clear to his mother that he would not tolerate her interference in his life, and that if and when he married it would not be because of duty. There was only one reason why two people should marry. Eirik understood that now. But for so long he had convinced himself that he did not need or want emotional attachments.

Following the death of his brother—the only person he had loved with all his heart—a loveless marriage had seemed appealing. He'd decided that he did not want to risk the pain of loving someone again. But a life without risk was dull and grey. He pictured Arielle's vibrant red curls and her sea green eyes. Her smile, and her gentle voice that was a song inside his head. She brought colour and light into his life. The question in his mind was, what was he going to do about her?

The helicopter circled above the Winter Palace and landed on the helipad. When Eirik walked up the steps of the palace a footman opened the door and Maks bounded out to greet him.

Gustav was waiting for him in the entrance hall. 'The dog is delighted to see you, sir,' he commented.

'I'm glad to see him.' Eirik patted his faithful companion's head.

'I fear you will be less glad to see me when I tell you that Miss Tremain…' Gustav hesitated, and premonition dropped into Eirik's stomach like a lead weight.

'What are you going to tell me about her? Where is Arielle?'

'Gone, sir. She said it was for the best.' There was sympathy in the older man's eyes. 'I'm sorry.'

Arielle pushed open the door of the pub. It was busy inside. The trawlermen had returned after several days at sea, and some of them looked as though they had been drinking all afternoon. No one took any notice of her as she walked up to the bar, carrying a few of her mother's paintings.

When she had bumped into the landlady of the Sailor's Rest in the local supermarket a few days ago, Arielle had mentioned that she was moving away from Penash.

'I don't blame you, love,' Julie had told her. 'It's no place for a young woman, living in that remote cottage. I hear that the owners who leased it to your father are planning to turn it into a bed and breakfast. I wouldn't mind a couple of your mum's paintings. She was a good artist and painted some lovely seascapes.'

There was a crowd of drinkers standing in front of the bar and Arielle tried to squeeze past them. 'Well, look what the cat's dragged in,' said a familiar voice.

'Shut up, Tamara,' Danny Bray muttered to his sister. Arielle did not understand why he was defending her. It was because of what Danny had told the journalist that she had fled from Fjernland.

'Well, I think you've got a nerve coming in here,' Tamara told Arielle. 'After what your father did.'

'Yes, what my father did, not me.' Anger rushed like scalding lava through Arielle. She'd had enough of being voiceless and picked on by the Brays and others who blamed her for crimes she hadn't committed. The pub grew quiet, and everyone stared at her. Good. Let them stare.

She pushed her windswept curls off her face and looked around the pub. 'Most of you have known me since I was a baby. I went to school with some of you, and all of you—*all of you*—knew what my father was like. He was a violent bully and he treated me badly. But not one person in Penash tried to help me or questioned whether Gerran Rowse should be allowed to bring up a child after my mum died. You accused me of being involved in my father's crimes, but I had no part in his disgusting drug dealing. As for poor Josh Bray...' her voice trembled '... I wish I could have saved him, but I was terrified of my father. I will regret for ever that I was a coward.'

'Never a coward, *skatta*. You are the most courageous person I have ever known, and a million times braver than everyone in this room.'

Arielle heard Eirik's voice but told herself she must have imagined it. He wasn't here in Penash. He couldn't be.

The crowd of drinkers in the pub moved aside and she stared at the impossibly handsome man who was standing in the doorway. His dark blond hair was ruffled as though he'd been running his fingers through it, although now he had shoved his hands into the pockets of his jeans, which had the effect of drawing her attention to his hard thighs.

'He's a prince,' someone said. 'Of that principality called Ferneyland or something.'

A few people bowed, and the pub landlady, Julie, came round the bar and curtseyed. 'We've never had a royal visitor in the Sailor's Rest before. I'd be honoured to get you a drink, Your Highness.'

'Thank you, but there is only one reason I am here.' Eirik's blue eyes blazed across the distance of the pub and held Arielle's startled gaze. 'I would like to talk to you, Arielle,' he said intently. 'Will you come with me, *elskeda*?'

She couldn't move, and her heart was thumping so hard that she was surprised it wasn't visible through her tee shirt.

'Go on, lass.' Julie nudged her, taking the paintings that Arielle was still holding out of her trembling fingers. Convinced that this was all a dream, she walked towards Eirik and followed him outside.

'You shouldn't be here.' She forced her voice to work.

'I had to come. You didn't go to the Winter Place and wait for me as I'd asked you to,' he reminded her, sounding oddly tense.

She lifted her chin. 'The last time I was there for the masquerade ball you had me smuggled into the palace secretly. I won't be hidden away or feel that I am a dirty secret ever again.'

'I'm sorry I made you feel like that. I want you to come back to Fjernland and I swear that you will only ever be treated with the respect you deserve.'

Her heart ached. 'I don't belong in your world.'

'You *are* my world.' Eirik held out his hand to her. 'Will you listen to what I have to say? If you decide that there is no future for us, I will respect your choice, even though it will kill me,' he said tautly.

He was talking in riddles. But she would agree to travel to the ends of the earth to spend five more minutes with him. When she put her hand in his, he gripped her fingers tightly. They walked down the cobbled street towards the harbour in silence. Arielle let him lead her aboard a small motorboat and her sense of unreality grew when he cast off and the boat chugged out of the harbour.

The sky was cornflower blue, and the May sunshine was warm on her face as the boat skimmed across the bay. The breeze ruffled the blond hairs on Eirik's forearms as he steered the boat. Arielle took the opportunity while he was looking straight ahead to drink in his chiselled features. He turned his head towards her, and his smile stole her breath. How she loved him! She quickly broke eye contact, afraid that he would see her emotions that she must hide from him.

She recognised this part of the coastline and minutes later they arrived at Pixie Cove. Eirik dropped the anchor and jumped over the side of the boat into the shallow water. Arielle made to follow him, but he scooped her into his arms and carried her up the beach. It felt so good to be held by him once again and feel his heart thudding erratically beneath her ear when she rested her head against his chest. As he lowered her to her feet, her body brushed against his and he groaned and hauled her closer.

'I told myself I would be patient and court you,' he rasped. 'But when you are in my arms, I can't think of anything but how much I want to do this…'

Eirik brought his mouth down on hers and with a helpless sigh Arielle responded to his kiss, parting her lips to allow his tongue to probe between them. She had left Fjernland a week ago, but it felt like a lifetime without him and for a few moments she was lost in the beauty and passion of his kiss.

But reality returned and she eased away from him. They were both breathing hard. 'You shouldn't have done that,' she choked out. 'Why have you brought me here?'

'This is where it began,' he said softly. 'I was saved from the sea by a mermaid. But in return for my life, she stole my heart.'

'Eirik…don't say such things.' Tears filled her eyes. 'We can never be together.'

'We will never be apart again.' He slid his hand beneath her chin and tilted her face up to his. 'Don't cry, *min elskeda.*'

A tear rolled down her cheek. 'You were angry when I told you about my father.'

'My anger was not with you.' His face twisted as if he were in pain. '*Faen,* when you told me that your father had hit you and was responsible for this—' he brushed his thumb gently over the scar on her cheek '—I felt so much rage and hatred for him. I wished I had been there to protect you as you should have been protected by the local community.'

'Gerran can't hurt anyone now.' But her father's notoriety would always cast a shadow on her life, Arielle thought bleakly. She bit her lip. 'Why did Danny Bray defend me in the pub?'

'I threatened to sue him for libel if he breathed a word against you ever again. When Bray realised that he faced being fined hundreds of thousands of pounds it made him reconsider his behaviour. |I have also taken out an injunction banning the media from printing anything defamatory about you.'

'But everything Danny said about my father is true and you can't stop the story from being in the newspapers.'

He smiled. 'It is old news already since a volcano named Vredkaempen erupted two days ago. Angry Giant, to give it its English name, is miles away from any towns, and no one was affected,' he assured her. 'The newspapers in Fjernland are full of reports about the volcano.'

Eirik slipped his hand into his pocket and withdrew a silk pouch. He tipped the contents out and held up a silver chain, which was attached to a pink pendant, carved into the shape of a heart. Arielle's breath caught when she recognised it was the piece of sea glass that she'd found smashed in her studio. She'd guessed that Danny Bray and some of his cronies had been responsible for the damage.

'You had told me that you found the sea glass when you were with your mother, and it reminded you of her,' Eirik explained. 'I asked a jeweller to create the pendant so that you can wear it close to your heart.'

'It's beautiful.' She studied the pink glass heart mistily, trying and failing to hold back her tears. 'Why did you do such a lovely thing for me?'

'Because I love you,' he said huskily.

Arielle's heart stopped beating. She lifted her gaze to

Eirik's face and the tender expression in his eyes made her tremble. 'You said you had no intention of falling in love,' she whispered.

He gave her a strained smile as he lifted his hand and brushed a stray curl off her face. 'And yet here I am, completely and utterly in love with you, *elskeda*. I think I have been since the last time we were here at Pixie Cove, and I know I will love you for ever.'

Arielle's mind was whirling. Happiness hovered within her grasp, but she dared not reach out for it. 'You can't,' she choked out.

Eirik wiped the tears from her cheeks with his thumb pads. 'Don't you want me to love you?' There was uncertainty in his voice, the vulnerability of the boy he'd once been who had yearned for his parents' affection.

'Of course I do, more than anything in the world.' She put her hand on his jaw and trembled again when he turned his face and kissed her palm. 'I love you with all my heart. But loving you is agony. I want to be able to love you freely and publicly.' Her voice cracked. 'Please don't ask me to be your secret mistress after you marry the woman who will be your Princess Consort.'

Eirik caught her to him and held her against his big chest. 'I don't want you to be my mistress, *min elskeda*. I want you to be my wife.'

She stared at him in disbelief and dawning wonder that he did truly love her. But love was not enough. He was bound by duty and centuries-old tradition. 'Oh, my darling, we both know that can never happen. I can't marry you. The people of Fjernland will never accept me, and your mother certainly won't.' Arielle pressed her finger against his lips when he made to speak. 'I cannot change who my father is and the terrible crimes he committed. You must choose a bride who is suitable to be a princess.'

Eirik's eyes blazed. '*You* are my Princess, and only you. The Fjernlandic people will fall in love with you as I did. As for my mother...' His jaw hardened. 'Princess Hulda is praying that you will accept my proposal because I have made it clear to her and Prince Otto that no other woman will be my wife.'

He took the sea-glass pendant and secured the chain around Arielle's neck. 'I will only marry for love, and I will only ever love you,' he said softly. 'I have persuaded my father and the National Council to change the principality's constitution so that if I die without an heir, Fjernland won't be returned to Danish rule. Instead, the democratically elected National Council will choose a head of state to lead the government.'

'Can you do that?'

'It's done, and it was surprisingly easy. But you can understand why my mother is desperate for you to agree to marry me, and for us to have children.' Eirik smiled at her stunned expression. 'I would like to have a family with you, not because I want an heir, but because I adore you and I'd love to have three or four mini versions of you.'

'Four!' Arielle stopped trying to fight the joy that swept through her, stopped being afraid to grab hold of the happiness that was standing right there in front of her in the form of a golden prince. Her Prince. Her fairy-tale happy ending.

'We don't have to have four, or any children at all if you don't want them,' Eirik said hastily.

'I do want your babies,' she assured him before she pulled his face down to hers and kissed him, telling him without words everything that was in her heart. 'But more than anything I want you to love me as much as I love you, for the rest of our lives.'

He captured her hand and pressed it to his chest above his heart. 'It beats only for you. Always and for ever, *elskeda*. My love,' he translated for her.

'Eirik…?' Arielle was sure she was dreaming when he dropped down onto one knee on the sand and took a small velvet box from his pocket. He opened it to reveal an exquisite, square-cut pink sapphire surrounded by diamonds that sparkled in the sunshine.

'Arielle, will you marry me and be my wife, my companion, my princess and my dearest love in this life and beyond?'

'I will,' she whispered. And then more loudly, because she had found her voice and would never lose it again. 'I will love you to eternity.'

Eirik slid the engagement ring onto her finger and stood up to draw her into his arms. He kissed her tenderly and with increasing passion until they were both shaking. 'Did you say that Pixie Cove is completely secluded?' he murmured.

'Yes, very few people know it's here.'

'Good.' He tugged her tee shirt over her head and unclipped her bra, giving a low groan as her breasts spilled into his hands. 'Because I have plans for us for the rest of the day and I don't want to be disturbed, my love.'

EPILOGUE

EIRIK STROLLED ACROSS the white sand on the private beach. Behind him stood an impressive castle that was the royal residence of Princess Catalina of San Sabinus and the Princess's new husband, an Italian Count, Bruno Oliveto. The principality was close to the heel of Italy, set in the azure-blue Adriatic Sea. The beach had a natural tidal pool surrounded by rocks that made it a safe place for children to swim.

Currently there were three mermaids in the pool. The two younger ones splashed in the water with their silver monofin tails as they swam. They were identical twins, with strawberry-blonde hair and deep blue eyes that appeared to be green in certain lights. The third mermaid was sitting on a rock. Her long hair was drying into titian curls and her sparkly green tail matched her bikini top. Eirik felt a familiar tug of desire as he studied his wife's voluptuous curves. Arielle's breasts were fuller now that she was halfway through her second pregnancy. A boy this time, but their son would not be Eirik's heir. In the future, Fjernland would be ruled jointly by his daughters, Princess Anna, and Princess Josefine.

'Papa, will you come and swim with us?'

'Look how fast I can swim. I'm faster than Anna.'

'No, you're not.'

'Girls,' their mother said softly. 'No arguing on the last day of our holiday.'

Eirik watched his little mermaids dive down to the bottom of the pool. 'Three years old and they are already amazing swimmers.' He waded through the pool to Arielle, the love of his life and the epicentre of his world. 'Will you mind going back to Fjernland tomorrow?' Royal duties took up much of their time, but they made sure that family time came first.

'Of course not.' Arielle lifted her face for his kiss. 'I don't mind where I am as long as I am with you.' It was a sentiment Eirik shared. 'The wedding was lovely, wasn't it?' She smiled. 'Catalina looked so happy with Bruno.'

'It reminded me of our wedding.' There had been three days of national holiday in Fjernland in celebration of the royal wedding, which had taken place in the Winter Palace. Eirik would never forget how his heart had leapt in his chest when he'd seen his bride walking towards him, an ethereal vision in an exquisite ivory lace wedding gown. Arielle was his princess in every way, and a month after they were married she had worn a fabulous diamond and sapphire tiara and stood by his side as the Princess Consort when he had been enthroned as Fjernland's Reigning Sovereign following Prince Otto's abdication.

His thoughts returned to the present as Arielle laid her hand on his jaw. 'Lina told me that she will always keep the memory of your brother in a little corner of her heart.'

'Niels would have wanted her to be happy,' Eirik said with certainty.

'Are you happy?' Arielle asked gently.

He smiled at his beloved. 'Do you need to ask? You are

my life, you and the girls, and our son when he is born.'
Family. They meant the world to him. Time had helped
to heal the pain of his brother's death. He too would always carry Niels's memory in his heart.

Eirik stood up and looked across the tidal pool and beyond to the ocean. A flash of silver caught his eye and he
thought he glimpsed a tail. It had been too big to belong
to a fish. Of course, mermaids and mermen couldn't really exist. Could they?

* * * * *

COMING SOON!

We really hope you enjoyed reading this book.
If you're looking for more romance, be sure to
head to the shops when new books are
available on

Thursday 7th
July

To see which titles are coming soon, please visit

millsandboon.co.uk/nextmonth

MILLS & BOON®

Coming next month

HIS DESERT BRIDE BY DEMAND
Lela May Wright

"Can you explain what happened?" Akeem asked. "The intensity?"

Could she? Nine years had passed between them—a lifetime and still… No, she couldn't.

"My father had a lifetime of being reckless for his own amusement—"

"And you wanted a taste of it?"

"No," he denied, his voice a harsh rasp.

"Then what did you want?" Charlotte pushed.

"A night—"

"You risked your reputation for a night?" She cut him off, her insides twisting. "And so far, it's been a disaster, and we haven't even got to bed." She blew out a puff of agitated air.

"Make no mistake," he warned, "things have changed."

"Changed?"

"My bed is off limits."

She laughed, a throaty gurgle. "How dare you pull me from my life—fly me who knows how many miles into a kingdom I've never heard of and turn my words back on me?" She fixed him with an exasperated glare. "How dare you try to turn the tables on me?"

"If the tables have turned on anyone," he corrected, "it is me because you will be my wife."

Continue reading
HIS DESERT BRIDE BY DEMAND
Lela May Wright

Available next month
www.millsandboon.co.uk

MILLS & BOON

THE HEART OF ROMANCE

A ROMANCE FOR EVERY READER

MODERN

Prepare to be swept off your feet by sophisticated, sexy and seductive heroes, in some of the world's most glamourous and romantic locations, where power and passion collide.

HISTORICAL

Escape with historical heroes from time gone by. Whether your passion is for wicked Regency Rakes, muscled Vikings or rugged Highlanders, awaken the romance of the past.

MEDICAL

Set your pulse racing with dedicated, delectable doctors in the high-pressure world of medicine, where emotions run high and passion, comfort and love are the best medicine.

True Love

Celebrate true love with tender stories of heartfelt romance, from the rush of falling in love to the joy a new baby can bring, and a focus on the emotional heart of a relationship.

Desire

Indulge in secrets and scandal, intense drama and plenty of sizzling hot action with powerful and passionate heroes who have it all: wealth, status, good looks…everything but the right woman.

HEROES

Experience all the excitement of a gripping thriller, with an intense romance at its heart. Resourceful, true-to-life women and strong, fearless men face danger and desire - a killer combination!

To see which titles are coming soon, please visit

millsandboon.co.uk/nextmonth